HER MOUTH BURNED
AGAINST HIS SKIN

Grazing Todd's neck with her lips, Janet was only vaguely conscious of how Todd had pinned her against the dressing table with his strong thighs.

"Turn around," Todd commanded abruptly, his voice thick with passion. Stepping back, he twisted her around, one hand cupping her breast. Janet clung to him as he made her face the huge mirror.

"Now look at yourself, Janet." Todd forced her head up, while his other arm imprisoned her at his side.

She stared at the image they made—he, big, grim, virile; she, her hair wildly disheveled, her eyes wide and stormy, her lips parted.

"You see a woman, Janet," Todd said implacably. "That's not daddy's little girl anymore. Look at yourself and *think*—does any other man make you feel like this?"

WELCOME TO...

HARLEQUIN SUPERROMANCES

A sensational series of modern love stories.

Written by masters of the genre, these long, sensual
and dramatic novels are truly in keeping with today's
changing life-styles. Full of intriguing conflicts
and the heartaches and delights of true love,
HARLEQUIN SUPERROMANCES are absorbing
stories— satisfying and sophisticated reading
that lovers of romance fiction have long been
waiting for.

HARLEQUIN SUPERROMANCES

Contemporary love stories for the woman of today!

Virginia Myers

SUNLIGHT ON SAND

Harlequin Books

TORONTO • NEW YORK • LONDON
AMSTERDAM • PARIS • SYDNEY • HAMBURG
STOCKHOLM • ATHENS • TOKYO • MILAN

To FLORENCE FEILER
my friend,
and literary agent,
in that order.

Published February 1984

First printing December 1983

ISBN 0-373-70105-5

Printed in Canada

CHAPTER ONE

JANET TURNED her clear gray eyes from Hassan's dark ones to the shoreline of Giza. It was closer now. Hassan was up to something. She could sense it, and she prepared herself to deal with it. She could feel his gaze still on her, admiring the way she looked—at least he had said so often enough, speaking as so many Arabs did, with a gift of poetry in his words. According to him her light brown hair had "shining amber lights," her face was a "delicate cameo" and she "walked like a princess."

Smiling a bit, she leaned back in the *felucca*, which moved lazily along the ancient Nile. She might as well enjoy herself. The worn triangular sail soared high above them and bellied out to catch the restless winds as they swept down out of the deserts. With only the three of them in it, the boat was light and inclined to rock leisurely on the slow movement of the water. Hassan would get to the point whenever he decided the time was right.

He was talking again in Arabic to the boat boy. The youth's brown face was turned upward, and his great black eyes were agleam with interest. Hassan's rapport with young people was good—she well knew that from her own experience. This was probably a good-natured persuasive lecture of some kind—"don't quit school...don't drink the river water." On his frequent trips to the States and in his letters Hassan had given her many such lectures. During her college years, after her father's death there in Egypt, she had needed his help and advice. And because of this kindness and his keen sense of humor, and maybe because he looked a bit like an Egyptian movie actor, she had somehow fancied herself enough in love with him to become engaged.

Now, within the next two weeks, she must tell him she had made a mistake. And she must do it in such a way as to salvage his pride and still hold on to his friendship. It wasn't—could not be—the end for her and Hassan. He meant too much to her. She wanted Hassan's friendship for the rest of their lives. But only his friendship. She had worried about how to tell him until two weeks before the school term started, then decided on a quick trip to Egypt, because her news was something she could not put in a letter. After he knew the truth, she would return to San Francisco and resume her art-teaching job at Terrace Grade School. She liked the work. It was a very gratifying way to earn her living. And she'd been aware for some time now that her teenage crush on Hassan was no basis for a marriage.

Hassan knew something was wrong about her sudden visit—which, he knew, too, she could not afford. Now he turned his attention to her again. "You look especially lovely today," he said lazily. "Exactly as I always think of you."

Janet's smile became strained. He had no idea how right he was. She had never let him see her in paint-smeared jeans with her hair bound up in a bandanna. Now she wished she had. Perhaps they would never have drifted toward the idea of marriage. But in a misguided effort to be agreeable, she had tried to please him by changing the way she looked. Lately she had realized that she really wanted her hair short and free. Instead, she wore it long and piled on top of her head because Hassan had been so disappointed once when she had cut it. Now her head was covered by a lacy straw sun hat that caught every stray breeze. She used eye makeup skillfully and only palest lip and nail color, because that was what he liked. Disregarding her own taste in clothing, she selected very feminine, often impractical designs in fabrics that always draped well. Janet's faintly Victorian look pleased Hassan, but she was ready to find her own style.

She smoothed her delicate soft-beige dress and looked with secret disgust at the thin straps of her pretty sandals. She would have been better dressed for a morning on the river in one of those tough little canvas hats, a cotton shirt, jeans and sneakers. She sighed gently and observed Hassan from beneath the drooping brim of the silly hat he thought so pretty.

Hassan was a good-looking man, dark, taller than the average Egyptian, but with the same natural grace and dignity. Even in chinos and an open-necked cotton shirt—things he usually wore in his work for the Bureau of Antiquities when he was out visiting any of the digs—he managed a kind of elegance.

Somehow she must guard his self-esteem when she broke the engagement. She must not violate the centuries-old Arab traditions that bound him to a sense of male pride like ropes of delicate steel lace.

She turned her gaze again to the shoreline and the increasing number of different kinds of boats clustered along the busy esplanade.

In the distance, back beyond the town of Giza, at the edge of the Libyan desert, was the cluster of pyramids and ancient mastaba tombs. Among those dead monuments so carefully wrought in ages past was that small hidden tomb her father had discovered shortly before his death.

"You are thinking of your father, Janet?"

Sometimes she wondered if Hassan could read her thoughts, and she quelled a sudden resentment. This would not have bothered her a few years earlier, but now it seemed a kind of personal intrusion, a subtle violation of her privacy.

"Three years is a long time, Janet. Life goes on."

"I know," she said remotely, aware he could sense her withdrawal and regretting it.

He spoke a phrase or two in Arabic to the boat boy again, and she watched the youth's muscular body, clad in its flowing galabia, respond in instant obedience. Their course altered under his skillful brown hands.

"I thought we were going back to Giza?"

"We are, all in good time. There is something I must speak to you about first."

She felt a kind of inward tightening, an increase of wariness, a this-is-it feeling. "About what?" she asked pleasantly. Sometime, anytime now, she'd have to face telling him she wasn't going to marry him.

"I want to talk to you about your father's excavation," he said, a half smile on his mouth. He knew she had something else on her mind and was prepared to do battle over it. Score one for him. She couldn't resist an answering smile.

"I want to talk to you about the possibility of your staying on in Egypt longer than just two weeks." He lifted his hand. "Wait. Hear me out. It may be necessary for you to stay on—just for a while."

"Hassan, I couldn't possibly. I want to get back to work. You know that. All right. I'm sorry I interrupted. Go on." She had seen his quickly veiled look of displeasure.

"Janet, your father's excavation meant a great deal to him."

Hassan sounded smooth and confident, for he assumed she would always listen carefully to him. He had been her father's best friend, had taken care of him like a brother during the final catastrophic illness. Then there was the help, including financial aid, he had given her so she could finish university—not to mention years of priceless friendship.

"They have reopened the excavation, Janet. The new man in charge wants to start clearing the burial chamber. He arrived yesterday."

"The new man?" She spoke without thinking, suddenly feeling angry. *Her father* had found that tomb. It was—would have been, had he lived—the high point of his whole career. But since the chamber had been resealed almost immediately after his discovery, no one knew yet what lay buried there in the earth. It might be—very possibly—an even more dazzling treasure than that yielded up from the tomb of the boy-king Tutankhamen. She realized she resented someone else taking up her father's work now. "Funded by the Ballard Foundation, I suppose," she snapped.

"Yes, of course. The foundation has never lost interest in your father's discovery, Janet. Of course they came forward again to fund it."

"They were quick enough to stop the funds and order the tomb closed when they thought there was going to be another Mid-East war," Janet countered. She was bending over slightly, staring at the peeled paint on the sliding panel beneath the seats. She focused on the dim gleam of the boat boy's battered tea kettle.

"One really can't fault them for that. Your father would have been the last to want to start clearing the tomb at that time—getting its priceless contents up aboveground and risk having them destroyed by rockets and mortar shells."

"I'm not so sure. He worked like a fiend out there until the last moments of his life. He died there, among the sand and rocks and rubble and all those treasures underneath. *He* hadn't stopped working, Hassan. I think he'd have kept on and taken the risk. At least until he was sure a major conflict was going to occur. A lot of unrest over here turns out to be nothing—you know that. He would have gone on. He would have," she insisted irritably, "if the Ballards hadn't stopped the funding."

"We cannot know that for sure, Janet." Hassan was frowning, worry in his fine dark eyes. "The government was about to close all such projects, anyway—they always do in the face of a serious war scare."

"They caused his death, those Ballards," she said suddenly. "He wouldn't have had a stroke if they hadn't suddenly snatched away his reason for living."

"Janet, that isn't fair. They were generous with your father."

"Oh, I suppose so. But I doubt they stinted on any of their necessities—like polo ponies, for instance. On the rare occasions my father spent any time in the States, I knew what he went through, aware there was work to be done over here and aware how well qualified he was to do it." She made herself stop. How odd—the grief she thought she had overcome suddenly welling up again.

"Janet, please." Hassan was embarrassed now.

The boat boy was looking astonished that a tourist lady would speak so sharply to a government gentleman. Then, with instinctive courtesy, the youth turned quickly and busied himself with the ropes.

"Well," Janet insisted, "I'm the one who made

coffee for him at two in the morning when he was sweating over writing a grant proposal—writing and rewriting it.''

"In any case, my dear, that is behind you," Hassan said firmly. "The tomb *has* been reopened. This other archaeologist will complete the dig. And in this you can—I feel you must—help. You should certainly want to help finish your father's work."

"Hassan, how in the world could *I* help? I teach art in an elementary school. I'm no archaeologist. I'm not even the slightest bit interested in the field." She bit off further comment; she had already said too much. There was no point in taking her anger out on Hassan. He had never shown her anything but kindness and love. In his position at the Bureau of Antiquities, in a nation rich in ancient ruins and destitute for money, he felt an obligation to encourage foreign contributions.

"On the contrary," Hassan smiled briefly, placating her. "There is great need for your help. Your father made pages and pages of notes when he reopened the burial chamber. But he did this, Janet, in his private shorthand system. He told me once that you know it, too, and he showed me one of your letters once, containing passages in that writing."

"He did teach me the system. I'd never have got through college so well if I hadn't used it for note taking." Suddenly she realized what he was getting at. "You mean, all his notes are in that shorthand?"

"Yes, I mean just that. He thought at the time, of

course, that the notes were for his own use only, and he had to work as fast as he could. He felt he had to get down in writing as much as possible, because any day the government might issue closure orders for all sites. He was down in the actual burial chamber—a room that had not been disturbed for five thousand years. It was littered with all sorts of things. No one dared to enter and walk across it for fear of crushing something priceless.''

Hassan was right about life going on. And until that moment Janet had believed she had got over her grief. But perhaps no one ever ''got over'' grief; they just learned to live with it.

It would have been easier, she knew, if her father had not been her entire family, but the death of her mother ten years earlier had left her with a sense of abandonment she could never quite escape. She tried to concentrate on what Hassan was saying.

''Without the notes, the man taking over the direction of the excavation is badly hampered. If the notes can be transcribed he can start clearing the burial chamber right away—without the work being delayed, you see? I told him—I took the liberty of telling him—that you would most certainly agree to stay on awhile to do it. I knew you would,'' he went on, lifting his hand against interruption, ''because you owe it to your father's memory. Your father was a man of great integrity, Janet. It would pain him deeply if he knew he had left work unfinished, incomplete, of no use to others.''

''How could the Ballard Foundation have cut off

his grant like that in the middle of the project?" she asked. "I've meant to ask you before."

"They didn't exactly, Janet. There is usually a clause in fine print someplace, giving the funder continuing control. They have to do that in case of unforeseen circumstances. In your father's instance, the original money was almost gone, anyhow, but when the hidden tomb was discovered, the foundation was more than willing to extend the original grant. They do that sometimes—make funding open ended if something promises some unexpected results. Your father asked for the extension and got it. That should prove to you how important it was to him to see the thing completed."

There was a hardness in Hassan's voice she had never heard before, and he was being very shrewd. He wasn't so obvious as to trade on what she might owe him, but he would trade on her loyalty to her father. There was no way she could or would deny that. She had loved her father deeply and was instinctively protective and defensive of his memory.

"Wouldn't father's photographs help the new man?" Janet asked. "I know he took dozens of photographs down there."

"The notes would still be needed to identify the items shown but anyway, the photographs are gone."

"Gone? How could they be gone?" In spite of her effort to control her irritation, she was angry. The startled eyes of the boat boy hastily turned away.

"I'm sorry," she apologized hastily to Hassan, "but how could all those just be gone?"

"How, indeed?" He laughed to cover his embarrassment. "Egypt has its bumbling bureaucracy. I turned in all the photos to the bureau, of course, but now they simply cannot be found. You must remember, it was a time of great confusion for us all. Another war was imminent, and the government was preparing. It was a real crisis. Any day, any moment, the order could come through to close all existing excavations. Foreigners were being moved out of the country because their safety could not be guaranteed for long. Egypt once again would be fighting for its life—as it has for thousands of years," he added dryly.

A faint film of sweat had appeared on Hassan's forehead, and Janet felt compassion for him. Egypt was Hassan's land, and he must love it. After all, he had been through the crisis and she had not.

"Your father was pushing, working as hard as he could—eighteen hours a day or more. The work itself was difficult and tedious because of the littered condition of the burial chamber. He dared not enter it in the normal way. He had his men construct a kind of platform hanging from ropes strung down the ninety-foot entrance shaft. It suspended him about a foot above the actual floor. There was a pad on the platform, and he lay upon this to make his notes. He would pick up an object from the cluttered floor, examine it, make his notes as quickly as he could and then replace it in the identical spot. If the notes are not transcribed, all this work will have to be repeated. Your father would hate to see the last hours of his life's work wasted, Janet.''

''How long do you think it would take me?'' she asked thoughtfully. Perhaps she should do this—for both her father and for Hassan.

He spread his hands. ''How long? Ah, Janet, you must look over the notes and decide that for yourself. There are,'' he added smoothly, ''eighteen hundred pages.''

''Eighteen hundred pages! Oh, Hassan! It will take forever. I can't expect the school to grant me an open-ended leave. I can't just resign from this job. I love it. Mr. Jamison, the principal, could never get a replacement before the term begins. I can't ask him to. He's got too much on his mind already. It's not one of those rich private schools, Hassan.''

''My dear, you haven't even seen the notes. Wait. Don't answer yet. You can look at them today, this afternoon. We are going to meet the new archaeologist, Dr. Ballard, now. He will be waiting for us at Giza. He arrived yesterday. He's already been out to the site, and he's gone over the notes himself. To-day he's supposed to meet with Dr. Houdeiby, my chief at the bureau—''

''Ballard! Did you say *Ballard*! Hassan! Is it one of *them*!'' She was surprised at the degree of her antagonism.

''Yes, it is. Todd Ballard. Did I not mention that?''

''No,'' she said firmly. ''You did not mention that.''

"Ah, then I am sorry. I should have mentioned that first, and my dear, I do apologize." He was being his most sincere; his dark eyes beseeched her.

"All right, Hassan," she said, relenting. "I'll start transcribing the notes and do as much as I can in the two weeks I'm here. If I can't finish, I'll take the rest home with me and complete them there."

Hassan looked dismayed. He started to say something but changed his mind, turning instead on the wooden seat to speak a phrase or two in Arabic to the boy. The youth wheeled the boat around and headed it in, neatly cutting between two other boats. Janet watched him, all his strength concentrated on earning a few extra coins. Chances were he had been born on the river and would die on it, as his fathers had before him and his sons would after him.

The *felucca* responded to his skill. Its sail tautened, and the boat veered out of the path of a sluggish motor launch as it plowed past them, leaving the sailboats gently rocking in the wake. The morning haze had lifted. It would be bright and hot soon, and the river traffic had picked up. Most of the other *feluccas*—the ever-present water taxi and freight carrier for centuries of Egyptians—were heavily loaded with the large white storage jars so widely used in the country, bales of hay, sugarcane or green alfalfa, animals or pigeons and chickens in crates. Mingled among these things were passengers of all descriptions—an odd blending of East and West, ancient and modern. There was a constant exchange among the passing boatmen as they called out greetings and messages to one another in Arabic, conducting their leisurely lives and businesses as others had for thousands of years. Allah had granted yet another day, so one must put it to use and enjoy life in the process.

They were close to the esplanade now and could hear the noise of the town. Some men on shore shouted in Arabic, and the boat boy replied. It was something amusing, because Hassan smiled and the youth laughed at the men on the shore.

Janet hoped that the boy would bring the boat in perfectly and that Hassan would tip him something extra. She had noticed that Hassan seemed good about that, sometimes even overly generous, as if he understood how much the people beneath him might need an extra coin. How could he understand? Beyond having been her father's and her own best friend, she really knew very little about him.

Janet picked up her straw handbag, watching fondly as the warm wind glued the boy's cotton garment to his slim body, outlining him against the vivid blue Egyptian sky. A man on shore had tossed a rope, and the youth reached up, catching it. Then he started to moor the boat.

"Watch your step, my dear. Can you make it?" Hassan helped her quickly from the boat onto the old stone steps rising out of the water.

Janet had not seen how much he had given the boy, but she had heard a pleased murmur of thanks. Then she was busy trying to keep the wind from snatching away her idiotic straw hat to send it sailing out over the Nile. She also had to keep the wind from lifting her skirt like a balloon. She longed to be in jeans and sneakers as she went carefully up the stone steps in the impractical sandals. She managed to avoid touching the edge of the water as it lapped and swished against the stones, carrying back and forth small pieces of floating rubbish and bright bits of orange peel.

"Can you hurry, Janet? Ballard is already here. I hope we haven't kept him waiting."

Hassan was tense. She could feel it, like static electricity in the air around him. Ballard was *important* to Hassan. She knew it and resented it. It was important to him to please Ballard, to placate him, keep him from becoming annoyed that he couldn't read her father's notes. And she admitted to herself, feeling disloyal, that she knew why. It was because Ballard was wealthy. An old American family, with old money, made before the heavy taxation. Now and then she had sensed this deep need in Hassan for money, this desire to subject himself to people who *had* money. She wondered why Hassan was like this. Someday she must learn the answer, someday when she and Hassan were just good friends. Perhaps then she would understand and not be repelled by the idea that Hassan seemed willing to do anything—anything at all—to please someone rich.

The wind whipped her skirt against her legs, and she could already feel a grittiness inside her sandals.

Hassan stepped forward, half bowing, holding out his hand. Feeling vaguely troubled and defensive for Hassan's sake, Janet assumed a smile and watched the man weaving his way purposefully through the swelling crowd.

Looking at him approach, she had the quick impression—felt the impact, almost—of raw strength held in check. It was in the quick toss of his fair head as he pushed a heavy lock of sun-bleached hair off his tanned forehead. It was in the impatient movement of heavily muscled shoulders beneath the cloth of a faded cotton plaid work shirt. It showed in the strong thighs straining against the worn denim of work pants. So this was one of the famous Ballard clan.

"Maybe I'm not a very nice person, Hassan," she murmured as they waited at the side of the pavement. "I'm going to do my best to like this man because he's important to you, but it may be hard going."

Hassan gave a quick nervous laugh and spoke rather sharply in Arabic to several street peddlers who were converging upon them, arms outstretched, draped with chains and strings of cheap jewelry. Bowing slightly, they backed away. Not so the dark-eyed, curly-haired children who darted about, laughing and shouting. A few women lurked in the background, their long black skirts trailing on the dusty pavement, their big eyes bright and curious above black face veils as they watched Janet with interest. There were also unveiled women in modern dress, apparently employed, who went about their business, seeming scarcely to notice her.

As Ballard came up to them, Hassan took her

arm, pushing her just slightly forward. "My dear, may I present Dr. Ballard? Todd, this is Janet Wingate. Miss Wingate is, as I told you yesterday, the late Professor Wingate's daughter."

"How do you do," Janet murmured. She would have extended her hand, but a sudden gust of warm wind snatched at her hat again.

"How do you do. You may have to exchange that hat for one of these." He gestured with a strong sun-browned hand that held one of the crumpled canvas sailor hats she had seen so often in Egypt.

Janet felt a momentary relief that she had not needed to let him take her hand. "Yes," she made herself say pleasantly. "I've noticed they do seem to stay put." Then she blurted out suddenly without meaning to, "Hassan tells me you're connected with the Ballard Foundation."

"Don't remind me." His sensual mouth twisted to an ironic grin. "I had to serve two years in the foundation's main office right after I did my doctoral work."

"I take it you didn't enjoy it?" She kept her voice level with an effort. There was a growing dread in her mind, something she couldn't quite identify. Why was she behaving this way?

"Not really." There was a quick glint of something like anger in his eyes—strange eyes. They were such a light clear brown that in the intense Egyptian sunlight they appeared almost golden. No, not golden, either, more like amber or topaz. "I'd made a deal with my guardian—one of my uncles— that I'd give a couple of years to the foundation if he wouldn't object to my studying archaeology instead of business management. So I paid off."

"Why didn't you like it?" she asked, going on in spite of a warning that sounded loud and clear in the bottom of her mind. *Don't say it. Let it alone. You don't want to know.* "I'd think that was a lot of fun—giving away all that money to worthy causes. There you were in some posh New York office shoveling it out for all sorts of reasons." She pretended not to hear Hassan's stifled gasp. "You must have been the best-liked man in the world."

"I don't think so. I was in Dover, Delaware, and I wasn't in charge of giving away anything." He was looking down at her intently, aware of the sudden hidden tension between them and not knowing why. "I spent most of my time there weeding out the undeserving applications—you'd be surprised what sorts of projects people want financed by someone else. It was good indoctrination in the many varieties of raw greed. A real crash course in the value of money and how to hold it. I became adept at saying no."

"Janet," Hassan interrupted desperately. He took hold of her upper arm firmly and gripped tightly. "Let's go inside someplace. There is too much sun out here for you."

"Yes, let's," Todd Ballard said, glancing around the esplanade. "It is too early for lunch, but we can get a cold drink in one of these cafés."

"Yes, yes," Hassan said eagerly, and added something in Arabic to the clustering children. They scattered back beyond his reach, laughing and dancing about.

"Baksheesh," they cried, holding out grubby little hands, "baksheesh."

"Dr. Ballard," Janet said with persistence, "in addition to saying no to new requests, did you have to monitor ongoing funding plans, too?"

There. She had asked it. Now she had identified the cause of the growing dread in her mind. Was this the man? Was this the one who had sent a cable or picked up a phone in some cool office and halted the funding of her father's project? She had to know.

He was saying, "That place is okay. I ate there when I was here before. To answer your question, yes. We—the foundation—always have a number of open-ended grants going, and I learned at an early age that things that are absolutely under control in the morning can manage to fall apart in your hands by noon." There was more than a trace of bitterness now in his voice. "Your father's project, for instance." He was standing very still in front of her, his topaz eyes intent. He was clearly aware of the undercurrent between them and not the least put off by it. "Being by that time an archaeologist myself, I hated like hell to halt the project, but—" he moved his muscled shoulders in a slight shrug "— you do what you have to do. Come on, we'd better get out of this sun for a while."

Janet felt sick. He, this arrogant man in front of her, with his tanned skin and his sun-bleached hair and his unlimited amounts of money, sitting in his air-conditioned office, had taken another man's whole life in his careless hands. He had picked up the phone or asked a secretary to make a call or type a memo. And here in Egypt her father had received his message. Here in the blazing sun and the blowing sand, with sweat running down his overworked body, he had heard or read this man's decision. Then her father's overworked body had rebelled. That quiet thoughtful man who had always been slow to anger could not handle the rage that must have exploded inside him. It had killed him, making him fall down on the sand among the rocks, while nearby workers dropped their tools and came running.

Stop it.

Janet turned swiftly away from the two men, trying to shut out the sudden resurgence of the old grief. She needed a moment—just a moment—to compose herself. Somehow or other, for Hassan's sake, for the sake of her father's unfinished work, she had to enter the small café and sit across the table from this man.

I can't do it, she thought desperately. *Not yet. Give me time. Give me a minute.*

CHAPTER TWO

THEY DID IT for her. The beautiful energetic children gave her the time she needed. In spite of Hassan's shouting at them and his gesturing, they clustered about. Some of the bolder ones had come closer.

"Baksheesh." They danced just out of reach, keeping up their chant. Janet had not needed Hassan to caution her against giving Egyptian children money. She had remembered from conversations with her father. Before coming to Egypt, she had, on impulse, included in her luggage several packets of colorful party balloons. Now she quickly opened her handbag.

"No! No!" Hassan said hurriedly. "No money, Janet. They'll be all over you like flies. Come. Come, we must go into the café. Dr. Ballard is waiting."

"Not money, Hassan." Janet was amazed at how steady her voice was. "Just some balloons. They deserve it." She held one up, waving it a little. The children converged on her. She ignored the glance that passed between Hassan and Ballard; Hassan was apologetic and Ballard calmly unreadable.

The small balloon fluttered bright and pink in the

shimmering sunlight. Janet put it to her lips and blew it up to about the size of a cantaloupe, then let it go. There was a wild hissing sound as it twisted about above the children's heads. Then she flung a handful of balloons into the air. The children went wild with joy, scrambling for them on the pavement, laughing, shouting, wrestling one another. The nearby adults were laughing, too, at the children's delight; even the peasant women's eyes gleamed above their black veils.

Janet watched them all, a blank smile on her face, until she was sure her emotions were under control. Then she turned. "I'm sorry," she said carefully. "I couldn't resist. Shall we go now?" She spoke directly to Ballard, testing herself.

"By all means," he said dryly, "if you're sure you're ready."

Their party escaped in the prevailing confusion and entered the small glass-fronted café with the large Coca-Cola sign over the door. Inside they passed a long refrigerated deli cabinet containing an assortment of chilled fish and shrimp. Crossing the bare plank flooring, they sat down at one of the square wooden tables covered with cracked oilcloth. Though it was too early for lunch, the small place was redolent with the aroma of dozens of small fowl roasting on spits. The spits were hand turned by three small boys and a little girl who seemed to be part of the owner's family.

"Those can't be chickens, can they?" Janet asked Hassan, trying to make conversation.

"Pigeons," Todd Ballard answered. "They are

pretty good the first hundred times, I guess, but you'll get tired of them before you leave Egypt.'' His light clear eyes regarded her intently. "You like children, Miss Wingate?''

"Very much. I work with them all the time. I'm an art teacher for elementary grades in a small private school.''

Without asking her what she wanted, Hassan ordered tea for her and himself and turned deferentially to Ballard.

"Coke is fine for me,'' Ballard said.

"I'd like that, too. I want something cold.'' Janet countermanded Hassan's order and heard without compunction his exasperated sigh. Blandly she continued. "Originally I came with the intention of staying two weeks, and now, this morning, Hassan has told me you're having difficulty with my father's notes.''

"Some difficulty, yes. I can't read them.'' There was an edge of sarcasm.

"My spring semester starts in two weeks. I can read them, of course, and Hassan has asked me to transcribe them for you.''

Todd Ballard had detected her underlying antagonism. He leaned back in the wooden chair, causing it to creak under his weight. He appeared mildly curious. "I'm not presuming to criticize your father's work, Miss Wingate. He obviously made his unreadable notes for his eyes alone. I daresay if the political situation hadn't erupted again, all would have been well.''

Their drinks were being served, and Janet stared

a moment at the glass before her, wondering if she could swallow any of it. Was this what hate felt like—this odd nausea and pounding of the heart? Surely not. She had never hated anyone in her life. She'd have to fake an appearance of cordiality for two weeks and wasn't sure she could. She placed her slim hands around the cold glass.

"Then you will stay on to transcribe the notes?" Again Ballard spoke directly to her.

"I'll start on them right away," Janet evaded. "I've used that shorthand system all my life. I think you'll both be amazed at how fast it goes."

If Ballard had noticed the evasion, he let it pass. "Hassan told me you'd be interested in doing it, so I haven't worried too much about it. I'm beginning to understand why everyone in the field depends so heavily on Hassan—he has a way of getting things done." Very neatly he was handing the problem of the unreadable notes over to Hassan, letting her know that if he were to be inconvenienced, Hassan would be responsible for it.

Janet seethed with a slow anger.

"I couldn't help noticing your instant rapport with all those kids. I suppose you come from a big family?" Smoothly now he was turning the conversation away from the notes.

"No," Janet said tightly. "I'm an only child." He hadn't even cared enough about her father to find out anything about him.

"So was I," Ballard said. He was giving her that intent look again. He wasn't drinking his Coke, either, but was twisting the glass around and around in a small circle of wetness on the oil-cloth.

He looked young—too young to be in charge of the excavation. He couldn't be much beyond thirty. And he looked like some magazine ad! He could have been a professional model. Yes, he'd make an excellent image for suntan oil. His heavy sun-streaked blond hair fell across his forehead again. The sunlight streaming into the room from the doorway bathed him in its heat. There were small points of light in his eyes, and his brown skin gleamed. The heavily muscled shoulders bespoke a strong swimmer. He looked anything but a scholarly type—more a man of action. She could picture him skiing, shooting the Colorado rapids, surfing. There was that aura of pure animal strength. Even as he lounged and relaxed it was apparent. She could feel it, like some sort of force field emanating from his splendid body.

He turned and glanced briefly toward Hassan. "Were you able to set it up with Houdeiby?"

"No, not yet." Hassan answered too quickly. "I'm going to telephone again in a moment." He turned to Janet. "My dear, I must find the telephone here. I've been trying to arrange a meeting between Todd and Dr. Houdeiby, my chief at the bureau. He is—how to describe it—a key man. It is important that Todd knows him. He can be of great help. But he is sometimes difficult to reach. I'll be right back." He was pushing back his chair. His attitude implored Janet to be polite, to be tractable, to please Todd Ballard.

When Hassan had gone, Todd Ballard was first to break the somewhat tense silence that had grown between them. "Shall we make it Janet and Todd, since we're going to be working together for a while?"

"Of course," she agreed. This man was important to Hassan, and Hassan was important to her.

She would just have to cope. Somehow.

"That's quite a stack of paper—those notes of your father's. I'm going to have you work from a photocopy, if you don't mind."

"No. There shouldn't be any difficulty. My father's writing is—was—large and clear, and he always used a black pen." She wondered how it felt to have always lived with people running your errands, doing your bidding, trying to please you. She could imagine Todd saying, "Make a phone call, Hassan. Take a memo, Miss Jones. Tell what's-his-name in Egypt to give up the most important thing in his life because I've decided that he should."

"The original notes are in the hotel safe, if you need to look at them anytime. I thought that would be the safest way to handle them. Incidentally, that's a fascinating shorthand he used."

"You've gone through the notes, then?" She stared blankly at the glass before her. *Please don't criticize my father,* she implored him silently.

"Yes. I tried to read them—thinking I could break the code, I guess," he said, twisting in his chair. "No luck. Oh, I could pick up a phrase here and there, maybe an isolated word, but nothing, of course, that would hang together. I have two ques-

tions for you, if you don't mind answering them."
He was restless in the small café, wanting to get up,
to be in motion.

"What are they?" she asked guardedly.

"Where did he learn to write like that?"

"It was his own system. He invented it—or it just
grew as he continued to add to it," Janet said, bit-
ing off each word briskly, trying to be businesslike.
"It is a combination of real shorthand symbols
from the old Pitman method—it's not used that
much anymore—mixed up with alphabetic and
some scientific symbols. It is really an excellent
system. I often use it myself. What was your second
question?"

"I'm not being critical, but why in the world did
he use it to make notes someone else might have to
read? I repeat, I'm not being critical of your father,
but I did wonder."

"Because he thought he had to, I assume," Janet
answered. She felt rather bleakly self-satisfied for a
moment to be keeping such good control of herself.
"He was in a hurry, of course. There was the threat
of another outbreak of war. Everything was in an
uproar. Rumors were flying. There was the possibility of a national emergency being declared by
the government. There was the danger that the
government would shut down all the excavations
until things settled down. That was before you
made the decision to halt the project yourself." She
paused.

He watched her for a long moment, moving
around to face her, sitting up straighter.

"That's what's really getting to you, isn't it? You realize, Janet, that the Egyptian government *did* come through with the closure orders less than three weeks later? The tomb was fated to be closed, anyhow, whether I ordered it closed when I saw how things were going, or three weeks later, when the governmental machinery came up with the same decision."

"Really? I didn't know that," she said carefully. *What difference does that make! He could have had three more weeks. Perhaps he would have been ready for the disappointment by then—perhaps....*

"Too bad he couldn't have just put all his thoughts on tape, instead of writing them all out. He must have had a tape recorder."

"He did," Janet said shortly. "But they couldn't get any tapes for it. Consumer goods—what is available here—have a way of becoming scarce at a war threat. Merchandise brings a lot better price later on the black market."

"Of course. I should have thought of that. Americans tend to get complacent about available consumer goods. According to some of the records—those written in standard English—your father was inside the tomb. What a discovery that must have been for him—to find an actual tomb hidden for more than five thousand years!"

"He was inside the burial chamber itself."

Todd gave a soundless whistle. "To be so close and then to have to withdraw. It must have nearly killed him."

"It did." Janet's voice was flat.

"What?" he asked softly, suddenly erect in his chair.

"I mean," she said distinctly, "it was the chance he had worked and waited for all his life, and then—suddenly—it was all snatched away from him." She swallowed hard. *Don't let me break down.* "My father suffered a stroke at the site. He never came out of the coma. If it hadn't been for Hassan—" She stopped, striving to hold on to her control, staring wide-eyed at the moisture-beaded glass.

"I *am* sorry. I didn't know that." Ballard's words sounded genuine. "What a rotten break for him. You, too. I've read several of his papers and his book, of course. He did a lot of good work."

"It's been a while. I'm over it now. Life goes on." She had to get out of the café, away from this man. "Oh! Hassan is coming back!" Janet stood up suddenly, bumping the table, making the glass of Coke teeter and almost spill.

In a swift reflexive motion Todd Ballard rose, too, and righted the glass.

"Thanks," she said breathlessly. "How clumsy of me."

She met Hassan halfway across the café, feeling Todd Ballard close behind her. She must get away for a while to think things out.

"Did you reach Houdeiby?" Todd was asking over her shoulder.

"Allah be praised," Hassan said, laughing, sounding in some strange way uneasy at the same time. "He is not only available, but he has been trying to reach us. He wants to confer with you, Todd. He says at the earliest possible moment. He's here in Giza now, over at Mena House, and he's invited us to lunch with him.''

''Good. Shall we go?''

Hassan touched her arm, and Janet, filled with dismay, fell into step between them.

Todd was driving a battered-looking vehicle that appeared to be part station wagon but stood as high off the ground as a Jeep with heavy tires. When they were inside, however, the ride proved to be quiet and fairly comfortable. The back section, including the seats, were crowded with boxes of gear, so she sat crowded between the two men in front. She felt she was too close to Todd Ballard, but there was nothing she could do about it. There wasn't room enough for her arms, and she tried to make herself small, leaning toward Hassan, trying to avoid any contact with Todd.

They were going, it seemed, directly to Mena House, where Dr. Houdeiby was already waiting for them. It was supposed to be a short drive, and she clung to this idea.

Crowded this close to Todd Ballard, she was again aware of the man's physical vibrancy. He seemed like some superbly healthy animal, and apparently he did have a brain he was willing to use. Somehow it didn't seem quite fair that the prodigal hand of fate had selected this one creature to so lavishly endow. And with such a heritage at his disposal, he must certainly have had all the women he wanted.

Suddenly, faintly appalled at herself, she became aware of everything about him—the muscular movement of his strong leg as it moved between clutch and brake, the hardness of his arm as it moved in frequent gear change because of the traffic, the occasional pressure of his arm against the curve of her breast. There was a metallic odor in the car despite the air conditioning, and she felt trapped, shut in some sort of box without enough oxygen, breathless. She was grateful that for the moment the two men seemed satisfied to talk to each other over her head.

Todd was saying, "Janet was telling me a little about her father at the tomb closing—you never mentioned if you were there at that time. Were you, Hassan?"

"What? No. I was not with him then." Hassan, who looked preoccupied, was clearly having difficulty concentrating on the conversation.

"You have no idea of the panic surrounding us then, Todd. I was a divided man. Wingate was my best friend. He was very disturbed that the work might be halted. I was mostly at the bureau, trying to find out how much more time he had—or if it would all be a false alarm. On the other hand, my country seemed to be getting ready for war again. I spent hours on the telephone and days in various offices, talking with other officials—I lost track of time."

Todd shook his head. "He didn't even get to take anything out of the burial chamber, did he?"

"No, nothing. It is all still down there, ninety feet below ground level."

Todd drove with skill, and driving wasn't easy in Egypt. Egyptians drove fast and used their horns constantly. Traffic was often impeded by a camel loaded with alfalfa or sugarcane. Camel drivers blandly ignored surrounding vehicles. In addition, carts loaded with produce or crated pigeons were impervious to the blare of the horns behind.

"Were you able to discuss the tomb contents at all with him before he—before the tomb was closed?"

Janet tried to lean farther toward Hassan. Todd had almost casually mentioned her father's death, only at the last moment remembering her presence. He didn't care about her loss. He cared only about what he would find inside the excavation.

"Not to really discuss." Hassan shook his head, squeezing himself against the door, trying to give Janet more room. "There was no time for discussion. We did talk a few times on the phone. Telephone service was unbelievably poor—everything was always tied up with priority military calls. Sometimes, late at night, I could get through—get patched through to his walkie-talkie down below. We talked, but we had no real conversations. There was too little time. I was always in a hurry, and he was always anxious to get back to his work or to steal an hour's sleep. My office has a little recording device. I remember now that I recorded his calls. I didn't want to forget in case he asked me for something I could get for him. He wasn't feeling well—having trouble with his digestion—too much tension, I suppose. He was eating, when he bothered to eat, only boiled unsalted rice and drinking hot *karkedeh*. You remember, Janet, that tea made from those little red flowers that grow up in Aswan and the Sudan. You had it chilled this morning for breakfast.''

"Hassan, you never told me you recorded any conversations with my father,'' Janet said thoughtfully.

"So I didn't,'' Hassan answered, sounding faintly surprised. "I must have forgotten. I remember thinking that I would listen again later, when I had more time. But I never did.'' He sounded somber, regretful.

Todd braked and swerved to avoid a motorcyclist.

Perhaps she could hear those last recorded conversations, once again hear her father's voice. "Hassan, will you let me listen to them? I want to.''

He was silent a moment. "Are you sure that would be wise? Even if it is possible—I am sure such things are filed away—the recordings might be difficult to find, and I would not know where to look.''

"I'd like to hear them, too,'' Todd said. "It might give me some insight into Professor Wingate's thoughts even before I have access to his notes.''

"I'll speak to my secretary,'' Hassan said promptly. "She will know where to look.''

Janet's lips tightened. Anything at all, it seemed, was possible for Todd Ballard. Okay. She would remember that. If she wanted hard information from

Hassan, she must see that Todd Ballard did the asking.

Hassan continued blandly, "I recall parts of it—things come back. I remember he commented more than once on the clutter. I'm not, as you know, an Egyptologist, merely a government official, but I've had to pick up some general information, of course."

Janet knew this was not entirely true. Hassan had a good post and did a good job. He also had a number of private business interests in addition to his governmental appointment. Her mind came back to what he was saying.

"He kept referring to piles of things that made his work more difficult. Nothing had been left in any order. Most of the furnishings for the dead had fallen apart centuries before, just where they stood. The gold fittings were lying about where they had fallen as the joints and wood disintegrated."

"Well, five thousand years might do that, even if no grave robbers ever found the tomb first," Todd commented. Janet could feel his body tensing. He was fascinated with her father's project.

"The sarcophagus was intact. I remember he said that, and we were pleased. At least," Hassan qualified, "he said the lid was in place. It looked undisturbed as far as he could tell from where he was just below the entrance shaft."

Todd came to a full stop behind a lopsided produce wagon and waited for it to turn onto a side street. Janet saw the quick flare of excitement in his eyes when he glanced at Hassan. What a coup it

would be for a young archaeologist—any archaeologist—to find an intact royal burial in Egypt these
days.

"Where was he inside the chamber, Hassan?" he
asked.

"Only just below the entrance shaft. He'd had
the workers build a kind of platform arrangement,
which they lowered into the tomb in sections. When
it was assembled down inside, they held it suspended by ropes about twelve inches above the floor.
There was a flat mattress on it, and Professor Wingate stayed there. He made photographs all the time
he was working—as I told you nobody can find the
photographs yet."

"You told me." Todd's voice was dry, and Janet
had to hold back a smile. He didn't like not getting
what he wanted.

"Then," Hassan went on, "Wingate would lift
up an object from the floor with a kind of pincer-
like tool, examine it, make his notes and put it back
exactly where it had been. It was slow work. The
floor was littered with all sorts of rubbish—"

"Rubbish! Are you sure?" A produce cart made
a turn, and Todd drove forward again.

"Yes, that surprised me, too. But he said it *was*
rubbish. Just leftover trash from the ancient workmen. Chips of stone. Bits of plaster. He said it
looked as if everything had just been thrown in together at the last moment as the workmen were fin-
ishing up. And some of the plaster work was
shoddy—careless. He didn't understand that,
either."

"Nor do I," Todd said thoughtfully. "That's out of character for those people. The workmen were always meticulous—they had to be. Ceremonies for the dead were vital, all locked into their religion. I've got to read those notes. If those men messed up on their jobs down there, then something was wrong."

Janet began to be interested in spite of herself. Growing up, her main focus had been her own developing artistic skills, and she had taken only a passing interest in her father's work.

"I'm really anxious to get at those notes, Janet. It's my good luck that you're here and able to transcribe them." Todd sounded excited.

Of course it was his good luck, she thought in exasperation. He was one of life's lucky charm people. So anything at all would happen if he wanted it to. All he had to do was hold out his strong hands and whatever he wanted would fall into them. She thought of her father, who had worked his way through university waiting tables. It was her father's discovery. Her father's triumph. It wasn't fair.

Todd moved beside her, leaning closer. "Look, Janet, see ahead there? That's the famous Mena House Hotel—one of the favorite places of the old British blue bloods, I'm told. I've been staying there—it's close to the excavation site. Hassan advises me to lease an apartment or house while I'm in Giza, but I'm not sure. I like the Mena House."

I . . . me . . . mine . . .

The man seemed totally self-centered. One would think, listening to him, that the secret tomb was his own personal possession, that *he* had found the carefully sealed entrance the ancient workers had so skillfully concealed centuries ago.

Janet breathed a shaky sigh of relief as they turned into the spreading grounds of the Mena House. It was breathtaking, set as it was amid forty acres of rolling lawns and ornamental gardens and pools. The rich cream-colored buildings themselves rose, almost at the base of the pyramids, in arabesque elegance like a lavish palace and seemed a vision from an *Arabian Nights* fable.

"I suppose you know, Janet, that Mena House started out as a royal hunting lodge," Todd commented. "Incidentally, Hassan, where does Houdeiby want to meet us for lunch? We're not exactly dressed for the Rubbayyat."

"I took the liberty of telling him that," Hassan remarked. "He said just come upstairs to the Khan el Khalili restaurant—that's fairly informal."

Janet was unprepared for the stunning luxury of the lobby. She got a dreamlike impression of gold-leaf murals depicting ancient Egyptian scenes on the walls; gleaming oriental rugs scattered over a marble floor; gigantic, intricately designed chandeliers of pierced metal. As they mounted the wide splendid stairway on the thick red carpet, Janet reflected that she could as well be in a palace. Briefly she touched the silken surface of the brown marble wall, which was topped by a richly polished pierced-wood railing along the sides. High above was the gleaming pounded-copper ceiling. The so-called informal dining room was a masterpiece of living greenery and artfully arranged fretwork baffles that gave an illusion of privacy to many of the tables.

As they entered, a portly Egyptian in a dark business suit rose from an alcove table by the windows and came to meet them. Just behind him strolled a woman about Janet's own age.

"Ah, Janet, let me present Dr. Idris Houdeiby, my associate at the bureau, and his lovely daughter, Nazli."

Janet extended her hand to Dr. Houdeiby as Hassan continued the introductions. She quelled an impulse to laugh as, with courtly grace, Dr. Houdeiby bent over her hand and kissed it. Hand kissing had always struck Janet as slightly funny, but she smiled graciously and turned to meet the "lovely daughter, Nazli."

She was lovely. She was a classic example of the most beautiful modern Egyptian women. She had black hair, swept back into a chignon; huge gleaming dark eyes; deep olive skin, and full voluptuous lips, which seemed at the moment somewhat sulky. She was dressed expensively, as were many of the well-to-do Arab women Janet had seen. The elegant simplicity of the casual linen skirt and matching pale yellow soft blouse bespoke designer labels.

"What a great pleasure to meet Hassan's dear friend at last," she murmured, taking Janet's hand gracefully in both of hers.

Janet felt, as one sometimes does, an instant wariness. Despite the other woman's courteous greeting, her attention had quite firmly settled on Todd Ballard, and Janet had the feeling it would not waver throughout the lunch. She wondered if there was some deeper reason than simply that Todd Ballard was a rich and attractive male.

She wasn't long in finding out. Hardly had the attentive waiter served their first course of chilled fruit than Dr. Houdeiby turned his full attention to Todd.

"Perhaps you do not know, Dr. Ballard, that my daughter, Nazli, is one of our leading young Egyptologists. Ah, yes, women here are entering the professions. As an American, you, of course, are accustomed to professional women, are you not?"

"Yes, of course," Todd agreed, picking up a fork. His light clear eyes held a look of detachment. In some subtle and inexplicable way he had removed himself slightly from the rest of them. It was the same remote look Janet had seen briefly on the esplanade. Somewhere in his experience he had picked up the knack of setting himself slightly apart, of withdrawing and erecting an instant invisible barrier around himself that, she knew, would be difficult for anyone to breach. He was a very private person, this clear-eyed man opposite her.

Somewhat put off by Ballard's coolness, Dr. Houdeiby nervously began to review his daughter's accomplishments, and as he did so, Janet could sense Hassan's growing anxiety.

Janet looked more closely at Nazli. So here was one of the emancipated Egyptian women who had been to university and had a career. She seemed

quite unperturbed in the face of her father's glowing tributes, making only a minimum deprecatory
gesture before eating her fruit.

Todd was lounging in his chair. He was looking
the Houdeibys over, making some sort of private
assessment. Perhaps he wondered what they
wanted from him or how useful they could be to
him.

"Nazli's best area of expertise is in the ancient
written languages—not only our Egyptian hiero-
glyphs, but also the Babylonian cuneiform." Dr.
Houdeiby was grimly persistent. Clearly he wanted
his daughter included in the Ballard project. "She is
most learned in all ancient writings."

Hassan made a hopeless attempt to deter the determined Houdeiby ambition. Exquisite tact was
mandatory, since Houdeiby was his superior at the
bureau.

"Todd has barely had time to—" he began, only
to be interrupted by Dr. Houdeiby.

"Nazli's background is sound. She did her gra-
duate work at the Sorbonne, and she worked a year
and a half at the temple at Dendera. Later she
worked ten months with the inscriptions at the
Temple of Khnum at Esna. Not to mention her early training experience at the Tomb of Seti I." Silently Janet gave Houdeiby good marks for trying so
hard to promote his daughter's career. She was
beginning to like the pushy little man.

Todd moved his muscular shoulders in a motion
resembling a shrug. There was a short silence from
the others. They were all waiting for his response.

Janet wondered how it would feel to always have everyone pause and wait for your decision.

"I think I could certainly use some help in translating the inscriptions. We'll be getting the crew together in the next day or so, and with Janet working on the notes, there should be no delay after we get the shaft cleared."

Dr. Houdeiby beamed, and Nazli's sulky lips opened in a wide smile, revealing perfect teeth. Janet was more interested in Hassan's reaction. His face had gone blank, and she realized in that instant how much he was opposed to Houdeiby's daughter's working at the excavation. She watched him as he made one last comment.

"Well, certainly, Nazli would be an asset to any excavation, and it's up to you, of course, but you yourself are an expert on ancient writings."

"Oh, I expect to be busy enough," Todd said easily. He had made his private assessment and decided against Hassan's obvious wishes that Nazli be excluded.

There was a spate of congratulatory comment—delight from Dr. Houdeiby and hollow enthusiasm from Hassan. The undercurrent was strong. Hassan most emphatically did not want Nazli working with the group.

How odd, Janet thought. She glanced again at Nazli, and accidentally their eyes met. Janet hastily glanced away in quick astonishment at the look of purest venom she had encountered. It had disappeared in half an instant, and Nazli reached over to lay a smooth hand over hers.

"What fun," she said pleasantly, "that we shall be working together. Isn't that nice?"

"Very nice," Janet agreed woodenly, suddenly aware that too many people at the table were looking at her now. Dr. Houdeiby rattled on happily, but no one was listening. Janet saw Nazli's fixed smile, Hassan's brooding stare and the gleam of malicious amusement in Todd's eyes. Somehow she had missed something. She had become a focal point—almost a target—and she didn't know why.

Yet. She corrected herself. She didn't know why *yet*. And she had better make it her business to find out, since she was going to be stuck in Egypt for two weeks.

CHAPTER THREE

BY THE TIME the three-hour lunch was finished, Janet had become extremely wary of the Egyptian woman and planned to avoid her as much as possible during the next two weeks. Nazli had established, in the most charming manner, several things: how much she envied Janet's slimness—which permitted the graceful wearing of inexpensive off-the-rack garments rather than fitted Paris designs such as she herself had to wear; how nice it would be to practice her English with Janet, since, having been educated in France, English was her poorest language; how very unfortunate and "inconvenient for Todd" that Janet's late father had made unreadable notes. This last remark was repeated at least four times. And finally, just before the group rose from the table, Nazli suggested, ever so kindly, that perhaps with her own expertise in languages, she could help Janet with the notes to get the work finished more quickly.

"That's very kind of you," Janet said, smarting under Nazli's barbs, "but it's awfully complicated. I think it would take longer to teach the system to someone else than just go ahead and do it myself. Thanks, anyway." Silently she had added, *over my dead body*, and hoped it didn't show in her expression.

"But you must not spend all your time working with your father's notes," Nazli persisted pleasantly. "You must take time to travel—some other places besides Cairo and Giza."

"Oh, I shall," Janet assured her. "There are so many things I mustn't miss."

Nazli laughed in pleased agreement, but Janet knew that the other girl's attention was divided. When she spoke again, Janet was positive that she raised her voice just slightly to catch the attention of everyone in the party.

"You must, by all means, visit the city of Ismailia."

"Ismailia?" Janet asked. "Why, Nazli? What is special there that I should see?"

"The Suez Canal—you must see that. Ismailia lies north and east from Cairo and is less than a hundred miles distant. You can visit it in only one afternoon if you wish. The town was laid out when the Suez Canal was built, so you see, by our standards, it is new."

"That sounds very interesting," Janet said agreeably. "I'll ask Hassan to take me." For some reason this seemed to amuse Nazli, and she laughed again.

"And if Hassan cannot find the time to take you," she said, "*I* shall. I know Ismailia. I have been there many times. Many." She seemed caught up in a moment of delicious private amusement, making Janet wonder if she would ever find out why.

In the lobby the lunch party appeared about to break up.

"Hassan, I assume you're taking Janet back to Cairo?" Todd asked after the two Houdeibys' effusive farewells. Janet watched them go. That *was* a designer outfit Nazli was wearing.

"Yes—ah, first I must speak a moment with Dr. Houdeiby. Janet, could you wait a few minutes?" Clearly Hassan had something else to say to the Houdeibys, and without waiting for an answer, he turned hastily away to follow them.

"Okay," Todd called. "We'll be upstairs in my suite. I have Janet's working set of notes there. She may as well look them over."

The Ballard suite was on the top floor, with a perfect view of that cluster of ancient mysterious pyramids that had attracted millions of people to Egypt through the ages. There was a golden haze in the air, so the images had a misty quality that added to a feeling of unreality. Janet was drawn against her will to the window and stood there, gazing out at them.

"Awesome, aren't they?" Todd murmured at her shoulder, and for a long moment they both stood as if caught in a spell. Janet found herself gazing at Todd. His strange topaz eyes looked remote and dreamy.

"You know, Janet, this may be the best place in the world just to 'stand and stare,' as the poet says."

A warning note struck in Janet's mind. She must not start liking this man.

Resolutely she turned back to the room. After the brilliance of the streaming sunlight it was difficult to see clearly in the relative dimness of his sitting room. The shaft of light from the window made a sheen on the rich carpet. It glittered on the edge of the thick faceted glass ashtray. It glowed richly on the polished wood of an elegant carved desk not really meant to hold an untidy stack of papers.

Todd pointed to the desk. "Let me shut out some of this glare. Turn on the desk lamp if you need to." He pulled a cord, and the drapes swung shut, as if to close them in together, as well.

Janet went to the desk, recognizing immediately her father's clear bold handwriting. Her throat suddenly ached with nostalgic longing.

"They copied well, didn't they?" Todd asked, coming to stand beside her.

"He worked so hard," Janet said softly, almost without thinking, looking at the stack of careful notes that had meant so much to her father and were to have been part of his great triumph.

"Here, you can take off the picture-book hat now," Todd said, and before Janet realized what he was doing, he had pulled it off her head and tossed it aside. "That's better. That looks good. I like the lamplight on that mass of hair."

Nervously Janet pushed at her hair. It felt as if it might uncoil and fall down. Todd was watching her, watching her sudden nervousness. The dreamy and remote look was gone from his eyes. He was a calculating predator again, and his attention was fixed on her so completely she felt an almost desperate need to escape. Escape from the small pool of golden lamplight and the rich dim room. Escape from the clear topaz eyes. She leaned, almost shrank against the desk.

"We got off to a bad start, Janet—I'm not quite sure why. My guess is that you're experiencing some resentment because I've taken over your father's project. If so, I'm sorry." His tone was persuasive, with an underlying note of amusement that Janet found belittling.

"I'm sorry I gave you that impression," she said stiffly, thinking of Hassan. For his sake she did not want to alienate Todd.

"If it's any consolation to you, I'd rather be working someplace on the delta. There are sites there in that moist earth that will become lost unless they are excavated—priceless things, maybe. This tomb at Giza, valuable as it is, could stay safely in this dry desert area for another five thousand years without excavation." He waited for some response, and Janet, ill at ease, could think of none. He shrugged. "Well, back to business, right? Would you like to leaf through these a few minutes until Hassan gets back?"

With a faint sigh of relief Janet turned to the desk and the notes. Whatever he had started to promote, her chill attitude had turned him off.

The notes, made from her father's closely but clearly written sheets, were in two stacks, each about six inches high.

Eighteen hundred pages.

Well, she could start by looking at them. She

reached forward too quickly and knocked the top few pages of one stack. They slid to the edge of the desk. To keep them from falling to the floor, both she and Todd reached for them simultaneously. Their hands collided.

"Sorry," he said, withdrawing his hand slowly, watching her intently.

Astonishingly, small tremors of shock moved through Janet's body like an electric current. Then a relentless wave of heat washed over her. A flush of embarrassment at her own visible reaction to this man's touch flooded her face as her hands jerkily sorted the pages into a neat stack again. He let the silence grow until she was impelled to look up at him. He was standing there, a half smile on his mouth. He knew exactly what her physical response to him had been.

"What color are your eyes, Janet?" he asked lazily, enjoying himself. "I thought they were gray. Now they've gone all dark."

"They change constantly," she said, attempting a lightness of tone. "I look in the mirror first thing every morning to see what color they are that day. It's a game. Now—since I never play games in the afternoon—I'll just go through the notes. Hassan should be here in a minute."

Todd shrugged, his smile widening slightly. "Oh, well, there's plenty of time." He was completely sure of himself. His meaning was clear.

"There will be two weeks. Exactly," Janet said bluntly. "I told Hassan I'd do as much as I could before I go home. Then I'll take whatever is left back to the States with me to work on the notes there.''

''And you'll just drop them in the mail to me here? In installments, as you finish them?'' He sat down on the edge of the small desk. ''That won't do, you know. Since you presumably corresponded with your father while he was here working, you must be familiar with the Egyptian mail service.''

''Two weeks,'' she said flatly, refusing to give him the satisfaction of moving away from him. Not one inch. She patted the stack of notes into an even neater block.

''You really like that job in San Francisco, don't you?''

''Very much. It's an independent private school, and the term is about to start. My principal, Mr. Jamison, wouldn't have time to get a replacement before the start of the new term. I have to be back on time.''

''Is it one of the old San Francisco schools? Heavy with history and endowments?''

''Terrace Grade School? No, hardly. It's existed for only five years—usually on very limited funds.'' She wished fervently that he would put some distance between them. ''Even so, they manage to offer some scholarships and partial scholarships for grades one through eight.''

The welcome ringing of the telephone interrupted her, and she was relieved when Todd left the desk to answer it. Then, with a sinking heart, she listened to his end of the conversation.

''Oh, Hassan. Are you ready for Janet now? I

see.. No, I have no plans at all yet for this evening.... Of course, I'll be glad to.... Don't worry, I'll see her back to her hotel. She'll probably want to rest before dinner.... Right. No problem. See you." He replaced the receiver and waited a moment before he turned back to Janet.

"Hassan's got hung up with Dr. Houdeiby—something down at the bureau, and they'll probably be there until midnight or so. He sends his apologies, and he'll see you in the morning. I promised him I'd take you to dinner—we can discuss your father's notes." A half smile played about his mouth.

Janet tried to hide her annoyance. "I don't wonder he has to work late," she said. "He took the whole morning off to give me a ride on the river, then take me to a three-hour lunch...."

Todd flung back his head and laughed, and Janet quickly turned her glance away. She mustn't look at that strong bronze throat. She mustn't let this man attract her.

"That's standard Egyptian practice," Todd said. "You can't believe their office hours until you've seen them. It's all part of their charm."

"I'm not charmed," Janet muttered. "Did I hear you say you'd see me back to my hotel? You needn't bother, really. I can take a taxi."

"Nonsense. I think Hassan and I are going to work well together, but I don't know him well enough to start breaking promises to him. Do you want to go now?"

ALL THE WAY BACK to her hotel Janet tried to think of a way to avoid going to dinner with Todd Ballard. She failed. No matter how convincing she might make her excuses, he was sure to think she was simply afraid to be with him. Somehow or other she must avoid any involvement. It could only lead to disaster. This was the man—and she was ashamed she had to remind herself of it—who had so carelessly hastened her father's death.

Despite her lack of enthusiasm for the evening, she started dressing an hour ahead of time. She struggled against growing fatigue. Sleep had come in brief intervals. The flight from San Francisco to Paris, the two-hour wait at Orly Airport for a connecting flight to Cairo—all to get a bargain rate. Then the constant underlying worry about how she would break up with Hassan without hurting him. Her tired mind and body were rebelling. Everything had gone wrong.

She almost fell asleep in the bathtub. When she did emerge, her hair dryer wasn't where she thought it was. It seemed to take forever to do her hair and makeup. She kept dropping things and forgetting what she was doing. Never had she felt so sluggish and inept.

She needed a lift.

She stood barefoot before the open closet where she'd hung her clothes. She reached in and plucked out the best garment she owned and gave a wintry little smile. Even what's-her-name, the catty Egyptian, would have been impressed. Nazli would have no way of knowing that it had been bought in one of San Francisco's several high-fashion thrift shops.

Janet held the hanger under her chin and walked over to the mirror. The expensive black chiffon was as filmy as fog. It was a border print of splashy red poppies that had been used for the bodice, supported by red spaghetti straps. The mid-length black skirt, full enough for dancing, draped beautifully and had an uneven pointed hemline. The wrap—in which she would probably freeze to death in San Francisco— was a matching red chiffon stole. She had recklessly bought delicate red sandals that didn't go with anything else she had. *Hassan won't like it,* she had thought. There was about the outfit not just sexiness, exactly, but *blatant* sexiness, which would not fit with Hassan's chosen image for her.

TODD BALLARD CAME PROMPTLY at seven-thirty. When she stepped from the elevator into the lobby, she saw a quick flare of interest in his eyes, and for a moment she regretted her choice of dress. Well, it was too late now.

"Beautiful," he commented, and she had to resist a sudden impulse to pull up the low neckline of the bodice.

Todd himself was dressed rather simply in a white jacket over black trousers, but she noticed the excellence of the fabric and the gold cuff links, set with a smooth dark blue stone.

"Lapis lazuli," he remarked, letting her know that he was aware she had noticed. "My little joke—I thought it appropriate since long ago, before the first wave of grave robbers, there was a lot of it in the pyramids.''

"They're very nice." She smiled politely. "Where are we going?" She was suddenly aware of other women turning their heads, and she suppressed a grin. It certainly wasn't her dress that caught their interest. But Todd seemed unaware.

"I'd like to eat at the Rubbayyat—so that means back to Mena House," he said. "The food is great there, you'll see. Then maybe you'd like to stay awhile and dance. It would be a shame to waste that outfit.''

"Not tonight, I'm afraid," she said firmly as he helped her into a small sleek car. She smiled a vague thank-you at the attendant who shut the door. This was not going to be a "date." She'd better get that settled. "I almost called to cancel dinner after I got back to my hotel, so I don't feel up to anything more strenuous than eating. The jet lag or something has caught up with me.''

"Okay." He settled himself in the leather seat. "But I do want you to see a room there tonight for yourself. I spoke to the reservations clerk. You can probably make faster progress on the notes if you're in Giza instead of in Cairo proper. I'll be there for quite a while, getting things going at the site.''

"Hassan made my reservations here in Cairo.''

"I know," he answered. "I talked with him about it yesterday, and he agreed that it might be more convenient if you are out there.''

Yesterday. They had talked about it yesterday

and settled it all between them. She thought about this a moment and then tried to quell her resentment at having arrangements made for her.

"This takes some getting used to, you know," she said—more shortly than she'd intended.

"What does?"

"This old-world system of making all a woman's decisions for her."

"Oh, I'm sorry," he said smoothly. "I guess I just assumed that Hassan was setting up things for you. Would you rather *not* stay at Mena House?"

There it was again, his adroit shifting of responsibility to Hassan. She bit her tongue, remembering how important he was to Hassan. "No, that's all right. Let it stand if you've already done it."

Let it pass. Two weeks isn't very long. She leaned her head back against the seat and closed her eyes, fatigue lapping at the edges of her mind.

"You're not asleep, are you? Or would you just rather not look at Cairo's nighttime traffic?"

She smiled, not opening her eyes. "I know it's there. I can hear it. I wonder how many horns they wear out in a year." She might as well try to keep things friendly on the surface. "I am beat, however. I'm functioning on less than two hours' sleep, so bear with me."

"Well, you're missing all the lovely neon signs in Arabic. Neon signs are a special art form when you can't read the language."

"Do you think they'll still be here tomorrow night?"

"Probably."

"Well, then, I'll pass for now. Incidentally, I'm glad you decided on Mena House for dinner. I think I'd like to take some of father's notes back with me tonight. I'm an early riser, and I can probably get a neat stack of them done before breakfast."

"Good. Remind me if I forget, will you?"

When they reached the opulent splendor of the Rubbayyat, Janet was surprised at her appetite. The food was, as Todd had said, excellent, and the service superb. After dinner they lingered over small cups of sweet strong coffee, and Janet had a vague sense of well-being and satisfaction that she seemed to have the situation in hand. Todd's interest was evident, and he was just waiting to make a move, but she had kept the conversation light and impersonal, avoiding eye contact, her hands out of reach so they could not accidentally touch his again. She thought—rather pleased with herself—that he might be getting the message.

"How does Hassan fit into the picture, Janet?" Todd asked thoughtfully after a longer-than-usual pause. "Is he your guardian or something? I gathered that he was a great friend of your father's."

"He was. And of mine." Then suddenly, on impulse, she added, "I'm engaged to marry Hassan," stressing it a little too much. There, that should quench any idea he had about a pleasant little two-week affair. Usually truthful, she felt a twinge of guilt at a flat-out lie, but it was in a good cause.

He stiffened slightly. This time she had surprised

him. Astonishment registered in his eyes. "I can't believe that."

"Why not, for heaven's sake?" she asked lightly. "It's true. He's certainly an attractive man. Dependable as Gibraltar. A gentleman, well educated—what more could I want? We became engaged some time ago, while I was still in college. Hassan stepped in and just took over after my father's death. I can never repay him for all—" She stopped. That was a wrong note. She shouldn't have said it. And there was something else lying bleak and bitter in the bottom of her mind. It was a lie. She was *using* Hassan, and it wasn't fair.

Suddenly Janet wanted desperately to go back to her own hotel. She began to make small leave-taking motions, hoping Todd would take the hint. She moved restlessly in her chair. She pulled the chiffon stole about her bare shoulders. She picked up, put down and picked up again her black evening bag from the table.

He refused to move, merely looking at her somberly. Finally, when she wanted to scream, he spoke. "If you marry Hassan, it will be the worst mistake of your life."

"Oh, really!" She tried to put a sound of amusement in her tone. "You're too much. When are you going to start writing an advice column on affairs of the heart?"

"Maybe someday. I haven't got around to it yet," he said. Then, refusing to be put off, he added, "Yesterday, when Hassan and I were getting acquainted, you and your father came naturally into the conversation. It's beginning to add up. The way I read it, and I'm usually right about women, you're still daddy's little girl. Sweet, helpful, always doing what daddy expects.''

He was getting much too personal—and too close to the truth for comfort. She had had a narrow escape from drifting into a meaningless marriage, stopping herself just in time.

"Okay,'' she said lightly. "Daddy's little girl has finished dinner and it's time for bed. Can we go now?'' She could have bitten her tongue when she saw his quick grin. They were both silent as he watched the color rise in her face.

"Believe me, anytime you say,'' he murmured, lifting his hand to signal the waiter for the check.

Janet made an effort to take control again. "I'm going to run into the powder room. Why don't you get father's notes from your room and I'll meet you in the lobby in about ten minutes?''

He agreed readily enough, but her moment of satisfaction at avoiding another encounter was soon dashed.

"Then we'll walk through the arcade,'' he told her, "over to the new section, and I'll show you the room I've tentatively booked for you. The guy offered a choice of two. You can look at both, if you like. I'll have the keys ready.''

When she met Todd downstairs ten minutes later, he had two room keys dangling from one hand and a thick pack of her father's notes tucked under his other arm.

Walking through the long marble-floored arcade

flanked by two rows of elegant shops, Janet made up her mind she would take the first room he showed her.

The room in the new section, when they reached it, opened off a wide corridor with oriental carpeting. The walls were decorated with large exquisite watercolors of village scenes from Upper Egypt. At intervals along the walls stood antique-chair groupings or settees. There was nothing "new" looking in this addition to conflict with the mellow charm of the older part of Mena House.

The room itself was lovely, much nicer than the one she had in Cairo. The walls were covered with a burnished metallike paper. The modern furniture included a king-size bed and a couple of easy chairs flanking a good reading lamp.

"There is plenty of space here for a desk," Todd said, standing just inside the door, surveying the room with one quick glance. Then, putting the notes down on the dressing table, he crossed the room. "All these suites have balconies," he said, opening the double glass doors. "And from here you should get a clear view of the pyramids. Yes. You see?" He turned back to her.

Almost without realizing it, she crossed the room, as well. The view across the lush gardens was breathtaking. From the balcony she could see a portion of the curving drive that wound through the grounds. She could also see a section of the main old building, its cream-colored towers rising into the black velvet sky.

Somehow or other she must manage to explore

something of this ancient fabled region that was Hassan's homeland, the country her father had loved so deeply. It seemed important to be—even briefly—part of it. Since she wasn't going to marry Hassan, she might never be in Egypt again. It gave her an odd feeling of loss.

"Are you thinking about what I said?" Todd's voice was oddly gentle.

"What?" She was startled. "What did you say? You mean about putting in a desk?"

"No, I don't mean about the desk. Look, we'd better get inside and shut this door, or the mosquitoes will get in—I didn't flip on the electronic debugging thing on the wall. No, I mean, what I said in the dining room—about a marriage between you and Hassan."

She made herself laugh, glad he was busy a moment with the balcony doors.

"Oh, come on. I'm a big girl. I know what I want in life." She walked away from him, crossing the room, looking around. "This room really is lovely."

She started to gather up the notes that had spread fanwise on the smooth polished surface of the dressing table. "I'll just collect these, and we can go."

"In a minute," he said directly behind her, causing her to stiffen, suddenly aware of his nearness.

Todd leaned forward and placed a strong browned hand beside hers on the dressing table. The lamplight glistened on the golden hairs of his wrist.

"He was a brand new father, wasn't he?" he demanded softly. "An available guardian waiting in the wings."

"It wasn't like that at all. I knew Hassan from—before. He had some business interests in the States. He has come to the States before—visited me. Many times! Well, a few times." She kept her eyes on the notes. Todd was close behind her, his mirrored reflection in front of her. She had a panicky feeling of entrapment.

"He's twice your age, Janet."

"No, not really. Well, not quite," she protested, pushing blindly at the stack of papers.

"It would never work. You're still just pleasing daddy—by marrying his good old friend, Hassan. Forget it, Janet. Save yourself. Get out and live your life. Enjoy yourself while you're young." His voice had become deeper, different in tone.

She looked up at him now, meeting his eyes in the mirror. She was terrified of what her own eyes might reveal but could not tear them away. He was right. This was what she had already realized, had already decided for herself. But having a fling with a millionaire playboy was no part of her plans.

She tried to straighten up, to salvage what she could of her poise. "You know," she said stonily, "I don't think you realize how arrogant you are. You've known me only a few hours, and yet you try to tell me how to run my life."

"Don't forget," he said softly, "when I touched you in my room this afternoon, sparks flew, lady.

You're the original Sleeping Beauty, and I got a good glimpse today of the fire underneath.''

"And you're the one to awaken this Sleeping Beauty and ignite the fire and so on? Really!'' She didn't veil her sarcasm.

"I intend to give it my best.'' There was an underlying grimness in his tone.

For the first time a ripple of near anxiety went through her. Surely he was too sophisticated—and had too many women at his disposal—to force himself on someone who didn't want him. She tore her gaze from his. "I'm going to marry Hassan!'' There it was again, the lie. Using Hassan, making him her protector, her shield.

Distractedly she half turned. The notes had started to topple, then slid off the table's edge, slithering in wide disarray across the expanse of carpet. She made a frantic attempt to catch at them, scattering them over a wider area. "Anyway, it's none of your concern!''

"Suppose I want to make it my concern?'' His voice had the quite implacable quality of a person unaccustomed to disagreement, a kind of smothering finality. "Would you like to know when I first realized I was going to be involved—was involved?''

"No, not really.'' She pushed aside the small bench and went down on her knees, blindly trying to gather up some of her father's notes, while Todd stood like a statue over her. She knew that her voice was constricted, that her hands were unsteady, that her clothing felt suddenly too tight and binding.

And there was, in the center of her mind, that tiny relentless core of cold clear honesty that said he was right—there was a fire underneath, an all-consuming fire, and his slightest touch had threatened to ignite it.

"It was when I first saw you on the esplanade, looking like an old-fashioned portrait. The wind snatched at the big straw hat and you grabbed at it—your eyes snapping fire. And all of a sudden I caught on—you hate that hat, don't you? It was then that I saw the woman inside the old-fashioned portrait, and—laugh if you want to—it was one terrific jolt. I haven't been hit like that since I was a teenager." He was laughing at himself, a kind of self-ridicule, but with an undercurrent of assurance and confidence.

In growing anger she looked up at him, her shaking hands full of papers. He saw too much.

She was about to protest again when he bent down. Placing his hands at her waist, he lifted her up as he might have a child. Nor did he release her then, but continued to hold her loosely, the warmth of his hands burning through the thin fabric of her dress. The notes dropped to the floor unnoticed at their feet. Slow heat began to course through her body.

"Don't," she said in heavy panic, pushing at his broad chest.

His hands tightened their grip on her body and he pulled her closer to him, beginning to move one hand slowly up and down her back, making her shiver with mingled excitement and apprehension.

Desperately she stiffened and pushed harder against him, twisting in his arms. Her foot slid on the slippery scatter of papers on the carpet and she lost her balance, instinctively clutching at his broad shoulders for support.

Catching her, he turned her effortlessly, just enough to place her between the dressing table and his own body. She was pinned against the unyielding wood by the male weight of him. The effect on her was stunning, and she couldn't even speak.

"Janet, don't be such an idiot. You can't marry Hassan. It's a sellout. You're buying emotional security, buying approval again."

"Stop it," she managed to gasp, turning and struggling in his grasp, her heart thudding. She must get away from the strong caressing hands that were sending molten fire through her whole body now. "You can't do this." She was pleading desperately, more with herself than with him.

Even as she pleaded, his hold on her tightened. With deliberate slowness he pulled her tightly against his body. One hand went up her back to her neck. She felt his fingers tangle in the back of her hair, forcing her head back, disarranging her chignon. Panic closed over her. "Please," she gasped. "Don't—"

His mouth came down on hers in a long slow kiss, moving against her own, forcing her lips apart. Her heart was pounding until it seemed she couldn't breathe. Pinned against the dressing table by his strong thighs, she tried to twist away, straining backward. But she was helplessly trapped. She could never escape him—or escape herself, she realized as an agony of deep desire passed through her body, until her very bones seemed to melt.

"Please—oh, please," she managed to moan, and felt his thrusting tongue. Against her will she began to go limp. Willing herself to fight him, she could only cling, her frantic fingers gripping his muscular body closer, closer—she couldn't get close enough. Dimly somewhere the phone was ringing. *Don't answer. Don't answer.* Vaguely she knew her hair was falling. There was the faint click as hairpins hit the dressing table. She felt his hard maleness against her loins and was forced to cry out in a surge of raw primitive need, arching herself against him. He started to pull down the thin straps of her bodice, and she pushed aside his hand to do it herself. Somewhere in the distance the phone rang and rang and rang.

"Turn around." He spoke roughly, his voice thick with passion. Stepping back, he turned her forcefully, one hand cupping her breast. She clung to him, gripping him, burying her face in his neck, her mouth burning against his smooth tanned skin—but he was turning her, twisting her around, making her face the huge mirror.

"Now *look*. Look at yourself, Janet." With one hand he forced her head up while he kept his other arm gripped about her, imprisoning her at his side. A shudder of intense anguish ripped through her as he partially let go of her.

"Hold me," she pleaded, not realizing she said it, clinging to his side, her whole body weak with desire.

"Now what do you see?" His implacable tone was a kind of shattering, rendering her helpless against him.

Vacantly she stared at the image they made—he, big, grim, virile; she, with her hair hanging in wild disorder, her eyes wide and stormy, her lips parted, unsteady.

"You see a woman, Janet." His voice bludgeoned her again. "That's not daddy's little girl anymore. You see? Now *look* and *think*—does Hassan make you feel like this?"

She struggled to focus her scattered mind on the reflection before her, knowing at the same time that he was letting her go.

"This is what I got a glimpse of this afternoon, Janet," he was saying. "And believe me, my love, I have no intention of letting you get away from me. I knew that if you ever let yourself be awakened, all hell would break loose. Now maybe you'll admit it, too. And something else! Listen to me, Janet!"

"Yes," she gasped, "yes." Maybe she had lost her mind. She couldn't think straight—she couldn't think at all; she could only feel.

"I don't intend to snatch a few stolen moments with you when Hassan's back is turned. We've got to get that straightened out. Is that clear?"

The phone by the bed was jangling again.

He released her and strode across the room to answer.

Janet stood shakily where he had left her, leaning forward, bracing herself on the dressing table, staring at her own disheveled image, adjusting to the idea that he was no longer touching her, holding her.

Slowly she began to concentrate on her reflection in the glass. Slowly, almost painfully, she attempted to put her shattered image back together again. Her shaking fingers fumbled at the thin red shoulder straps. Two were broken, and she twisted them together, tucking the loose ends behind the others. Then distractedly she tried to cope with her hair, straining to hear what he was saying across the room, every cell of her body intent on the sound of his voice.

"Oh, yes, we were probably in the corridor. We've been looking at the two rooms. Yes, of course, that's all right." Todd spoke coolly, obviously in control of himself. "No, that's quite all right. You did well to try to locate me if the call is from the States. Please put them through. I'll take the call here."

There was a long pause as he listened. She worked vacantly with the smooth coils of her hair, getting it all back in place. He appeared so intent. He had contacted someone in the States. But who in the States? A woman? She held her breath, wanting him to say something, to utter some revealing phrase that would tell her who he was listening to. Her hands were motionless as she strained to hear some nuance, some intonation when he answered whoever it was.

What difference does it make? she asked herself. It didn't matter *who* he was talking to.

"Well, it was very kind of you to call. I'll certainly tell her. She'll be relieved to hear it, I know." He spoke a few more words and then hung up.

His voice had been gracious. No, not exactly. More like cordial. It wasn't a personal call—it was business. Relief eased through her. Her appearance was in order now. She was feeling calmer. She'd gone a little crazy for a time, and she'd better think about that later—try to get it all sorted out when she got back to the privacy of her own hotel room. She watched him. This tall muscular man had made her feel like someone else.

He hung up the phone, and then slowly he turned around to face her.

She was ready for him now. "I'm going back to my hotel," she said, marveling at the steadiness of her voice. She picked up her handbag. "And I'm going by myself in a cab. I want to be by myself—*by myself*, I said," she added as he took a step toward her.

He stopped and waited. Grimly she gathered up the stack of notes, glancing at him at guarded intervals, wary of him. No one had ever affected her like this before. It was exhilarating and oddly frightening at the same time. From the bottom of her mind came a remembrance of something she had heard in the past—that one person was always the lover and one the loved. How comfortable and secure to be the loved. She had let her first boyfriend, Nicky, love her—and she knew now she had never been able to return his love.

But this man, there, now—how was she going to deal with this?

He simply waited. He had the same measuring calculating look on his face she had seen before. When she had stacked the notes, she faced him again.

"Whatever you wish," he said finally. "Don't you want to know first what Mr. Jamison said?"

She froze. "Mr. *Who*!"

"Mr. Jamison, the principal at Terrace Grade School in San Francisco. I knew you couldn't possibly get through eighteen hundred pages of notes in two weeks, so this afternoon I telephoned San Francisco and spoke to your Mr. Jamison. It's ten hours earlier there, so I got him out of bed. He's a very agreeable guy, isn't he?"

"Mr. Jamison," she echoed blankly. "What—why—"

"You are now on an extended leave-of-absence."

There was a thick ugly silence between them.

"I'm *what*! They can't. There's *no way* they can find my replacement in time. Mr. Jamison would never—"

"But he did, Janet. Very graciously. He said he'd work something out with two of the other teachers. You're not to worry. He said to tell you the rest of the staff joins him in sending good wishes for your temporary work here on this project. He said to remind you to send some picture postcards to your classes."

"What have you *done*!" She was shaking with anger.

"I personally haven't done much of anything," he said smoothly. "I just picked up the phone and made a call. I did say in passing how highly you thought of Terrace Grade School and that you had mentioned it was new and had no endowment income. I mentioned, too, that I would speak on the school's behalf to the board at the foundation. It seemed to solve the problem.''

"I just picked up the phone and made a call.'' Just as he had stolen three precious weeks from her father's life, causing him to die before his time.

Damn him. He had trapped her there, and what could she do about it? How could she fight it? Hassan would be on his side. Mr. Jamison was desperate for money for the school.

A shudder of sheer fury ripped through Janet. The room was suddenly a red haze. She lifted the stack of her father's notes high over her head and threw it at him. The papers scattered wildly about his head, but she didn't wait to see them fall to the floor. She tore across the room, wrenched open the door and slammed it behind her.

CHAPTER FOUR

JANET AWAKENED slowly, relunctantly, feeling resentful as she drifted up layer by layer from sleep into a state of vague seething anger. It was ten o'clock before she was fully conscious. Then her fury became clear.

Todd Ballard.

Mechanically she went through the motions of brushing her teeth, showering, dressing, her mind all the while intent on him, rehearsing imaginary confrontations with him during which she made brilliant, scathing, cutting remarks, reducing him to abject apologies for his high-handedness.

As she sat down to wait for her continental breakfast, honesty compelled her to recognize a heavy uneasiness at the uncontrolled passion of her response to his lovemaking. Oh, she must be careful from now on, very careful.

Looking out her window, four floors above a teeming Cairo street, Janet did what she always did under stress: she reached for her sketch pad and, almost without conscious thought, began to sketch unrelated details of the scene below her.

The sidewalks thronged with masses of people in both European and Arabic dress. Veiled women in

long black draperies that touched the dusty pavement mingled with office workers smartly dressed
in the latest modern styles. There were many young
tourists in the international uniform of blue jeans,
along with men in business suits and men in flowing
galabias of cheap cotton or fine expensive woolens.
Some wore the bedouin head drapery and some had
on small bright knitted skullcaps that clung to the
back of the head. Now and then she saw a red
Turkish fez.

And there were many races in Cairo, the original
crossroads of the ancient world: the slender black
Nubians with their soft easy laughter; the hard
sinewy bedouins with their clear sharp eyes, who, in
centuries past, had swept down over Egypt like
desert winds from the Sahara; the darker stockier
pure Egyptian, who had lived in this place along the
Nile since time was young.

The people below seemed to find an unlimited
amount of time to pause, linger, talk, laugh and
touch one another. Janet's pencil began to move
more quickly now and went on until her breakfast
arrived.

With it came two written messages from the desk
and two bulky brown envelopes. One of the messages was from Hassan, saying that he would pick
her up at one o'clock for lunch. She held the one
from Todd Ballard in her hand a long time, staring
at his laconic comment: "You forgot the notes. See
you later, Todd."

There was no hint of an apology. She crumpled
up his note and tossed it in the trash basket by the

dressing table. He had certainly proved his point—a few minutes in his arms and all her defenses had melted. A hot embarrassed flush stung her cheeks. So big deal, the laws of sexual chemistry were still valid. He hadn't taught her anything new. Some men attracted; some didn't. It had nothing to do with looks, education, background or personality. It had everything to do with yin and yang, female and male—woman and man. And such basic attraction either existed or it didn't.

Janet tried to banish the subject from her mind and reached for the brown envelopes. The first one contained about a two-inch stack of her father's notes. The second contained a similar stack, but of blank lined paper. Todd thought of everything!

She did not want to talk to Hassan about Todd—not now, anyway. The realization sprang full-blown into her mind. Before she had time to wonder why, the old familiar dread of breaking the engagement rose again.

Forget it, she told herself in exasperation. She couldn't leave now until she had finished with the notes, or Mr. Jamison would lose foundation support. Focusing on the task at hand, she began to read her father's clear black handwriting, deciphering his notes carefully, page after page.

It was dull going.

Anyone who chose archaeology as a lifetime career, she reflected, must have the patience of a saint. The first fifteen pages were a meticulous and painfully precise description of clearing the downward shaft into the tomb. Perhaps to another archaeologist such laborious detail might be fascinating.

It wasn't long until her back ached from sitting hunched over the low table. Deciding to use her sketch pad as a sort of lapboard, Janet tore off the top sheet, pausing to criticize the small sketches she had done earlier.

There was an interesting top view of two Egyptian men in native dress as they embraced in greeting—she had captured the movement in the drape of their garments, the quick eager friendliness she had noticed from her window. Another sketch showed a loaded camel in the street. The animal's face was good—she was at her best with faces—but she had skimped effort on the small tattered tassels decorating the bridle. There was another face—in detail only—an uptilted masculine chin with the suggestion of a rather sensual-looking mouth, lips slightly parted. Even unfinished, the sketch had caught a distinct feeling of male self-confidence, almost arrogance. Somehow it was appealing in spite of it. Sexy. A smile touched her own lips. Where had she seen that—''

It was Todd Ballard!

She felt a warm sting of embarrassment in her face once again and ripped off the page, crumpling it angrily into a ball. She threw it toward the basket, but it fell short.

Picking up the next page of notes, she set to work again. In spite of the tedious descriptions, she found herself falling under the spell of the situation as it had occurred. The notes began to hold a quiet suspense that became stronger with every page she finished. She could imagine her father and his workers slowly, relentlessly, chipping away, carefully removing the stones and rubble that blocked the long downward entrance. There was a slanting passage cut into the side of a slope, then a shaft straight down to the hidden tomb. All these facts were important in ways she did not yet understand.

The notes implied it was significant that no monument at all had been erected aboveground over the tomb site. For some reason a sacred tomb in a place of royal burials had been hidden from the world. It was important that the surface of irregular stones had been cleverly matched to the natural stone formations, so as to have remained unnoticed for centuries.

Janet worked steadily, page after page, becoming more immersed in her task. When the telephone by the bed rang suddenly, her hand jerked, making an irregular line in the middle of a word.

Hassan. Lunch. Hastily she pushed the notes aside. She would persuade him to have a quick meal so she could get back to work. However, she discarded the idea the moment he spoke. She could tell by the sound of his voice that he was not alone. A moment later she put back the receiver thoughtfully. They would be lunching with Ballard. Well, now was as good a time as any to lay down some ground rules.

She strode into the dining room to meet them, head high, notes tucked under her arm. She saw the men immediately at a corner table as they rose to greet her. Without a word she thrust the transcribed pages at Ballard.

"You've already started," he said in surprised pleasure. "But that's wonderful."

"Before you read those, I want to mention one thing," she said crisply, seating herself in the chair that Hassan had pulled out for her.

"And what's that?" he asked, glancing up. He was smiling, deeply pleased with the notes. The excitement made his eyes gleam.

"I think we'd better review this business of your arbitrarily changing my plans for returning home. I don't like it."

Hassan's face flamed. "Janet!" He sounded appalled.

The delight vanished from Todd's face, and he slowly put the notes on the table.

"It was ridiculously high-handed. I can't imagine why I let it pass," she continued.

"Janet, *please*." There was anger in Hassan's tone, and he would have said more, but Todd lifted a hand to stop him.

"No," Todd began quietly. "She's absolutely right. It was ridiculously high-handed of me. And I do apologize, Janet." He even bent his fair head in a small gesture of humility. "There's no excuse, really, except that I was so disappointed about the notes—and wanted so badly to begin work. I'm not usually such a steamroller about something."

I'll bet, she thought.

"What would you like to do about it?" He was

looking at her intently, with every evidence of sincerity in his expression.

What would she like to do about it? It took her a minute to realize what he was getting at. What could she do? Reverse his plans now and go back home on schedule? And what would that do to her father's project? What would that do to Mr. Jamison's newly minted dreams of an endowment for Terrace Grade School? Todd was, in his polite way, having the last word.

There was nothing much she could do about it—now. She knew it, and he knew it. Their eyes met and held.

"I just want you to know how I feel," she said. "I don't like decisions being made for me. Is that understood?"

"Absolutely, and I appreciate your being candid," he answered with grave courtesy. There was something almost too serious about his manner, and she looked searchingly at him. But his bland expression revealed nothing. He had retreated behind his barrier again.

Hassan, miserable with embarrassment, interrupted. "Well, my dear, I hope you don't think I'm making any decisions for you, but since you will be helping with the notes, I've changed your hotel accommodations to Mena House—rather than here."

Janet had a strong feeling that Hassan was covering up something about the move, but in a rush of sympathy for Hassan, she pretended to believe him. "Whatever you think is more convenient," she said, picking up the menu.

"These are good," Todd commented pleasantly over the notes. "Very good. Your transcriptions will help a lot."

Janet watched the pulse beat at the base of his tanned throat, and her lips suddenly tingled. The night before her mouth had clung briefly to that same spot at the base of his throat.

Stop it. Her fingers tightened on the menu, and she tried to concentrate, but she had the odd feeling that there had been an obscure battle and that she had lost it.

LATER, WHEN SHE HAD PACKED for the move to Mena House, Janet glanced around and noticed the crumpled sheet of sketch paper near the trash basket. Picking it up, she spread it out on the dressing table. The two Arabs embraced each other still; the camel's bridle tassels were still not correct, but the man's mouth was right. Exactly. She looked at it a long time, noticing the fullness, the strength, the curve drawn just so. Carefully she tore off her half-finished portrait and thrust it into her handbag, as she left the room.

"Where's Hassan?" she asked when she reached the lobby.

"He's sorry, Janet, but he had to get back to the bureau. I told him I'd drop you at Mena House. Right out there," Todd added to the bellman carrying her bags, gesturing toward his car. "Those notes will be a terrific help," he added pleasantly with his dazzling smile.

Janet decided to keep the peace, since he seemed

to be trying to maintain things on a professional basis. She got into the car.

"Well, I'm glad they're useful. It all hasn't come together for me yet, but I suppose it will, though I'm afraid that only another archaeologist could get excited about chips of black basalt. They seemed important to father."

"They are. Basalt dates things rather firmly. The chips had to have come from Cheops's mortuary temple, so his pyramid was already being built. Then the type of paving that covered and concealed this tomb shows very clearly that the hidden tomb already existed before those four small pyramids were built during Cheops's reign. They were for his queens. So whoever was put in this hidden tomb was there *before* any of the queens died.

"All the details add up. As soon as the initial work is finished, we can start right in on clearing the burial chamber. Then we'll know a lot more about who the person buried there was and why the tomb was hidden in the first place."

He was looking straight ahead, driving automatically, his mind on that ancient hidden tomb, apparently totally unaware of her beside him.

Perversely Janet resented this, and knowing exactly what she was doing, she decided to capture his attention again. "He mentions some furniture later on," she murmured.

"What did he say?" Todd asked, suddenly intent.

There. She had him again.

"Something about a chair that had fallen apart down there. He was looking at it from across the room, using field glasses. It was wood, or had been wood—most of that had rotted away—and was covered with gold casings. It seemed important to him that the struts supporting the arms were made to show three twined papyrus blossoms."

"No lotus?"

"He didn't mention any. Is that important?"

"Very." He thought a moment. "It wasn't an earlier *king*, then. You see?"

"Not really. You mean a king wouldn't have had papyrus blossoms on his chair?" Janet wished again that she had known more about her father's work.

Todd smiled suddenly, his eyes glinting, and her heart jumped.

"Yes, a king would have had papyrus flowers, but he would also have had lotus blossoms—symbolic of both Upper and Lower Egypt. There were two separate kingdoms in the beginning. These were later combined, much earlier than this tomb, apparently. The pharaohs afterward had to do a careful balancing act, always including symbolic things from both kingdoms so they wouldn't antagonize either."

She laughed, almost at ease. "Politics were about the same then as now—is that what you're saying?"

"Right. Politics as usual." He was turning into the Mena House drive now, still smiling. "Do you think you'll be working on the notes again this afternoon?"

"I guess so. Did Hassan say anything about this afternoon?"

He stopped the car at the entrance. "He did to me before you came down. He's going to join me later at the site—I'll be out there most of the rest of the day. We'll all have dinner together, and we can go over how things are coming along and make some plans. I've already got the same foreman who worked for your father. He's getting the crew together."

"Who is 'all'?"

"The Houdeibys. Hassan, you, me." He opened the door on her side, leaning across her to do it. The touch of his arm against her breasts sent a shock of awareness through her whole body. "Let's get your bags up to your room. I'll see you up." He slid out behind her and tossed the keys to one of the two attendants coming toward them.

In the elevator Todd continued. "I know that your first interest in life is certainly not archaeology, and I know this must be a rotten way for you to spend a vacation."

"Not really," she countered. "I do have an interest—they are my father's notes, after all."

"Anyhow," he went on blandly, "you'll have one break. Nazli told Hassan this morning that she'd stop over to see you this afternoon. That should break the monotony."

"Oh, great," Janet said flatly, and could have bit her tongue, because Todd glanced at her quickly, holding back a smile. He never missed anything.

Inside the room he paused while she glanced around. She was recalling with sharp intensity the previous night's torrid encounter. Carefully she avoided looking at him. She must say something—anything—to break the tension that suddenly charged the air.

"They've brought in a desk," she commented, walking over to it.

"Yes. Is that where you'd like it? I had it put in front of the windows. It doesn't block the balcony door, but you can look up at the pyramids once in a while."

Todd had come to stand beside her. His tone was deceptively tranquil, and his studied calm seemed to promise the beginning of excitement still carefully submerged. *So,* she thought savagely, *he feels it, too.* Warmth moved languourously through her body, and Janet turned away from him. "It's a beautiful desk," she remarked, her voice strained.

"Are you still uptight about last night? Don't be, Janet. I'm not going to leap at you every time we have a moment alone."

"Thanks a lot."

"But I accomplished my purpose."

"You did *what*?" she snapped, turning to look at him angrily. "Well, I must have missed it. What was your purpose—aside from moving in on some other man's territory! I had just finished telling you, if I recall correctly, that I was engaged to Hassan. If your purpose was to show me that you have no respect for Hassan—or for me—you succeeded."

"Don't get your back up, Janet. I think we're both too sophisticated to go along with any 'shocked maiden' charade. You've suffered a loss, a deep grief over your father. I'm sorry, because I know what that is. Now you're letting yourself drift into a marriage of convenience. You can do better with your life than that. I wanted just to—"

"What? Wake me up?" she asked levelly.

"Well, let's just say I wanted to get your attention. We can leave it at that for now, I think."

"We can leave it at that permanently. My life is my business, Todd Ballard. I don't want any advice from anyone else on how to live it. You and I are crossing paths—very briefly—while I transcribe the notes my father left. When I hand you the final page, you will have seen the last of me. After that, except for some very unlikely accident, we'll probably never run into each other again!"

He looked at her speculatively. "And that's what you want?"

She meant to answer instantly with firmness and decision, but the full force of what she had just said thudded into her mind. When she left there she would never see this man again. It caused her to falter. "That's the way it is," she said finally, not sounding firm or decisive, only dull and somewhat lifeless.

He looked at her for a long moment, and then he said quietly, "We'll see." He walked to the desk, which was actually a writing table with a single wide shallow drawer. He pulled the drawer open. "Hassan had a little box of things your father had been using—pens and such. He thought you'd need them. I put them here.''

"Thank you." Her voice was tight with sudden anger. He had handled her father's possessions. He should have left them for her to retrieve. Janet went to stand at the desk, looking down into the partly opened drawer. "Well, I needn't keep you any longer. I may as well get to work again,'' she said.

"I'll see you at dinner," he reminded her.

"Yes," she answered, refusing to look at him, still focusing on items scattered in the drawer. She kept staring at them until she heard the door close behind him. Then resolutely she turned and opened the case containing the notes.

She arranged the notes and the blank paper on top of the desk and then, faltering only slightly, took up one of her father's familiar black pens and set to work. And while she did so, in the back of her mind, there was a derisive flash of self-contempt. She was escaping, trying to shut out the potent image of Todd Ballard. With the meticulously detailed account of items left in a forgotten tomb she was trying to bury two ugly little facts: one— that the man Todd Ballard had carelessly and selfishly erased her father's life before it was his time; and two—that she, her father's daughter, found the man Todd Ballard nearly irresistible.

With an almost total effort of will she tried to blot out Todd Ballard with the small dead things in the ancient tomb. It became an uneasy game she played. Her father's notes told of the gold-encased beams and poles that must have supported a tent-

like canopy over a royal bed. She studied the notation carefully. Her father had said "royal." But
Todd had said the chair was not a king's chair unless there were both lotus and papyrus in the designs. Stubbornly she wrote down the phrase "royal
bed" just as her father had it. "Royal" probably
had to apply to more than one member of the king's
family. Wishing desperately for the misplaced
photographs, she transcribed her father's description of the gold-encrusted frame and the lionlike
golden feet. There were also the remains of a gold
inlaid box that contained cloth fragments of what
could have been the bed curtains. Here her father's
writing seemed hurried, as if due to some inner
urgency or excitement.

Surprising carelessness in packing here—fragments of plaster and mason's rubbish. Why
would workmen's trash be mixed in with royal
bed curtains. Must examine these closely.

And while she wrote the words, Janet despised
herself for the inner gleeful voice that reminded her
she could fascinate Todd Ballard with this question
that evening. She pushed the idea out of her mind
and went doggedly on, copying the partial inscription from the lid of the box her father had been able
to read from his position beneath the shaft. Her
father had indicated writing he could not see clearly
by leaving dashes. "Beloved Lady—Lord of the
two crowns, Snofru, the Horus; Nebmaat—"
Then, in a side note to himself, her father had writ-

ten, "Royal wife? Royal mother? Check references known family members." Then came an additional note that gave her a sudden glimpse of his frustration:

Deplore lack of artwork on walls for some guidance. Nothing. Rough plaster. Sloppy work. Strange! Feel sickish again. Should have tried to eat something. No time. Never enough time.

Janet sat back suddenly in the chair, letting the pen drop from her fingers. It was the first time her father had inserted such a personal note. It seemed like a dim cry for help from a man who had never asked for help. She thought of him down in the hidden tomb, ninety feet below the surface, on the platform over the floor, scratching away at the notes, working against time, trying to get it all down, feeling sick, surrounded by the rough plaster walls that told him nothing of what he wanted so badly to know.

Suddenly she was crying. The tears rained down, drenching her face; deep wrenching sobs racked her body. The old grief at her father's death three years earlier, pain she thought had gone, swept through her again. She went and sat on the bench in front of the dressing table, hunched over, rocking back and forth. Gradually, as the force of emotion spent itself, her ragged tearing sobs became slow and tremulous and tired. Feeling leaden, she finally got up and washed her face in cold water again and again. Her eyes were almost swelled shut.

Janet had no heart for resuming work on the notes now, and she lay down on the bed. She would rest a few minutes. Thinking this, she plunged into the deep black sleep of utter exhaustion.

A long or short time later, she struggled into wakefulness, aware that the telephone by the bed had been ringing repeatedly. She groped for, then fumbled the receiver off the hook and answered the call, her mind fuzzy, her voice thick.

"It is Nazli! Nazli Houdeiby," the tiny voice was saying. "Ah, I have awakened you. I am so sorry. I am downstairs. I come—came to take you to tea with me. Didn't Todd tell you I would come for this?"

Tea.

Janet stared at the opposite wall, trying to think clearly.

"I'm sorry," she said. "I guess I was asleep."

"I know. I can tell by your voice. I am so sorry to have awakened you. But now that you are awake, do please let us have tea together and a nice chat?" The voice, relentlessly bright and cheerful, was insistent, not about to be denied.

"Yes...all right," Janet said. "Look, I'm—not dressed." She gazed down in dismay at her rumpled clothing. "Give me half an hour, will you?"

"Of course. I'll wait. I am by the pool, okay? You'll remember that? The pool? I'll watch for you."

"Yes, fine." Janet hung up and stared blankly at the disordered bedspread.

She felt better after a quick shower and noted with relief that somehow or other her hair had stayed under the cap and not got wet. *But I'm going to cut it short,* she vowed to herself in a quick gust of anger. Then she dressed in an attractive blue gray sun dress of fine cotton that would pass even Nazli's inspection, since it had come from the same thrift shop in which she had found the black chiffon with the red poppies.

She had a general sense of where the pool was because she could see it in the distance from her window. At ground level she could no longer see it, so she began a leisurely stroll through the gardens. Nazli, she knew, would have to be at the Oasis, one of the restaurants.

Janet passed the colorful tables, shaded by a spreading canopy that came up almost to poolside. It was busy now, with the teatime and cocktail crowd present. She glanced around for Nazli, her eyes scanning the suntanned people, many of them still in swimsuits, some, who had come from the hotel's riding stables, in riding clothes or jeans. They were clustered around the bright tables as deft waiters weaved among them with loaded trays. She found Nazli waving to her, seated near the sign advising that guests were granted temporary membership in the Riding Club. She had a swift image of what Todd Ballard would look like in riding clothes and banished it from her mind instantly.

"I'm sorry I kept you waiting," she said to Nazli. "But I haven't caught up on my sleep yet."

"Of course. I understand." Nazli said, looking at her rather intently.

Janet realized that her eyes were still puffy from crying. By nature reserved, Janet usually felt a sense of embarrassment about giving in to emotion. But not this time. She didn't regret the sudden onslaught of grief, because it appeared, in some odd way, to mark the end of her mourning, and it left her with a sense of relief.

Sipping a tall glass of iced tea, Janet began to feel better. The tranquillity of the scene around her seemed to seep into her soul. The eternal sun of Egypt laved her in its warmth. Janet's eyes roved idly over the dancing blue water of the pool, the green velvet of the spreading lawns. The vines and shrubs hanging with bright flowers moved continually in the soft warm breezes. Soft waves of sound rose and fell around her. There was the sound of occasional voices from the pool, subdued talk from the surrounding tables, the drone of bees in the shrubbery and the soft whispering of the palm fronds as they moved against one another.

"Nazli, this is really a lovely place," Janet said.

"Yes, I suppose." Nazli glanced around, vaguely surprised. It was obvious that her mind was elsewhere. "Would you like another biscuit?" She pushed the small plate of cookies toward Janet.

"No, thanks, I think not." Janet was about to suggest more tea, but Nazli pushed back her chair.

"Perhaps we have finished, then?" Nazli had a

way of ending a phrase like a question. "I have an errand to do. Please come with me. You have been working too hard on the notes, Todd said. I want to take you for a little drive." She almost laughed, but checked it.

"What's so amusing?" Janet asked, looking the other girl full in the face.

"Forgive me. I don't laugh at Americans, really. It is just that some of the rich ones are so—ah—eccentric, are they not? I think Todd Ballard will live here at Mena House all the while he is working on the tomb. Imagine that! Usually one lives at the dig and the living conditions are—" she spread out her hands gracefully "—very simple. Very simple. You see? But somehow Todd is working on a dig that is close to a deluxe hotel. That is very funny?"

Janet managed a tight little smile, absolutely sure in her own mind that Nazli was laughing at something else entirely.

Nazli chattered pleasantly as they left the Oasis and walked along by the pool and around to the entrance of the hotel.

"My father is well-known here, as you see," Nazli said complacently, waving when the driver of a luggage-laden hotel van honked his horn in greeting as he drove by with incoming guests.

At the hotel entrance a doorman and two bellmen sprang into action when Nazli appeared. The two women were helped with great ceremony into one of the small black taxis.

"I was out at the site for a while," Nazli said, and Janet heard the excitement in her voice. "Todd is very pleased with the notes you have given him so far. He had the men open the first passageway. He's having the workmen string in the electrical wiring.''

"Where are we going?" Janet asked after a moment. She felt obligated to make some approving comment about the city, except that she could find nothing appealing in the drabness that totally surrounded them. They drove through a series of dreary neighborhoods, dusty streets and grimy stucco and brick buildings, all of which seemed in great need of repair and paint. Bedraggled washing was suspended on sagging lines hooked to window ledges and rickety fire escapes. Here and there a small carpet hung out a window. There was an occasional tree with dust-laden leaves. The narrow concrete sidewalks were often cracked and broken, or they simply stopped in mid-block, so that people continued walking on the hard packed earth. Occasionally, house plants drooped sickly in tin cans or pots on window ledges from which faded paint had long ago peeled or worn away. And over and through everything was the continuous movement of the warm restless breeze—slowly twisting the garments on the lines, pushing at the drooping tree branches, causing a hanging rug to flap tiredly against a building and picking up bits of trash or rubbish from the street, to whirl it listlessly around in the heavy air.

"We are going to Hassan's apartment," Nazli said. "That is my errand. The light in Todd's big electric torch burned out, and he needs one until the rest of his things come. I told him that Hassan has several, very strong, like searchlights, and I will bring one back with me.''

The taxi stopped in front of a slightly better-looking building. While the driver held open the door for them, Nazli issued orders in Arabic like a gracious young queen. Apparently he was going to wait, because as they entered the building, he got back into his cab, flipped on a small transistor radio and settled back.

Janet shrank as she entered the building. Surely Hassan didn't live here, she thought. He was so fastidious and particular in his manner and dress. She had seen him in very different circumstances on his visits to the States and even in Egypt he gave the appearance of affluence. Silently she followed Nazli down the narrow hall and up the flights of concrete steps, past linoleum-covered landings. Nazli stopped on the third floor.

The apartment was less depressing than the outside entrance had prepared Janet for, although the entrance from the hall opened directly into the dining room. With a distinct sense of dread, Janet stepped into the small high-ceilinged room. Her own reaction unnerved her—there was no reason to feel this way. She cared for Hassan deeply, but the implied intimacy of going into his apartment when he was not at home repelled her, and she wondered how she could have been idiot enough to have thought seriously of marriage to him, for marriage was certainly the ultimate intimacy. She glanced around, keeping her face blank to the inquisitive glance Nazli sent her.

The ungainly little room was furnished with care-less mismatched pieces. A rather ornate wooden sideboard was against one wall. The center of the room was occupied by a chrome dining table sur-rounded by chrome chairs upholstered in yellow vinyl. On the table a glass vase held an assortment of blue and white silk flowers that were slightly dus-ty. Poor Hassan, who so much enjoyed luxurious living. He must spend very little time there.

Then she noticed that one of her paintings was hanging much too high on the wall. Hassan had re-framed it in heavy gilt-painted carved wood. The little picture of a small bridge in the Japanese Tea Garden in the park at home cried out for its own delicate bamboo frame.

"I see you noticed your picture," Nazli said. "Hassan has the other one you gave him in the bed-room. That pale one of the vase of blue iris—you remember it, too?"

"Yes," she said, dreading to see what kind of frame he had put that one in.

She followed Nazli into the sitting room, which looked out over the narrow street.

"Look at this dust," Nazli said in annoyance, giving one of the pale Swedish-modern tables a swipe with her hand. "Hassan pays a cleaning woman—much too generously—and this is the job she does. I must speak with her again. Well, come, let us find the torch."

She was acting like the lady of the house, and

Janet got the message immediately. So that was her problem, then. Nazli herself had plans for Hassan and wasn't going to step aside conveniently when Janet appeared.

"I'll show you the rest of the apartment," Nazli was saying. "I've managed to make it livable—but only just, as you see. I keep telling Hassan he should live better, but he wants to put all his income into this or that. So I do the best I can. Down here is the kitchen."

She led the way down a short narrow hallway. Obediently Janet peered into the kitchen. The cupboards had been painted so many times that the doors didn't close properly and stood ajar. The bathroom had apparently been a closet at one time.

"Now here is the bedroom," Nazli said sweeping into it rather grandly, then stopping short just over the threshold. There was simply no room to sweep grandly through the bedroom. It was unbelievably crowded. The massive king-size bed, covered with peach-colored satin, took up most of the space. But in addition, two wardrobes flanked the door of the single walk-in closet and the large double dresser. This seemed more like Hassan—it was here he must keep the expensive elegant clothing that made him look like a super-rich oil sheikh when he visited the States.

Janet stood in the doorway, watching Nazli rummage with great familiarity through the dresser drawers, ostensibly looking for the flashlight. She was putting on quite an act. At one point she sorted through a stack of clean undershirts. Shaking her head in disgust, she took out one with a rip in it, rolled it up in a tight ball and pushed it into her handbag. She was giving a very good performance of the loving and concerned mate.

"I'll wait for you in the sitting room," Janet said, turning away. "I'll look around for the flashlight there, too."

Maybe it was that simple. Maybe Hassan had now found someone of his own people he really cared for.

And Nazli had a key to the apartment! Janet suddenly recalled that Nazli had used one of the keys on her own key ring to open the door.

Still thinking about this, she absently pulled open the front of a small drop-leaf desk, painted green, which stood against the sitting-room wall. Perhaps the flashlight was in it.

When open, the leaf slanted downward and a flat manila envelope slid toward her. Janet picked it up to replace it. Labeled with Hassan's flowing Arabic writing, it gave her no idea of the contents. As she pushed it back among the mass of other papers that jammed the desk, the top gaped open and a small tremor of shock went through her at the photograph she saw. The envelope was stuffed with papers, some handwritten notes in Arabic but mostly newspaper clippings. Frowning, she reached in and riffled through the mass. Many of the clippings were in English, some in French and Arabic. There were a number of other photographs. *Todd Ballard*. What in the world was Hassan doing collecting a fat file of data on Todd Ballard? *Why?*

Then immediately came the thought—*time*. It had taken Hassan time to collect all this information. Yet he had never mentioned to her until the last minute that Todd Ballard was taking over her father's unfinished work.

"I found it!" Nazli's triumphant voice rang through the apartment.

Anxiously Janet thrust the thick envelope back into the mass of papers and quickly shut the desk. She must not put it off any longer. Too many unanswered questions were piling up. She must talk to Hassan—and soon.

CHAPTER FIVE

FINALLY—AT NEARLY MIDNIGHT—Janet managed to get some time alone with Hassan. She was tired and her nerves ragged. She had a strong impulse to put off what she must say until later, but grimly she made herself get on with it. Hassan had been extremely elusive since her arrival. She had better use this moment while she had it.

"Come out here," she called to him. "I want you to see the view from my balcony. What do you think of that?" She gestured extravagantly toward the dark outline of the pyramids against the velvet sky. Her voice sounded false to her own ears, and she caught a speculative look in Hassan's fine eyes. He was too clever, and he knew her too well.

He laughed softly, reminding her subtly to keep her voice down, as people strolled about in the gardens beneath the balcony. He pushed forward one of the rattan chairs and brushed off the canvas cushion so she could sit down. She seated herself, murmuring a belated thanks.

"You are pleased with the room Todd got for you, then?"

"Yes, but frankly, it's nearly the only thing about Todd Ballard that I'm pleased with at the moment. For one thing, are we always going to have this chummy little family-group dinner arrangement? He just seems to assume he's authorized by God to decide when and where we'll all eat.''

Hassan laughed, choosing to treat this as a joke.

Janet gritted her teeth. "I'm not joking, you know. I'm up to here with Todd Ballard," she persisted.

"Janet, Janet, you were 'up to here,' as you call it, with Todd Ballard long before you even came to Egypt. Now isn't that so? Why do you think I kept from you the information that he was going to be in charge of the excavation? I have known for some time, but I did not tell you.''

She tried not to resent the tone of authority he was using, as if she were a somewhat unruly child and it was his place to control her.

Hassan seated himself on the rattan ottoman and took one of her hands in both of his, holding it fast in his warm grasp. She resisted an impulse to pull away. His hands were much softer now than she remembered. Nothing at all like Todd's hard strong grasp. A small tremor went through her as she tried to shut out the sudden recollection of Todd. Mistaking it for excitement, Hassan pressed her hand tighter and commenced to move his own, stroking back and forth, sometimes on the back of her hand, sometimes on the palm. With effort she refrained from pulling her hand away from him. A little flare of panic darted through her mind. Although they were engaged to be married, Hassan had always been gentle and somewhat chaste in his lovemaking—if it could be called that. Because at first she had been rather young, or because of his friendship with her father, or because his own position had been part-guardian, part-friend, part-fiancé, he had limited his advances. Now that she was clearly a self-sufficient, self-supporting adult he need not. She was astonished at the silent violence of her resistance. She strove desperately to keep her mind on the conversation, acutely aware of his caressing hands, definitely suggestive now.

"Why did you keep it from me—that Todd would be here?" Despite her effort her voice sounded ragged and breathless.

"Because I was delighted that you were coming and I didn't want you to change your mind. Didn't someone say that all was fair in love and war? I love you very much, my dear. You cannot imagine how overjoyed I was when you wrote you were coming for a visit."

"Hassan, listen, I—I have to talk to you." Now she did pull her hand away from him, unable to stand the relentless stroking another second.

"Of course. What is it?" Immediately he was all concern.

Desperately she tried to focus her thoughts. "Keep in mind Hassan, that I'm American and inclined to be a little outspoken sometimes."

He gave a little indulgent laugh. "Be as outspoken as you like, my love. You've never been anything else, and I adore you the more for it."

This she knew was a polite lie.

"About going to your apartment today—Nazli insisted on taking me there. I—there is something—two things, actually." She stopped in mid-sentence to collect her thoughts. She mustn't sound petulant or aggrieved.

"Ah, yes," Hassan said softly.

"We were looking for that large flashlight, you know. The one she wanted to get for Todd. Well, Nazli was in the bedroom, searching through the drawers of the dresser, and I went into the living room. And in the living room I looked in a desk for the light. An envelope fell out—a big one. You know, a brown manila envelope."

"I know the one," Hassan said quietly. His tone was almost soothing, as if he were speaking to a nervous child. "It is information about Todd that I have collected. It is labeled on the front." He was being either very open and candid or very clever. She wasn't sure which.

"It is labeled *in Arabic* on the front," she countered.

"Ah, yes, of course. But that is what it says. Inside are—"

"I know what's inside. It's stuffed so full that it gapes open. You must have everything ever written in any paper or magazine or journal about him. Why, Hassan?" There. At least she had that much out.

"Why?" he echoed, faintly astonished, sounding genuinely puzzled. "What do you mean, 'why'? Because I wanted to know all about him."

"But why did you, Hassan?" Here her courage

failed. This was as far as she could go. She simply could not reveal to him her own uneasiness about what appeared to be his absorbing interest in money, his almost slavish attention to anything Todd Ballard wished.

"Why did I wish to know about him? Because it is my duty to know, Janet. Part of my job at the bureau." There was laughter in his voice now. "Do you know how rare it is to encounter an archaeologist with unlimited money available to him? This country—my country—has unbelievable archaeological deposits yet undiscovered. Of course I know about people in that field—all about them, or as much as I can learn. We depend on these rich foreigners to find our treasures. And believe me, to my way of thinking the greatest treasure in Egypt at this moment is the open-handed young Dr. Ballard."

It was plausible. Very reasonable. There was no real flaw in Hassan's logic, so he must be right. Except for what her father had always referred to as a "gut feeling" when something was wrong. She sat silently for a long moment in the velvet semidarkness, gazing unseeing at the massive outlines of the monuments to three dead kings. The gut feeling didn't go away. It told her that Hassan was up to something and was suddenly confronted with it. What better defense than a display of candor?

"There was something else, was there not?" Hassan's soft voice startled her. Apparently he was going to get everything straightened out, allay any doubts she might have. The gentle indulgence of his tone was condescending. She struggled against the old feeling of awkwardness at being treated like an intractable child to whom he must explain everything slowly, carefully and with unfailing kindness.

Janet looked at Hassan. His near-exotic face was thrown into dark and light relief in the reflected glow from her room. Whoever did marry Hassan would never be an equal partner to him. The insight came and went sharply and clearly in her mind. He was too Eastern. Regardless of the Western tailoring, regardless of the excellent education he had received in European and American universities, he had started life in Egypt and would always remain Egyptian. And whoever married him would adapt.

"Well, my dear, you did say there was something else," he reminded her softly in the silent pause that stretched between them.

"Yes." Janet straightened in the chair, taking care to keep her hands out of his reach. "I wondered about Nazli. Forgive my bluntness again, but to get right to the point, I was given the distinct impression she's in love with you. At the apartment this afternoon she—" Janet paused because Hassan's low laugh interrupted her. He leaned closer, reaching out, and she slid her hands down beside the chair cushion.

"And I am in love with you. So what have we here—a triangle, an impasse?" He laughed again, sliding his hands around Janet's waist. "Nazli is an adorable—but very unruly—child. She has fancied herself in love with me since the first week of my work at the bureau for her father." His hands were caressing her. "I remember the first time she came down to the office to see her father. She wore a white middy and pleated black skirt and had a brief-case bulging with textbooks. I thought she was a delightful child. I still do.''

Janet put her hands against Hassan's upper arms in an unconscious attempt to hold him away from her. He was getting too close.

"She's much more than a delightful child, Hassan," Janet said grimly. "She's a woman, a very desirable woman, I'm sure, and she's madly in love with you."

"Nonsense. She's had a crush on me for years. One of these days she will find her real love, and I'll lose her. I can't say I won't regret it. There is no man alive who doesn't enjoy being adored."

"She—has a key to your apartment," Janet said breathlessly. Hassan half rose from the hassock and leaned over her, his head and shoulders blotting out the night sky. "Where did she get it?" she persisted, turning her face slightly. *Don't kiss me! Please!* she entreated silently.

He was really laughing now. He couldn't keep it out of his voice. "She got it from me, my darling. She invented all sorts of excuses until I finally gave in and let her have it. She's had it for two—three years, perhaps. Janet, it means nothing, and it is a big help to me, I must admit. You can't imagine the errands she runs, the favors she does. And I, lazy man that I am, take shameful advantage of her. She's been a combination assistant-sometime secretary-errand girl—I don't know what else." There was a subtle change in his voice. Panic shot through Janet. He was going to kiss her. Not the sweet, gentle, chaste kisses of the past, but for the first time a lover's kiss.

Desperately she tried to put it off. "She took one of your undershirts—it had a rip in it. She—"

"*Janet*—you can't be *jealous*. Oh, my dear, come here. Inside a moment." He appeared to be delighted with the evidence of possessiveness.

"But she took it—" she insisted as he pulled her up from the chair and into her room.

"And she will mend it for me—or have her housekeeper do it—I'm never sure who actually mends the things she takes. Forget about Nazli!" His voice, husky now with the beginning of passion, held a definite command, and he expected to be obeyed. "I love you—nobody else. I'll make you forget about her. I'll make you forget everything."

Janet steeled herself for the kiss, knowing she couldn't hurt him by rejecting it. She was caught suddenly unawares. There seemed nothing she could do but submit for the moment. She let herself be crushed against his body and felt his face against her throat, felt his lips moving against her skin. *No,* her mind screamed silently. *Let me go.* She willed herself not to go rigid in Hassan's unwelcome embrace. She could do this for him at least and not humiliate him by letting him know how she felt, without any warning, any explanation. She wished desperately that the maid hadn't come in and turned down the bed.

"My dearest—my beautiful—" he was muttering.

Then his mouth captured hers and she endured an endless kiss, hating it, frantic for it to end. Against her will she twisted, trying to break free, but could not. Real fear shivered through her. He was too big and too strong. She was helpless, and knew it. It made her feel sick. *Please. Let me go.* She felt him force her lips apart and couldn't stop him. She submitted for another long moment, and then she stiffened in his arms, unable not to. She felt appalled, violated, and she couldn't help showing it.

"Janet—Janet." His voice was tender, soothing. "My dear, you're not *afraid*. Not of *me*." The concern in his tone had to be real, but he continued to hold her loosely, not releasing her, swaying a little in a kind of rocking motion. "My dearest little girl."

"I—I'm sorry," she said, hating herself, filled with guilt. "It's just that—you've never really made love to me before. I guess I just—wasn't prepared." *Tell him. Tell him now. Break the engagement,* she thought frantically.

"Of course not. And I was too demanding too quickly. Forgive me, my darling. And you're tired, of course. It is late. It has been a long day."

"Yes, it has." A wild sense of panic seized her. She mustn't let him smooth it over. Nothing was really understood. She had to speak to him, reasonably, sensibly. And there sprang into her mind the uneasy idea that he had purposely distracted her with the sudden advance.

"We have to talk, Hassan. There is something I must—"

"Forget about Nazli, Janet. It is nothing. I swear to you."

"Not Nazli. That doesn't matter. It's something else." Janet stopped. She must be getting hysterical. Nazli mattered. She mattered a great deal if she and Hassan were having an affair, if Nazli had a prior claim and really loved him. She gathered her thoughts together. *Talk to him. Explain.*

"You're right," she said flatly. "I'm for bed. We can talk tomorrow." It was a cop-out, and she knew it.

He stood by the door watching her thoughtfully for a moment. He was aware that something was wrong, that there was something more, something she hadn't yet said. Knowing Hassan, how clever he was, she wondered if he could tell what it was.

"All right," he said calmly. "We'll make time to talk tomorrow. In fact—" he paused a moment, then went on "—I'll drive out tomorrow morning and we can have breakfast together. I'll be here by nine. Is that all right?"

"Nine. Of course. That's fine." Even as she said it, Janet felt a sinking sensation at the coming confrontation. What would he do? What would he say?

"Then I'll drive you out sight-seeing. You've visited almost nothing since you got here. I'll drive you over to Ismailia—how would you like that? I was born and spent my childhood in Ismailia. Did you know that?"

"No, I didn't. Thank you. I'd like that."

She stood staring at the door after he had gone

out, feeling herself become tense, uneasy. He *knew*.
He knew she wanted to break the engagement, and
even now he was planning to circumvent her. He
was determined to marry her, and for the first time
she wondered why. Then she realized she simply did
not believe he loved her. She wondered how long
she had sensed it. She could have understood his
determination readily if she had been an heiress, but
she wasn't. It didn't really make sense. She must be
wrong. He really must be in love with her. Well, she
wasn't in love with him. She set her lips in a firm
line. Somehow or other, regardless of everything,
she would have to make the break. Feeling the way
she had in his arms, any attempt at a marriage between them would be a disaster, and she knew it.

So what now? Sleep, at least for a while, was out
of the question. Her mind was churning with anxiety. She would work on the notes for an hour or so
until she calmed down. One after the other she
kicked off her high-heeled shoes and padded over to
the closet, starting to undress as she went. After a
tepid shower, and clad in her robe and slippers, she
curled up in the reading chair beneath the lamp,
notes in hand, again using her sketch pad as a lapboard. Page after page she transcribed, gradually
pushing her present problems to the back of her
mind. In their place she could see—almost feel—her
father's difficulties as he wrote faster and faster on
the hanging platform inside the airless tomb, ninety
feet below the hot sandy surface.

"Moved spotlight. Many more personal effects
revealed in addition to yesterday's food containers

and dishes. Woman's effects.'' Janet trasncribed carefully. So the "Beloved Lady" mentioned before had taken with her into death all her personal things. Janet flexed her fingers to ease out a slight writer's cramp and went on.

See scatter of large golden rings on stone floor, end of sarcophagus. Appear to match in size to pegs in open box (portable container) described in previous notation. Lid, when found, may have inscription. Ring size varies. Obvious leg bracelets graduating from anklet on up calf of wearer. But why not inside their box? Could box have been thrown into tomb, breaking open to scatter contents? Odd. Beautiful inlay work on rings. Green dragonflies of malachite with touches of blue lapis lazuli. Exquisite.

Janet paused, lifting her eyes to look out over the balcony into the distance. It was late. There was no one in the garden beneath her room; no voices drifted up now. Very dimly she could see the pointed outlines of the pyramids that had stood there so prominently against the horizon for so many centuries. But behind them, hidden and unseen for all those hundreds of years, had waited this small secret tomb of some long-dead royal woman. For the first time something changed subtly for Janet. Sometime while she had been writing about those golden leg rings, the notes about the tomb were transformed from an odd professional puzzle encountered in her father's work into a fragment of living history plucked from another century. A woman not too different from her had been the beloved of someone, had eaten some food from a golden plate, had drunk something from a golden cup and put upon her legs lovely golden bracelets decorated with green and blue dragonflies. Had Beloved Lady paused and looked at the delicate design with pleasure? Had she smiled her pleasure at someone else? For the first time Janet understood her father's fascination for this work. She understood Todd Ballard's impatience to learn what was in the notes. It was all *real*. These were people. People who had come and gone but had left behind them little fragments of their lives so the people who followed could know and learn. She picked up the pen again.

    Another box. Larger. Lid intact but fallen half off. Can see part contents. Alabaster cosmetic jars. Marbled brown and white. Dark caked substance. Black or dark blue. Kohl. Without doubt eye shadow to protect her eyes from sun. Inlaid inscription on box lid. Must get stronger light to read whole inscription.

And here the writing changed slightly, became larger, more hurried, as if her father had suddenly become very excited. "Name visible. We have a name!" Then in faster, larger, bolder writing he had written, "Her name is Eyes-of-Love."

Janet stopped writing, although her gaze traveled on through the next few lines of the notes. More sedately her father had added: "Name not uncommon that period. Must check names known queens this dynasty."

"We have a name," her father had written. Bemused, Janet leaned back in the chair slightly. She could stun Todd Ballard with that one tomorrow. "I worked on the notes last night," she would say. Casually. Just toss it off. "And we have a name." In her mind she could see the tensing of his lean body, could feel the intent gaze of the clear light eyes on her, only *her*. And he might say, "A name! What name? Tell me the name! Let me see!" And his strong brown hands would reach out.

Her eyes focused suddenly on the dressing-table clock. It read three o'clock in the morning! Good grief. She'd better get to bed. Feeling a bit stiff, she uncurled in the easy chair. She carefully put aside the stack of notes. Then she stopped, motionless, as she stood watching the door of her room in fascination. A broad flat envelope was being slowly pushed beneath it; it made no sound on the soft carpet. Half smiling, curious, she went quickly to the door and opened it—and wished she hadn't.

Todd Ballard, down on one knee, about to slide through a second envelope, looked up in surprise. "I thought you'd be in bed."

"I—almost was. I mean, I've been working on the notes and suddenly noticed the time and—What *are* you doing?"

He grinned sheepishly and held up the second envelope for her to take. "Oh, sort of delivering a peace offering, I guess. I got some prints earlier down in the bookshop and I was looking them over in my room, and then I remembered that your Mr. Jamison had suggested you get some picture postcards for your classes, so I thought maybe these—''

He reached over and picked up the other envelope. ''I've got some good comparisons for them, I think.'' He opened the envelope and let several prints slide onto the carpet, then fanned them out. ''This is all late-eighteenth-dynasty stuff. I'm fascinated with it myself,'' Todd said, pointing out details in the pictures. ''Look how light—how free—how natural. See how the flowers bend by the water. You can almost feel the breeze. And look at the ripples in the water where the ducks are swimming. And look at this of the two girls talking—any minute she's going to lift that fan and use it. And the way she's got her head back—you can almost feel how warm it is.''

''They're lovely. And yes, you're right, she's too warm and any minute she's going to fan her face and her neck.'' Without even thinking about it, she went down on her knees in front of the spread of prints. ''But these don't look at all...Egyptian,'' she said in wonder.

''No, they don't, do they?'' He reached over and took back the other envelope. ''These are what you think of as ''Egyptian.'' He pulled three or four large prints out of the envelope and spread them like a gigantic hand of cards with his strong brown fingers. ''See? Look at the rigidly controlled figures, the ritualistic gestures. The Egyptians painted this way for centuries because this was the

accepted tradition and they were tradition-bound."
He was looking at them thoughtfully, totally absorbed. "Yet they're beautiful—in their way."

"Yes," Janet agreed slowly, "they are. There is
something compelling in the almost brutal austeri-
ty. But *these*," she added, her voice softening,
"these are so lovely." And she turned to the first
ones he had shown her, noticing again the graceful
lines of motion, the pale muted colors.

"I knew you'd like those best." His preoccupa-
tion was gone, and his voice was soft, personal and
pleased. She had the feeling he liked them best, too.

"How did they come to be among those
tradition-bound artists?" she asked, trying to re-
establish the impersonal mood.

"These are from Ahknaton's brief reign—one of
the great dreamers of all times. While he held the
double crown of Egypt this is the way his artists
painted. I think I'd give everything I own to be able
to see his city the way it was—the graceful houses,
the reflecting pools. I think you'd have loved it."

"I'm sure I would have," Janet said. She had an
odd sense of something tenuous and shimmering
between them for an instant.

"If. . . you ever want to see where it is—I mean,
was—I could take you there. Sometime." The instant she had sensed had passed, and he knew it, as
well. He bent his fair head over the pictures and
began to gather them up. "Well, I know you want
to get to bed. I do, too. There's a lot to do tomorrow." He stood up and held out one hand to help
her. "I hope your classes like the pictures."

She held out her hand, anticipating his touch. "Oh, they will. They'll love them. And thank you," she added breathlessly. She took the pictures and the large envelopes, clasping her arms around them. "What's out there now?" she added. "Is there anything left of that city?" *Wait. Don't go,* she silently begged.

He turned at the door. "Not much. Part of one stele with a carving of the royal family—Ahknaton and his queen, Nefertiti, and some of the little princesses. It's at Amarna, out in the desert. Just that one stele and the sunlight and the sand. And if you run your hands through the sand there, you'll find—oh, hundreds of those little white disks the tourists call 'pharaoh's pennies.'" There was an odd little pause. "Well, good night," he added, and suddenly he was gone.

She leaned against the door after he'd left, still holding the pictures, wanting intensely to see Amarna—to see Amarna with the sunlight gleaming on the sand and on his hair.

Ridiculous.

Oh, he was a spellbinder, that one, when he put his mind to it. On the other hand—he *had* remembered pictures for the kids in her classes.

Janet set her alarm again and called the desk to make sure she'd be ready when Hassan came. It had been a mistake inviting him to her room, and in case he took it as a standing invitation, she wanted to be up and dressed when he arrived. She realized in the back of her mind, without thinking too much about it, that Hassan's gentle indulgence might well be a shell of politeness. She had a vague feeling that beneath his courtesy lay implacable hardness. For all their times together, for all his kindness to her, she knew very little of the real man. She had got a fragmentary glimpse that evening of violent surging passion hastily checked. Hassan was—she groped for the right word, slowly untying the cord of her robe. He seemed somehow indestructible. If provoked, would he become a harsh enemy? Now where in the world had she got that wild idea? She kicked off her slippers and crawled into bed.

"THIS IS EGYPT'S DELTA," Hassan said the next morning, slowing the car to little more than a crawl. "You are surrounded by it—I think the most fertile land in the world. The 'Land of Goshen,' it is called in your Bible."

Janet took off her dark glasses and looked around, squinting slightly in the brilliant morning. It seemed the whole earth was drenched in sunlight. It pressed with heavy warmth against her skin. It cast the dark, rich, loamy soil into sharp black shadows. It shimmered in the golden air around them. It was true what her father had always said, "The sun of Egypt is like no other sun." As far as Janet could see, on either side of the road, were lush fields of plowed land.

"Are you thirsty yet?" Hassan asked.

"No, thanks." She smiled absently. There was something almost hypnotically tranquil here, and she felt it seeping into her, lulling her senses and filling her with a vague feeling of peace as the car sped along the smooth two-lane highway.

"Let me know when you are. I brought along an ice chest with some cold drinks," Hassan said. They were passing through villages at intervals now, and Janet's sense of peace began to recede at the ubiquitous evidence of what seemed, to her American eyes, bare-bones poverty. The small square houses of mud brick were scattered on both sides of the highway on grassless hard-packed earth. Some houses were partially covered with crumbling fragments of old plaster. All had domed dovecotes on their flat roofs for the ever-present pigeons. Some of the larger houses had low walls fencing off sections of yard. Scruffy dogs lay about the yard, and cats sunned themselves on wide window ledges or draped themselves over the curved tops of the walls.

Here and there people had improvised with odd bits of material they had bought, so that a centuries-old mud house could have a patch of shade in the yard provided by a resplendent piece of corrugated yellow plastic. In one instance a missing gate in a crumbling wall had been replaced with a discarded Coca-Cola sign. And one house had been fitted decades ago with wooden window frames that were beginning to crack and come away from the house. They had been covered recently with a thick coat of paint in a vivid electric blue. One house with most of the plaster either still intact or mended had been painted a stark white and contained a row of partly finished hand-painted murals in bright primary colors. There were figures of a camel, a pickup truck, a bus, an airplane, a donkey and what appeared to be a flatbed truck, in varying degrees of completion along the side and front of the house.

Hassan stopped the car. "That house—you see? He has made the hajj. He has been to Mecca. So now he paints his house to show all the ways in which he traveled in his pilgrimage. It is the custom."

Janet was enthralled. "Who paints it? Does he do it himself?"

"He can if he can paint. If he can't, there is usually someone in the village who can paint well enough to make recognizable figures."

"It's really not bad for someone who hasn't been trained," Janet said. "Do you think he'll get around to putting a saddle and bridle on the camel?"

Hassan laughed. "Oh, yes, but there is never any hurry about it here. This could take several years. Nobody will mind. After all, I'd guess the house has been there for a couple of centuries at least. Would you like to put the saddle on the camel? Shall I go and tell him you are an artist and offer your services?"

"Oh, Hassan! Could you!"

"It might take hours," he warned. "We may not get back to Cairo until midnight." But even as he said it, he was opening his car door to get out, caught up in her enthusiasm.

Already several men villagers and some children had approached and were standing about at some distance from the car, some watching intently, some smiling slightly as if in welcome. Most wore the native dress of loose ground-length galabia, with skullcap or twist of cotton covering the head.

Hassan was immediately surrounded by a growing crowd as he spoke rapidly in Arabic. Response was immediate; everybody talked at once, gesturing and pointing. Perhaps they weren't so poor, after all, Janet thought. Two of them wore glasses, and she had caught the flash of more than one wristwatch in the sunlight.

Two teenage boys were sent on errands and went running in different directions across the plowed fields, holding up their garments, their brown legs gleaming.

Hassan returned to the car. Several women had come out of the house now. They had on long black dresses and face veils and stayed in the background.

"I've told them that you are an artist from America and that you admired the paintings."

She got out of the car. "Did you tell them I wanted to paint the saddle on the camel?"

"No, that will come later. I told them you might, that I would ask you if they wished me to. I told them that I thought you would consider it an honor."

"I would," she said simply, catching his arm for support as she walked over a patch of rough ground toward the house. This was the *last* time she would wear high-heeled sandals out in the boonies. Hassan could like it or lump it.

"Actually, the man who went to Mecca would be delighted to have a professional artist add to the mural. Those two boys you saw—he sent one to locate something for you to stand on and the other one to find the camel and saddle it. You get a live model." He laughed. "You really enjoy this, don't you? Your eyes are shining like stars."

Janet couldn't help laughing herself. All of a sudden Egypt her old enemy was slipping away, and in its place was a new but ancient land, filled with delightful people.

"Prepare to stay awhile," Hassan warned as they approached the group. "You don't rush a visit here—it takes time."

It did. The better part of an hour elapsed while the props were assembled, the paint mixed and Janet was placed atop two crates, one a flat wooden fruit box and the other of open-work orange plastic that had at one time held pop bottles. There had been much conversation and laughter, with Hassan translating and some of the children commenting in village-school English.

By now what appeared to be most of the village had been assembled, and Janet had a rapt audience for her work. Enjoying herself thoroughly, she sketched in the high brown saddle in broad strokes, working quickly. The boy with the camel held it reasonably still by feeding it leafy green sprigs of something. From time to time, however, it would give an agonizing scream and spit a dollop of foamy saliva onto the ground or blow its nose at the boy, who moved nimbly aside each time. Now and then there were murmurs of appreciation from the onlookers. A burst of applause greeted the first red tassel she added to the bridle, and she felt a little rush of pride. When the picture was finished, a veritable bedlam arose. The crowd had swelled to fifty or sixty people, filling the yard, sitting on the wall or peering over it from the field. Everyone had something to say. One small correction had to be made. After looking at Janet's work for some time, the man who had been to Mecca remembered that when he had made the pilgrimage, there had been some gold threads in the red bridle tassels, and Janet obligingly added them from the tube of bright yellow paint he provided.

It was another hour before Hassan and Janet could leave, and when they did, the back of Hassan's car was loaded with two large bags of fresh peanuts, several melons and a sack of ripe tomatoes.

"What in the world are you going to do with all that produce?" Janet laughed when at last they were on their way again.

"It's not my problem," Hassan grinned. "You painted the picture for the man. It would have been unthinkable to leave without accepting some token in return. So it's *your* produce. I'll carry it all into the lobby of the Mena House for you if you like."

Janet collapsed with laughter at the idea of all her humble gifts being carried into that splendid lobby. As she wiped her eyes, she thought, as she had thought so many times before, what a wonderful friend Hassan was. If only he didn't want marriage, too, if only he would settle for friendship.

Now road signs prohibiting foreigners from leaving the main highway began to appear, and they had been stopped at two checkpoints. Both times Hassan went into the small sentry structure with Janet's passport and his own identification.

"Security gets tighter the closer we get to the Suez," he had explained, "and of course no cameras are allowed in this area. It is sensitive defense territory."

Janet didn't care. For some reason she couldn't identify, she wasn't eager to take pictures of this place, anyway. She didn't like it. Some of the villages now were partly rubble, with many deserted houses without roofs; here a long gap in a blasted-away wall; there two intact rooms of a house remaining, into which a whole family crowded. It was after noon, and the sun was high and hot. Janet caught a flashing glimpse through an open front door of what appeared to be a dozen or more people. They were seated inside on the floor, lined up one after the other against the walls. The small room was literally crammed with people escaping the intense heat for a while.

But despite the many signs of devastation among the dwellings, people continued to work the land with an astonishing blend of ancient and modern methods. On one side of the road a large government irrigation system had been installed over several acres.

"There's a vast water table underneath all this," Hassan said, slowing down slightly. "And the government is putting in modern irrigation systems as funds are made available. The crop increase is excellent. Egypt's oldest struggle has been to keep food production level with population increase.''

Janet gazed somberly at the field, covered with a low green haze of plants coming up through the soil. Above them a network of spiky metal pipes several feet high rose starkly.

Meanwhile, on the other side of the road, another farmer was still making do with the ancient type of waterwheel his ancestors had used in biblical times. The wheel stood silent and still now in the blazing sun, a great wooden circle with metal dippers attached, mounted on the edge of a long water ditch crossing the farmer's plot of land.

''Coming back later this afternoon we can stop and watch one of the old wheels working, if you'd like. The farmer will be delighted to show off the equipment. You might like the sound of the wheel too—it creaks in a kind of musical rhythm. Sometimes, when I was a boy, it would almost put me to sleep.''

''Did you ever work one of the things?'' Janet asked. An odd feeling of inexplicable apprehension came and went quickly.

''Oh, yes,'' he said easily. ''When I was a teenager. I worked a couple of years on a farm outside Ismailia. Somehow I didn't mind it. It would kill me now, of course, I'm so out of condition. I enjoyed it then. It let me stand waist high in the water ditch, and I could often douse water over the rest of me. It was a good feeling, and I still love the sounds—the running water, the buzzing of insects, the birds, the faraway voices coming from the houses now and then.''

"Were your people farmers?" Janet asked.

"No." His tone was abrupt, and there was an unaccustomed frown on his face. "I just worked for a farmer awhile."

Hassan slowed down, pulled the car over to a wide place in the road and stopped. The hot silence around them made the noise of a car settling into immobility seem too loud. Hassan turned in the seat and delved among the bags of produce for the ice chest. The smell of ripe warm tomatoes and cantaloupe hung about them, heavy and cloying.

"Coke, Sprite or orange soda—which would you like?" he asked.

"Orange soda, I think."

He took out two orange sodas and wiped the water from the bottles with an immaculate linen handkerchief. He opened the caps with an opener on his gold key chain and handed a soda to Janet. It was cool and delightfully refreshing.

"That's a lovely handkerchief," she commented, noting the fine fabric and delicate monogram embroidered in an off-white.

"A gift from an old and dear friend. I don't have many handkerchiefs left, but they've lasted a long time." He was staring thoughtfully at the wet cloth he had placed on the sunny dashboard, his mind far away for a time.

"I've wanted to have a quiet talk with you for some time, Janet," he said after a while. "One of the reasons I think that your father was pleased to approve our marriage was that we are—were—both men who moved upward by our own efforts.

Neither your father nor I was—what you might call—a 'born gentleman.' Both of us had poor beginnings.''

''I know. Father did all sorts of things to pull himself up.''

''So have I. You asked if my father was a farmer. He was not. We were of the landless poor. My father was a domestic. He supported our family by working as a houseboy for well-to-do British or French families, usually officials of the Suez Canal Company or business firms related to shipping. We all lived in a tenement in Ismailia. We were seven children—three from my mother, who died before she was thirty, and four from my stepmother, who had lost half her teeth by the time she was twenty-five.''

Janet felt a welling up of pity and rejection. *No, she thought desperately, I don't want to hear this. Don't tell me these things. Don't open your heart to me, because I am going to leave you, and you will hate it afterward that I know these things.* But courtesy or kindness or something she couldn't name, made her sit still and listen, with her hands gripping the cold wet bottle.

''His hours were deplorable and his workload, unbelievable. The wages were next to nothing. The theory was that native servants were all thieves—which they had to be—and would steal enough to make up the difference. My father took food from the kitchen where he worked, so he brought home some food every night to supplement our diet. There was a rather definite system among the servants as to who got what, but it evened out among them in the end. My father never let his wife beg, but we children were encouraged to pick up money by begging from every tourist in sight. Everything we got belonged to the family—it all helped. None of us ever considered that the money was ours. We would go tearing home and hand it to mother. She always put it in a small clay jar she kept for that purpose. Ah, you've finished. Would you like another?''

Hassan reached over to take the empty pop bottle, and Janet released it, her fingers a little stiff.

''No, thanks. That was wonderful. I'm ten degrees cooler.''

He laughed. ''Not really. It just seems like it.'' Carefully he twisted in the seat to put the bottles in back. ''I still have the little jar,'' he continued thoughtfully, reaching for the ignition key.

''What jar?'' Janet asked, confused.

''The little clay jar my stepmother kept our money in. I have it in plain view in my apartment. You probably didn't notice it. I've kept it all these years. It reminds me of where I started and where I am going. It keeps me from taking things for granted, things such as fine linen handkerchiefs and always having enough to eat. It is my talisman.'' He started the engine and eased the car back onto the highway.

Janet breathed a shaky sigh of relief. Maybe he would stop talking now. Then her heart sank.

''I knew I could tell you this,'' he was saying. ''All my ancestors were *fellahin*. I am a peasant.

Nazli wanted you to know that, I think, believing it would turn you against me. But I realized it wouldn't. I knew you wouldn't hold my poor beginnings against me. Americans don't, as a rule. Usually it's what you are that counts, not what you've been, and it was time I told you. I know all about you—your father and I used to talk for hours. It's only fair that you know about me. We must have no secrets. Do you not agree?''

Janet gulped. "Yes, of course. Not only fair but sensible.'' Then she grasped it as an opening. "In any relationship *honesty* is essential. Hassan, please. Don't go yet. Please park a while longer. I— I have to tell you something, too. *Please*,'' she added almost sharply.

He pulled over again to the roadside, well off the paving. The car wheels crunched on the pebbles, then came to a halt.

"Something has been on your mind since you got here, hasn't it?'' he asked kindly in a tone she knew well, a tone he had used in the past to comfort her, to solve her problems. "Don't try to be brave, Janet. Cry all you like—I have a big shoulder.'' He had used that tone when he had talked to her about her father's death on his first visit to the States afterward. "Why didn't you tell me you needed money, Janet? I have money, and it is yours. I promised your father I would care for you,'' he had lovingly scolded her. He made her give up an extra night job and paid her school fees from then on.

Janet stared straight ahead, not able to look at him. It wasn't easy being beholden to someone.

Mentally she clung to the idea that she had kept precise records of the monies he had spent on her education, vowing even then to pay him back. There was no way, of course, that she could pay him back for the other things—one can't pay back kindness except with kindness, or love except with love. And she didn't love him—not the way he wanted her to. She was going to be brutal, not kind.

"I've been thinking about our engagement, Hassan." All right. There it was, out in the open between them.

"And?" His tone, level and calm, told her nothing. "Shall we settle on a date? Is that what you wish to discuss?" He wasn't making it easy for her.

She couldn't answer for a moment, and he continued.

"No, of course not. It is something quite different, isn't it? Then please tell me, and we shall resolve the problem."

"Yes. Hassan, I'm sorry to say this, but more and more this last year or so I've got away from the idea of marriage," she began carefully.

"How can a woman 'get away from the idea of marriage'?" he asked gently. "Explain to me, please." A kindly chiding tone. He was going to cajole and humor her, gently guiding her to a correct decision. "Shall I help you clarify your thinking. . ." was a phrase he had used once, and it had made her choke with resentment at the time.

"I like my work. Very much. I intend to go on with it. I don't want to marry until later—much later. Perhaps when I'm thirty or so. Women in the

States combine marriage with careers now, as I'm sure you've noticed on your visits. I intend to do that. If not teaching, then something else to do with my painting." Despite her best efforts Janet felt breathless, and her words seemed jerked out of her rather than stated. "So you see—" she muttered, not daring to look at him. But *dammit*, she shouldn't hang her head like a guilty schoolgirl. She lifted her chin sharply, still looking straight ahead, and continued in a firmer tone. "I know how you feel about wanting a large family. I want one, too. Being an only child was no fun. But the fact is, since I don't plan even to marry until I'm thirty or so, that isn't fair to you. I should think you'd want a family sooner than that." She bit off the rest of it. She wouldn't—would *not*—remind him he was seventeen years her senior. He was sensitive about that. She swallowed hard. Might as well say it all. "There is also the problem of my—my independence. That has annoyed you in the past—don't say it hasn't. You've chided me often enough about my—my—attitudes. I am what I am. I can't change, Hassan. I've tried. I can't be molded and shaped into the submissive kind of wife you want and need. It would never work. Believe me, it would never work." She was almost pleading with him. "You're an Egyptian. And I'm an American," she added desperately.

"You forget, Janet," he said calmly, "that I shall be an American, too. I thought that was understood—you know my plans to emigrate to the States. My job at the Bureau of Antiquities is a stopgap. You know that. My field, my real field, is business. I'm a moneymaker. I'm good at it. I already have some business interests in the States. I have money piling up in the States."

"I know," she said desperately. "I know about your interest in the restaurants in Marin County. And I know that you and your partner there have discussed expanding to a chain and franchising. You can still do that, Hassan. I'd love it if you lived in the States, but you don't have to marry me to do it. People come to America all the time. You must already be on a quota list. I'm surprised you haven't come before this. I never want to lose touch with you, Hassan, I want—I want us always to be friends."

She made herself look at him now.

His face was completely blank. A slow mottled color began to darken his naturally swarthy skin. His eyes were unreadable, utterly blank.

"You and my father were best friends for years. I want *us* to be best friends, too," she plunged on wildly. "Please understand. *Please.*"

"I do understand," he said, a tinge of grimness to his tone. "The fault is mine. I should have brought you over here immediately and kept you here until I was ready to emigrate. You must understand that leaving one's homeland takes time, takes many arrangements, that I have certain obligations here, responsibilities."

She looked at him in astonishment. The phrases "brought you over" and "kept you here" repeated themselves in her mind. Nothing she had said had really sunk in. He was planning to "clarify" her thinking again. Dull anger began to throb in her head.

"I could have sent you to the American University in Cairo. What a fool I was." Hassan struck himself on the forehead. "But it never occurred to me."

"Hassan. You haven't really *heard* anything I've said!"

"I've heard everything you've said," he answered shortly. "And I've heard enough, Janet. You're talking nonsense. Stop it. Please. You've always been a good girl. Studious. Ladylike. Your father said many times that you had never given him a moment's worry. And I've always been gentle with you because you never *seemed* to need any sort of correction or punishment." He was reaching for the ignition key.

Correction! Punishment!

She reached over and caught his arm. "Just a minute! Just a damn minute! Friendship is one thing, Hassan, but trying to run my life is another."

"Keep quiet!"

The sudden flare of naked rage in his eyes made her quail despite her own anger.

"The subject is closed for now, Janet," he went on in a more controlled tone. "But there is *no* possibility of canceling our marriage plans. It is what I want and have waited a long time for. You know how family-oriented I am. I should have married long before now. I should have had half a dozen children by now. I haven't married. Why haven't I?

Because I waited to marry *you*. It is what your father wanted. I realized last night from your withdrawal that you have not yet awakened to sexual desire. I am sorry. I hurried you. Perhaps I frightened you.'' He started the engine and eased the car onto the paving again.

Not awakened to sexual desire. Janet had a swift mental image of her response to Todd Ballard's lovemaking. She remembered kissing his throat, opening his shirt, pleading with him not to push her away. *Not awakened!*

''Very well!'' Hassan's foot slammed down the accelerator and the car shot ahead, jerking Janet's head back. ''I'll be patient. You can take your time. But believe me, my girl, the betrothal will stand. You've grown away from me, got too involved in your career. We'll have to get to know each other again. We will start from the beginning.''

''Oh, Hassan,'' she wailed. ''No.''

''You will thank me,'' he continued grimly over her protest. ''The day will come, when we are back in the States, when we have a wonderful family around us, that you will laugh at this.''

''I will never laugh at this,'' she cried bitterly.

''Enough. No more, Janet. I've taken all I can.'' His voice shook suddenly, and she was horrified that he would break down. She couldn't stand that.

''Take me back to Cairo. Please, Hassan. Let's go back,'' she pleaded. She didn't want to go on to Ismailia, to Hassan's birthplace, to see the house where his family had lived so miserably.

He increased the speed. "We are almost there. No point in going back when we are this close."

Janet lapsed into helpless silence, sitting tensely beside him, clenching and unclenching her hands as he increased the car's speed. She could feel his smoldering anger, a palpable ugly thing between them. The traffic was heavier now, and he drove with a kind of wild abandon that terrified her, weaving in and out of cars, trucks, buses and all manner of vehicles.

"Hassan, be careful!" she gasped once as he cut in front of a van full of tourists. She heard the scream as the van's driver braked and caught a glimpse of startled faces. They missed crashing by a hair.

"Don't worry about my driving," he shot back. "I've never wrecked a car yet. I learned to drive in a Cairo taxi—working nights while I studied at university days." He had slowed fractionally, but now they roared ahead again. Janet closed her eyes, feeling the sting of tears beneath her lids.

"This is Ismailia," he said after a few minutes. "What's left of it, that is."

"What—what has happened to it?" She stared around her as he began—slowly now—to drive about the city.

They passed a section of pretty pastel-stucco villas, with well-dressed children playing in the gardens. These must be the homes of the Suez Canal employees, Janet thought. Elsewhere were wide desolated areas. Few streets were without demolished buildings. Piles of rubble and trash were heaped between those buildings still standing, some of them pitted with great holes dug out of the walls.

"What *happened*?" He repeated Janet's question with thinly veiled contempt. "You Americans continue to astound me. What happened is that Ismailia—my city—was built on the edge of the Suez Canal. It is—has been for decades—a target, Janet. It is here first and last that the bombs fall and the rockets come tearing through."

He pulled the car to a stop in a block of tenement buildings—or what had been buildings. Janet stared in dark fascination up the ugly street. Possibly a little more than half the buildings were still standing, some of them tottering drunkenly, looking as if they might disintegrate into dust at any moment. Some were condemned and had boarded-up windows bearing faded signs in Arabic and English forbidding trespassing on pain of fine, imprisonment or both.

It was a dead city out of a nightmare, weirdly teeming with stubborn vibrant life. The street was crowded with a mingling of slow vehicles and pedestrians. Women draped in black strolled leisurely along with great baskets or jars on their heads, balancing them without apparent effort. Men went about the business of earning a livelihood. Tiny shops crowded together at the ground floor of the remaining buildings. A produce vendor had improvised a shop where none existed by erecting a flat roof of scrap lumber as a sunshade. His floor was a neat fiber matting smoothed upon the bare ground. He conversed with two other men as he carefully stacked pomegranates into a rusty-red pyramid next to a similar stack of brilliant oranges. Tiny wooden tables surrounded by a collection of rickety wooden chairs of all periods and designs were strewn up the entire street. Men in worn galabias or Western dress sat at the tables, drinking small glasses of tea or just smoking and talking. Some of them had horsehair fly whisks that they snapped slowly now and then over a shoulder to drive off the buzzing flies.

"This is our street. We lived here," Hassan said after a time.

A heavy sense of melancholy descended upon Janet, weighing her down into a sea of depression. How could they survive there? Yet they were surviving. The adults were busy. Dusty lively children with curly hair and brilliant eyes, their laughter ringing out, played about on rubble, improvising games out of nothing. A tin can painted yellow and holding a plant stood brightly on a portion of a fire escape that still clung like a metal vine to the side of a building. Even the condemned structures were illegally occupied. From the top floor of one a woman was hanging a red plaid shirt from a window clothesline.

There were some attempts at rebuilding. A new apartment house reared up starkly in the middle of the block, square and unlovely.

Janet knew she should say something. Hassan was waiting for her to speak. She had to swallow twice. "Did—did you live here all your life?" she finally asked.

"No, just the first few years. I left when I was eleven. It was a good life, really. Simple, but good. My father was a provider—we were seldom hungry. He was a man of kindness and sensitivity. He always remembered to bring home the discarded newspaper for our mother from the house where he worked. She couldn't read. She just used it to cover the table where we ate—she wanted things nice for us."

Janet sat stiffly, filled with a mingled anguish and anger. He was doing this deliberately—making her feel guilty because she had never been hungry, had eaten her meals from a cloth-covered table. She passed her tongue over her lips. Well, let him have his say—he had earned it.

"I wish you could have heard my father laugh He had a fine laugh. He was always making jokes. Our building was one of the oldest in the city, and he always said it was lucky it was wedged in between two others—they were the only things that held it up."

"Which one is your building?"

"We are parked in front of it—that is, where it was. It received a direct hit one evening about sundown and that finished it."

Janet stared hypnotized at the pile of rubble between two other buildings. She had to ask it. She had to. She finally got it out. "Your family?"

"All gone. All dead. I hadn't got home yet. I survived. I went home to that." He was looking somberly at the bricks and fragments of old plaster and dirt before them. "I couldn't believe it. I spent the next two days digging around in the rubble, looking for somebody—anybody.''

"Didn't anyone help you? Weren't there any Red Cross people? Any Civil Defense people?''

"The Red Crescent was here, working around the clock. I eluded them for two days, running like a rabbit anytime one of them showed up. Childlike, I kept thinking I'd find my family. And I had found our money jar. It still had some coins in it. I slept in the ruins sometimes curled around it with it clutched against my stomach. I had sense enough to keep the money hidden. When I got hungry, I found something to eat in a garbage pail that still stood behind a ruined restaurant.''

"Stop it,'' she said, her voice ragged.

She stared at the broad face in somber repose, the remote faraway look in the dark eyes that had seen too much. Dread slowly built in her mind. *I can't let him down,* she thought in helpless misery, *I can't.*

CHAPTER SIX

THERE WAS A HEAVY BALL OF LEAD in Janet's stomach. All the way back to Cairo after a ghastly lunch she'd had to keep swallowing. They had eaten in a barnlike dining room in some inn or hotel. There had been no cover on the wooden table, and she'd found she couldn't meet Hassan's eyes. The eager waiter had pressed her with dishes of hot heavy food she hadn't wanted, redolent with aromatic spices and slick with rich oil. The windows at one side of the room had been removed, and the hot breeze had moved in and out, sometimes bringing little swirls of fine sand. A couple of small dusty birds fluttered and squabbled up near the ceiling. The hovering waiter had batted at the droning flies, and gradually Janet's clothing had begun to feel damp and limp.

They arrived back at Mena House a little after four, and Hassan, professing worry at her queasiness, insisted upon seeing Janet to her room but did not, as she had feared, insist on coming in.

She shut the door behind him and leaned against it for quite a while, too drained and listless to move. Wearily she started taking off her clothes and went toward the shower.

A nap would be nice, she thought after shower-ing, as she lay lax and naked on the bed, staring up at the ceiling. But perversely sleep would not come.

Well, she had got no place with Hassan that afternoon. That was certain. Somehow she had to reach him, had to make him understand and release her. She had to see the break with him through. She couldn't just pack up and run away.

The terrible temptation just to leave, go, run, shivered a moment in her mind. She sighed, know-ing she'd never do it. According to her personal ethics, one never ran away from a problem, and if one started something, one had to finish it. Other-wise the code would be violated. *So number one,* Janet thought, *I must work out the Hassan prob-lem, and two, I must finish the notes.*

Suppressing a small wave of homesickness, she got up from the bed, feeling cool and fresh now in her slim nakedness. It was almost six o'clock. The afternoon heat had probably abated, and a gentle breeze moved the curtains at the edge of the French windows. Her hair felt like silk, flowing loosely over her bare back and shoulders. She put on the coolest long garment she had brought, a floor-length, cream-colored peignoir with a low round neck and three-quarter sleeves. It was made of light handkerchief linen and edged at the neck and sleeves with narrow flat lace of gossamer-thin thread. She had long ago worn out the accompany-ing nightgown. The peignoir, too light to have got much wear at home in San Francisco, felt cool as it rested lightly on her bare skin. Swinging back her mass of golden brown hair, she seated herself at the writing table before the notes. She was reaching for the pen when the phone rang.

Hassan. He had said he would call. Reluctantly she picked up the receiver.

"Janet? Janet, are you there?" It was not Hassan. It took her a moment to place Nazli's voice. Her tone had a rough huskiness that made it sound unfamiliar.

"Yes, this is Janet. Nazli? I didn't recognize your voice."

"Ah, yes. I have this small—what is it—asthma, sometimes. No, not asthma. Allergy. Sometimes I have that. The allergy. Today I have it."

"Oh, I'm sorry," Janet said perfunctorily. "Do you take anything for it?"

"Sometimes I do. Yes, I did." She lost interest suddenly. "Janet, we wish—my father and I—for you to come to dinner with us." There was a feeling of tension in Nazli's voice that conveyed itself to Janet clearly from her choppy sentences, the breathy quality of her voice and her more pronounced accent.

"That's very kind of you and your father, Nazli, but I thought Hassan was going to call and I don't know—"

"Ah, yes. I forgot. I should have mentioned first. I have a message from Hassan. He regrets, but something has come up. He is out at the site with Todd, and they will be late. Todd got all the wiring in and the passage was almost cleared today, did you know?"

"No, I didn't. I haven't been in touch with Todd today. Hassan and I went to see Ismailia, and we got back rather late and—to be very honest, Nazli, I really couldn't eat any dinner tonight. I felt a bit sickish after lunch today. Will you and your father give me a rain check?"

"But of course," Nazli agreed quickly, and then rather blankly added, "A rain check?"

"That means I can't accept this time but I hope you ask me again. It's—it's American, sort of slangy."

"Oh, for sure we'll ask again. Janet?" Suddenly Nazli's voice changed. There was more urgency in it. "Are you too busy now? Too sickish? I mean, I am down in the reception, and I wish to run up to see you. For just a moment. I have brought you a present."

Janet was nonplussed. Her old reliable gut feeling told her that Nazli Houdeiby hated her with blinding intensity. There was no reason she would want to bring a present.

"Really, Nazli," Janet started to protest, then decided not to. "Of course, come on up," and then for good measure she added pleasantly, "we can have a little visit." If this was an olive branch, she might as well accept it.

Janet hung up the phone slowly, wondering if she should order something up from room service to offer to Nazli. But before she could make up her mind there was a sharp rapping at the door, and when she opened it, Nazli swept grandly into the room. Janet didn't like Nazli, had not liked her from the beginning and probably never would like her, but she had to admit that Nazli certainly knew how to enter a room with a flourish. Even now, a bit disheveled and wearing jeans and a cotton shirt, her arms filled with parcels, there was a regal tilt to her chin, a kind of controlled grace in her body that was almost queenly.

"Ah, what a day," Nazli said dramatically, flinging the packages down on Janet's bed. "I was out at the site. Oh, such fast progress is being made. That Todd. How he works. And he speaks Arabic so good. I mean, well. He says jokes, you know? He jokes with the workers sometimes. He makes them laugh and they work harder. Not so many Americans know Arabic well enough to—ah—say jokes in it."

"I'm glad that Todd can be funny in Arabic," Janet said dryly, and bit off an acid comment that she hadn't found him funny at all in English. "You certainly have been shopping, haven't you," she said instead, looking at the jumble of packages.

"Yes, yes. I worry about you terribly." And with this startling statement, Nazli leaned over and ripped open a package. As she did so, Janet took a closer look at her face. It bore marks of strain that told her the Egyptian woman's hearty enthusiasm was totally false. Nazli was more than upset; she was profoundly shaken. The usually competent hands were unsteady, and it was possible—probable, really—that at some time that day she had cried—cried long and hard. What an odd turning of the tables this seemed to be.

Feeling sobered and sorry for her, Janet retreated toward the balcony, mentally trying to think of something to say to fill the gap.

But Nazli rushed on. "I spoke with Hassan, and he wants you to visit the site day after tomorrow. The passage and the shaft will both be clear."

That was it, then. Hassan had said something, done something, as a result of their confrontation that morning.

"And you said yesterday about jeans—things to wear at the dig—so I have them for you. You see?" Nazli turned from the bed, holding up a pair of designer jeans and a couple of fancy T-shirts. In the sunlight coming in from the balcony window Nazli's face looked for a moment ravaged, her eyes haunted. Then she moved quickly, and the image vanished. "Here, also a hat. You must have a hat. But I was not sure of the size of the hat—you know, with all that lovely hair I was not sure. Will you try it, please?"

In silent astonishment Janet took the round cloth hat and put it on. It fit, of course, because the mass of her hair hung down her back. "It's fine," she said quickly. "Just fine."

"But with it up, you know? On top? Will it fit with the hair up? You must not be in the sun without a hat, you know." Nazli was definitely agitated. It came through clearly. She was worried sick about something.

"I can arrange it," Janet assured her quickly. "Don't worry. It's just right." She tried to put enthusiasm into her voice, staring at herself in the mirror, at the thin lace-trimmed peignoir, the round little white hat on her head. "I love it. But Nazli, you can't buy clothes for me. Please, you must let me—I was going to get some things, anyway...."

What in the world should she do? Could one decline a gift from Nazli without offense? Janet had learned enough about Egyptians from Hassan to understand some of the intricacies of the complicated system they had for polite behavior.

"Oh, yes, yes. You must accept!" Nazli plunged on, an edge of desperation in her voice. "It is my gift to you. I was going to get you a gift, anyway, when Hassan told me you were coming, but I didn't know what to get. Now today I know. So it is all yours, *this* things." In her excitement she was mutilating her English again and didn't know it.

Janet went rather still for a moment, recognizing that beneath the surface of their encounter Nazli was almost pleading with her.

Placating.

Hassan must have asked—told—ordered—Nazli to make friends with her, and Nazli was trying to obey.

"Everything is lovely," Janet said warmly. "Just exactly what I needed." She turned and picked up the jeans, sure without checking that Nazli had got the right size. She realized, suddenly appalled, that Nazli had bought everything at one of the poshest shops in the hotel. It must have cost her a small fortune. "Oh, marvelous," she added, looking at first one gaudy T-shirt, then the other. "I *love* them." The yellow one had a profile picture of Queen Nefertiti on the front, surrounded by black lettering that stated Land of the Pharaohs in a circle. The beige T-shirt had a pyramid and a camel, backed by a vivid red ball representing a setting sun. Beneath it glared one word, also in red, Egypt.

"It is what most Americans buy, you see?" Nazli said eagerly.

"I can't thank you enough. Really, Nazli, I do appreciate this," Janet rushed on, assuring Nazli how perfect everything was, how kind it was of her to think of it, until she sensed an easing of the other woman's tension.

When Nazli had finally gone, Janet stood looking at herself in the mirror for a long time. The hat was good, exactly what she had been going to buy for herself, exactly the plain tough little cloth sailor hat she had seen on so many people in Egypt. Just enough to keep the sun off, she supposed. Then, still wondering uneasily about Nazli's sudden change of attitude, she returned to the desk. If there was one thing she was now sure of, it was that Nazli Houdeiby was deeply in love with Hassan al-Emary. And after Janet's own confrontation with Hassan earlier, in an attempt to break off the engagement, Nazli had spent some time with him. During that time Nazli had changed—or Hassan had changed her—from the confident sharp-tongued adversary she had met on the first day to the badly shaken and placating woman of this afternoon. Hassan had probably not missed any of Nazli's waspish digs and barbs at the first meeting, and very likely he had thought carefully of the uncomfortable questions she herself had asked him after the visit to his apartment. Now he was setting out to change her mind about breaking up, and one of the details had doubtless been to quell Nazli's exuberant antagonism. Hassan was very thorough.

Well, he had certainly admonished Nazli, and as much as Janet disliked Nazli, she felt sorry for her. She had never believed for one moment the "delightful unruly child" version of Nazli that Hassan had so glibly invented. Nazli was—probably had been for some time—his mistress. Janet was sure of it. She hoped that someday, when she herself was long gone from there, that Nazli might be Hassan's wife, if that was what she wanted. The more she thought of it, the more right they seemed for each other. They had her blessing, for what it was worth.

She took up her pen with an odd sense of anticipation. "The passage and the shaft will both be clear." The day after tomorrow she would go out to the site, to the stone room in the ancient earth where *Beloved Lady's* things lay strewn about. Had Todd read the notes yet? Had he even picked them up? Did he know that the lady's name was Eyes-of-Love? With a new eagerness she bent over her work.

Her father had moved the spotlight again. From the notes Janet could almost see what he had seen. The light, trained on a disorderly pile of objects in a corner, revealed a veritable hodgepodge of possessions. A bedstead had been shoved in crookedly, on top of which a round box with a lid had been stacked or tossed. There was a small table turned upside down, on top of which were two or more—it was difficult to tell—graceful wooden chairs that had withstood the ravages of time quite well.

"Old kingdom," her father had stated with assurance.

Delicate hardwood, painted surface , largely intact. Designs of leaves, flowers, twining vines, very stylized. Pearl gray or white ground. Effect: fragile, elegant, light. Completely different from heavy lavish use of gems, gold and bright enamels of later dynasties.

She knew he was thinking of the chunky, gaudy, decadent pieces from the celebrated tomb of Tutankhamen, the tragic boy-king of a more recent time. She thought for a long moment of all those pharaohs who were never permitted to keep their secrets forever as they had planned. For now and then, here and there, in bits and pieces, they were forced to yield their hidden truths up to the tireless modern seekers who would not let them rest. People such as Todd Ballard and her father, who sought out all the old treasures in a kind of relentless love, wanting to lay them bare for all the world to see. But it was better so. Otherwise even the ancient *things* would die and be lost, and something should be saved.

Even now Eyes-of-Love's things were dying. At some time during those long centuries in the hidden stone room the pretty and delicate bed—Eyes-of-Love's bed—had started to collapse. Only because the supportive space beneath it had been stuffed with other items had it remained intact. Meticulously her father described everything.

Very small gray enamel chest with one drawer. Probable game box. Round box with lid, tooled leather, design unclear. Metal-hinged flat box. Empty bird cage, probably bamboo. May be dome-shaped but misshapen now from weight of collapsing bedstead above. Papyrus scrolls falling from beneath bed. Some writing visible. Very dim from here.

Bemused, Janet put down the pen and flexed her numb fingers. She had accumulated quite a stack of pages, and she had had to turn on the lamp. She was familiar with examples of Old Kingdom furniture. Her father had loved it. She still had a reproduction of a small side chair he had given her because it was the only Egyptian piece she had really liked. It stood now in her bedroom in San Francisco. She loved that little chair and had often thought how lovely a whole room of such furnishing might be—light, airy, delicately beautiful.

And that royal lady, Eyes-of-Love, had lived that way, in such a room, in such a house, somewhere, sometime. These were the things she had used in her daily life, because these were the things that had been placed in her tomb when she died. Then, for his own urgent reasons, someone had rudely thrown, tossed, shoved Eyes-of-Love's bed into the corner and stacked things on it and under it and sealed up the room, hiding it all away, then had hurried on, leaving everything locked in endless time. Time was being unkind to Eyes-of-Love's things. Time—century after slow century—passed by and was breaking down her pretty bed and laying a film of dust on her game box. Time was dimming the writing on her scroll to erase all the words, and time would go on crushing the bird's cage until it was nothing but splinters of wood falling one by one to the stone floor.

But she, royal lady, had once lain in that painted bed and dreamed her dreams. Or had she loved someone there on a long warm afternoon? She had sat at the painted table and pulled open the single drawer of her game box. Was someone across the table to laugh with her as they played? Or alone, she had picked up the scroll to open it and read. Were there love poems written there? Was the bird in the cage singing its heart out while she read?

The phone rang stridently. The sound shattered Janet's bright fantasy, but vestiges of it lingered, and her voice was warm and slightly unsteady when she answered.

"Hi, Janet?"

Todd Ballard. Janet came back to earth with a thud.

"I just read those notes you left at the desk for me this morning—about Eyes-of-Love."

There was an eager warmth in his tone that made her smile. So Eyes-of-Love had cast her spell on him, too.

"Have you—finished any more?" he asked.

"Yes," she answered. "Some. Maybe twenty pages more, give or take."

"Have you had dinner yet?" There was no mistaking the warm excitement underlying his tone. "I'd like to talk to you about the notes."

She glanced quickly at the clock. It was almost nine.

"No. I'm not having dinner tonight," she explained. "I had a very late lunch."

"Oh." He sounded disappointed. "Okay. I'll eat alone, then, but I'd better do it soon. I'm starving to death. It's been a long day. We thought you'd like to come out to the site day after tomorrow. Did Hassan tell you the entrance will be clear? Would you like to come?"

"I'd love it," she evaded, trying to cut short the conversation. Janet tried not to think about Todd after the phone call. To this end she granted herself a brief interval of dreamy musing over the pictures he had given her and then determined to put them out of sight until she returned to San Francisco.

She had scarcely started to work again when there was a knock at the door. "Who is it?" she asked, getting up. Good grief! Not Hassan, she hoped. Janet didn't want another scene with Hassan yet. She hurried over and opened the door a hesitant crack.

"It's only me, Todd."

She pulled open the door, feeling suddenly defensive. He had gained a small advantage with the pictures, and now he was following it up.

"Thought I'd stop off for the rest of the notes

to—'' his startled glance swept over her thin garment ''—to read while I have dinner,'' he added. Then his mouth curved into a quick grin. ''Hey, I like your hat.'' He was dressed in casual slacks and a soft shirt, open at his neck, about which lay a small gold chain. The delicate fragility of the chain accentuated his strong suntanned throat.

She stared at him blankly for a moment, realizing with dismay how thin the peignoir was, then snatched off the little hat she had forgotten she was still wearing.

''It's something Nazli picked up for me,'' she said. ''To keep the sun off my head. Here, I'll get you the rest of the pages I've finished.'' She turned and hurried to the desk, feeling unbelievably naked beneath the loose peignoir.

Get rid of him. Fast, she told herself.

She was turning as she heard the door shut, and hoped that her quick flare of apprehension didn't show in her face. ''Here they are,'' she said briskly, hurrying toward him, thankful it was dark outside so she wasn't backlit from the window. Maybe, just maybe, he wouldn't know she had nothing on underneath. Ha! Fat chance.

He took the notes almost absentmindedly. Looking at her, his clear eyes glinted with small golden lights. She sensed his excitement and it made her more wary. His eyes kept coming back to her loose flowing hair.

''How are you going to get all that hair into that little hat?'' The grin was a lazy smile now.

''You have enough problems,'' she said tartly,

"without worrying about my hairdo. Don't sweat it. I'll manage, believe me."

"Oh, I do." He stood there, half smiling, eyeing her appreciatively, enjoying himself.

"Look," she said uncomfortably. "I don't mean to rush you, but you've got the notes, and I'm not exactly dressed for company."

"I noticed," he said, and gazed again at her hair. "You're almost a blonde, aren't you? I see a lot of gold." He reached out and touched a curling strand, his fingers almost but not quite brushing her breast. "Were you blond as a child?"

She felt a slow uprush of warmth in her body and an impulse to move toward him, to capture his hand in hers and press it against her body. She *wanted* him. The idea was shocking. No other man had made her feel like this before. She wanted him to touch her, kiss her, make love to her.

Why not, she thought crazily. Why not? Janet crushed the idea instantly. "No." She was embarrassed at the sound of her own voice, husky and breathless. "I mean, not really. I was—"

He moved closer and a tremor went through her.

No. Go away, she thought to herself.

"I was always streaky like this," she managed to say as his hand clasped the side of her neck and moved up the back of her head.

"Okay," he said. "I'll go." His fingers tangled in her hair. Then he tightened them on her head and pulled her toward him. "In a minute," he added, tossing the notes onto the bedside table, laughter still in his voice.

"No! Now just a minute!" Janet made a quick attempt to escape, but his other arm circled her, holding her close. She pushed with all her strength against his shoulders and gasped at the raw shock that went through her when their bodies came together. Gripped against his rock-hard body, she could feel the pounding of his heart and knew the surging excitement that filled him. Underlying her panic was an intoxicating awareness of her power to arouse him.

"All right, stop it!" She made herself struggle against him, twisting and turning as he lifted her slightly and buried his face in her neck.

His warm mouth moved in soft brief kisses against her throat, behind her ear, around her lips. He began kissing her protesting mouth.

"No!" she gasped. "I told you—you said you wouldn't—you promised—"

"Right. I did, didn't I?" There was no laughter in his tone now, but he did release her partly, letting her go slowly, reluctantly, his hands lingering, caressing her rounded hips.

She felt her hands go limp against his shoulders and stood trembling before him, hating it intensely that he was letting her go. Her fascinated gaze took in every detail of him—the ridges and pads of hard muscle in his shoulders, the gleaming sun-browned skin, the troubled angry eyes that held her hypnotized, unable to move away.

"What is it with you, Janet?" Todd spoke with an effort, his voice unsteady now. "You know—and I know—that you don't want me to go. You

don't really mean it. Isn't that true? Well, *isn't it*!"
His voice turned harsh.

"Yes," she gasped, unable to lie to him when
every cell in her body yearned for him. "All right,"
she went on desperately, "I don't deny it. I admit it.
Are you satisfied? There is...an attraction, but
that doesn't mean—"

"An *attraction*," he said in soft disbelief.

"Doesn't mean anything's going to—I won't let
you—"

"You won't *let* me?"

Her body was filling with molten fire. It made her
breasts taut. It melted her bones. It stopped her
breath, and she couldn't speak. Some wanton part
of her silently shrieked, *fool—fool. Don't let him
go.*

"Janet," he said in a grating whisper. "Right
now, this minute, you want me to make love to you
more than you've ever wanted anything in your
life—and you won't *let* me." He spoke in a kind of
furious male outrage. Even as he said it, he pulled
her close again. This time she didn't resist. It would
have been too false, too dishonest.

Oh, why not?

He tumbled her onto the bed and fell onto it with
her, pinning her down with his weight. She gave a
gasping sob as he pulled her close and without
thought, her lips parted to meet his. These were no
gentle, fleeting kisses now, but the deep ravaging of
her mouth, which demanded—and got—her wildest
response.

She gripped him close, her hand sliding beneath

his shirt, across his strong back. One slim bare leg twined about his. She was stunned at the force of the tide engulfing her. She had no will but to hold him, no thought but wild exultation. She could only arch her body against his, moaning in an anguish of desire.

"I want you," she whispered between kisses, scarcely aware of her own words. "I want you."

There was a sense of rending when he pulled away from her, pushing her back against the pillows. She tried to stop him. She pulled at his shirt, fumbling at the buttons.

"Janet," he said thickly. "Janet, wait a minute."

Even as he said it, she knew they were going to stop. It was too soon. They were going too fast. There were too many barriers between them.

"Oh, no," she wailed, twisting her head on the pillow.

"Janet—listen a minute." He slid away from her, down to a half-kneeling position beside the bed. "I'm rushing you. It—isn't fair." He was trying to control his voice, but the words came out in painful jerks. "I don't want to treat you like this."

A long shudder went through her body. He was right.

"Janet, we have to take some time...come to some understanding...get our heads together."

He was *always* right. Slow anger began to build inside her. "Well, I told you to go," she gasped. "You wouldn't. You had to come on like some macho—"

"I know, I know. I'm sorry. That was a mistake."

Her robe had come undone, and he pulled it closed across her breasts. His hands were shaking.

She pushed his hands away, sick with longing. "I'll do it myself," she said miserably.

"We have to talk, Janet."

"Just go, please." She pushed him back and slid her legs off the side of the bed.

"Listen to me, please." He moved closer again, still kneeling. His hands almost without his volition were kneading her thighs in long slow strokes.

"There's nothing to talk about—stop that!" She pushed at the tormenting enticing hands, and he sat back.

"I'm sorry," he said. "Here, you lost a slipper." He fumbled under the edge of the bed to retrieve it.

Janet steeled herself against the touch of his hands as he slid the slipper onto her bare foot. Then she stood up, holding the light robe together, and he had to move back. She gave herself the grim aching pleasure of watching him stand up, taking in the slow strong muscular grace of his body. Then she turned away.

"We have to get things settled. This business between you and Hassan." His voice was steady now. "Do you want me to speak to Hassan? I will if you want me to. I can handle it."

Outrage, like a shaft of naked lightning, shot through her. "Do you want me to speak to Hassan?" As he had spoken once about her father, halting his life work, halting his very life.

"No!" She spoke harshly. "Don't say anything to Hassan!" She turned, her eyes blazing at him. The arrogance of him, the effrontery. *I can handle it,* she thought to herself.

"Well, then, we are going to have a talk, Janet— you and I. I won't hassle you with it tonight, because you're upset. But we'll have to sort things out. We'll discuss things tomorrow. Rationally and sensibly." He picked up the pages of notes.

"Not likely!" she snapped, her anger increasing. She was angry at him, angry at Hassan, angry at herself.

Todd slammed down the notes. "Then we'll talk now."

"No. Wait." She crossed the room a little too quickly, putting some distance between them.

"Then agree to have it out tomorrow, Janet. I'm serious." It was that deadly calm voice again. One way or another he had to win. He was crossing the room, implacable, relentless. "This is a stupid situation, Janet. Surely two people with even average brains can work it out. We're going to reach some sort of understanding tonight or tomorrow. Make a choice. It's up to you."

She stopped at the writing table in front of the windows and turned to face him, feeling like an animal at bay. "All right," she said thinly.

"All right *what*? And speak up."

"All right," she yelled. "We'll talk tomorrow!" She stood rigidly, her back to the table, terrified he would put his hands on her again, hating herself because she wanted him to so badly, hating him because he knew it.

He reached over and plucked a strand of her disordered hair, caressed it between his fingers for a moment, then turned and walked out of the room, forgetting about the notes.

When he had gone, she sank down shakily into the desk chair, still burning with desire, filled with helpless rage—mostly directed at herself.

Todd was right, of course, right to have stopped their headlong plunge into passion. She couldn't—absolutely must not—get involved with him. And she must never let herself get into another situation like this one. She knew she couldn't control her response.

She sat at the desk, head drooping, her long tangled hair hanging over her shoulders. Well, say this much for Todd Ballard—he was a wonderful lover for somebody else. It was a sobering experience, frightening in a way, being with a man like that. It was so different from the pallid excitement of being with other men who had made her heart ache with pity. She pushed back her hair wearily, and it caught in her fingers.

She hated long hair.

The telephone, shrill and loud, shattered her thoughts. *No, Todd. Don't call. I can't talk to you now.* She hunched over, letting it ring several times before going over to answer it.

"Janet? Are you all right?"

It was Hassan.

Her heart sank. "Yes. I'm fine." Her voice sounded all right. "I guess I'm out of breath. I—was in the shower," she improvised. "And then I ran in to answer as soon as I heard the bell."

"I'm sorry I couldn't call you before this," Hassan was saying. "Have you had dinner? Would you like me to take you somewhere?"

"No. No, thank you. Really. I've been working on the notes, and I guess I'm tired. I thought I'd make an early night of it. I was just getting ready for bed."

"All right, my dear. Sleep well. I'll see you in the morning and we'll work things out. Good night."

"Good night, Hassan." She put back the receiver.

"Work things out." Everybody was going to work things out for her. After a moment, her lips set, she picked up the hotel phone book and flipped through the pages, found the number she was looking for and dialed it. The phone rang twice before it was answered.

"Is this the hairdresser?" she asked.

"Yes, madame."

"I wasn't sure you would be open this late."

"Oh, yes, madame. Does madame wish someone sent up?"

"No, thanks. That won't be necessary. But I'd like to come down. I can be there in ten minutes. I want my hair cut. Short." She hung up the phone, feeling a little better. It wasn't much, but it was something.

CHAPTER SEVEN

IT TOOK JANET a long time to dress the next morning. She kept going back to the mirror to stare at her reflection. She had forgotten there was a lot of natural curl in her hair. When worn long, the very weight of it had straightened it out to gentle waves. Now, with no weight, it tended to spring into bright little curls here and there. In the clear morning light, the sense of wild freedom and exhilaration she had felt at the hairdressers'—all out of proportion to the simple act of getting a haircut—had totally vanished.

But it had been fun, a kind of relief and letting go.

There was one thing that could be said for Egyptians—they were enthusiastic and immediately got into the spirit of things, whatever was happening. Three hairdressers had cut and consulted and cut—pondered, deliberated, cut, laughed, experimented and cut—talking endlessly all the while. One small boy, a child of one of the hairdressers, had the task of keeping the floor around her chair clean, which he did thoroughly, darting in and out with his long-handled brush and dustpan.

Janet's hair was now a shining close cap. There

was a curly fringe across the forehead, a graceful wisp or two in front of the ears and tendrils and wisps at the nape of her neck.

"Oh, very chic, madame. Hand madame the glass. Oh, charming, madame, so charming!" All three hairdressers beamed their approval.

The total effect *was* attractive in a pixielike way.

"Oh, madame, monsieur will love it."

This had been a bit sobering. Actually, both messieurs of the moment were going to hate it. Well, what was done was done.

Janet's thoughts were interrupted by an unexpected telephone call from Dr. Houdeiby. He called her "my dear" and asked with avuncular fondness if she still felt "sickish." Janet had to think a moment to recall that the last information he had had of her was the afternoon the day before, when she'd declined a dinner invitation from Nazli. She smiled at how quickly the Egyptians picked up foreign slang and casual phrasing, especially Americanisms. She had liked this kindly fussy little family man and assured him that she was again fit.

"Splendid, splendid," he said enthusiastically. "Then please join us for breakfast. We are going to meet at the Mena House Café. It is in your building on the ground level."

"Yes, I've passed it," she answered. "Have you talked with Hassan? I think he was going to call this morning."

"Yes, yes. He will join us. We have decided to discuss your sight-seeing program—which we must not neglect. Nazli says you have worked much too hard on the notes, and Dr. Ballard is very pleased.'' From here his conversation meandered for several minutes—apparently Egyptians never hurried at anything of a social nature.

Janet sat looking thoughtfully at the phone for some minutes after she had hung up. Somehow or other, interspersed with the chitchat about her enjoyment of travel, her reactions to Ismailia, whether she had yet tried Egyptian beer, Houdeiby had managed to work in several mentions of Hassan, whom, it was clear, he held in great esteem. It had been almost as if—but this was surely ridiculous—almost as if he were pushing Hassan at her.

Was Hassan's friendship with the Houdeibys so intimate that he had told them she was trying to break the engagement? The idea made her uneasy. This was between Hassan and her. Janet didn't like the sudden feeling she had of being badly outnumbered in some sort of contest.

She took a last look at her appearance. She had decided to pass up the jeans until she visited the site and instead had put on a light blue denim wrap skirt, with matching blouse of fine cotton and white sandals on her bare feet. Picking up the white cloth sailor hat, Janet left the room. She delayed putting on the hat for the moment, to give the world the full benefit of her new hair style.

The determined Houdeibys, father and daughter, met her at the door of the Mena Café, and both stared at her in astonishment.

''I had it cut last evening,'' Janet explained, cool and pleasant, pleased at the casual tone of her voice. "I discovered it was just too warm here for long hair."

"But Hassan likes long hair," Nazli blurted without thinking. "I didn't think he would permit—" She stopped herself.

"But it is charming—charming," her father cut in quickly. "So modern, so—so American. Come, now, let us breakfast. Hassan will be along in two moments." His round face held a cherubic smile, but the round brown eyes were worried about something. "You see," he added, "we are having our rain check now," and escorted them into the café. "Hassan asked us to order for him. The café has an excellent hearty English breakfast," he explained when they were seated outside on the stone terrace.

They sat beneath overhanging branches of a tree that swayed continually in the warm breeze, lazily moving patches of shade and sunlight over them. The hotel was waking up. Muted sounds came to them: a motor in the distance sputtering out, a snatch of conversation too far away to understand, a distant peal of laughter. There was a deep sense of leisure, of having unlimited time at one's disposal. Janet could feel herself relaxing.

Freshly squeezed orange juice arrived in chilled glasses, as well as a pot of steaming coffee. The Houdeibys, father and daughter, were having a friendly squabble in mingled English and Arabic with an occasional phrase of French about the sight-seeing route. From the English portions Janet gathered they were taking her to a church, a mosque and a bazaar, in that order. It was finally decided which bridge they would use to cross the Nile first.

The hearty English breakfast came—scrambled eggs, sizzling sausage and English bacon, stacks of hot buttered toast—and Janet started at it with enthusiasm. She was enjoying every bite and had for the moment forgotten Hassan. Janet remembered him only when she saw the smiling black-clad waiter putting down a plate of food in front of the vacant setting.

She noticed that Hassan was standing stock-still, a little distance from the table, staring at her. She swallowed a bite of half-chewed toast and took a quick sip of coffee, burning the tip of her tongue. An uneasy silence had settled over the table; even the waiter was affected. Bowing, he backed away. A slow ugly red suffused Hassan's face.

"Please say you like it, Hassan," Janet said, sounding more at ease than she felt. "I decided suddenly just last night. It's much more comfortable this way."

"And very pretty, too," Hassan agreed politely, coming to the table and taking his place. "Be patient, my dear. I must become accustomed to it."

The words were pleasant and kind, but Janet was sobered. Once again she had seen the flare of raw rage in his expressive eyes. He had seemed somehow outraged, as if she had committed some unpardonable error. Janet put down the cup suddenly. He believed, he was sincerely convinced, that she had no right even to change her hairstyle without his permission. It made her a little sick, and she could feel herself tensing, getting ready to face him down if need be when they were alone.

Then Dr. Houdeiby smoothed the moment over by a flood of conversation. Janet could have kissed him in gratitude. She realized at the same time that Hassan was dressed in his work clothes. "Aren't you coming sight-seeing with us?" she asked.

"No, I'm sorry." Hassan was in command of himself again. "I have to go out to the site with Todd first, but I shall meet you later back here. I have a surprise for you—something you wanted me to do. I have done it."

"What is it?" she asked, searching her memory.

He laughed, no vestige of anger showing now. "A surprise, I said. You'll know this afternoon. Say about four o'clock."

NAZLI DROVE her father's small black sedan with the same kind of dramatic flourish she did everything else. Miraculously they all escaped certain death a dozen times, and Janet's leg muscles were tired from pushing against imaginary brakes.

"Abu Serga Church—Saint Sargius," Nazli said over her shoulder as they walked down a narrow cobblestoned alleyway with ancient masonry rising on both sides. Even in her low-heeled sandals Janet had to watch her step on the uneven stones.

Her first thought when they entered the church itself was, *how small*. Janet paused just inside the door and looked slowly around, her eyes adjusting to the dimness. She experienced a feeling of great age, of slow time passing. She tried to take it all in—the stiff narrow pews; a freestanding pulpit; an intricately carved altar; a red banner bearing a picture of the Madonna in gaudy primary colors; other pictures, early Christian images, framed, on the walls.

Dr. Houdeiby spoke softly just behind her. "This is the oldest Christian church in Egypt—they think it probably dates from the fourth century."

"Are we going down into the crypt?" Janet asked, her fascinated gaze traveling over the inlaid ivory or mother-of-pearl in the intricate wooden screens.

The trio went down the steps that sloped dangerously from centuries of wear, until they were in the low-ceilinged crypt. The air was dank.

"They say this was where the Holy Child was kept while he and Mary and Joseph hid in Egypt," Dr. Houdeiby said, looking thoughtfully around at the walls. He placed one hand very lightly against the stones. "Dry. That is good. There was seepage here from the Nile, but it has been attended to, I see."

From the Abu Serga Church they went through a small dusty garden to the Old Cairo Synagogue that seemed, if anything, even smaller than the church. The gate was arched with narrow wrought iron topped by a Star of David. A patient spider was weaving a fragile web between two of the iron tips, and Janet watched the web move in the faint warm breeze. Inside the synagogue, a tiny scarecrow of a man in a faded galabia spread out for her ancient Hebrew manuscripts on scrolls, and Janet marveled that anyone could read the dim, ornate, handwritten words of ancient Hebrew.

A short distance from the synagogue, opening on the cobbled alley, was an attractively clean shop specializing in bright brass and copper trays and other utensils. All about the floor were scattered large leather ottomans in vibrant colors, great poufs with exquisite hand-tooled designs of Egyptian scenes.

"Could we stop here a moment?" Nazli asked. "I must get a little gift for a friend."

Janet and Dr. Houdeiby seated themselves on two of the hassocks while Nazli progressed regally about the shop, attended slavishly by two male clerks. The proprietor brought bottles of cola on a brass tray for Janet and Dr. Houdeiby to drink while they waited for Nazli. Janet rolled the cold bottle against her forehead.

"Nazli is buying a wedding gift for an old school friend," Dr. Houdeiby commented, his gaze following his daughter fondly as she shopped.

"How nice," Janet answered. "When is it to be?"

"In two months." He sat up straighter on his round leather ottoman and added with elaborate casualness. "When do you think you and Hassan will have a wedding day?"

Janet groped for an answer. She didn't want to lie to this kind little man. "We haven't really discussed it much," she finally said. "There's been so much else to do since I got here."

"Hassan was so happy when you decided to visit

Egypt. And it has been such a—forgive me, I speak frankly, as a friend, for I am an old friend of Hassan's—but it has been such a long engagement. A good and patient man, Hassan.''

Janet took a deliberate sip of her cold drink. Hassan had discussed it with him, and in his own fumbling little way he was pitching Hassan's cause. She couldn't really be annoyed, but it did make her uneasy.

"And a brilliant man. Such a brain for finance. You know this, of course. You know how well he does in his business interests."

"Yes, more or less. He doesn't talk of business too much with me.... Nazli keeps going back to those inlaid trays," Janet commented, trying to change the subject. "They are lovely, aren't they? Probably pretty expensive, though."

Dr. Houdeiby gave a forced laugh. "Ah, ha, but the time will come when the wife of Hassan al-Emary won't even have to think of price, is that not so?"

"I don't know what you mean."

"Well, after Hassan has gone to the States, he will be a very rich man. You mark my words, my dear young lady, a rich, rich man."

Janet set her empty bottle carefully on the floor. "Everybody in the States isn't rich, you know."

"But the *opportunities*—" Dr. Houdeiby spread his hands and cast his eyes upward. "When a man of such talent as Hassan's is in a place of such opportunities—" He stopped again, as if words had simply failed him.

When they returned to the car, Janet braced herself for another harrowing drive through more Cairo traffic. They were in an older area, and Nazli had to manage carefully to get around a donkey-drawn produce cart loaded with piles of fragrant alfalfa. She had to stop at the mouth of the dusty street while a man tugged a camel overloaded with sugarcane from in front of them. Nazli kept her hand firmly on the horn until this was accomplished, and Janet, looking out the window, observed another man praying. She had noticed a number of times that the Muslim Egyptians had an innocent unselfconsciousness about praying in public in any place they happened to be if the time came for them to pray. This man, of early middle age, had spread a minute red carpet out on the ground. He now crouched with his forehead touching it. The simple image was snatched from Janet's view as the car lurched ahead and they were on their way again.

"We go now to the Citadel, where we will see the Muhammad Ali Mosque, often called 'Alabaster Mosque,'" Dr. Houdeiby said, settling back comfortably. "I taught Nazli to drive. Don't you think she does well?" Janet nodded politely.

"It is on a hill, you know, the Citadel," Nazli interjected. "One can look around and see all of Cairo, all of it. One sees the Nile, too. One even sees the pyramids of Giza, all from the Citadel. It is a good showplace for visitors, yes," she said.

"Why is it called the Alabaster Mosque?" Janet asked.

"Because all the walls are made of alabaster. You will see."

Janet did see and was enthralled. She and Nazli padded around for an hour, their feet covered with small cloth bags. Dr. Houdeiby followed behind them in his white socks, which became very grimy.

The fretwork, the beautiful tortured twisting of arabesque carving, the countless glowing crystal-ball chandeliers suspended overhead and the cool alabaster walls cast a kind of spell all their own. The rest of the world seemed far away. Janet sat down once on a bench, looking across the vast expanse of the main room. It seemed even more vast and empty because there were no chairs or pews. The worshippers, when they arrived to pray or meditate, did so seated in rows on the floor.

Dr. Houdeiby came to sit beside her while Nazli spoke with the agreeable old caretaker, who was now extinguishing the lights in the great crystal clusters overhead. They had been a sight worth seeing.

"Ah, yes," Dr. Houdeiby said, "it is a fortunate woman who marries Hassan. He will give her every-thing. She will want for nothing."

It took Janet a moment to realize he was taking up their conversation precisely where he had left off in the brass and copper shop.

"Well," she demurred, "I know he has an in-terest in some restaurants in Marin County, but I hardly think that means—"

"Oh, but it *does*," Dr. Houdeiby said fervently. "You mark it. Hassan will be a rich man, *very rich*. He has great plans. You will see."

He had broken the spell of the mosque, and she breathed a sigh of relief as Nazli came toward them.

"Ah!" Dr. Houdeiby gave a crow of surprise. "It is Dr. Ballard!"

It was indeed Todd Ballard, just entering the great room. He paused at the door, looking around. The outside sunlight glinted on his bright hair. He was dressed casually again, with the soft shirt open at the neck.

Janet had a wild impulse to run like a rabbit when she saw him but made herself resist it, sitting there frozen on the bench, waiting for his eyes to find her—which they *would*, any second. There seemed to be no escaping him. Her breath caught slightly when he saw her. He lifted a hand in casual greeting, then strode purposefully toward them.

Nazli whirled around to greet him first. "You got my message where we were going? Good. Did Hassan finish out at the site?"

"Yes, and he went back to the bureau for a while. There's nothing more I can do out there until those treads come. How are you, Janet? Dr. Houdeiby? Have you had lunch?" he asked after the exchange of greetings.

Janet felt somewhat pleased at her own display of composure, which, she felt sure—well, reasonably sure—matched his own. During a long restless night she had vowed to keep as far from him as possible during the rest of her days in Egypt. Her immediate aim at the moment must be to get away from him as quickly as she politely could.

"Lunch? Is it time for lunch?" Nazli cried. "But, yes. It is two already."

"Two?" Dr. Houdeiby's round face was a study in astonishment. "I think I must get to my office."

Janet felt a sinking sensation. The Houdeibys were deserting her. She bid them a polite goodbye and thanked them quite sincerely for the morning of sight-seeing.

When they had gone, Todd stood looking down at her with a blank expression. "I picked up the latest batch of notes. Thanks for remembering to leave them. Where would you like to go to lunch?"

"Actually, I'm not keen for any lunch right now. I'd like to go back to the hotel and freshen up a bit."

"Okay, whatever. We can talk there, I guess. But all things considered, I thought you'd rather our talk be in some public place."

"Talk?"

"Yes, talk. We made a deal last night. We were going to talk things over today—come to some understanding. Incidentally, what happened to your hair?"

"My hair?" Confused, she reached up and touched the short tendrils. "Oh, I had it cut."

"I'd already guessed that." His tone was acid. "I didn't think that was a wig spread all over the pillow last night."

"It—it's too hot here. I just wanted to get rid of it. I take it you don't like it." She would ignore the reference to the night before. He was right about one thing, though. He had trapped her into "a talk," so it had better be in some very public place. She couldn't trust him—that had been proved. Then the little core of honesty in her mind, that inconvenient, uncomfortable, relentless little voice, spoke up again. Actually, she couldn't trust herself, either. And *that* had been proved. Conclusively.

"Oh, it's not bad," he was saying thoughtfully. "With your looks I don't suppose it matters much how you do your hair."

His hand moved slightly, and she knew instantly he had wanted to reach out to touch her hair and had halted the impulse. She felt a gust of thin anger at herself, at her own instinctive physical response to the half gesture. Escaping him, leaving him in Egypt, was going to be simple enough—getting him out of her mind *afterward* was yet to be coped with.

"Well." He was smiling slightly. "Are you making up your mind what you want to do for lunch? I suppose you'll let me know if you reach a decision." He tried to make it sound like a joke, but it didn't quite come off.

"How about that new hotel—Ramses Hilton? Could we go to one of the restaurants there? I've heard a lot of good comments on it."

"Sure. Come on."

The top was down on his little white sports car and she pulled the brim of the sailor hat down firmly. This proved to be unnecessary, as it was slow going in the afternoon traffic.

"Any special place there you want to go to?" Todd asked as they waited interminably behind an overloaded bus while additional passengers managed to squeeze in.

"No. I've never been there, just heard about it."

"They give a good choice of restaurants. They've got the Garden Court off the central lobby. Or we can use their Egyptian Corner, if you like the local food. Or there's the Grill, which is their main dining room. Or their Terrace Café, a twenty-four-hour coffee shop just up one flight in a sort of open mezzanine."

"That would be fine," Janet agreed. "I'm not that hungry. I just want something light."

"The 'open mezzanine' part is what got you, isn't it?" he prodded in grim amusement. The traffic came to another dead stop.

Todd always knew what she was thinking. She pretended not to have heard, gazing with a show of absorption into an open door of a store crammed with a mix of Western and Eastern merchandise.

"Fascinating, aren't they, these native shops," he asked dryly. "That's a Woolworth's store. I don't suppose you have them in San Francisco."

Then Janet realized that beneath the graceful Arabic script printed on the sign, there was also printed clearly in English *Woolworth's*. If only he wouldn't watch her so closely.

She felt embarrassment flush her face.

"Look, I can do without the sarcasm," she said. "We're having this 'talk' only because you've insisted on it and—and due to our relative positions here, I can't very well—" She broke off, not knowing how to finish.

"All right," hc said immediately. "I apologize if I've seemed to take advantage, Janet."

"Okay, then. We'll consider that a truce has been declared," she agreed politely.

Once seated in the bright open coffee shop overlooking a portion of the elegant lobby, Janet was more than satisfied with her choice.

"Is that real marble covering all those walls down there?" she asked.

"Solid rose granite from Aswan," Todd answered. "They wanted this to be a showcase for Egypt, and they did a good job."

"It's beautiful," she breathed, turning her gaze reluctantly to the expensive menu again. She was feeling less tense now. Todd's manner was casual, pleasant, showing none of the urgency she had sensed while in the mosque and during the drive over.

In fact, he did not even let the conversation take a personal turn until she had enjoyed as much as she could of the magnificent fruit salad and yogurt she had ordered.

A silence developed between them—and lengthened until she began to feel slightly uncomfortable. Todd's mouth—that beautiful, sensual, expressive mouth—almost smiled, and then became still again.

"Is it all right if I open our discussion now?" His voice was deceptively humble, and she glanced up sharply to meet his eyes. That was a mistake. They were looking straight into hers, their clear depths questioning, troubled.

"It's why we're here, isn't it?" she asked, keeping her voice noncommittal.

"Yes—and thanks for agreeing to come. I say that in advance. That's in case we end up in a big fight and you storm out without knowing how much I appreciate it. I know you didn't want to." He sounded totally sincere.

Janet put her hands in her lap, out of sight, because she had felt a small tremor. He was going to be persuasive, turn on his charm. It must be an old story to him. She had seen women's heads turn as he passed, had seen the flare of interest in their eyes.

"You may not like some of what I'm going to say, but I'm going to be completely honest, Janet."

"Sounds like a good beginning," she said cordially.

"I'm sorry I came on so strong in the beginning—I'm apologizing again. Two apologies in one afternoon. You may not believe it, but that's a kind of record for me."

"Oh, I believe it," Janet said softly, then regretted the tinge of viciousness in her tone. "Scratch that. I shouldn't have said it. I was the one who demanded no sarcasm."

"Forget it." He smiled, but the barb had hit home. "In some ways I've had things easy. Through the simple happenstance of being born into the Ballard family, I was cast into a certain role. *I* didn't choose it, Janet. Some things are ordained for you the instant you're born. That's not my fault, Janet. If it's any comfort to you, I've taken plenty of blows, too. Different blows, maybe, from those your father took. But, and this you're not going to like at all, I've been programmed from way back—by women, mind you—to *assume* willingness on their part. Most of them are out for what they can get. I'm not irresistible, and I've got sense enough to know it, but my money often is."

Janet carefully and deliberately refused to look at the smooth tanned skin, the strong muscular shoulders. A sense of pure physical strength seemed to emanate from him. That invisible force field was back between them, and she felt it to the marrow of her bones. She gripped her hands together in her lap to keep from reaching across the table to touch him.

"I'm finding you very resistible at the moment," she lied.

"Really?"

It was spoken softly. She barely heard it. He knew, had known instantly, how she felt.

"Okay, let's skip that for the moment," he went on. "I had no business making a pass at you when you told me to get lost. I misunderstood. I didn't think you meant it. I—"

Janet interrupted. "And you remind me here that I crawled all over you, that I gave a pretty good demonstration of the willing woman, didn't I? Is that what you were about to point out?"

"No, as a matter of fact, I wasn't. My next line is to be my—what would be the formal phrasing? My declaration? Yeah, that sounds right. I'm serious, Janet." He was half smiling, but diffident somehow, tentative. It clutched at her heart.

Maybe he meant it. Oh, why couldn't things be different?

"I fell in love with you. It's that simple. And I nearly went into cardiac arrest when you said you were going to marry Hassan. I couldn't deal with it. I just tried to move in."

She crushed a mad impulse to hide behind Hassan again. No. She had used Hassan for the last time. It was unfair. She waited for Todd to go on.

"So what...do you want to do?" For the first time his voice was unsteady for a moment.

"Todd, I'm sorry you said what you just did about loving me. You'll be embarrassed about it later. There is nothing for us. You and me. Nothing." She half turned in her chair.

"Now," he said with sudden soft fury. "There. That's it. That's the goddamned stone wall I run into with you. Why, Janet? Why? I can't be the only man who's ever wanted you. There must have been others. What do you do—stonewall everybody? It's me, isn't it? Something I've done. Janet, tell me. *Please.*"

Oh, God, he was pleading.

Then sudden rage swept through her mind. She maintained a stricken silence for a long moment, refusing to let herself speak. *You killed him, you arrogant bastard. You caused my father's death.*

"Janet, what is it? What have I said? Here, do you want some water?"

"No," she replied, her voice scarcely audible. "Thanks." She fought hard for composure and won. When she spoke again, her voice was simply dull and flat. "Todd, I'm going to say this only once, so listen well. I mean it. I'm being flat-out honest now. You have enough pure animal sex appeal to turn on any woman, and I concede that."

"But what?"

"I *am* attracted to you—I'd be stupid to lie about that. But understand this, I am not going to get involved with you. In *any* way. I decided this for my own reasons, which are valid to me and which you have no right to question. Am I getting through?"

"Clearly." There was instant withdrawal.

"And furthermore, *I don't have to* explain my reasons. To you, or to anybody. Is that clear?" Her voice was low, but cutting. She had the feeling her words were falling on him like blows, but she made herself go on. "I will finish the job I've taken on here. Then I will go back home. And that's it. That's *it*, Todd. Do you understand what I'm saying?"

He waited a long moment to answer her.

"Yes," he said finally. "I understand what you're saying, but you've left out one important fact." His face was closed, blank.

"What fact?" She was striving to identify something. Then she did. The beginning of fear. He hadn't even raised his voice, but beneath the low polite tone lay an implacable hardness as cold as the centuries-old rose granite of Aswan. Had she gone too far? This man was important to Hassan, to Mr. Jamison. "The fact is that I am not bound to accept your decision on anything that concerns both of us. And I don't accept it. One way or another, my love, I'm going to change your mind. Am *I* getting through?"

"Yes, and that closes the subject. I want to go back to the hotel," she said stonily. "I'd prefer to go in a taxi by myself. I suppose you'd make a scene if I tried to. Right?"

"Right. A scene like you wouldn't imagine. Now come on. You're going with me."

THE DRIVE BACK to Mena House was made in empty silence. Janet glanced once or twice at his profile. It might have been carved in stone. She sighed with relief when Todd left her at the hotel entrance and the powerful car roared away.

Inside her own room she dropped her bag onto the bed and took off the hat before she realized the balcony doors were open and the radio was on.

"Hassan!"

"Hello, my dear. Did you have a nice time?" He walked in from the balcony and put down an empty glass by his briefcase and a small black something. A camera? He reached over and snapped off the bedside radio.

"Yes," she said distractedly. "Very. The Houdeibys are—are lovely people, aren't they?"

"I think so. Well, aren't you going to ask about your surprise?

"Are you surprised?"

"Surprise?" she echoed stupidly.

"Yes. I promised you at breakfast."

"Of course." Janet tried to sound enthusiastic. "What is it?"

"This." He went to the table and picked up the camera. No, not a camera. A cassette recorder.

"You said you wanted to hear those tapes I made of phone calls with your father. So I found them. And here is one I want you to hear—I had forgotten we even said these things. Listen now. Just this part."

Her father's voice. Shock bludgeoned her mind. *No. Not now,* she protested silently.

"Listen to this." He pressed down the key.

But her father's voice, husky, vibrant, so familiar, so dear, came out of the machine. Stunned, she could do nothing but stand there and listen.

"Awful connection—can you hear now?"

"Ah, yes, that's better." Hassan's voice came in smoothly. There was a clearing of the connection, and the voices were louder. "I agree, everything goes too fast these days. No time to stop and think, stop and talk awhile."

Her father laughed. Janet backed up against the dresser, leaning against it, her legs suddenly weak. As if hypnotized, she strained for every word, every intonation. He had laughed out there at the site during those last hectic days of his life. Hassan had made him laugh, had pleased him.

"Talk—what's talk? You mean *conversation*? I've forgotten the meaning of the word. But...." The rest of the phrase was lost in the sound of their mingled laughter now. When her father spoke again, his tone was serious, the laughter gone. "I got your note, Hassan. Muhammad brought it this morning."

"It was something difficult for me to say," Hassan's voice came. "There are too many people at the site. I couldn't say it on the phone. But something made me want to say it now. I wanted, I really wanted to talk to you about it, to explain—''

"Explain? What? Friends don't need much explanation. Hassan, I'm delighted. I couldn't be more pleased."

"I thought—" Hassan's voice, diffident but relieved. "The difference in age."

"Nonsense. I haven't been much of a father to her, and I do worry. I've left her here and there, first one boarding school, then another, and she's really all I've got. If I know she's going to be your wife, I'll never have to worry about her again. There is nothing I want more for her."

"I have not spoken to her, of course." Hassan's voice, diffident again. "I don't know—"

"Janet adores you—always has. I'm sure of it. She's intelligent and perceptive, sensitive. I know she'll realize how fortunate she is."

Hassan shut off the machine, abruptly cutting off her father's voice in mid-sentence. Another shock. It tingled along her raw nerve ends. He was gone again. Dead.

Hassan walked over to her.

"You see, my dear?" he asked softly. "You heard his words. Your father's words. Your father wanted you to be my wife, Janet." Reasonable. Kind. Determined. "I'm tired of waiting. I want to marry you while you're here in Egypt. Now."

She stared up at him blankly, trying to think. She felt wooden, emotionless, unresisting. There was a sense of remote disbelief as she let him take

her in his arms, as he pulled her close with a new
kind of self-assurance and locked her body against
his.

CHAPTER EIGHT

AFTER HASSAN FINALLY LEFT, Janet worked feverishly on the notes into the early hours of the morning, trying to shut out the vivid recollections of his insistent advances, the determinedly increasing intimacies, the feeling—unspoken, but there between them nonetheless—that he was being patient with her, but that the patience would in time end, and when it did, there would be complete submission on her part, with no question about it. Small shivers of apprehension and distaste ran through her now and then, causing her fingers to grip the pen more tightly for a moment, to pause in the middle of writing a word while she tried to shut out all memory of the scene between them. But he had left the recorder with her and emptied his pockets of several other cassettes. They were there in a casual heap on the polished wood surface, small mechanical aids to pull her father's voice from the grave, urging her toward Hassan.

Macabre! Morbid! She got up and swept the lot of them into a drawer and slammed it shut. It was her own fault. She should never have asked to hear them. She went back to work on the notes, trying to concentrate, to put everything else from her mind.

She hated Hassan's lovemaking.

She put down the pen and stared at the half-finished page. That simply didn't make sense. She loved Hassan, had loved him for years. He was very dear. She had thought, quite honestly for a long time, that she could ask nothing better than to marry him. He was good, kind, wise. And she hated his lovemaking. It was no use telling herself that she was a woman and he was a man and that if she agreed to the marriage after all, things would work out between them sexually.

Because things would not work out when she froze every time he touched her.

On the other hand, Todd Ballard—without half trying—could elicit a sexual response from her by a glance, by a half-made gesture, by *not* touching her.

Grimly she bent over the notes again. She divided the remaining pages into stacks, shuffling them from stack to stack, estimating. If she could transcribe this many pages each night, it would take ten more days. Or if she did that many, it would take only six. She set a definite goal, working it out so she would get it all done within the original two weeks of allotted vacation.

She sent down for coffee at midnight and worked on doggedly until four o'clock. Then her sleep was broken with angry, fragmentary dreams that eluded her the moment she woke. She could only remember they were about her and Hassan.

THE JEANS fit beautifully. Trust Nazli to know what she was doing when buying clothing. They were smart and comfortable and altogether suitable. A flip of a coin told her to wear the yellow T-shirt, which she had just put on when Nazli arrived to take her out to the site.

Nazli was driving a small ancient Jeep with U.S. ARMY still stenciled dimly on its battered surface. She seemed to pay considerable attention to the shifting of gears, still managing to grind them agonizingly, which set Janet's teeth on edge.

Nazli ground to a stop behind a tourist bus. The closer they came to the pyramids, the more buses they had to cope with.

"Hassan says he thinks he may persuade you to marry him right away. Is this true?" Nazli asked, jerking out the question with a taut averted face. Apparently her valiant effort at cordiality wasn't going to withstand the idea of an immediate marriage for Hassan to someone else.

Janet's heart sank. She was really in no condition to play diplomacy games with Nazli this morning. Nor did she want to grapple yet with how she was going to cope with Hassan's demand for marriage immediately. She had put him off briefly on a plea of "I'm thinking about it," but that was only a reprieve, and she knew it. It was rather amazing that Hassan had accepted it at all, since he clearly wasn't too keen on women "thinking" in the first place. It was probably his old loyalty to her father that made him easier to deal with.

"He mentioned it, suggested it, I mean," Janet said guardedly.

"And what did you decide?" Sheer venom undercut Nazli's conversational tone.

Janet replied with careful politeness, but her voice was drowned out by what sounded like the shriek of tearing metal as they resumed their journey.

"I'm not sure I can work it out," she repeated. "I told him I'd think about it." That seemed a safe noncommittal answer. "You know, Nazli, sometime during my stay here I want to go inside the Great Pyramid," Janet added as they passed the cluster of ancient monuments. "Do you think I could?"

"Of course it can be arranged," Nazli said. "Everything that you wish can be arranged." Then to soften this acid comment she added, "Most, that is many, tourists do. It is no problem. Just be sure first that you are not claus—claus—"

"Claustrophobic?"

"Yes. Just be sure you are not that."

Somewhat beyond the pyramids and Sphinx, Nazli cut off the highway onto a side road that soon disappeared into the hard-packed desert terrain. They continued an up-and-down course for a short distance. The pyramid complex was still in clear view when they came upon a wooden shed and the site of the hidden tomb.

No wonder the tomb had not been discovered for five thousand years. The wonder of it was that her father had discovered it at all. She sat silently in the Jeep for a moment, surveying the scene. There were ten or twelve workmen milling about, their grimy galabias flapping about bare ankles. The shed door stood ajar, an open crate near it. Coils of rope, stacks of short metal rods and odds and ends of tools lay about. There was a crooked stack of large, coarsely woven baskets that Janet had seen briefly before, slung over the backs of workers carrying loose earth from an excavation.

The tomb itself—that must be the tomb—was a gaping hole in the sloping side of a bleak sandy hillock. The face of the hillock had been scraped away, exposing the entrance. Beside it were jagged chunks of rock that must have been used to seal it up and that had been removed.

For days Janet had been transcribing the notes on Eyes-of-Love, and now, suddenly, with a tingling sense of shock, she became aware that the tomb was indeed real. She could go through that dark hole in the side of the slope and then down to the stone room and she would see the painted bed with the broken birdcage wedged crookedly beneath it.

Todd Ballard, half crouching, came out of the low opening in the slope. He had on worn jeans but was bare from the waist up. He wore a sweatband around his forehead, and the shimmering Egyptian sunlight gleamed on his smooth, heavily muscled chest and shoulders. But for the disordered fair hair above the sweatband, he might have been an ancient king freshly anointed with oil.

The fantasy abruptly disappeared.

"Hi. You made it. Well, we're just about ready. Two more treads to put in the passage." Todd spoke with a calculated casualness, wiping his dirty hands on a piece of rag that he then tossed back into the hole. It was as if their angry scene at lunch yesterday had not happened. Janet wondered what he was feeling. Whatever it was—if anything—was not about to be revealed. She could feel her own anxiety increase. Her heart thudded. Her lips felt dry.

"Have you completed any more of the notes?" Todd began walking across the hard-packed sandy soil toward her.

"Yes, quite a few," Janet answered, thinking of the stack of fresh pages she'd left at the desk.

"Good." He turned to Nazli. "Nazli, I've been down this morning. Maybe you'll want to spend some time down there today. Get the inscriptions from what's visible. And maybe we can get a scroll or two from under the bedstead without dislodging anything."

"Yes, we must try that," Nazli answered absently, her mind apparently still on something else. "I want very much to start the translating. Is Hassan here? I have a message for him from my father."

"Not yet—maybe in a few minutes. I'm expecting him. We have cold drinks in the shed." He opened the Jeep door. "The guys are just about through in the passage. Come over and have something while we wait."

Janet braced herself for his touch as he helped her from the Jeep. She would reveal nothing. Nothing.

"After we start taking out the tomb's contents, I'm going to have some very bright students from

Cairo and American Universities help. They are coming over later today for a first look. Nazli, thanks for recommending that Idris Sibai from American. He's going to be a real help with the remaining wood pieces.''

''Yes, he's an old friend,'' Nazli said, and Janet felt a flash of annoyance because they were shutting her out.

Todd opened the door of the wooden shed, and she stepped inside, unable to see much because of the dusty dimness. Janet got the impression of stacks of various kinds of objects and implements. There were a couple of heavy wooden benches against the walls, a scarred, slant-top wooden desk on tall legs, and a long work table against the wall.

It was her father's workplace. At home he had mentioned the high, old-fashioned desk he stood at sometimes. He had found it at a bazaar in a mixed lot of battered secondhand furniture. She went to the desk and touched it lightly, wondering if Todd knew her father had bought it or if he cared about such details.

''All we've got is cola and lemon soda. No, here's some ginger ale, too.'' Todd swished his hands around a mass of half-melted ice inside a plastic cooler. He took out two dripping bottles of cola and one of lemon soda and removed the caps before handing each over.

Todd blotted his hands on his jeans, and Janet concentrated on her lemon soda. She would not look at the shining wet skin of his strong forearms.

She would not look at the damp fabric clinging to his muscular thighs.

There was the sound of a motor outside. "I'll see if that's Hassan," Nazli said, moving to the door.

"There is something I think I should mention to you," Todd said rather tentatively after she had gone.

"And what is that?" Janet asked crisply.

"Apparently Hassan knows about us—you and me."

Janet set her soda bottle down on the desk with a thump. "Knows *what* about us? What is there to know?"

The strong shoulders shrugged. A faint smile came and went. "Hassan's a big boy, Janet. He doesn't miss much. Apparently he picked up right away on what you so casually referred to as 'an attraction.'"

She lifted the bottle and took a sip, stalling for time. She had to ask it. "Was he—upset? Angry?"

"Yes, to both. Upset and angry. Has been for a couple of days."

"Well, what happened? What did he say?"

"*Say?* He didn't have to *say* it, Janet. You must know better than that. You've known Hassan longer than I have. He naturally prefers an indirect approach. Hassan's an operator—no disrespect intended—and he wants to make the most of his new association with me. And you can wipe that look of contempt off your pretty little face. Not me, personally. He could care less for Todd Ballard, but he cares a lot about what doors Todd Ballard

could open for him. He couldn't have been plea-
santer.''

"You still haven't said anything. What 'indirect'
method did he use?''

"He said he had decided on marriage right away.
By that he made it clear that he meant soon. Like in
a few days.''

Janet knew he was deliberately trying for a reaction. Todd was watching her intently. She was glad
the light in the shed was dim, as a quick flare of apprehension must have shown briefly in her eyes. She
put down the bottle of soda. If she drank any more,
she'd be sick.

"Feeling a little queasy, are we?''

"The soda's just too sweet, that's all.''

"You looked sick for a second, Janet. Are you
beginning to get the idea maybe that marrying Hassan isn't what you want? Relax. I can see out the
door from here. That wasn't Hassan who just
came. Now what Hassan did not tell me, and I must
say he omits things very smoothly, but what he did
not say, was whether you agreed. Did you actually
agree to marry him while you're here? I mean next
week, the day after tomorrow?''

"We...talked about it,'' she answered after a
moment. That wasn't exactly a lie. Next week. The
day after tomorrow. One thing about Todd Ballard,
he would be good with a bludgeon if he ever needed
to be.

"What did you tell him?'' he prodded.

There was an interval of thickening silence in
the dim shed. Tiny dust motes moved slowly in

the shaft of sunlight that came in the half-open door.

"And you're not going to answer. Okay. That's answer enough. You're scared to death of the marriage trap, Janet. Good for you. You're smarter than I thought you were."

"Thanks a lot." Janet said the words absently, thinking how cold his voice was, so filled with contempt when he referred to marriage. Somewhere, sometime in his life, something had happened to turn him against marriage—commitment of any kind, perhaps. It had shown for just that instant in his light clear eyes, blank and bleak. Whatever had happened must have been ugly, and she had the feeling he had lived with it a long while.

Her pulse quickened. Hassan knew all about this man's past. He had made it his business to know. And even now it was all there in a thick manila envelope stuffed into Hassan's cluttered living-room desk. There was no way she could read those clippings—could she? How could she do it? Oh, surely not. But the idea lingered. There was a kind of fascination about it.

"What?" She realized suddenly that he had asked another question.

"I said, 'What do you actually know about Hassan?' Really know, Janet, from your own knowledge?"

"Why, I—he's—was my father's best friend! For many years they worked together. I know all I need to know!" Anger rushed through her. The appalling nerve of this man! Maybe Hassan couldn't raise her pulse count, but he was a better man than Todd Ballard.

"Simmer down," Todd said easily. "It was only a question. And you answered it." He left just enough pause between these comments to prick her curiosity.

"What do you mean by that?"

"Just that I suddenly have some unanswered questions about our friend, Hassan, that's all. As I understand it, all his business interests are on the other side of the world. Yet he's been content to fiddle away his time here in Cairo as a minor official, waiting around for you to reach the age of consent. I'd just like to know why. Why hasn't he been in the States all along if he's so crazy to get there?"

Janet started to speak, then shut her mouth firmly. She would not defend Hassan to Todd Ballard. She pushed away from the tall desk and walked toward the door. "I've had about enough of this," she finally said icily.

At the door she paused. No matter what Hassan's investments were, they were nothing compared to this man's resources. She turned. "Let Hassan alone," she added with an effort. She had a panicky vision of Todd Ballard picking up the telephone in his suite at the hotel and making one or two calls, putting wheels in motion, causing things to happen—things that vaguely threatened Hassan and all Hassan's plans. It wasn't fair. "I asked him that myself once," she went on uncomfortably. Once again she must placate Todd.

"And what did he say?"

"He said it's difficult to uproot—to leave one's homeland. He has commitments here, responsibilities. These things take time."

There was a long pause. Then he said, "I see," in the most noncommittal voice she had ever heard.

She waited a moment longer in the drawn-out silence. Apparently he wasn't going to say anything else, not another word, just stand there looking at her absently as if he were thinking of something else.

Outside she experienced an increasing sense of dread. Todd wouldn't let it alone. Just as he hadn't let her plans alone. He'd called Mr. Jamison, he'd called the Ballard Foundation and he'd managed to get his own way. She felt fiercely protective of Hassan. She would have to do something.

Nazli sat disconsolately on a block of stone by the opening in the slope. She was tossing a bit of black basalt up and down on her dusty palm. Janet looked at her.

There was Hassan's responsibility—the one he had to extricate himself from before leaving. Janet felt sure of it. That stunning Egyptian girl in designer jeans tossing the dusty rock up and down.

"The treads are all in place," Nazli said, standing up and tossing aside the chip of basalt. "Ah, here comes Todd. I guess someone told him."

"The treads," Janet learned as she stepped inside the opening after Todd, were metal and wooden rods fixed at one-step intervals on the decline of the stone passage.

"You don't have much heel on those sandals, do

you?'' Todd observed critically at the entrance. "Well, hook into the treads as well as you can. Sand on stone can be slippery. I'll go ahead, and if you fall, I'll stop you.''

Not likely, she thought grimly, and moved forward with great caution, stretching out her hands on either side to touch the stone walls. She didn't fancy having to extricate herself from his embrace in the narrow passage. She had expected that Nazli would go down with them, but she had elected to wait for Hassan's arrival aboveground.

After a few steps the light was different. The brilliant golden sunlight did not penetrate too far and was replaced with the shivering white glow from a series of bulbs.

"Don't panic if the lights fail,'' Todd said, moving just ahead of her. "You know what the power is like in Egypt.''

"Yes, it's the first luxury-class hotel I've ever been in where they provide a supply of wax candles just in case.''

Todd laughed. His voice had a soft intimate quality that sent a tingle of excitement through her. He paused a moment, testing a tread with his foot, kicking at it slightly. She thought she could almost feel an echo of the jolt in her own body. The wavering electric light made thin shadows caress the mounds and hollows of his shoulder muscles as he moved.

"Thought it seemed loose, but it's okay. Come on. Two more steps and we go down. How are you on heights, by the way?''

"Heights?" She stopped in her tracks.

He twisted around to look at her upturned face.

"Well," he said, sounding somewhat uncertain, "you've been working on the notes. You know we're going down. It's about ninety feet—not quite that, maybe, since we've been moving downward since we entered the passage."

"Ninety feet?" she said, and was immediately embarrassed at how shaky her voice sounded. She swallowed. The slithering sand on the stone floor and the rough texture of the walls beneath her fingertips made her stunningly aware of the vast difference between transcribing notes about a ninety-foot shaft and actually climbing down it.

"Is this going to be too much for you? You want to go back?"

Never, she thought. "Of course not," she said in a crisp tone. "Thanks, anyhow, but I'll manage okay."

"Your father had iron rungs put all the way down, you know. So it's just a matter of climbing down one step at a time and holding on to the rung above. A few of them needed replacing, but they're all firm now."

"Good. Let's go."

The shaft, not exactly square, seemed less than three feet wide. It was a bottomless pit full of flickering light, with the iron rungs much too far apart down one wall. Taut ropes suspended from fastenings in the floor around the shaft entrance hung down one side of it. These must support the platform her father had worked from.

Janet set her jaw and watched Todd start down. As soon as he was out of the way, before she could change her mind, she followed him. The rungs were like a ladder of sorts. She had climbed down ladders before. She could pretend it was the ladder on the side of a pool. Or maybe she could imagine climbing down into the galley of a cabin cruiser on San Francisco Bay. One step after another. It must be two football fields long. Or ten. Janet tried to be deliberate and not hurry for fear of panicking. Once she scuffed against Todd's hand on a rung below, and he said, "Easy, now. Watch it."

Her legs were cramping. She just noticed this when they reached bottom.

"Don't jump onto the platform. Just ease down. Here, I'll hold you." He was standing on something, in a room, reaching up.

Janet felt his hands slide up her hips and around her waist. She relaxed her grip on the iron bars and let him lift her down, feeling intensely the pressure and warmth of his clasp.

"Well," he said, "this is it. What do you think?" There was a soft exultation in his tone.

She went down slowly to her knees on the padded platform. He didn't even seem aware of her, only of the room.

She looked around. It was all so familiar. She had been transcribing the notes for several days, so it was small wonder that she felt no surprise. She recognized one thing after another, starting with the massive outer sarcophagus of alabaster, now grimy with age, into which would have been fitted the smaller gold-and-jewel-trimmed one. Yes, the heavy alabaster lid appeared in place and secure, just as her father's notes had said. And she recognized the sagging bedstead. No, she thought, it was not the same design as her bedroom chair. Similar, but not identical. Somehow she had imagined it would be. And there on the floor was the scatter of large golden rings inlaid with blue and green dragonflies. It was all in such a terrible jumble. They shouldn't have done this to Eyes-of-Love's things. It was a violation.

"What are you thinking about?" Todd asked.

Janet turned her head to find him watching her again.

"I was thinking about what must have happened here five thousand years ago. They must have had a reason for crowding it all in here like this. I wonder if you'll find out what it was."

"Ah, wouldn't I love to?" He smiled rather wistfully, and she wanted suddenly to assure him that he would definitely find out anything he wanted to.

"It's a violation, though, isn't it?" he asked thoughtfully. "You feel it, too, don't you? I can sense your reticence."

"Well, yes, I do feel like an intruder here."

"It's what we are really, intruders. This place was meant to be sealed up forever, and we've broken into it. We'll study it all, make notes about it, write about it and add it to our already vast store of information." His voice was sober. "It's supposed to be helpful in some way that's never really clear to me. Yet now and then I get this feeling I'm...tres-passing.''

Their eyes met in a moment of complete under-standing.

"You'd like to go up now, wouldn't you?'' It wasn't really a question. He knew.

"Yes,'' she said quietly. He was such a strange mixture. Sometimes he was so unfeeling about the needs of others. Then again, as now, he could show sudden insight and sensitivity.

Outside in the blazing sunlight Janet took in a gulp of air and stood watching a funnel-shaped cloud of dust trail after a departing car.

"You missed Hassan,'' Nazli said. "He had to go right back. Do you want to return to the hotel now?'' The Egyptian woman was taut with some suppressed emotion. Her voice revealed it. Janet saw Todd's eyes move impassively over her stiff body. Anger. That's what it was. Nazli was furious about something.

"If you have something else to do, I'll take Janet back,'' Todd offered.

"No, no. It is fine. I have an errand, anyhow,'' Nazli said, moving off toward the Jeep in her regal stride.

The short trip back to the hotel was made in steaming silence, and Janet looked forward to bid-ding Nazli goodbye at least until she was in a better mood. However, she was dismayed when Nazli turned the Jeep over to an attendant and got out when she did.

"We must have a little visit,'' Nazli said, her eyes

roving restlessly about the grounds. "This way. Come this way. We'll go sit in the lawn chairs." She charged off determinedly across a wide expanse of lawn toward some canvas chairs set around an umbrella-shaded table.

Janet sighed and followed her. Might as well see it through, she thought.

"Do you want something?" Nazli asked as they seated themselves.

"No. Nothing, really," Janet answered. She watched Nazli wave away an approaching waiter, then slump down in her chair and go into a sullen silence.

"You are very modern, sophisticated, is it not so?" Nazli asked at last.

"Reasonably so, I guess," Janet said warily.

"But you are American," Nazli muttered. "Sometimes they...you...are different, very... um...not sophisticated. Stifflaced."

"Straitlaced. I suppose some people are, yes."

"Are you, then?" Nazli's great eyes looked at her somberly.

"Nazli, I'm not even sure what we're talking about." Janet's patience was wearing thin.

"We are talking about Hassan and all this business about marry and not marry, marry and not marry. You can't behave in this manner. It is not...not appropriate. Did you find something out about Hassan that makes you offended? Did you? Tell me what?"

There was really no reason for her to tell Nazli anything, Janet thought, and she mentally counted to ten. She was about to answer when Nazli plunged on.

"You see, he is an older man. Very sophisticated. So you have to understand this. There cannot be a nonsense about being offended because he is... um... a man of the world. So if he has had love affairs and mistresses, it does not matter, you see?"

Then suddenly Janet's patience snapped. "For heaven's sake, Nazli, shut up! I'm aware of Hassan's masculinity. I wasn't born yesterday. He's hardly the celibate type. I know he's had affairs— probably many. I know you're his mistress now. I'm not going into shock over it. We're all adult human beings—" She stopped at the look of raw shock on Nazli's face.

"No! Not! I am not. Not his mistress! Never!" She clutched her shaking hands against her mouth and stared wide-eyed at Janet over them.

"But you said—you just said—you used the term 'mistress' yourself."

"I know. I am sure—I mean pretty sure. There was... is... was... one mistress. And I don't take offense, you see?"

"One? Oh, come now, Nazli. Hassan is in his forties."

"I mean, one person—many women, yes, yes— but one especial person," Nazli stumbled on wildly. "But I *understand* it."

"What do you mean, 'was'? That's past tense, Nazli. Where is she now, this woman? Did she— die—or something?"

"No, no, no. She is in Alexandria—at an apartment there. On the Corniche. I pretend I don't know this, you see?''

Janet had only a guidebook idea of Alexandria, Pearl of the Mediterranean. Cleopatra had received the crown of Egypt there, met Caesar there, taken Marc Antony as her lover and died there.

Was Nazli telling the truth? Janet didn't believe her denial for an instant. Nazli, not as clever or sophisticated as Hassan, had revealed in many ways the deep intimacy between them. They were sleeping together—Janet was sure of it—probably had been for some time. There was a wry twist to her lips. Maybe Hassan didn't increase her own pulse rate, but he didn't seem to have any difficulty with other women.

''I'm going to the hotel now,'' Janet said, getting up out of the canvas chair. ''This little visit is finished.''

Nazli caught at her hand, gripping it. ''You must not mention—''

''All right!'' Janet said in exasperation. ''We'll just forget it—but tell me her name?'' she added as a sudden thought occurred to her.

''Her name?'' Nazli whispered, horror-struck.

''Yes,'' Janet said patiently. ''The woman in Alexandria. What is her name?'' If Hassan could not be persuaded to forget about the marriage plans, it might just be helpful to mention the name of a lady in Alexandria. Janet wanted to part from Hassan as friends, but just in case—

''Oh, no,'' Nazli moaned softly.

''The name, Nazli. If you don't tell me, I can always ask Hassan.''

A SUPERROMANCE™
the great new romantic novel she never wanted to end.
And it can be yours
FREE!

She never wanted it to end. And neither will you. From the moment you begin... *Love Beyond Desire*, your **FREE** introduction to the newest series of bestseller romance novels, **SUPERROMANCES**.

You'll be enthralled by this powerful love story... from the moment Robin meets the dark, handsome Carlos and finds herself involved in the jealousies, bitterness and secret passions of the Lopez family. Where her own forbidden love threatens to shatter her life.

Your FREE *Love Beyond Desire* is only the beginning. A subscription to **SUPERROMANCES** lets you look forward to a long love affair. Month after month, you'll receive four love stories of heroic dimension. Novels that will involve you in spellbinding intrigue, forbidden love and fiery passions.

You'll begin this series of sensuous, exciting contemporary novels... written by some of the top romance novelists of the day... with four each month.

And this big value... each novel, almost 400 pages of compelling reading... is yours for only $2.50 a book. Hours of entertainment for so little. Far less than a first-run movie or Pay-TV. Newly published novels, with beautifully illustrated covers, filled with page after page of delicious escape into a world of romantic love... delivered right to your home.

**EXTRA BONUS
MAIL YOUR ORDER
TODAY AND GET A
FREE TOTE BAG
FROM SUPERROMANCE.**

← Mail this card today for your FREE gifts.

Canada Post
Postes
Canada
021

Nazli gave a dramatic shuddering sigh. "Mrs. Fugate. She is Mrs. Fugate, that English lady."

"*Mrs.* Fugate?"

"She is a widow. She and her husband, Captain Fugate—I never knew them exactly—used to come to Egypt in the winter and then sometime he died, poor man, and Mrs. Fugate stayed to live here."

Janet paused a moment longer. "Nazli," she said with grudging kindness. "Don't worry. Things will work out all right. You'll see." Then she turned and started across the green lawn, thinking about a woman in Alexandria—whom Nazli didn't know exactly—in her apartment overlooking the sea.

Could it all be true?

CHAPTER NINE

DESPITE GROWING LASSITUDE, Janet made herself begin work on the notes as soon as she returned to her room. She tried to concentrate on them, to forget the nagging questions that refused to be shut out of her mind.

Janet bent over in her chair and rubbed her thighs—she'd have some aching muscles the next day from the unaccustomed climb down into the tomb. An intense wave of homesickness swept through her. For a moment she felt physically sick, but it passed. Todd had said there was ten hours' difference in the time between San Francisco and Cairo—maybe that meant that right now great drifts of wispy fog were coming in through the Golden Gate, gently draping themselves around the orange metal of the bridge, lapping like slow waves up the hillsides across the bay. Janet longed intensely for the misty caress of fog against her face.

Merciless nagging questions drove the image from her mind. There was Hassan still to be dealt with, and they were still poles apart, since she wanted out of the engagement and he was determined on marriage "next week or the day after tomorrow."

Then she had a recollection of Todd Ballard in the work shed at the site. And her conviction remained that—somehow or other—Hassan needed protection from him, that Todd could in some way prevent Hassan's emigrating to the States. Hassan had worked too long and too hard to be denied his prize now, as her father had been denied his. Janet straightened up with an effort. She was beginning to feel rotten, absolutely rotten. This was what anxiety did to a person. If one was mentally down, one's body got sick. It was all in one's mental attitude.

Determinedly she picked up the pen, and from nowhere she recalled Nazli's frantic disjointed revelation on the lawn about the "one especial person" who, Nazli had convinced herself, was Hassan's ex-mistress. Poor Nazli, tormenting herself with jealousy when she really didn't know what Hassan's relationship with the woman was—if there was a woman there at all. *Forget it. Get to work,* she admonished herself.

But it was not so easy. There was the memory of the way the shadows had flickered over Todd Ballard's shoulder muscles. It would take a while to clear away the last of Todd Ballard from her mind after she got home. And she thought about Todd as he was in the shed, when he had seemed so quietly relentless, "Feeling a little queasy, are we?" Todd's phrase sprang to mind, and her skin was suddenly bathed in dampness. She knew with quick dread that she was going to be sick. It wasn't mental. It was in her stomach. She was suddenly convulsed with nausea and dashed wildly for the bathroom.

Rinsing her face with cold water, she worked her way through the mild sense of panic she was encountered on the very rare occasion of being sick. "Extremely healthy persons," her father had once told her, "get sick so seldom it confuses them. They can't cope. Just assume you will live, and go find something interesting to do."

She paused in patting her face dry and looked in the mirror. Her face did look a little pale. She decided that a couple of days isolation with the legitimate excuse of a tourist complaint might get her through the rest of the notes; so there would be nothing to hold her here when two weeks were up.

USING HER ILLNESS —and she was more or less queasy part of the time—Janet was able to hold on to her privacy for two and a half days. She transcribed a mountain of notes. The stack seemed to melt away under her hands, and although she fell exhausted into bed in the early morning hours, her interest never flagged in the fascinating fragmentary image of Eyes-of-Love that continued to emerge.

Meticulously her father had pieced the bits together.

Evidence definitely points to Eyes-of-Love being part of royal family. Otherwise permission would *not* have been granted for this site adjacent to royal mastabas...royal princess is good possibility, as Cheops's royal queens elsewhere.... Sister, perhaps.

Then later her father had painstakingly examined the inscription on a broken box of scrolls and identified under which king's reign she had been born.

Reign of Snofru, Cheops's father. Good indication, then, that Eyes-of-Love could have been dowager queen, Cheops's mother. Strong evidence that if Eyes-of-Love's original tomb elsewhere and discovered and broken into, king would order a reburial near own tomb construction site.

Janet gazed out across the balcony at the cluster of pyramids. So thousands of years ago, when Eyes-of-Love had lived, the Great Pyramid had not even been completed. And the man who finally had it completed had probably been the child of Eyes-of-Love.

As Janet hurried on with growing interest, she got phone calls from the others and visits from both Hassan and Nazli. Hassan stopped in morning and evening, bringing little gifts, usually confections. He was arranging to take her to Luxor with him next week, since he had to make a trip there for the bureau.

Nazli came briefly every day after she left the site, still in her dusty jeans. She gave fragmentary bulletins on how the work was going. Todd had taken on another assistant, a doctoral candidate from American University, who was x-raying the small mummified birds they had found. Todd planned to hire one more person. Nazli herself was working on some scrolls in the shed. No, they had not got the bedstead out, but it was propped up, so the scrolls could be safely taken. Todd had an air conditioner put in the window of the shed, which was very loud. Nazli had switched back to a cordial mood, possibly because she had Hassan pretty much to herself.

Todd sent red roses and a note the first morning. "I tried for red poppies, but they didn't have any, Todd." He had remembered the black dress with the wild border of red poppies! This insight sent a wave of color washing over her face and neck, and when she placed the flowers on the dresser, her hands were unsteady. She stood there a long moment, looking at her hands, feeling the heat in her face. She was so vulnerable where Todd was concerned.

She could not prolong her hiatus any longer than two and a half days because Nazli, on an errand for Hassan, stopped in for a visit without calling first. Nazli discovered her eating the Mena House version of a cheeseburger—and with great gusto—while she worked at her writing table, surrounded by transcribed notes.

"You are well again!" Nazli exclaimed with a great show of pleasure, and Janet had to admit she felt fine once more and yes, she would join them for dinner.

After Nazli left, Janet pushed away the rest of the

cheeseburger, as there was no possibility of eating it all, anyway. She had already eliminated the top half of the bun, which appeared to be a small loaf of bread. Without a scale she could only estimate that the burger contained at least a pound of beef and half a pound of cheese!

The evening turned out to be one of those Janet privately termed "a family dinner." In addition to her and Hassan, there was Todd Ballard and the Houdeibys, father and daughter. Feeling somewhat guilty about her feigned illness, Janet wore very little makeup, hoping to appear pale and frail. She regretted it when she saw how much the skillful use of makeup enhanced Nazli's already vivid beauty. Janet felt like a mouse.

As in most groups with a common work interest, the dinner conversation was mainly shoptalk, and Janet's interest in getting out to the site again heightened. They had cleared a lot from the chamber, and everyone was hard at work photographing and classifying artifacts. Some journalists had come and gone and would come again when the sarcophagus was finally opened. The discovery of an intact royal mummy would be enough to warrant at least a mid-size media event. She made a comment to this effect, and a small pool of silence developed at the table.

"But it wouldn't be a *royal* mummy, my dear," Hassan said, smiling. He placed his hand over hers on the table with just the slightest pressure. Hassan was telling her tactfully to leave it all to the experts and not to make embarrassing mistakes.

Janet tensed up and then relaxed. After all, they hadn't read as far in the notes as she had. The information that Eyes-of-Love was probably the royal mother of Cheops would be a neat little bombshell. She pondered a moment and then couldn't resist tossing it into their midst.

"Well, you can't know yet." She smiled, withdrawing her hand. "You haven't seen the notes I've done today. My father has a pretty logical theory of who Eyes-of-Love is—was. He believes there is good evidence to think she was the wife of Snofru, Cheops's father. She was in his reign. It would have been late in his life."

"Oh, no, cannot be," Nazli cut in quickly. "Not possibly. We know who she was. We—"

Her father was making small tchk-tchk sounds that silenced her.

"I just transcribed the notes, Nazli," Janet said more sharply than she had intended.

An embarrassed silence fell. Todd broke it in the cool, remote, in-charge tone she had heard at their first meeting. "As it happens," he said smoothly, "we just learned today that Eyes-of-Love was not a royal woman at all. But that's the purpose of archaeology in the first place, isn't it? Turn over another stone—find another truth?"

Janet felt a flush of anger in her cheeks. "Are you implying my father made a glaring mistake?" She was conscious of Hassan stiffening in his chair beside her.

"Not at all," Todd said pleasantly. "Professor Wingate was too dedicated a scholar to make glaring mistakes. And he offered his analysis as a theory only, didn't he? I'm sure the evidence of the moment led him logically to his theory, but at that time, remember, he did not have access to the information we gathered today.''

Before she could answer Hassan interrupted, placing his arm around her shoulders. ''Nazli's been working on one of the scrolls from beneath the bedstead. It's not in bad shape. The work has been slow going, but she can read quite a bit of it. It seems Eyes-of-Love was simply one of the king's favorites. It was Cheops, though. There appears to be no doubt about that.'' His voice was kind, placating. He wanted very much for her to shut up and stay quiet.

That tomb had been her father's crowning achievement and there, casually about the dinner table, they were repudiating his theories. She couldn't let them do that.

''The king's 'favorite'? By that, I assume you mean his concubine? Of course, I'm not an expert, but that doesn't make sense to me. If she was just one of the palace hookers, how did she get to be buried in the royal compound?''

Todd hid a quick grin, and Hassan looked annoyed and pained as he always did when she jarred his schoolgirl image of her. Dr. Houdeiby filled the gap.

''Ah! That is the big puzzlement!'' he said in such a loud voice that the people at the next table glanced over.

''I think we can assume that the king's favorite

automatically had a certain...social standing,"
Todd cut in. "In any case, why don't we put it on
hold for now? We'll be learning more every day.
Have you got a lot of the notes done, Janet? You
apparently didn't waste any of your con-
valescence."

"Quite a lot," she said tightly. There was nothing
Janet could say to rebut them, to further defend her
father. She was not one of the experts. She had no
credentials. "In fact," she added with some angry
satisfaction, "I'm almost through the notes. I'll be
able to go back to San Francisco on the return ticket
I brought with me—no problem. The transcription
went awfully fast once I got into it." Never would
she reveal to any of them the long nights hunched
over the writing table, the cramping fingers, the
countless cups of coffee ordered up from room service. She had never worked so hard in her life.

"Ah, yes, well..." Hassan said. "That is something we must discuss, my dear."

Ah yes, indeed. The matter of the marriage that
Hassan wanted to occur "next week or the day after
tomorrow."

Suddenly more than two days of almost ceaseless
work began to take their toll and Janet was bone
tired. She was able to get away early, pleading
fatigue, but even then Hassan insisted on seeing her
up to her room.

Janet expected he would talk to her about the
coming trip to Luxor. "What did you want to say,
Hassan?" she asked wearily. "I can see there's
something on your mind."

"Don't look so grim." He smiled. "Something nice. Todd is going to offer you a very interesting job with the excavation."

"He what? What in the world could I do—beyond transcribe the notes—which I've just about finished?"

"He needs a sketch artist to render some detailed drawings of various objects."

"Oh, Hassan! Really! Look, I may as well get it out in the open. You know, anyway. You just haven't said anything. Todd Ballard doesn't want me as his sketch artist. He wants to go to bed with me. Please don't look so shocked. Sooner or later you're going to have to realize that I'm not a little girl anymore. I grew up, Hassan!"

Hassan looked pained. "I am aware of Ballard's motives. I will deal with him in my own way," he said stiffly.

"Yet you want me to stay on in Egypt and work for him."

"I want you to stay on in Egypt for a time, yes. When I said I would deal with his interest in you in my own way, I meant it. It must be done diplomatically. No unpleasantness."

Janet turned away, angry at him and feeling sorry for him at the same time. Todd had been right. Again. Hassan would try to keep Todd away from her without damaging what he perceived as his friendship with a man of Todd's importance. It made her want to cry.

"The detailed fine-line drawing he wants is one of your best skills, Janet," he persisted. "And he already helped you to get an open-ended leave of absence from your Mr. Jamison."

Janet sighed. If she refused, Hassan might stay for the next three hours trying to convince her. She fell back on her standard tactic with him. "I don't know. Let me think about it."

Tired as she was, it took a while to get to sleep. Hassan's attitude toward Todd made her uncomfortable. They were adversaries, but it was all so secretive and hidden under the surface. Yet open combat over something wasn't either man's style. Hassan would try to manipulate and maneuver as if he were playing a chess game. Todd would quietly arrange to hire the best possible chess players to play the game for him. *Well,* she asked herself angrily, *what did you expect—a* High Noon *shoot-out between the two by the pyramids?*

The pyramids!

Janet sat upright in bed. She had forgotten the next day's visit to the Great Pyramid. Sometime during the dinner—early, before she had become angry with them about her father's theory—Nazli had mentioned that she wanted to show Janet inside the Great Pyramid. Somehow or other it seemed that Todd would be the logical one to do it. She wasn't sure now how that had come about. Janet lay back, fuming in the darkness. She *must* get to sleep. The last time she looked at the clock it was three-thirty, and Todd had said he'd leave a seven o'clock wake-up call for her at the desk.

JANET STOOD SILENTLY, waiting for Todd on the hard sand, looking at the Sphinx from an angle.

The massive lion's body was in strong repose, with the kingly head in royal headdress held upright so the broad beautiful—mutilated—face could go on gazing into the distance through the centuries. She felt a compelling sense of infinite silent strength and of endless serene patience. There, bathed in the golden sunlight of an Egyptian morning, the Sphinx seemed to be watching, as it had watched for thousands of years and would watch for thousands more.

"He gets to you, doesn't he?" Todd's voice spoke softly at her side. "They call him Abu Hol—Father of Terror. Do you see that?"

"No," she said thoughtfully. She saw no threat of terror in the Sphinx. "I see strength certainly, but serenity, too. And *patience.*"

"Oh, yes, patience. Willingness to wait for something forever." Their glances crossed briefly, each recognizing something in the other, a shared understanding. Then the moment was gone.

Janet turned, smiling politely, because the guide had joined them.

"This is Mahmoud. He's going in with us. He says no one has entered yet today—it's a little early for the tourist crush."

Mahmoud bowed and smiled, his teeth showing very white in his ebony face. He was one of the many Nubians who had emigrated to Egypt years ago when the original high dam was built at Aswan. He was young—scarcely twenty, Janet thought—and his white galabia and the white twist of cotton on his head, though worn, were immaculate. He seemed in no hurry at all and stood beside them, gazing with them at the majestic image of the Sphinx. He said something softly in Arabic, and Todd replied, apparently telling him to change to English, because he did.

"You see," Mahmoud said, pointing to the massive image, "he has the lion-body to fight and the man-head to think."

"Well put, Mahmoud," Todd commented. "Shall we get started?"

They started across the sandy waste toward the Great Pyramid. It rose like a symmetrical rocky mountain straight ahead of them.

"How do we get in it?" Janet asked.

"There's an entrance in the north face. Originally one entered about fifty feet above the present entrance. Then they took pity on the tourists, I guess, and opened it just about ground level," Todd explained. He was wearing newer-looking jeans today and a white T-shirt. The familiar little canvas hat clung to the back of his fair head, with his sunglasses resting in his hair just in front of it.

Janet didn't see the entrance until they were almost upon it.

"Watch it, now," Todd cautioned. "Let Mahmoud go first. The entrance slopes downward, and the sand sifts in." Mahmoud went into the opening ahead of them, and Todd gestured her in, then followed along behind her. "We're going down for a few yards—not far. Then we're going to go up a kind of gangway arrangement. Take it slow and easy, because it'll be narrow and steep. But there's a handrail. and hopefully the lights won't go off.''

"I have the lamp, m'sieur,'' Mahmoud's soft voice came reassuringly.

"Good,'' Todd answered as they came to the end of the downward ramp. "Well, this is it. Ready?''

They were at the beginning of a sharp upturned square tunnel.

"It's so low!'' Janet was startled.

"Right. Sorry, I forgot to mention that. You have to kind of lean over. It's only about four feet high.''

"Okay,'' she said, beginning to feel doubtful. "How long is the tunnel?''

"Oh, maybe a hundred and twenty feet.''

Determinedly Janet followed the guide, remembering for the first time that she was knowingly and willingly climbing slowly up into the center of a mass of great stones that had been fitted tightly together to form this mountain. But it was five thousand years ago that they had fitted tightly. Were they still tight?

"How much stone do you think this took, Mahmoud?'' she asked about halfway up.

"More than two million, madame,'' came Mahmoud's reply.

She watched his bony black ankles climbing steadily ahead of her step after step. She was getting a cramp in her neck from her half-crouched position. There didn't seem to be enough air.

"And each stone weighs about two and a half

tons," Todd said behind her in a conversational tone.

The electric light in the tunnel flickered off. Then it flickered on again. Then it went off, plunging them all into thick blackness. Startled, Janet straightened and cracked her head against the stone ceiling of the tunnel. An instant of wild panic seized her, but she fought it.

"Easy, easy. Mahmoud has a light." Todd's hands were at her waist, firm, reassuring. "Just a second, now, just a second. Are you okay?"

"Oh, yes," she said, trying not to sound tense. "Just a little bump on the head. I'm fine, really." She had a compelling impulse to sag backward, to curve her body against Todd's body and rest there. She wanted intensely to have his arms slide around her and pull her close and hold her there.

There was a tiny spark by the wall, then another. Mahmoud was trying to strike a match against the dusty stone.

"Hang on." Todd's voice close behind her had laughter in it. "This is the kind of thing you only do once so you can say you did it."

Janet laughed. The momentary panic was gone. "It'll make a great dinner-party story," she agreed as Mahmoud's small alcohol lamp flickered into life. It gave a sickly wavering glow in a circle around them. Beyond that lay the thick darkness of the tunnel up into the tomb's center. The moment the lamp was burning steadily the lights went on again, and they all three laughed.

"I think they do that power-failure routine on

purpose," Todd said, "to give the tourists a thrill. Okay, let's go, we're more than halfway to the grand gallery."

"Is that it?" Janet asked. "The burial chamber?"

Todd paused a moment before answering. "Not exactly," he said. "The grand gallery is great, though. You can stand up and breathe. It's more than a hundred and fifty feet long and—how high, Mahmoud?"

"Twenty-eight feet high, m'sieur."

"And after that?" Janet asked, her breath coming shorter. She felt she had been climbing for an hour.

"A short passage—maybe twenty feet. But honesty compels me to admit that it is only three feet high."

"Oh, no!" Janet laughed.

"Sorry. That one we do on hands and knees or in a lower crouch than this."

Janet felt a glorious moment of freedom when they emerged into the grand gallery and then felt less claustrophobic through the short passage into the actual burial chamber.

She looked around the big room with a sense of anticlimax. It was more than thirty feet long, she thought, and maybe twenty feet high. It was gray, dusty, bleak. No decorations. No painting. No furnishings.

"All stripped by thieves centuries ago," Todd said, divining her thoughts. "Grim, isn't it?"

"Where are we now—inside it, I mean?" she asked.

Todd thought for a moment. "We're close to the center of the mass—a little over a hundred forty feet above ground level."

"What's that?" she asked after a moment, pointing to what seemed a massive stone box about six or seven feet long and half as high. Then she realized what it was. The Pharaoh Cheops had lain there inside it in all the splendor of his death. But living, what had that man been to Eyes-of-Love? They had all said she was his "favorite." Had she been? And if so, how long? Till her death? She had died first, because it would have taken the king's supreme authority to place her small hidden tomb in the royal tomb area.

"His sarcophagus. It's alabaster but doesn't look like it under all that dirt. That's the lid over there."

Janet looked pensively around the great room, with an uneasy feeling of melancholy touching the edges of her mind. She glanced up and met Todd's eyes. There was a faint movement in his body, as if he were about to start toward her. "Even the ceiling is stone, isn't it?" she asked hastily.

"Several stones," he said. "Nine, I think. But all fitted together so well that you don't see the cracks. That was a fascinating bit, wasn't it? And if you're trying to distract my attention from you, forget it. You can't."

"Where's what's-his-name, Mahmoud?" she asked, her breath a little short.

"What's-his-name Mahmoud took a hike. He'll be back."

"You mean you sent him away?" Her heart was suddenly thudding.

"More or less." He came toward her now, slowly, his gaze never leaving hers. "I told him I wanted to speak to madame a few minutes. He took the hint."

"Good grief!" Janet gave an exaggerated laugh. "Don't tell me you've decided to make a pitch *here*!" She flung out her arms in a wide gesture, taking in the massive stone room.

A reluctant grin curved Todd's mouth, and golden lights glinted in his eyes. "Thought did cross my mind," he conceded ruefully, looking around. "Just think. Smack in the middle of the Great Pyramid. Terrific idea, actually. And it would be a first for me, I admit."

Janet felt color rise in her face.

"But then," he went on, "I decided to pass it up. You said last night you've almost finished the notes."

"Yes, I have," she answered, regretting intensely that she had made him withdraw.

"I didn't show you Mr. Jamison's letter, did I? It includes a note for you. He's a nice guy, isn't he?" He was trying to sound conversational, but he failed.

"Very," Janet said, realizing Todd's tension and recognizing her own. They had better get out of here.

"He's delighted. The foundation has already been in touch with him. But I'll give the letter to you when we get back to the hotel.

"Did Hassan mention that I'd like you to do some sketching for the project?"

"Yes, he mentioned it, but — "

"He'd like you to stay on a while, you know, that's why he suggested this."

"*Hassan* suggested it?"

"Does that surprise you? It shouldn't, Janet. He wants to marry you, but you're dragging your feet on marriage. Hassan doesn't like that, obviously. So he'd jump at any opportunity to keep you here awhile longer until he can work things out. Why don't you stay on awhile, Janet? You've got an open-ended leave from your job. I'm not trying to con you that I'm doing any favors for Hassan. I want you to stay on for my own reasons, as you very well know."

"What do you mean, time for Hassan 'to work things out'?" she asked sharply. "What's there for him to work out?"

"I don't know," Todd said thoughtfully. "Yet."

"What do you mean, 'yet'?" She was instantly defensive again about Hassan. "This is none of your affair, Todd. Hassan is—maybe Hassan has a different set of values than you do, but he's had a different life. Any person is the result of what's. . . what's happened in his life so far—" She broke off in mid-sentence and went on in a calmer tone. "Your association with Hassan is a professional one only. It's really out of line for you to inquire into—"

A subtle change in Todd's eyes stopped her. It was as if some sort of curtain had come down. He had withdrawn and shut her out, and she felt immediately that she had hit on the truth. He *was* investigating, making inquiries, looking into Hassan's affairs and—passing judgment on him.

"This work you want done—is it just accurate line drawing? Fine detail? Is that all?"

"Yes," he said distantly.

She gulped. "How long would the job last?"

"Hard to say. Several weeks. A few months. We won't be working at the site all the time, you know, because in April the windy season starts. That can be hellish out there in the sand."

"All right," she said uneasily. "I'll give it a try."

The drive back to Mena House was made in almost total silence.

Perversely Janet's smoldering anger at this man made her more intensely aware of him physically. She was mesmerized by the curve of his strong leg, the gleam of browned skin on his forearm, the crisp ends of honey-colored hair that showed at the back of his neck beneath the canvas hat. The familiar warmth of her response to him began to spread through Janet's body, filling her with restlessness. She wanted to stretch, twist, move—to do something, anything, for release from the tension.

"Would you like breakfast—brunch, or something?" he asked as they turned into the hotel's drive.

"No. No, thanks," she said too quickly. "I couldn't eat anything now. Thanks."

Something in Janet's voice made Todd glance at

her intently. She looked away a moment too late, so that their glances locked for a split second.

"All right," he said after a moment. "Stop by my suite before you go back to yours, and I'll give you Mr. Jamison's letter."

No. She couldn't possibly. She didn't dare. She was transfixed by the pulse beating at the base of his throat steadily and hard. She could reach out, touch his throat, feel the beating beneath her fingers. *Make an excuse! Get away!* she cautioned herself.

His unspoken question hung in the heavy silence that grew between them.

She took a shaky intake of breath.

"I'll—just stop for the letter," she said finally. *Liar,* she thought.

Janet walked into the hotel beside him with a strange feeling of captivity, as if she could not, even if she wanted to, turn and walk away from him. An alien sensation of being helpless against him, of being possessed, seized her. It aroused a feeling of snarling resentment in her mind that did desperate silent battle against the swirling throbbing desire that seemed to fill her. Every cell in her body was intensely alive. She had a crazy longing to loosen her clothing, to get the friction of the T-shirt away from her breasts.

She watched him pause at the reception desk and speak briefly to the clerk there. Then the elevator doors opened, and she stepped before him into the empty elevator. Janet could feel him behind her, and she turned, willing herself not to look at him again, not to see the smooth sun-browned hands, not to see the curling wisps of sun-bleached hair edging the crumpled canvas hat, not to recognize the raw need that churned inside her. She must leave him, get away.

He stood slightly apart, watching the lights move along the panel, not touching her, not even close to her at the moment, moving away. He was thinking about something else—not even aware of her. Sheer fury licked along her raw nerves. *Damn him.* Her body was aching, and she made herself wait stiffly beside him as the doors slid open. Then she walked stiffly beside him down the hall to the door of his suite and stood there while he unlocked it.

He strode into the room and tossed his hat and dark glasses on a chair. "I left it over here somewhere, I think." He crossed the room and moved some papers about on a corner table.

She stayed by the door, letting herself watch him for a moment. He *knew*—he must know—exactly what he was doing. He had seen that instant of raw hunger in her eyes downstairs, and he was deliberately tormenting her, punishing her for past rejections. Oh, surely not, she thought.

"Here it is," he said, and came toward her.

She took the letter and would have turned to go, but he let his body touch hers, sending a wave of shock rippling through her. He was reaching around her, behind her, doing something to the door. It clicked firmly shut behind them.

"Oh, Janet, Janet," Todd whispered in her hair. He began kissing her gently along her temple, his strong warm hands sliding up beneath her T-shirt over the small of her back, caressing slowly, taking his time. A small tremor of anticipation moved through her.

She wanted him closer, closer, and strained toward him. But he held her firmly where he wanted her, moving her constantly this way and that so that her taut sensitive breasts brushed continuously against his hard chest. Teasing her. Tormenting her. It was driving her frantic. When Janet could stand it no longer, a desperate moan escaped her, and she slid her arms up around his shoulders, forcing her body against his. The shock of the contact coursed through her, taking her breath away.

It was her small victory, for he gripped her close then, letting their bodies be molded together so that she could feel the hard powerful length of him. She raised her hungry mouth to his, and he began to kiss her gently, elusively, enticingly, holding back the deep ravishment of her mouth that she so blindly craved.

Then she gained another small victory, for he pushed her slightly away and swung her up in his arms and strode toward the bedroom. Exultation flashed through her like ragged lightning at her power to arouse him, the age-old triumph of the female. She began to kiss his neck, never moving her warm clinging lips from his skin, her hands of their own volition stroking and kneading his shoulders and back.

Todd dropped her onto his unmade bed and swiftly peeled off his T-shirt. Janet gripped the rumpled sheets in an agony of longing. The maids hadn't been in yet. This was the bed he'd slept in, just as he'd left it. She twisted over and for an instant buried her face in his pillow, breathless, her heart pounding.

Then his hands were on her again, gently turning her over to face him. He was leaning over her. "Janet?" His voice was unsteady. "I guess we'd better talk."

"No," she said, not able to meet his eyes. Her resolutions and decisions were forgotten. They weren't important at this moment. She knew with a kind of sweet madness that the most important thing—the only vital thing in her world at this time—was to touch this man.

She lifted her hands, fingers spread, and passed them across his bare chest, letting them follow the curves of the muscles, lingering enticingly. She got the response she desired as she felt a shiver pass through him. Then he caught her hands and forced them back over her head, bending down.

"Janet..." he tried to warn her, his voice ragged. His face was very close now, and with a kind of slow reluctance his hands loosened.

She twisted her arms loose and twined them around his neck, pulling him down closer, her hands stroking the smoothly muscled skin of his back. Then she touched his mouth with hers, inviting him sensuously with the tip of her tongue, knowing full well what she was doing.

A shudder ripped through him and he came forward, letting her bear some of his weight, seeking her mouth. And she was teasing, enticing, moving slightly this way and that, until he was desperate. Janet knew instantly the moment to become pliant against him and let him capture her mouth. He ravaged it for an endless mindless interval while she gloried in it.

Then, shaken with the force of their desire, they drew apart for a moment, neither one able to speak, nor wanting to. They needed only the unsaid messages of lovers learning, exploring, discovering, scaling the shattering heights they knew awaited them.

He pulled her up with rough tenderness and in one quick motion peeled off her T-shirt and tossed it onto the floor. Groaning, he buried his face between her breasts. "I knew this—I knew it," he whispered against her flesh. "I knew you wanted this when you looked at me in the car and in the elevator...."

"You knew?" Janet was half laughing. "You could have touched me then. You tormented me."

He gave a half laugh, half sob, an exultant sound. "No, no. But I didn't dare start anything. I was almost crazy myself with wanting you. It nearly killed me...."

You killed my father. You caused his death, you bastard. The idea smashed into her mind. What was she doing? She stiffened, pushing at him, staring up at him wide-eyed.

He went deadly still, astounded by her sudden rejection. Then slowly he stood up beside the bed, looking down at her, uncertain, confused. "Now just a minute. What is this! Two minutes ago you couldn't wait . . . and now . . . and now . . . .''

Stiffly, aching with desire and fighting against it, Janet began to crawl off the bed on the opposite side. She was bitterly ashamed.

"I . . . I'm sorry. I shouldn't have let it get out of control.'' She crossed her arms over her naked breasts. "Where's my . . . my . . . .''

In one swift motion Todd turned, snatched the T-shirt off the floor, balled it up and threw it at her. It landed on the bed, and with shaking hands Janet picked it up and struggled to put it on.

Slowly, like a wounded wary animal, he came around the bed and stood watching her. "No,'' he said roughly, reaching over to help her. "Put your arm through here, you little jerk.'' Then, "Oh, Janet, what did I do? What did I say to turn you off, to make you freeze up like that?''

"You didn't. Not exactly,'' she replied with an effort. "I—I—'' She looked around distractedly. "Where did I leave my hat—my bag?''

"How the hell do I know? Oh, maybe they're in the other room. Janet—'' He was pleading.

She looked at him fully, meeting his eyes without flinching. She saw confusion and naked hurt. She took a shaky breath. He didn't really deserve this.

"You didn't turn me off, Todd,'' she said steadily. She owed him an explanation. "It's something else entirely. Something I . . . I have to work out. I'm sorry about today. I'm not a tease—please believe me. I . . . just for a while . . . went a little crazy. It won't happen again.'' She made herself take a step, then circled around him toward the sitting-room door.

Todd doubled up a powerful fist and slammed it into his other palm. "Damn it! It's this business about Hassan, isn't it? How does he do it? Tell me, how can a guy like that inspire such mindless loyalty?"

Inside the sitting room Janet turned. "What do you mean, 'a guy like that'?" she asked dully. She was still sick with longing for him. Little aftershocks kept running through her body.

"That's what I'm in the process of finding out." His expression was one of mingled hurt and defiance.

Wearily, she went toward the hall door.

"Maybe you'd like to go with me tomorrow." His tone was challenging. "I'm driving over to Alexandria for lunch. Then I'm going to see someone. A Mrs. Fugate."

She whirled to face him.

"How did you find out about Mrs. Fugate?"

"I have certain resources. I'm going, Janet. You can't stop me. Do you want to come with me?"

She looked at him for a long moment, measuring his mood. She must keep on top of this, ascertain what he was doing all the time. Hassan didn't have a chance against this man.

When Janet spoke, her voice was harsh and grim. "What time do you want to leave?"

CHAPTER TEN

JANET AWAKENED the next morning with a sense of dread after a troubled restless night. She felt increasingly uncomfortable about the trip to Alexandria. It seemed so sneaky, checking up on Hassan behind his back. She decided in the shower that it was too sneaky, and as soon as she came out, she telephoned Hassan's apartment.

"*Zayak?*" It was unmistakably the voice of Nazli, thick and indistinct with sleep, still only half awake. Janet struggled for a moment between irritation and amusement. She might have known that at some point she was bound to surprise Hassan and Nazli together in an intimate situation. She would have to handle it as tactfully as she could.

"Hello! Nazli? This is Janet," she said crisply.

There was a smothered gasp at the other end of the line, then a long silence, during which Janet wondered how Nazli managed to keep the affair from her father.

"Ah, Janet. How lovely to hear from you! And how lucky I was just on my way out the door! I might have missed you!"

Oh, good grief, Janet thought, *we're going to go through a little charade of my just happening to call the apartment when Nazli just happened to be stopping there on an errand.* She cut off Nazli's next predictable line. "Actually, I wanted to talk to Hassan a moment," Janet said as patiently as she could.

"Oh, too bad. He is not here. He is gone. Can I help you?"

"It's not important," Janet answered carefully. "I was just going out for a little sight-seeing trip this morning with Todd Ballard and I wanted to check in with Hassan first, of course."

"Of course." Nazli's voice was suddenly thoughtful. "I am sure this would please Hassan, you know?" She spoke slowly, and it was clear she was choosing her words carefully. "Hassan likes everyone to be happy together and sometimes, you know, you seem—what is it?—annoyed with Todd. And really, Todd is such a superior person, very superior, you know?"

"No, I don't know," Janet said rather more sharply than she'd intended. "But he did invite me on this little sight-seeing trip, and I did say I'd go. Will you leave a note for Hassan? Tell him I'll call again when I get back?"

"Yes, yes, yes. For sure. I'll even put down the time."

"Thanks a lot, Nazli. Well, I've got to run. See you later." Janet brought the conversation to a quick close before Nazli remembered to ask where she and Todd were going to sightsee.

Janet wore a smooth cotton sun dress in pale beige with touches of white embroidery. It had a short jacket she could put on if Todd chose a posh place for lunch and she wanted to look a bit more dressed up. She added the white straw hat with the turned-down brim she had bought at one of the hotel shops, paying more than she could afford, and she clutched a natural straw handbag.

Todd was driving the white Jaguar again. He looked casually elegant in cream slacks and a caramel turtleneck of very thin knit. They began their sporadic progress through the morning traffic of office-bound workers.

Apparently he had decided on a wary truce. Okay, she could go along with that.

"I'm sorry to get you out so early, but it's a little over two hundred and twenty kilometers—one hundred and thirty-two, if you like it in miles—and I didn't know how much time we'd need in Alexandria."

"I brought my guidebook," Janet said. "If our—whatever it is—afternoon call takes only a few minutes, we might see a couple of the sights." She was trying to imply they were on a wild-goose chase and knew he got the message, because a half smile touched his sensual mouth.

"Well, we'll be seeing Alexandria's world-famed Corniche," Todd said, "because that's where Mrs. Fugate lives. In one of the apartment-hotels there. And we'll be having lunch at the San Giovanni, not far from there, at Stanley Beach on El Gaish Street—205, I think, but if that's not right, I can find it. They have that excellent Mediterranean shrimp with lemon and butter. Beyond those two places, it's up to you. Where else would you like to go?''

"I think maybe the Roman amphitheater and the Christian catacombs. If there's time," she added doubtfully. So he had a specific address. Trust Todd Ballard to have bought the best information possible.

"I'm taking you there through the delta," Todd said, managing to change lanes without apparent effort. "Then I'll bring you back by the other highway through the desert. The desert way is just a little shorter, but I thought you'd like to see both routes."

"I saw some of the delta with Hassan," she said, remembering the hideous visit to Ismailia.

"They've got a fast paved highway on both routes now, so we'll make good time." He reached over and flipped on the car radio, and the monotonous droning of Arabic music filled the car. He turned the radio down to a gentle murmur. "If that gets too much for you, flip it off or find another station, if you like."

She settled back to listen and to watch the traffic, keeping her eyes away from Todd as much as she could. Now and then the announcer broke in with Arabic. She wondered again if any non-Arab—even Todd, who was supposed to be fluent—could master that combined k and h in the back of the throat the way they did.

When they reached the open highway away from the heavy traffic, there was a newsbreak, also in Arabic, with an intriguing sprinkling of English words. She picked up the words "London" and "Washington" and "American Congress." Newscasts in a foreign language always made her feel so isolated.

"Have you ever been to Ismailia?" she asked after a time, thinking again of that patched-up city.

"Yes. Not recently. It was some time ago. Why?"

"Hassan was a child there. Or did you already know that?" she couldn't help adding.

"Yes, I knew it."

"He had a pretty rough beginning, you know." She sounded wistful and hadn't intended to.

"A lot of people have rough beginnings," Todd answered slowly. "You're very protective of Hassan, aren't you?"

"Hassan is very dear to me," she answered simply.

"But not as a lover or a husband, I gather," he answered. "Or you wouldn't be stalling so much on the idea of marriage." There was in his tone an underlying sound of confidence that was irritating, but she couldn't rebut it. She'd given him a clear idea of where he stood with her and, by extension, where Hassan stood.

Janet and Todd arrived in Alexandria about eleven-thirty, and since each had taken only a continental breakfast before leaving Cairo, they decided on an early lunch. They had a table by the window at the San Giovanni that overlooked the sparkling sweep of blue sea curving into the long crescent-shaped shore, with its ancient whispering palms, graceful mansions, hotels and apartments. The leisurely two-hour lunch was a delight. They lingered over a meal of large delicate shrimp rich with pure butter and piquant with fresh lemon juice.

Janet began to feel a sense of ease and relaxation she had never felt before with this man. During the drive through the lush delta, a tentative rapport had been established between them. Beneath the surface of the casual and pleasant conversation—at which Todd was proficient—there had been a hesitant reaching out. There was also a sweet secret satisfaction because she sensed how hard he was trying to bridge the gap and how careful he was being. She was being *wooed*—and only this old-fashioned word seemed to fit. It gave her a wistful glimpse of the man he might have been if he were not the man he was. It was a brief lovely fancy, and playing with it awhile left her feeling slightly tremulous in vague anticipation.

"We still have a little time," Todd said after lunch as they walked slowly along the old street to where he had left the car. "Would you like to take a look at the Roman amphitheater?"

"Yes, that would be nice," she said, feeling ambivalent.

The amphitheater was surrounded by a parklike area with grass and colorful flowering vines and trees. Small wooden benches had been placed at intervals about the rim.

Janet left the dusty path and stood on the verge of grass to look down into the theater itself, where the Roman conquerors had held their games and entertainments during their sojourn in Alexandria. Rows of stone benches rose in a widening circle from the arena. It had the solid timeless look of all Roman structures.

"The Romans went everywhere, didn't they?" she mused.

"Just about," he agreed. "Let's go down into the theater and sit awhile."

"It's so old," she murmured when they had descended about halfway and were seated on the curving stone bench.

"Not really by Egyptian standards," he said, looking out across the open arena before them. The shimmering sunlight was caught in golden tendrils of hair at the nape of his strong neck, and Janet suppressed a yearning to reach over and stroke them as he went on. "This only dates from about 30 B.C. That was just about three hundred years after Alexander founded the city. With Egyptian antiquity you're usually thinking in thousands of years, not hundreds." He moved one browned hand over the warm pitted stone, almost caressing it.

"So, on to Cleopatra—the one and only," Janet murmured.

Todd looked at her, his eyes smiling. "Not exactly. All the Ptolemy queens were named Cleopatra, but she did eclipse all her relatives, since she's the only one most of us remember. Sometimes these brighter-than-life people happen along in history. People who stand out from everybody else."

Todd was a brighter-than-life person himself,

Janet thought, and felt a familiar hunger for him. She wondered wearily if she would ever be free of it. Long after she was back home, would she still yearn for this man at odd times and places—whenever she caught a partial glimpse of a tall fair-haired man with broad shoulders, whenever the sun was beginning to feel too warm on her skin?

He was looking at his watch. "We'd better start. We're due there at three."

Janet was instantly alert and apprehensive. "You mean you actually have a specific appointment?"

"Yes." He glanced at her in mild surprise. "Did you think I was just going to barge in unannounced? I do have a little more finesse than that."

"Oh, I'm sure you have plenty of finesse," she said grimly. "Just for my satisfaction, how does a perfect stranger make an appointment with another man's—"

"Another man's ex-mistress?" He completed the question for her. "It's not hard. One just. . . ." He was standing up and looked down at her.

"And you are positive, of course, that she is an ex-mistress, not just an old family friend or something?" She stood up, too, anger roiling in her mind.

"That's what we came to find out, isn't it? I simply telephoned ahead, introduced myself as an associate of Hassan's who was spending the afternoon in Alexandria and asked if I might stop in. I talked to a Frenchwoman named Elise Montand, who seems to be some sort of companion-housekeeper. She was brusque but accommodating. She said three o'clock because madame naps in the afternoon.''

"Just like that! You really astound me, Todd. How would you feel if someone went around investigating your life, prying—''

"Feel? Nothing much anymore. Since I've always been a target. I'm used to it. My educated guess is that your idol Hassan knows more about me than I'm learning about him. He's a smart operator. He'd have made it his business to know.''

Janet looked away quickly, remembering with sudden clarity the fat envelope of clippings and notes in fine flowing Arabic script she had discovered in Hassan's cluttered desk.

"That struck a note, didn't it?'' Todd said dryly. "Well, come on, let's go.''

Todd pressed the bell of Mrs. Fugate's apartment at five minutes past three. It was on the top floor of one of the graceful white buildings on the Corniche. The elevator was a wrought-iron cage that rose and descended in a series of shivering jerks. It settled with an audible thump four floors below. Todd pressed the bell again just as the door opened, revealing a small stocky woman aged between forty and sixty. She was dressed in a faded cotton print dress.

"M'sieur B'lard? Madame?'' she asked, stressing the last syllable of his name.

"Yes. I'm sorry we're late,'' Todd answered, glossing over the fact that Janet was not Madame Ballard. They followed the Frenchwoman through a short dark hallway into a rather cluttered sitting room. A spacious room with the lofty coved ceilings of a bygone era, it was now crowded with heavy furniture. Janet noticed marble-topped Victorian tables ostentatiously carved, as well as many corner and wall shelves loaded with small statues and ornaments and dull with dust. There were several wicker plant stands holding anemic greenery, mostly tattered-looking ferns.

"Oh, come in. Do come in." It was one of the pleasantest voices Janet had ever heard, melodious and sweet with a faint lilt. A young voice. But the woman herself seemed old, quite old and very frail.

Janet forced herself to smile to conceal her surprise and extended her hand, suppressing a shiver as she felt it clasped in the chill, fragile, birdlike hands of Mrs. Fugate. She was *years* older than Hassan. Mrs. Fugate's dress of draped gray jersey, high at the neck, hung loosely on her emaciated form. Her short hair, fine and loose with streaks of white, floated about her head in thin wisps. Her fine fair skin was a network of tiny wrinkles, and she had the palest blue eyes Janet had ever seen. There was only a dim echo of a sort of English-gentlewoman prettiness she must once have had.

"How very nice of you to call," Mrs. Fugate was saying in her incredibly sweet voice. "I do hope I remember to tell Hassan how kind it was of you. My memory is not the best anymore." The ladylike face turned to Janet; the faded-watercolor eyes held a question. "I cannot recall that Hassan mentioned—"

"Oh, this is not Mrs. Ballard," Todd was saying

easily. "This is my associate, Jan. She's an artist. She's going to do the line drawings of artifacts from our excavation."

"How fascinating. Do sit down. Elise will bring us some tea and cakes in a moment. I have tea twice in the afternoons these days. I find I don't eat much, but I like to eat more often, so I have a tea before my nap and also afterward. I'm so fortunate that Elise has returned."

Jan. My associate. He had included little shreds of fact, but what Todd had said added up to an outright lie. Oh, that Todd was a smooth one. Janet sat down in a stiff Victorian "lady's chair," designed without armrests to allow for wide skirts. And because Victorian ladies did not lounge, the back curved away from her, providing no support. Janet sat up straight, feeling tenser because of it.

"Elise was away for a while, then?" Todd asked conversationally, appearing quite at home, although his light brown eyes glanced around, missing nothing of the shabby elegance of the room or the frail elderly woman who was their hostess.

"Elise was our maid for many years—I refer to Captain Fugate and myself—and later, after the captain's passing, she stayed on as my only staff when Hassan disposed of our house in Heliopolis and we took an apartment. Hassan was just a boy in university then." She paused a moment before adding with a hint of breathlessness. "Always such a helpful boy. The captain, my late husband, met Hassan when he had to visit the doctor. Captain Fugate's health was never the best, which is what brought us to Egypt. The captain used to visit the American Hospital as an outpatient, and it was Hassan's taxi he always called. We did not keep a car, you see. Hassan was so kind to the captain, such a help." Her voice trailed into silence. She seemed lost in some dreamy recollection from the past.

Janet moved restlessly on the stiff Victorian chair, reading uneasily between the lines. It wasn't fair—prying into Hassan's past like this, taking advantage of this little old lady's innocent ramblings. But another glimpse of Hassan's past had been revealed. She could imagine the Fugate household— the ailing captain, clinging to life; his ineffectual lady-wife, unable to cope. And Hassan, as he was then, the tough hardy peasant from the rubble of Ismailia, streetwise now and driving a Cairo taxi, looking for the main chance, with his earthy vigor, his strength, his laughter, his intense *aliveness*.

A silence fell and lasted so long that it became uncomfortable.

"Oh, dear, where was I?" Mrs. Fugate resumed speaking in faint surprise. "Forgive me. My mind sometimes wanders."

"I believe we had mentioned Elise, your maid," Todd reminded her, his voice somewhat subdued. Well, at least he hadn't brought her back to the remark about Hassan disposing of "the Heliopolis house." Had Hassan been living with the Fugates then? Did he take over their aimless lives?

"Oh, yes. Elise was forty at that time. She had saved some money and wanted to return to France.

I was so sorry to see her go, but she had a family responsibility there...and she wished to marry...."
Mrs. Fugate's voice trailed off and the room was filled with another growing silence. Somewhere else in the apartment, a whistling tea kettle shrilled wildly a moment and was silenced. There was a clink of china. Then Mrs. Fugate continued. "Elise remained in France—I'm sorry, I can never recall the name of the village—for twelve years. Or was it eleven? We kept in touch, you know. Then, when the situation changed, Hassan persuaded her to return to Alexandria. Did I mention that Hassan had finished university and was establishing himself in his career?"

"No. You were living in Cairo at that time?" Todd prompted, while Janet's mind silently begged him to stop it, to let the old woman alone. She shot a venomous look in his direction, but he ignored it. Trust Todd to keep pressing onward, Janet thought bitterly. Mrs. Fugate was helpless against him. Like many of the very old, she was lonely, hungry to talk of the past that filled her mind, responding eagerly to the slightest show of interest.

"Ah, yes," she murmured. "We had an apartment near the university. Hassan matriculated much sooner than the others he started with, of course," she added complaisantly. "He is so clever and worked so hard, and, you see, he had more time for study, since he didn't have to drive the taxi anymore."

"Yes, that would have given him more free time," Todd conceded, smiling at her. "It must

have been a big help to you—his being so clever. I
suppose he managed all your affairs for you after
Captain Fugate passed away."

Stop it, Todd. Let it alone, Janet commanded
him silently.

"Oh, indeed, yes. And he was so good with the
window box, you know? I like growing things
about." She gestured vaguely to the potted ferns.
"Hassan always kept a window box blooming for
me."

Janet's lips twisted ironically. She let her glance
travel to Todd's face. *Skip the window box, Mrs.
Fugate. Todd doesn't care about the window box.
He wants to know what Hassan did with your
money. Is that what started all his business ven-
tures? What else did Hassan dispose of besides the
house in Heliopolis?*

There was china rattling in the hallway, and the
housekeeper, Elise, entered with a tray. She put it
down in front of Mrs. Fugate. Then she held out
the cups one by one, while Mrs. Fugate shakily
poured out the tea, letting some of it spill into the
saucers.

"Elise, I'm trying to recall," Mrs. Fugate murmured. "What were those yellow flowers—such a
common flower, really—that Hassan had such
good luck with? You remember, sometime before
you left, in that box outside our bedroom window."

"Nasturtiums, madame?"

"Yes, of course. Do you take cream or lemon,
my dear?" she asked Janet. When the tea and small

bready cupcakes had been handed around, she added, "Before the captain's passing, he spoke several times of adopting Hassan. We had no children, you see, and he worried about how I would manage." She sighed.

Janet shot a triumphant glance in Todd's direction.

"Did the captain adopt him?" he asked, ignoring her.

"No. With his illness...and the Egyptian bureaucracy he never seemed ...." Her voice trailed away.

Janet put her cup down on the small marble table with a clatter. Well, that should answer their questions. So much for the theory of Hassan's hidden mistress.

"We really must be going, Mrs. Fugate. Don't you think so, Todd?" She started to rise.

Todd looked at his watch. "Oh, we have quite a while," he said coolly, and turned back to Mrs. Fugate. "Do you like living in Alexandria?"

"Oh, yes, and Hassan has some business interest here. From before he decided to remove to the States, you understand. He tells me so many things, but I forget. He manages to come about once a month—taking care of everything, you know. He is so indulgent."

"But he won't be able to come so often, now that he's moving to the States," Todd said carefully.

Stop it, Todd. Let her alone.

"No," she murmured, "but you see, he has arranged for Elise to return permanently from France. He is so good about arrangements."

Todd glanced at Janet, a quick look of veiled contempt, and Janet looked hastily away.

Mrs. Fugate took a sip of tea and a drop dribbled down her chin. Elise, with a small economical gesture, picked up a grayish linen napkin and blotted it away. Mrs. Fugate gave her an absentminded smile.

Janet's heart went out to the Fugates, drifting, childless, and Hassan, the tough wily peasant youth, suddenly sweeping into their lives. Well, at least he had given them that.

Janet closed her eyes a moment, willing Todd to get up, to leave. But he would not. He accepted another cup of tea and continued his quiet relentless questions. Without actually saying so, he let Mrs. Fugate assume that he and Hassan might enter a joint business venture in the States.

This brought a surprising response from Elise Montand, which she delivered in her small dry voice with a heavy French accent. The little Frenchwoman knew exactly how much the Heliopolis house had brought and what Hassan had done with it. Her intent was to give Hassan a good reference to the inquiring M'sieur B'lard, and in so doing she revealed too much. There was a quarterly "allowance" from Hassan for the two women to live on, and somehow or other Captain Fugate's trust fund had come under Hassan's control. Twice Todd spoke directly to the housekeeper in French, and she replied in that language, which effectively shut Janet out.

Finally Janet could stand it no longer. She stood up. "Todd. We really must go," she said in a strangled voice.

"You're probably right," he answered leisurely, putting down his cup.

Once in Todd's car again, she could contain her anger no longer and raged at him as he worked his way through Alexandria traffic. "Well, are you satisfied? Did you enjoy—"

"No!" he shot back. "I'm not too happy about hassling two little old ladies. But I found out a few things I needed to know."

"Like Hassan bringing more happiness into that poor faded woman's life than she—"

"Knock it off, Janet. Let's get Hassan down off his pedestal for a minute, shall we? Be honest for a change. Can't you face the fact that there was an ugly side to it? Hassan took them for every cent they had."

"It wasn't like that. It couldn't have been. She worships him. It's obvious."

"He conned them, Janet."

"You don't know that!" she blazed.

The very air in the car seemed to palpitate with their mutual antagonism. Janet couldn't look at him, instead staring blankly at the surrounding traffic. They were inching their way through a crooked narrow street of small shops and eateries. Ahead of them was a tourist bus and behind them a tourist van. Beside Janet was an open pickup truck loaded with animal carcasses destined for a butcher's shop. A workman in a sweaty, blood-smeared T-shirt half reclined on top of the meat, smoking a cigarette. His eyes caught Janet's for an instant, and he flashed her an engaging grin. Then he was gone as the pickup lurched ahead.

"Yes, I do know it, Janet," Todd snapped. "I've had a lifetime's experience of learning to recognize opportunists when I see them."

They were leaving the town behind now, getting onto the highway back to Cairo. "But he takes care of her," Janet said desperately, almost pleading. "Don't you see? Hassan doesn't have to do any of this. I know... I realize... I'm not stupid, Todd. He was young and desperately poor. All right, he was an opportunist. He saw a chance and took it. And now he doesn't need her. He's—he's got all the money there was. All right, I admit that. He undoubtedly took her money, *but she doesn't even care!* You heard what she said. She has no interest in it—can't even remember what he tells her about that sort of thing. He's kind to her. He's taking care of her—seeing that she's happy—even after he doesn't need her!"

"Oh, Janet, knock it off! He used her! He uses everybody he can! He's using you...." He bit off the sentence, staring grimly ahead at the desert road, which ran like a black ribbon through the undulating sand dunes on either side of it.

"What...do...you...mean?" Janet said through her teeth. She waited through a long ugly silence for him to answer. "Stop the car!" she finally demanded. "Right now! Pull over to the side! I want you to listen to me!"

In grim silence Todd pulled the car to a stop on the shoulder of the road. As soon as he did, it was evident that a strong wind had arisen. Neither of them had noticed it with the car in fast motion.

"Okay, let's have it," he said, turning to her, his face closed and forbidding.

"What do you mean Hassan is using me?" she asked levelly. "You'd better explain that."

"I will. As soon as my information is complete. I don't need proof, just common sense, to tell me Hassan doesn't give a damn for you, Janet. You could have two heads and he wouldn't notice. Marrying an American citizen is just a fast pass to U.S. citizenship—which apparently is his current burning desire. I don't need evidence to see that. What I would like evidence for is to find out why he didn't go through regular channels, get on a quota list, wait it out. He's had plenty of time. When I find that out—you want proof? I'll come and dump it in your lap, my sweet. We'll see what you think of your hero then."

"That's just guessing. Wishful thinking. You made a big play for me and it didn't take—"

"Hell it didn't," he snapped.

"And now you're taking it out on Hassan. You're trying to paint him as a villain, a renegade, a—a—"

"A con artist," he interrupted.

"No! An opportunist, yes. Maybe. But Mrs. Fugate needed somebody, some sort of family. Hassan gave her that. He was loving. He was kind to her—is kind to her now."

"And Hassan will be kind to you, too, even after your usefulness has ended." Todd's voice softened. "Janet, you don't want to marry him. There is nothing between you and Hassan except an old obligation. There *is* something between you and me. We both know that."

Slowly, deliberately, he extended his hand, reaching across her. He let his fingers rest lightly on her bare shoulder and trail down her arm. The very lightness of his touch was maddening. A tremor moved through her body, and he felt it. He moved imperceptibly closer as a blast of hot desert wind flung sand angrily against the car window. The surging blast of the desert wind outside matched the surging need inside her, and she tried to hold herself rigid under his touch.

"Take me back to Cairo—we'll never agree on this," she said raggedly.

"But we agree on one thing, don't we?" He was trying to keep his tone casual, but failed; the beginning of passion underlined his words, and he couldn't hide it.

A sense of purely female triumph pierced Janet at her power to arouse him. She felt a sense of satisfaction as old as Eve and—against her own will—strove to hold on to it a moment longer. She deliberately leaned her head back against the car seat, knowing she would feel his mouth against her throat—*knowing* it.

Even knowing it, prepared for it, she could not suppress a small gasp at the intense pleasure that tingled through her body. Nor was she prepared for his seeking, gently strong hands sliding beneath her arms, the thumbs touching, caressing the nipples of her breasts, which tautened in swift response. She could not stifle a low moan, and it sounded a warning in her mind. She must stop him. Before it was too late. She must stop him right away.

Janet pushed against him hard with all her strength.

Todd pulled back, his mouth twisting sardonically. "We've come to that stopping place again, right? At times like this I wish I smoked. At least I'd have something to do with my hands. You know, I could light a cigarette. . . look casual. Like I was taking it in stride." His voice was harsh with emotion. "Like I hadn't really noticed. Well, I notice! It tears my guts out. And I think you know it! I think you do it deliberately. You get a real charge out of watching me bleed." His voice steadied; his tone hardened into bitterness. "Does it do something for your ego, playing God with another person's feelings, deciding what someone else will or won't have, making arbitrary decisions about other people's hopes?"

"You tell me," she shot back. "You're the master at that game aren't you? What did it do for your ego when you arbitrarily decided to halt work on the tomb my father had discovered? You stopped his life's work—*his life's work, Todd!* You might as well have put a gun to his head—the result was the same. He died of it. You killed him!" There! She had finally said it, thrown it in his face.

His body recoiled from her as if he had been

struck by an invisible force. He made a hoarse sound, then said something unclear that might have been, "Oh, my God." Next he turned, wrenched open the car door and plunged into the angry sand-laden wind that pushed and pulled at the car.

"Todd!" she cried, leaning over toward the open door. A hot gust of wind swirled into the air-conditioned interior, enveloping her for a moment, throwing sand in her face, and then swept out like a restless demon. For a moment Janet didn't see where Todd had gone, and she knew a wild sense of panic. Then she saw him standing—or rather leaning over—bracing himself against the hood of the car that gleamed in the brazen desert sun.

"Todd, don't! You'll burn your hands!" she shouted, and slid across the seat to go to him. Then she stopped and sank back, shaking. Let him alone, she thought. Let him alone for a minute. He was escaping from her. He wanted a moment of privacy away from her. She should give him that much.

Janet watched, scarcely breathing, as moment followed slow moment in Todd's desperate inward struggle for composure. She watched the punishing wind toy with him spitefully, whipping the honey-colored hair about his eyes, plastering his clothes against his muscular body, molding it as if with gleefully lustful fingers like a second skin, over the hard curves and planes of him. Twice he shook his head like a stunned animal or a fighter before he falls. Slowly he straightened up and began to brush the palms of his hands together while the frenzied wind pushed and pulled and swirled about him. Then he was coming back.

She slid over into her own seat and waited with dull dread. She had a vague feeling of having finished something, not a sense of completion, but a sense of having destroyed something, smashed it.

"It's hot out there," Todd said woodenly. He was looking rather blankly at the reddened palms of his hands. "And that wind is a devil today."

Janet couldn't answer. She didn't know what to say, didn't know if he expected any answer. She could only sit silently, unable to take her eyes from him. She saw everything about him with utmost clarity. She could almost feel the smarting of his red sensitive palms.

"I'm sorry I forgot to shut the car door," he was saying with laborious politeness. "I let the inside of the car get hot." He reached over and turned the air conditioner up as high as it would go, and they were enveloped in a heavy gush of cold moist air.

Again she had nothing to say. He had sand on him, all over him, it seemed. Glittering grains of it clung to his fair hair, rested on his eyelashes, lay like dust on his face and neck and arms. He kept brushing at it absentmindedly, as if the grittiness bothered him.

"How long have you lived with the idea that I caused your father's death?" He asked the question in the same tone in which he had spoken about the wind and the weather.

Janet felt a moment of violent regret. She should not have told him! Some things were better left unsaid; some words better left unspoken. Who was she to sit in judgment? "I—ever since—it happened." She managed to keep her tone as noncommittal as his.

"Hell of a thing to live with," he muttered, starting the car. He gunned the engine, and the powerful car leaped forward, tearing strongly through the furious wind. There was a long interval of silence during which Janet stared as if hypnotized at the black roadway that stretched ahead of them toward Cairo. Always, just some distance ahead, was the sheen of water they never reached. A mirage.

He spoke three more times during the journey. Once he said, "This is early for a wind of such force. It feels more like what happens the last of March or in April."

And Janet watched for miles after that as aimless shallow waves of sand swept this way or that across the highway, however the willful wind drove them, whipping them along.

Once she said, "There are some little flecks of blood on your jaw. Did you know?"

And he answered, "No, but I'm not surprised. Blowing sand can slowly rip a guy's hide off. I was dumb to go out in it. But skin will grow back. This car will probably need a new paint job, though. We should have stayed in Alexandria until this settled down."

Much later, as they approached the smog and snarling traffic of early evening in Cairo, he said, "You've made your point, Janet. I'm convinced. Because of what you've told me we're in a no-win situation. I won't bother you again. Just try to put it out of your mind—if you can. I'm sorry. I apologize for being so hard to shake." He was humbled, beaten, and it twisted her heart when she should have been glad.

She searched for the right answer—for any answer. "It's too bad we ever met at all," she managed finally, her voice sounding as dull and lifeless as his.

He was right, and she was right. She kept telling herself this as she entered the hotel and went to her room. It was an ill wind that had brought them together. It was better to stop the relationship now, before it had really begun.

With part of her mind she saw the man behind the lobby reception desk recognize her and wave a brown package. She paused at the desk and took the package, smiled a vacant thank-you and accepted her key, then continued toward the arcade that led to the hotel's new section. When she paused before her room to unlock her door, she couldn't remember having walked through the arcade. She had got rid of Todd Ballard. For good. She would somehow—sometime in the future—forget Todd Ballard. Completely. Carefully, piece by piece, she would root out her memories of him, lay to rest the ghost of what could have been. Honesty made her admit it would be the hardest thing she would ever do. She'd have to work at it. She must close the book. She must forget him. *Forget* him.

Mindlessly Janet sat down in the chair by the window, still holding the package. It was a large bulg-

ing manila envelope. Finally she looked at it, really
looked at it, and recognized Nazli's distinctive
handwriting. Surely Nazli hadn't bought her something else! She had scrawled a hurried message right
on the front:

> Dearest Janet, it is best always to learn more
> about a friend—is it not true? Please give back
> when finished.
>
> Much love, Nazli

No! Oh, *no!*

Janet tore open the envelope and watched,
stunned, repelled, as all the clippings and notes and
pictures of Todd Ballard fell out into her lap and
spilled over and slid to the floor about her feet.

CHAPTER ELEVEN

JANET AWAKENED AGAIN AT 5:00 A.M. She'd had another bad dream in which Todd was telepathically saying, "A lot of people have rough beginnings." He was about to add something else, but a little boy, who was also Todd, was standing there crying—silently, because his lips were pressed together. He was half turned away from the woman who gripped his hand, looking at someone else. Janet couldn't see her. In the boy's face was the helplessness of all children who have no control at all over what happens to them, who know with some age-old wisdom that they must just endure.

Janet reached over and snapped on the bedside lamp. She would *not* go over to the dresser and leaf through any of those clippings and notes again. Every time she did that her heart ached anew.

Talk about rough beginnings.

No wonder Todd Ballard had never married and established a family. No wonder he wanted none of it. No wonder he distrusted it—even feared it. She had known instinctively that day in the dusty shed at the work site that something terrible had happened to Todd Ballard to turn him against commitment to a relationship of any kind. It was something ugly, she had thought, that he had lived with a long time.

Indeed, yes. Most of his life. Probably even now his nightmarish early years plagued him. Somewhere along the line she had made her peace with the idea that Hassan's beginnings had shaped the man he had become. But no less had Todd's beginnings shaped the man he was now. Neither man would ever be free of his childhood. There had been a kind of psychological maiming of them both.

She sat up and pulled up her knees, clasping her arms around them, then resting her head on them. *Janet,* she told herself, *you do have the greatest luck falling in love with the wrong man. Well, maybe next time, kiddo.*

Her neck cramped slightly, and she lifted her head, which was a mistake, because she was looking again at the mass of scattered clippings she had dumped on the dresser. She tried to will herself to stay where she was and not get up and leaf through them once more. She wished she had known the facts earlier. Perhaps she could have handled Todd differently. But differently how? Been kinder maybe, in rejecting him? She didn't know. She was too tired to think.

Wearily she got up, as she had known she would, and walked over to the dresser. Her hands slightly unsteady, she began to turn over the bits and pieces of paper that represented Todd Ballard's life. Her action seemed useless. A kind of masochistic penance. A mental self-flagellation. In shuffling the clippings around, which one would she see first?

The clipping about his father's suicide? That one was very small—just one brief photograph before Ballard influence was brought to bear and the matter hushed up. It had all happened before she had been able to read, but even so she had always retained a vague idea from somewhere of the Ballards as a scandal-haunted clan. She had been right.

But maybe she would uncover a nice article. Hassan had collected everything about Todd: his university graduation; his winning of some sailboating trophy; and many many small items mentioning rumors of an impending marriage—always denied by "a spokesman for the family."

With numb fingers Janet picked up and hastily turned face down the article about the second Ballard custody battle. How many lawyers had been set up for life from fees collected during the long fight over where one small boy would live? She picked up another clipping and shivered slightly, putting it aside. It was about the kidnapping. "Child stealing" the newspapers had called it. Before laying down the article, she read the headline, "MOTHER SOUGHT IN MISSING-HEIR MYSTERY," then below:

Mrs. Angela Ballard, divorced wife of the late millionaire Quintin Ballard, is being sought for questioning concerning the whereabouts of their young son, Todd, who disappeared from his school six days ago. The boy's uncle and present legal guardian, Tait Ballard, could not be reached for comment, but a spokesman for the family stated. . . .

Janet stood by the dresser, thinking. Had it been Angela Ballard the boy in the picture had looked at with such helplessness, the figure the camera hadn't caught?

Better read some of the articles from the professional journals about Todd's work here or there after he reached adulthood, she told herself. Janet glanced over to where she had stacked the journals neatly to one side. It was to Todd's credit that he had come out of the mess as whole a person as he was.

She picked up another clipping, a larger one printed on the glossy paper of some Sunday magazine insert. It was about a new scandal that had been quickly hushed up. It featured news of violent recriminations within the family and an investigation of mismanagement of Todd's inheritance. Then it mentioned another sudden change in the boy's custody, this time to grandparents who had previously declined the responsibility. The tone of the piece was overly emotional, a "sob story," a "poor-little-rich-boy" story. The uncle he was taken from was always referred to as "his favorite uncle" and the grandparents were pictured as grim recluses. Janet wondered how much of the story was true.

Todd's face in the picture told her nothing. He was thirteen or fourteen and was wearing a blazer with a school emblem on the pocket. He was looking full into the camera with a closed expression. As far back as then he had learned to withdraw, to shut himself off from others, to protect himself. No wonder the career he had chosen for himself dealt mainly with people who'd been dead for hundreds of years, Janet thought.

"I fell in love with you," he had said that day at lunch. But he hadn't meant marriage. He hadn't meant commitment. She could remember just as vividly his harsh comment in the work shed: "You're scared to death of the marriage trap, Janet. Good for you. You're smarter than I thought you were."

Maybe she should try to get some more sleep if she could, because tomorrow she—what was happening tomorrow? Janet almost groaned. The trip to Luxor with Hassan. Hastily she began pushing the clippings together into a stack. Curse Nazli for sending them. She should forget this, wipe it out. Todd had survived. He had a pretty good life now—incomplete, but that's the way he wanted it.

"RUNAWAY BALLARD HEIR CAUGHT." Suddenly a headline leaped up at her—something she had missed earlier.

Fifteen-year-old Todd Ballard, missing from his school for the last two weeks, was picked up by uniformed police today in Los Angeles. The officers were acting on a tip from a pawnbroker in whose shop he was trying to sell a wristwatch and a portable radio. The youth refused any comment to reporters, but a reliable source has disclosed that his mother was recently released from an institution for the cure of alcohol addiction. She is said to be ill and in destitute circumstances. It is believed that the youth....

Janet turned away from the dresser and went back to bed. The thing was, she kept telling herself, not to start crying. Because once she started, she might not be able to stop.

HASSAN BOOKED ROOMS FOR THEM in Luxor, four hundred miles south of Cairo, at the nineteenth-century Winter Palace, in the original hotel, not in the new section.

"A little slice of the past," he laughed. "You can see how wealthy Britons lived in the past century when they came here to escape the English winters."

Hassan, always a smooth conversationalist, seemed more voluble than usual—and had since he had picked her up at her hotel early that morning. He seemed tenser than usual, too, and Janet wondered absently if it was because he anticipated rejection of his marriage plans.

Janet looked around the room with a sense of mild disbelief. It was like stepping back into the gaslight era, although she could hear the efficient hum of the air conditioner in the background. There was an iron bed, painted white and surmounted by a vast white canopy, with white net side curtains drawn back.

"To keep off mosquitoes at night," Hassan said. "They just leave the curtains in the room for show now, though, as no one needs to open the windows for cool air anymore." He went over and touched the netting lightly. "I advise you not to close them, because the falling dust would probably choke you."

The heavy Victorian furniture consisted of a tea table and two chairs, a dresser and a tall wardrobe standing against the wall. This section of the hotel had been built before the era of the walk-in closet.

Janet took a tentative peek into the bathroom and encountered another first. She had never seen such a high bathtub in her life. Over this was another modernization—a spindly shower pipe and head, surrounded by a plastic curtain on a ring. The bathroom was huge, with wide shuttered windows overlooking a small area of the garden. She could picture a retired British civil servant standing before the small oval mirror, shaving with a straight razor and looking out into the sun-drenched Egyptian morning.

"This is a landmark," Hassan was saying. "I wanted you to see it. When I come here on business, I usually stay at the little Beau Soleil on the south edge of town. It's clean and adequate, but there's no elevator, and there are showers only in the baths. Air conditioning costs extra." He laughed ruefully when he said it.

Janet smiled politely. He was letting her know again that he was putting them up at a four-star hotel just for her benefit, reminding her again of her continuing and mounting obligation to him. Since coming to Egypt, she had tried several times to pay her own way, but each time he had been deeply affronted. To have Hassan pay embarrassed her, and it was a problem she hadn't solved yet.

Janet knew he had a business appointment now, and she wished he would leave her alone for a while. She was tired from lack of sleep and from coping with the madness of the Cairo airport. She had the beginnings of a throbbing headache and couldn't recall where she had packed her aspirin.

"I'll be back in time to take you to dinner," Hassan said. "Will you be all right here by yourself until then? If you want anything, just ring that bell or call the desk. I spoke to the desk man when I registered. I have to make a phone call—someone I wasn't able to get in Cairo. There's a line out of order, being repaired. These things take forever."

"Thank you. I'll be fine."

"Before we left, Nazli gave me photocopies of some of the tomb translations she's made. She thinks they will interest you since you're working with your father's notes."

"That was nice of her," Janet commented. It was probably something amounting to absolute proof that Eyes-of-Love was not of royal blood as her father had theorized. Well, what difference did it make? The controversy seemed remote now, far less important than it had.

"I'll get the copies from my luggage before I go and have the boy bring them to you. He'll expect a ten-piastre note, but give him twenty-five. He can probably use it."

"Never mind. I can certainly handle a tip," Janet demurred as Hassan took out his wallet and dropped a limp dirty little bill onto the tea table. The tiny piastre notes were so much smaller than the overlarge pound notes.

"No, no. It is my pleasure. Try not to be too bored. I see no one tomorrow but you. I'll take you through both temples—Luxor and Karnak."

"I'm looking forward to it," Janet said in a good imitation of enthusiasm, and braced herself for his parting kiss. He was back to the old chaste gentle kisses—which was a relief—but she wasn't sure how long they would last. As long as Hassan was pushing for an immediate marriage, she supposed. He was trying to please her, building up Brownie points.

Should she marry him? He wanted so desperately to get into the States permanently. The idea popped into her head from nowhere. He had been through so much, and he was so dear. And Todd Ballard was out of her life for good.

There would never be another love.

This idea had a momentarily stunning effect, so that when Hassan gently released her, she sagged back against the hard iron bedstead. She wouldn't love anyone else. That had been it. The insight stunned her with a kind of terrifying clarity. She had come face to face with the one great love of her life. Then she had turned and walked away. She felt numb and didn't understand it. She should be hurting. Maybe this was some sort of shock and the realization would come later. Later the reality of her loss would come crashing down on her. So there wouldn't be any love now, she thought, feeling hollow. So why not marry Hassan, then? Why deny him when she had no hope of a real love herself? At least she could do that much. She would certainly never love Hassan as a woman passionately loves a man, but would he care? Secure in his supreme male confidence, would he even notice? If she married him and went through the motions of fulfilling wifely obligations, he would simply assume that she had become as besotted with him as the vivid Nazli, who dogged his footsteps in Cairo.

He had got as far as opening the hall door to leave.

"Hassan?"

He turned, eyes questioning, his mouth smiling. Hassan did have a nice smile. He was a nice man.

"You don't always have to kiss me as if I were a six-year-old child."

There was a moment's pause, and then the door clicked shut. She watched him come back, willing herself to be relaxed and pliant when he took her in his arms again. She lifted her face, lips parted. She clung to him, deliberately responding to the deep lingering kisses for an endless interval, overcoming her inner reluctance and holding her resistance at bay by sheer force of will. Then she had to break free. She went rigid against him, pushing at him, tearing her mouth away.

He let her go instantly, all kindness and contrition. "Ah, my sweet, dear, little girl," he murmured in her hair. "You try too hard. You go too fast. You need not, my love. I'm a patient man. And I am not such a roué that I don't treasure genuine innocence when I find it."

Janet steeled herself to endure his embrace, which she had once thought so comforting. Eventually he left, and she climbed onto the high bed, staring up into a mishmash of grimy white netting.

It would never work.

Hassan as a father figure was absolutely super. Hassan as a husband was all wrong. Well, sleep was out of the question. She crawled off the bed and was opening her bag to unpack when there was a combination rapping and scratching at the door.

It was a young porter in the usual white floor-length garment, bringing the translations from Nazli. She took the envelope and gave him an order for bottled water and a pot of tea. She had found her aspirin. While she waited, she added another twenty-five-piastre note to his tip and opened the envelope. Inside were several sheets of paper covered with Nazli's bold writing. Dear Nazli, the faithful pen pal. She tossed them onto the tea table and rested her head on her folded arms. Ever since she had awakened that morning she had felt suspended in space, like a forgotten puppet still dangling lifelessly after the show was over and the theater dark. One of these days she would start feeling things again. Then she would know what it was to have lost Todd Ballard. Correction: to have thrown him away.

But what else could she have done? Could they have had any life together given the impossible situation in which they found themselves? It was doubtful. Very, very doubtful. She would soon have become miserable in any relationship that fell short of the marriage and family she had always counted on. Just as Todd would have become miserable placed in such a situation if he bowed to her wishes. Even if they could have reconciled the obvious problems, there would still have been the image of her father and of his dying, to haunt and bedevil them. There wasn't a chance. It was a no-win situation, as Todd had said. *Just your regular average Romeo and Juliet,* she thought ruefully, *the circumstances already in place when the young lovers enter.*

After the porter had come and gone, after the remaining tea was cold in the pot, dusk filled the room. Janet got up and figured out how to turn on the small dresser lamp without having the ceiling light blazing. She sat in the pool of lamplight and started to read the translations Nazli had sent. Maybe, Janet thought, she could get interested in Eyes-of-Love again. She should get interested in something, certainly. After reading the first paragraph four times and not grasping anything in it, Janet put down the papers on the table again. She reached over and pulled open the white painted louvers at the window. Okay. She would just sit. Until Hassan came back she would simply stare out into the famous gardens. Gardens were supposed to be soothing to the troubled spirit.

AFTER A LEISURELY BREAKFAST the next morning in the vast, rather barnlike Winter Palace dining room, Hassan took Janet through the spreading ruins of Luxor's temple. They were all that remained of the ancient god Amun, whose worship had lasted thousands of years, and of his powerful priesthood, which had held sway over Egypt for so many centuries. They walked the short distance from the Winter Palace, along the busy edge of the Nile, as the journey was too short to bother with one of the small black horse-drawn carriages that bounced along the dusty street.

"We'll take one of those to Karnak, if you like." Hassan smiled.

"Yes, I'd like that," she said with a show of enthusiasm. No point in dragging down Hassan's mood by her own depression.

The little carriages, some open, some with the tops put up, were obviously very old and left over from another century. They were kept in exquisite condition by their drivers. Janet had watched them in the rank across the street from the hotel porch as she waited for Hassan to inquire about his phone call again. Those not engaged in transporting tourists were lined up, with most owners busy dusting the shining black sides or polishing the bright brass bells or arranging the colorful tassels decorating the horse's mane and bridle.

When she and Hassan reached the temple, they walked up the avenue of ram-headed sphinxes. Hassan smiled and waved away the proffered services of two hopeful guides who had not recognized him at first. Janet had to watch her step because many of the avenue's paving blocks were missing and the ground was uneven.

"This avenue once stretched from here clear to Karnak," Hassan said. "You will see the other end of the avenue there."

Janet looked at the battered pitted stone faces of the serene rams that lined the pathway. She tried to ignore feelings of ultimate defeat and futility that the magnificent ruins aroused in her. She cataloged them: a door opening in half a wall; some steps leading to vacant air; and giant granite statues of gods carved with exquisite beauty, lying in great broken chunks in the dust.

"It was all completely buried for thousands of years—discovered again less than a hundred years ago. It took over two years to dig everything up again, and what you see now is all that is left. Time takes a heavy toll."

"Todd said the country is probably still rich with undiscovered treasures," she began, and then stopped. The less she said about Todd to Hassan, the better.

"Very true," he agreed pleasantly. "When we get to the big black statue of Ramses II, I'll take your picture, if you like. You won't come up to his knee. Afternoon sun would be better here, of course, but I'll do the best I can."

They spent two leisurely, though rather somber hours wandering among the vast ruins. Hassan commented knowledgeably on the huge broken statues, the stumps of carved columns contained inside and outside of partial rooms: a shrine with two walls missing that still housed a god's image; a wide colonnade between two vast halls in which kings had held court; all of it naked and open to the vivid blue Egyptian sky. Janet wondered pensively in passing how many centuries it had taken for the last of the great roof to go. When had the last stone of it, burned by the endless sun, lashed by the angry wind and scored by the cutting sand, cracked and fallen in pieces among the rest of the rubble?

They had lunch in a new luxury hotel, where Hassan was greeted by name and much gracious bowing. It was almost four when they were ready to leave for Karnak. Hassan was helping Janet up into the small black carriage when the red-clad doorman came out the heavy glass doors and asked Hassan to return. Hassan's long-awaited telephone call had come and had been transferred from the Winter Palace.

Janet waited for him in the carriage outside. A feeling of drowsiness had been induced by the larger-than-average lunch and the heat. Putting up the carriage's cracked leather top afforded little relief except to protect her from direct glare, as the sides of the carriage remained open. Dust from an occasional passing horse drifted in, and a few slow-moving flies hovered listlessly in their strange flight patterns. Now and then the driver, seated on the high seat at the front, flicked the tip of his horsehair fly whisk against the side and the flies moved out of the way.

When Hassan came back, Janet thought sleepily

that even he was getting too much sun, for an un-healthy flush mottled his face. As soon as he was beside her, the carriage jolted forward, and the horse started out at a leisurely pace through the molten afternoon. Janet leaned her head back against the leather seat. It was stickily warm, but she was too lethargic to straighten up. Several slow miles passed before she realized the charged quality of the silence between Hassan and her.

Uneasiness began to push her mind back to full wakefulness as she struggled against the lassitude that held her. Something had gone wrong. Hassan was angry. It showed in the heavy silence, in the slight shaking of his well-shaped hand on the leather seat. The cause of his anger was something to do with the long-expected phone call that had finally got through Egypt's faulty communication system. Bad news of some kind. Janet bit back a polite question, for something warned her not to ask him about the phone call. Not yet.

When they neared the temple at Karnak, about thirty minutes later, Hassan seemed to have re-gained his poise. Only his darkened face and the crisp edge to his speech, his clipped words spoken in an almost British accent, revealed that some inner rage still moved just beneath the surface. Hassan was going to speak of it just as soon as he was sure of his own self-control. Janet had an urgent need to delay his revelations, to fend them off somehow. They got out of the carriage and walked up the frag-mented avenue of the remaining ram-headed sphinxes.

"Oh, Hassan, what a magnificent gate!" Janet wanted him to start talking about the temple, but her awe was not entirely feigned. "It's huge!"

"A little over a hundred and fifty feet tall," he said. He sounded remarkably calm, his voice steady, his words no longer clipped but blending easily into one another. And he sounded almost American again—an accent he had carefully tried to cultivate ever since she had met him. "Maybe fifty feet thick. And you'll notice it's still in almost perfect condition."

They went through the gate of the complex into the great court. Small temples built by different kings were on either side, and on through the opening into the vast Hall of Columns. Janet stopped just beyond the threshold. Here and there groups of tourists wandered, looking lost among the giant stone forest of carved columns soaring upward toward the limitless azure sky.

"This part is much older than the court we just came through," Hassan said, "and of course these pillars once held up the roof, which is now long gone. Everything goes eventually, I guess." His tone of voice was thoughtful as his eyes traveled up the nearest pillar, past the broad round base, along its curved and exquisitely decorated surface and on up to the intricately carved capital, which was one of those still intact.

Janet stared at the massive columns still decorated with the remains of the thousands of illustrations the ancient Egyptians had so loved.

"There must be at least a hundred of these—at least ten thick, aren't they?"

Hassan was looking at her, his eyes veiled. He knew what she was doing. Stalling. Holding him at bay. "Actually, it's a hundred and thirty-four, but you're right about the width. And let's see, this hall has over fifty thousand square feet. It's bigger than any other temple, for any purpose, anywhere else in the world. Impressive, yes?"

"Yes, I'm impressed," she agreed quite truthfully.

"Then you'll want to see all the rest of it, then, 'every nook and cranny,' as your father used to say. Come along. I'll show you."

Before they finished Janet's legs were aching. Beyond the Hall of Columns was a long colonnade, and Hassan commented on the remains of other columns, statues, images, shrines and sanctuaries. There was the ancient shrine to Amun, and directly across from it a mosque for present-day use had been built. Hassan knew about the building materials, the limestone, black and pink marble from Aswan. He knew about the dynasties, and he possessed an amazing amount of information about the artwork and how one era differed from another. Janet was aware he was overdoing it, telling her more than she wanted to know. Certainly more than she could absorb and retain from one visit. Well, she had asked for it, she had to admit, so she couldn't fault him for it. When she thought she was about to drop, he led her through another opening.

"Now, through here—no, we're going this way. Watch your step. Some of the paving is gone. I want you to see the sacred lake." A fleeting smile touched his mouth. "They've added some new touches to it you may appreciate—umbrella tables and soda-pop vendors. Could you use a cold drink?"

"Yes, I certainly could," Janet said fervently.

It was almost seven o'clock, and most of the tourists had gone back to their hotels. Most of the tables were empty. Janet headed for the closest one and sank down into one of the chairs surrounding it. Hassan seated himself opposite her. A vendor was coming toward them with a Styrofoam cooler in which several bottles of soft drink floated in ice water. Janet chose something light orange to drink with a brand name in a language she could not read. Nothing had tasted so good to her in a long time. She tried not to gulp it down.

The umbrella of metal strips laid thin shafts of the lessening sunlight across their hands and the table top. Janet took off her little cloth hat and shook out her hair, which felt damp and which stuck in small tendrils to her forehead. She was thinking of the huge white bathroom with the tall tub back at the Winter Palace. Hassan's voice brought her back to the present with a thud.

"The phone call I was waiting for finally came through," he began. Even as he said it an ugly flush began to rise in his face. "Why did you not inform me of your visit to Alexandria with Todd Ballard?"

Janet decided quickly to tell a half-truth, but as always the ploy made her uncomfortable. "I called your apartment, but you had gone," she said. That neatly omitted her surprising Nazli out of a sound

sleep and also Nazli's suspicions about a secret ex-
mistress. The last thing she wanted was a confrontation with Hassan at this moment.

He muttered something in Arabic and suddenly
leaned over, placing his face in his hands.

"Hassan, please," she whispered. "It doesn't
matter. None of it matters now. Your—your hands
are shaking again. They were shaking in the carriage. They—"

He lifted his face and looked at her, his eyes
agonized. Then he straightened up. "Adrenaline,"
he said bitterly. "It shoots into the bloodstream
when a man has an urge to kill an enemy or is
threatened. Then when the man just sits there and
does nothing about it, some shaking occurs. Pay no
attention. It will pass."

"Oh, Hassan," she said, placing her hand on his
arm, feeling the tremors. "*Not* an enemy! Not me!
I'm so sorry. I was going to talk to you about it. I was.
Really. And don't blame Todd. He was just—just—"

"Yes, what was he doing there? Tell me." It was
almost a command, spoken in his politest voice,
which was as hard as Aswan granite. He had re-
gained his composure, and he was in control.

"We—he—we went to see . . . ." Janet remembered with intensity the kind confused little old
lady, and she was choked with guilt. They had had
no right.

"I know who you went to see."

"Then you must know why, Hassan."

She meant to go on, but he interrupted with soft
violence. "I will not have her badgered. I—"

"She wasn't! We didn't! It wasn't like that at all, Hassan. Todd was very—very gracious, very pleasant. She was pleased. She was, Hassan! She enjoyed the visit. She didn't understand—I mean...." Her voice trailed away.

"Allah be praised for that, anyway."

There was a long interval of silence between them. It seemed as if they were engulfed by silence—the vast ancient temple complex behind them; the shining oval pool before them; the vendor with his battered plastic cooler, waiting quietly at some distance in case they gestured him to come back.

"I suppose Ballard got the information he wanted."

"More or less." Her own voice was steadier now. "About...you know...her finances, and so on. It doesn't matter, Hassan."

He muttered something again in Arabic and looked bleakly out over the ancient lake.

"Whatever that means," Janet said, stroking his arm a little. "You'll have to translate if you want an answer."

"It wouldn't exactly translate. It has to do with our friend Ballard's ancestors. You know, of course, Janet, why he's digging into my personal life?"

"Yes, I know. But there is no need—I mean, he'll stop now. I'm quite sure."

"What makes you quite sure of anything a man like Ballard will do? He hasn't suddenly lost interest in you, has he?"

"He should have. I—he and I—had our final confrontation. I made sure of that." A sudden sharp anguish swept through her.

"Don't underestimate a man like that." There was a small tremor in Hassan's voice again. For the first time since she'd known Hassan he sounded beaten. "He won't stop now. He could finish me." He said something else, but his voice had dropped so low she missed it.

"What?"

"I said, 'And probably will.'"

She was worried now. She tried to push the thought of Todd and her to the back of her mind as she watched Hassan carefully. His face had lost color, become grayish. His lovely eyes were dulled, as if he might be falling asleep.

"Are you all right?" she asked tentatively.

"Oh, yes," he said after a moment. "I'm a survivor, as they say. Given a little time I'll spring back. I always have."

"Hassan, there's no need for him to do anything else," she said with more assurance than she felt. "We had it out. You and I talked about it before. He was interested in me. Well, I'm not interested in any liaison with him. So I stopped it. He apologized for...for having been so persistent. He said he wouldn't bother me again. Well, that's what he said. I'm just telling you what he said," she added at his look of bleak derision.

"But he didn't say he would not bother me, did he?" Hassan waited a moment. "No, I thought not. I know a great deal about that man, Janet. He doesn't give up. He may stop his attentions to you if he's said he would. But if he's out to discredit me, he will. And incidentally, Janet, he can without too much trouble," he added wearily. "What else is he going to do, do you know?"

Hassan seemed to look ten years older. She wanted to cry.

"I'll talk to him when we get back to Cairo, Hassan. We were both upset when we had our last... confrontation. Now we'll have some distance from it, and...I'll talk to him. After all, I'll be seeing him. I'll be working out at the site if that arrangement still goes. He hired me himself. I could go on with it, talk to him, make him drop it."

"Drop what, Janet?"

"One other thing he said. Oh, I know he's given it up now. I'm sure. He wanted to find out why you didn't apply for American citizenship in the usual way—why you waited so long."

"He can find that out easily enough," Hassan said dully. "Records exist."

"Why? What do you mean?"

"I would have told you, Janet, all in good time. I wasn't trying to hide anything. Your father knew. I just hadn't got around to mentioning it."

"Told me what?" She didn't want to hear it but made herself ask.

"I've been in prison. Twice. Once here and once in Algeria. This was long ago when I was very young. It seemed like forever. Time passes so slowly for the young." His voice trailed away, and there was another long interval of silence, as if he were recalling his youth and the slow days in prison. "That was during my political—what do you call it in the States—phase? Yes, my political phase."

"Surely that wouldn't stop you from being admitted to the States, would it? Good grief, Hassan, political activists thrive in the States. They always have, I'm pretty sure."

He was looking at her as if from a vast distance. "It certainly wouldn't help me any."

"But you aren't still active in politics, are you?"

"No! I was an ignorant child, spouting slogans. I began to grow up. Then I began to learn. I came back here, got myself educated. Money, Janet. That's the only security. Money is the only answer."

"Oh, surely not, Hassan," she objected.

"Anyhow, the past has been long buried. I'm a different person now. I have a good reputation—well earned, I might add. But going through regular channels would drag it all up again. You see, none of my present professional and business associates—except Houdeiby—knows anything about that period. I would be a difficulty, an embarrassment, certainly. I talked all this over with your father many times. It seemed simpler just to wait and emigrate as the spouse of an American citizen. Since I've always cared about you and later I wanted to marry you. . . ." His voice trailed off.

Janet felt a tightening in her throat. Hassan had always been able to reach her, despite the clear small voice of doubt in the bottom of her mind. How much of this was true? All true? Partly true?

Had he really discussed it all with her father? Or was he giving her a carefully edited version of the parts he knew might win her sympathy, now that Todd had forced his hand? Was this just Hassan, the survivor, surviving?

It was true he had impeccable credentials now, at least in his work and present social connections. Dr. Houdeiby idolized him. Her father had counted him a friend. And he was certainly one of the kindest people she had known. She looked carefully at his face. He had leaned his head back against the chair, slouching down, his eyes closed against the shafts of sunlight. He looked utterly defeated. In another ten years would he still be in Egypt, where there were limits and restrictions on income, always struggling for more money to try to satisfy his insatiable needs? He was an opportunist, yes, but it didn't seem fair, somehow. He shouldn't have to pay for the rest of his life for his early mistakes. Shouldn't the punishment fit the crime, more or less?

"You've been to the States as a traveler a dozen times, Hassan," she said. "Rather than wait for me to grow up, why didn't you just marry some other American woman? You certainly could have."

He opened his eyes. They showed a flicker of astonishment. "I never wanted to. I've always loved you. And I promised your father—"

"Oh, Hassan," she murmured in hopeless fondness. Hassan wasn't quite the villain Todd made him out to be. Villains came tougher than this. Too tough to modify their villainies to fit their personal loyalties. Villains weren't supposed to follow their hearts, only their heads.

A party of late tourists wandered out of the temple and headed for a table some distance away. The soda-pop vendor got up and started strolling in their direction.

"What about Todd Ballard, Janet?" Hassan asked gently. "Are you being hurt by him? Is it really finished?"

She wasn't going to lie.

"I'm sorry, Hassan. There was an initial...attraction. On my part, too. I think that if circumstances had been different, something might have happened."

"Ah, I see. What circumstances, my dear?"

"I can't—couldn't have lived with the idea that he caused my father's death. It would have been too much. I couldn't have handled that over the long road, after the first bliss of the honeymoon. Besides, I don't think that Todd will ever marry anybody. And I don't really want anything less."

"What a wise child you are," he murmured. "Then there is nothing in the future for you and Todd Ballard, is there?"

She made her voice as emotionless as she could. "Nothing."

"And because your heart is hurting from this... disappointment, you are shutting me out, also. Yes? We are all to suffer." He waited a moment, then added softly, "Why?"

Why, indeed? It didn't make sense. At least one of them should come out of it all with something.

"That's a good question," she said remotely, feeling a little numb.

"I know you've made up your mind not to marry me. I've known it since you came here. But will you change it now, Janet? Will you marry me, anyway?" His face was very close, the beautiful eyes haggard, desperate.

Her mouth felt dry as she realized what she was going to do. "All right," she said steadily. "Yes, I'll marry you. Somebody should win."

CHAPTER TWELVE

ALL DURING THE FLIGHT BACK to Cairo Janet had a premonition Todd was going to meet them. She was convinced he would come striding through the hurrying crowd of every race and description that surged back and forth like a restless tide in the overflowing airport. Janet thought she looked terrible, but she didn't care much. Her blue seersucker skirt was grimy, and she was wearing a sleeveless top that made Hassan slightly uncomfortable, although he didn't make any comment. Out of consideration for him she tried to keep a light sweater over her shoulders, but it continued to slide off. She longed for her quiet cool room at Mena House.

She gave a shaky sigh of relief when it was not Todd's tall muscular form that came forward out of the waiting mass of people but the portly beaming Dr. Houdeiby. For one mad moment she wanted to kiss him, but instead she settled for holding out her hand with somewhat more enthusiasm than usual. When he bent to kiss it, he reached for the single paper parcel she was carrying.

"Ah! I see you have bought from all the shops in Luxor," he said with great gaiety. "And very wise, very prudent. You will make Hassan a good wife, indeed. Indeed.'' He turned to Hassan. "Permit me to carry some of these, Hassan." He began tugging at the purchases Hassan was carrying for her. So Hassan had already talked to him from Luxor by phone, had told him she had agreed to the marriage, and probably how soon. She tried not to be annoyed. Certainly she had known that the two men were friends and that Houdeiby was promoting Hassan's proposal with great fervor.

"I bought some cotton things. Since I'll be working at the site, you know," she said pleasantly. "My father always told me that the long-fibered Egyptian cotton was the best in the world."

"Ah! It is! It is! And it lasts very long, very long. Forever. You will see."

"Well, it's certainly beautiful, I must say that," Janet agreed. She had got some cool short-sleeved blouses in light colors and white, so finely spun as to be feather light. She had found several short skirts she liked in heavier weaves, some with vividly printed designs adapted from the ancient paintings.

"There was no place to park—I mean, it was too far away. So I have my driver driving around and around. Come, let us get your luggage." Dr. Houdeiby bustled on ahead of them.

Another small sigh of relief escaped Janet. Promising to marry Hassan in the warm silent afternoon by the sacred lake at Karnak was one thing. Coming back to Cairo to face Nazli, who was in love with him, was something else again. It would be a rough few minutes, and she dreaded it. She tried to tell herself that it was for the best, that

Nazli would get over it, and would find someone else, but the words rang hollow in her mind.

Not to mention coming face to face with Todd Ballard. *Yes, I'm going to marry Hassan. Yes, as soon as he can arrange things. It's for the best. Let it alone. Let him alone. Let me alone.*

But she would have to be careful, very careful. Todd could still easily cause them trouble if he chose to. By now Mr. Jamison was counting on some funding, and there were probably other things about Hassan that were best not exposed to the light of day. His early life had been so precarious.

She was glad when they reached Mena House again. Its old cream-colored walls and turrets were washed in golden sunlight. There was almost a feeling of homecoming. It might be a long time before she again saw the real hills of home in San Francisco, topped with wreaths of swirling fog drifting in from the bay. This had to be home for the moment. She would dig in and do some of the best work of her life and hope that work would at least block Todd out of her mind, if nothing else. And somehow she would hold Todd off, hold him in check, until Hassan had been cleared for legal entrance into the States.

Hassan and Dr. Houdeiby saw her to her room, dropped her parcels onto her bed and then left with surprising alacrity. Odd. Egyptians usually indulged in prolonged farewells, as if reluctant to go. As the door shut behind them, Janet could hear them begin speaking in rapid Arabic. They had lapsed into their own language several times on the drive from the airport and then quickly reverted to English. It was clear they had much to discuss.

Almost instantly Janet was aware that she was not alone. She froze for a moment, her hand still outstretched from pushing the door shut. *Not Todd. Oh, please. Not Todd.*

"Nazli!"

The other girl got out of a chair on the balcony and walked slowly into the room. With the light behind her it was impossible to see the expression on her face. She was not in her usual working clothes, designer jeans and a cotton blouse. Rather, she had dressed up, as for a special occasion. Perhaps to bolster her own courage. Janet got a swift impression of an amber summer dress in what must be raw silk and high-heeled sandals in the same fabric.

"Welcome back to Cairo," Nazli said, pronouncing "welcome" as if it were two distinct words, as most Egyptians seemed to do. "Ah, I see you followed my advice and did some shopping in Luxor." Her attempt at enthusiasm failed, giving the words a hollow sound. She advanced to the bed and glanced down at the parcels, and Janet got a clear look at her face. It was gaunt. The great dark eyes were haunted.

Janet felt slightly sick. Nazli was going to be hurt by this, was already hurt by it. She did not like the other girl, but at the same time she had no desire to hurt anyone at all. Life was too short.

"What happens, then? Tell me." Nazli jerked the question out, avoiding Janet, bending over and starting to pick up and put down again unseen the various paper bags and packages of clothes from Luxor. There was a mindless aimless quality to her activity that stirred Janet's compassion. They hadn't even told her! Though they were clearly discussing it between themselves, they hadn't even bothered to tell Nazli. That was really rotten. Anger tingled along Janet's nerve ends. They could have been honest with her.

"I. . .Hassan and I. . . ." Actually, it wasn't that easy.

Nazli had looked up, was staring at her, making no pretense of being calm now, very vulnerable. She was still bent over, stone still, waiting for the blow to fall.

"We discussed it, Nazli. It seemed that in the long run—given Hassan's personal situation—that he—we should go ahead with the marriage plans. There just seemed no better way. I mean, that seemed the best way." Janet wanted desperately to reach out and touch Nazli, comfort her somehow, but she knew instinctively that the gesture would not be welcome, that it would just add a final touch of humiliation.

A long shivering sigh went through Nazli's body, and she straightened up slowly. "You don't even love him," she said faintly, almost to herself.

"Oh, but I do, Nazli," Janet protested. "Hassan has always been very. . .dear to me." She felt she had to defend the decision, justify her actions somehow. "It will be a good marriage for him. I'll be a good wife—you'll see. It's not a mistake, really. It's for the best."

She started to say something else, but there was a knock at the door. The moment, the sudden sound at the door, or what she had said—something seemed to ignite Nazli, and she exploded into sheer rage. Her face twisted, and her teeth bared. She snatched up the bedside lamp and lunged at Janet, screaming in Arabic. Then she threw the lamp and came plunging after it, clawed hands outstretched. Janet knew a moment of stunned terror. Then the lamp, still connected by the cord, was halted in midair and crashed down in front of Nazli, causing her to stumble and fall awkwardly on top of it. She landed in a twisted heap, entangled in the cord, the crushed lampshade and the shattered ceramic base. There was pounding on the door, and something crashed against it.

"Janet! Open the door! It's me! Todd!"

Nazli, not even aware of what she was doing, lay huddled in a heap on the floor, clutching the mangled lampshade close to her body, rocking back and forth, crying in great wrenching sobs that seemed to tear through her body.

"Oh, Nazli...please ...." Janet, choking with pity, hovered over her a moment, then rushed to the door and pulled it open.

"Be quiet! It's all right. I mean—" She sagged against the wall, shaking. "Come inside."

"Good God, what happened? Did she fall? Nazli, are you all right?" Todd, still in his work clothes, knelt quickly beside Nazli and put his arms around her, trying gently to loosen her hysterical grasp of the broken lampshade. It was slightly smeared with blood now, since she had apparently cut her arm on part of the shattered ceramic base. "Janet, get something. Get a towel."

Janet, sick with revulsion at the ugly scene, hurried into her bathroom and with shaking hands snatched up a clean towel from the stack, then came back with it.

"It's not too bad, see?" Todd was saying soothingly, as to a child. "Look, it doesn't even come through the towel. Look, Nazli, you're okay."

Under his gentle ministrations the stormy weeping gradually subsided. Nazli's arms went lax, and the lampshade rolled to the floor beside her. Carefully Todd helped her up, questioning her gently all the time. "Can you stand? Move this other arm, okay? Put that foot flat on the floor. See? Nothing's broken. Nothing's even sprained. Just one little cut. That's not too bad."

Janet, small shivers of shock still running through her, jerked spasmodically as someone else knocked at the door. She had not reached it before it was opened with a passkey and an assistant manager poked his head tentatively inside the room.

"Madame? Is madame well? Does madame wish—Ahh!" He broke off in dismay when he saw Nazli and the ruins of the bedside lamp.

"Miss Houdeiby stumbled over a lamp cord and somehow had a bad fall," Todd said smoothly.

"I get the doctor." The hotelman darted to the phone, but Nazli forestalled him.

"No, no, no. Not at all. It is not necessary. It is a

small thing only.'' Her voice quavered a moment, then steadied, and she was in control again. In unspoken agreement the three of them acted out a little charade for the assistant manager.

Janet had no idea of how much of Nazli's screaming in Arabic had been heard outside in the hall, how much some servant had had time to report to him, but he politely went along with their explanation. With a gentle show of sympathy and many apologies—Janet wasn't sure what for—he secured a bandage for the cut, had the broken lamp replaced and ordered someone downstairs to bring around Miss Houdeiby's car. Then with one last apology, he left to escort her downstairs. Nazli had completely regained her poise and walked out the door with her head high, reminding Janet once again of a young Egyptian queen.

A moment after the door had shut behind them Todd spoke.

''What the hell happened?''

''She stumbled over the lamp cord and fell,'' Janet snapped. ''That's what you told the man.'' She paused uncomfortably, remembering what a help he had just been. ''That was bitchy, wasn't it?''

''Yes, but I'll let it pass. I heard some of it—you forget I understand Arabic. She was furious. I got the crazy idea that your life was hanging by a thread. It upset me, so I tried to beat in the door.''

''Thank you. I—I'm glad you did. I appreciate it. And I apologize for being so—''

''Okay. You don't have to grovel. Let it go.

What happened?'' He was flexing the fingers of his right hand as if it were hurting. ''That's a terrific door. As long as you keep it locked, you're safe from everything.''

Janet took a shaky breath. She'd have to tell him, too. Unconsciously she straightened her shoulders. ''She...ah...lost her temper. And, well, she just picked up the lamp and sort of came at me.''

''And got tangled up and fell?''

''More or less. I think she tried to throw the lamp.'' She waited for his next question. It came.

''What made her lose her temper? Something about you and Hassan? That much I got from what she said.''

''While Hassan and I were in Luxor we talked things over.''

He stopped flexing his fingers, became completely still, almost visibly bracing himself. ''And?''

''I told him to go ahead and make arrangements for our marriage. Soon. Right away. It seemed the best way to...solve things.''

He gave a quick intake of breath and turned away abruptly, walking aimlessly out to the balcony and back. When he stood in front of her again, his face was hard, but his eyes looked haggard.

''That's it, then.''

''That was already it, Todd,'' she said wearily. ''We've been all over this. It shouldn't matter to you one way or the other what I do with my life now.''

''It does matter.'' He grated the words out between his teeth.

"Well, it—this part of it—is your own fault! You won't let him alone. You keep digging and dig-ging...."

"You're practically admitting there is something for me to find, aren't you? Or he wouldn't be so frantic to slide into the States as the husband of an American, right?"

"No, I didn't say that. Oh, Todd, let it alone. And how did you just happen to knock on my door five minutes after I got back?" she added angrily. "It's almost as if you had someone watching for me."

"I did, actually. Not here. At the airport. I thought it was worth a small investment." He had slowly withdrawn again and had spoken with cool detachment.

"Oh, Todd," she said desperately. "All right, I think we both know I don't care about Hassan the way a—a—wife would. But that doesn't matter. I do love him. I care enough to want him to have what he wants. It's vital to him, don't you see? Please try to understand. You and I—that was a mistake. We both know that. And I'm sorry. You'll never know. Look, if I tell you what he did that he's so worried about now, will you stop digging around? Will you let up? It's not so bad, really." She had gone to stand in front of him, peering up at him beseechingly.

"What makes you think he told you the truth?" It was like a slap in the face. "I think I'll do my own digging, thanks."

She turned away and collapsed into one of the

chairs by the balcony doors, gazing at him hopelessly.

He leaned back against the dresser, half sitting on it, his long legs crossed at the ankles, hands thrust into his jeans pockets. "What about the loose ends? I'm not referring to myself, of course, because I'm no problem now. But did you and Hassan get around to tying up any of those?"

"Loose ends?" A small warning clicked in the back of her mind. *Go away. Leave me in peace,* she screamed inside.

"Assuming an instant marriage—instant here in Egypt taking somewhat longer than in the States—I would say that within three or four weeks you'll be married to Hassan. To share his board—and bed— until death or something else do you part. Did you know that a Muslim man can divorce his wife by simply saying, 'I divorce thee'? He may find it a little more complicated in the States if it happens there, but I'd trust Hassan to figure out something. Are you even slightly familiar with Muslim marriage laws and customs?"

"I'm assuming that Hassan is familiar with them," she said coldly. "He's never given me any reason to distrust him. If there's anything I need to know, he'll fill me in." She found she couldn't take her eyes from his face. He looked the way he had at thirteen in the school blazer, detached from his surroundings, viewing things distantly from behind his personal barrier.

"But in the meantime," he continued smoothly, "what about my work? The notes? The line drawings you promised to do for me? You could start on those immediately, if you're still agreeable. I found a whole cache of discarded or forgotten hand tools yesterday. Is our personal hassle going to mess up my work as well as my life?"

"It shouldn't," she said with an effort, reluctance dragging at her voice. Dread slowly began to build in her mind. What would it be like out at the site with all three of them—Nazli, Todd and her—all inwardly seething, yet somehow trying to keep up appearances.

"You mean, business as usual?" There was a faint note of incredulity in Todd's tone.

She straightened in the chair. "I don't see why not. It will take a while—the arrangements. I can't just sit around doing nothing. I'd rather be working at something."

"I thought brides-to-be were always busy—shopping, planning, entertaining."

"Is that necessary?" She stood up to face him, leaning slightly against the arm of the chair because she felt unsteady.

"No. I guess you've had all you can take for today. And if I were a real nice guy, I wouldn't needle you, but baby, you've sure ripped my life apart."

"You'll survive," she said grimly.

"Is your standing up a hint for me to go?"

"Well, why don't you go? No offense intended, Todd. I do appreciate your help with Nazli, but—" Suddenly she sat down again, ripples of delayed shock running through her body. Probably that adrenaline Hassan talked about. "I do need some time alone. I have to, uh, adjust."

"To the idea of marrying Hassan? Why? You've been engaged to him, haven't you, since you were in kindergarten?"

"No, not that." It was painful to say it. "It just occurred to me that Nazli hates me. That's a first for me. I've never been hated before." In spite of her effort at control, Janet's voice shook. It was a shocking thing, but somehow or other she had managed to drive another human being to the breaking point. She had a quick mental image of Nazli's face, twisted with rage, coming at her. She shut her eyes a moment.

"Okay. I'm going."

She opened her eyes. He was over by the hall door. How had he got there so fast?

Todd paused, looking at her. "You okay?"

"Yes. That is, in a while. My father gave me a good system for coping with things. Everything passes sooner or later. The first step is to decide how long a bad time can last. A week? A month? Whatever. Then think positive. Like, 'A month from now this will be over and I will be doing such and such again.' I'm allowing three months for this present hassle. I can cope with three months all right, a day at a time. Because in three months all this will be past. Hassan and I will be in the States, and I can begin forgetting about this. It will have passed for Nazli, too. Maybe she will already have started rebuilding her life."

Todd looked at her uncertainly for a long moment, as if deciding whether to say something. "Are you sure about that last part, Janet?" he asked finally.

"What last part? You think Nazli won't get over this?"

"Oh, Nazli will come out all right."

"You think *I* won't be able to put all this behind me and go on?"

"You won't put Nazli behind you, Janet," he said matter-of-factly, "because she will be right there, in the States, probably on Hassan's doorstep, as soon as she can get there."

Janet stared at him, dumbfounded.

"But she lives here. Works here. And she knows now that Hassan is going to marry me. They hadn't even told her that. I had to tell her. But she knows now, Todd. She won't come to the States if she can't have Hassan."

"Her plans to emigrate are already in the works—have been for some time."

"How would you know that!" she demanded.

"Because as her present employer I've had a routine inquiry from the U.S. Immigration people."

"But—" Janet fought a rising uneasiness. "But Nazli will cancel all that now." She tried to make her voice decisive. "She must have applied for papers because of all Hassan's talk of living there—she's been crazy about him since her school days. I know all about it."

"Do you want me to dig around and find out when she cancels the proceedings?" There was just a tinge of sarcasm.

No. This was between Hassan and her. She would have to take care of it herself. "No. Thanks, but no thanks. I'll cope with it—if it turns out there's anything to cope with. I'll give Nazli the benefit of the doubt. Since Hassan and I have agreed about the marriage now, she knows she can't have him."

"Does she?" Todd opened the hall door to leave. "Are you sure she can't, Janet?"

CHAPTER THIRTEEN

THE SOUND OF THE AIR CONDITIONER in the shed at
the site was a combination of whir and hum, with
an occasional grinding noise. Its vibrations also
rattled intermittently against the worn uneven win-
dowsill. Janet was comfortable in one of the light
cotton outfits she had bought in Luxor, but Nazli,
having built up a lifetime of tolerance to the heat,
had a light sweater over her shoulders.

The women avoided looking at each other and
spoke with careful, slightly exaggerated courtesy
even when just the two of them were present. When
any of the men came into the shed for something,
Nazli made an obvious attempt at a somewhat hollow friendliness—which probably didn't fool anyone. But with the inbred courtesy patterns of her
culture other Egyptians recognized a face-saving
gesture when they saw one and honored it. Todd,
familiar with Middle Eastern customs, went along.
Janet couldn't tell whether he did this from innate
kindness—she knew now he was capable of deep
kindness on occasion—or whether he simply wanted the dig to move forward smoothly. He avoided
coming into the shed at all if possible.

Janet focused again on the half-completed drawing before her and took some bleak satisfaction in the quality of her work. She was using as a surface the slant-top high desk her father had bought and alternately stood or sat on the tall stool. Before her was an assortment of three carpenter's chisels in varying sizes with round wooden handles designed for easy gripping by the ancient hands that had used them. She had finished drawings of the chisels that morning.

Everyone continued to wonder and comment about why an odd lot of tools had been left behind and sealed into the tomb at all. A flat pointed trowel, she knew, had also been found in a corner, uncleaned, bits of plaster still clinging to it.

The day before she had drawn from several perspectives a T-square and an adz. Now she was drawing the drill, a more complicated tool. One of Todd's young assistants, Yusef, a Coptic Christian from American University, had set it out for her. Janet recalled how Yusef's eyes had suddenly glinted with mischief. "Do you want to drill a hole in that shelf? The window ledge?"

She had had to laugh. "I'm sure Dr. Ballard would like that! He handles these things as if they were eggshells."

A bedouin opened the door of the shed and put his head inside, murmuring something to Nazli.

"Ah!" she said. "They have repaired the telephone again. And it has been today so serene. Maybe the wind will stay away awhile so the line will remain up. It will—"

At that moment Janet heard the odd noise the telephone bell now made in ringing, which thankfully saved them from going through another of their stilted little discussions of Egyptian weather. Well, she shouldn't knock it. Talk about the weather had helped Nazli and her over some uncomfortable moments there in the shed together.

Nazli leaped for the phone with the grace of a cat. "You almost did not hear that, did you?" she demanded.

"Hardly at all," Janet agreed.

In an excessive display of goodwill in front of Todd and Hassan both, Nazli had demanded that the workmen muffle the strident bell, as it had startled Janet into spoiling an early drawing.

Janet sighed. This evening she would cross off another day on her pocket calendar, suppressing a wisp of homesickness. She had to keep reminding herself that she was not going back to her life as it had been. She would be going back as Hassan's wife. Her small apartment would not do for two people for very long. And her job? Uneasiness stirred in her again. Still unresolved was the question of whether, as Hassan's wife, she would go on with her teaching. It was but one more of the problems that seemed to be slowly piling up.

"I'm going," Nazli said, hanging up the receiver. "That was the Papyrus Institute. That last scroll is completely unrolled now. I shall probably be there the rest of the day. I'll be back if I can. Will you be all right?"

"I'll be fine, thank you," Janet said firmly. Nazli

in her current pose of denmother, or whatever it was, had begun to be tiresome.

"There are still cold drinks in the—"

"In the cooler. Yes, I know. Thanks." Janet finished for her.

"And here, so you do not forget, are the translations I made for you of the poems. In this envelope. I think—I am very sure, and I will be sure later— that she herself, Eyes-of-Love, writes these things. It is about her lord, the king. You will see."

Janet gripped her pen tighter, waiting for Nazli to remind her again that Eyes-of-Love had not been royal, as her father had at first thought, but only a concubine. She was determined not to show her irritation, but this time Nazli did not mention it.

"Okay, I will go now. The institute number is there. Call me if you need to."

Janet breathed a faint sigh of relief to have the shed to herself again and worked steadily on in peace. She was surrounded by a rare and wonderful silence. There had been no blowing sand at all that day, dashing itself against the windows. No sudden powerful gusts to make the old shed creak or the door rattle. And not once had there been that sound the desert wind often made—half moan, half wail— as it rounded the corner of the shed at a certain velocity. She hated the sound. It made her scalp prickle. The capricious winds of Egypt, which had been daily mounting in intensity as the spring progressed, seemed to have gone completely. Thanks be to God. At least for that day.

She went as far as she could go with the third partial drawing of the drill, then laid down her pen to walk around the room and stretch her legs a bit. She was studying the drawing again carefully for possible flaws when Hassan arrived. She turned from the drawing board and raised her face dutifully for his kiss.

"Those are exquisitely perfect, my dear," he said, looking at the drawings.

"Thank you," she answered, and let a silence fall, which was more noticeable because of the unusual quiet outside. They were at odds again. She was going to ask him what, if anything, he had found out about Nazli's plans to go to the States, and he knew it.

"Did you read the poems Nazli translated for you?"

"Not yet. I'll take the envelope with me when I'm through here and read them this evening."

"You are through now, my love. It's almost seven o'clock, didn't you know? I've come to pick you up." There was a false note of heartiness in his tone, a phony joviality that annoyed her all the more because it was so condescending, as if she were a child to be put off simply by distracting her attention.

She picked up the envelope Nazli had left and slid it into her tote bag. "Have the watchmen come?"

"Yes. Come along, we'll go."

Deliberately Janet hoisted herself back up onto the high stool in front of the tall slant-top desk and settled back. "This would be a good time to talk, then."

"I don't think so." Hassan smiled as the shed door was pushed open.

One of the bedouin guards stuck his head inside. His long garment still hung limply in the hot still air outside, and his rifle lay loosely across his back, with the strap holding it around his chest. It was vital to have plenty of nighttime security at an open site that still had priceless artifacts both above-ground and below, as well as an unopened sarcophagus.

"Have all the workers gone?" Janet asked, smiling at the guard. This was one she had met before and knew that he spoke fair English.

"Most, madame," he said, giving her his wide grin. "Only some—two, perhaps—three, perhaps—with M'sieur Ballard. Down," he added, gesturing, meaning down inside the tomb. Then he bowed to them both and withdrew, shutting the door behind him.

"You heard what he said, almost everyone's gone but Todd, and he always works as late as he can. Hassan, this is important. Have you talked with Nazli?"

He was silent a moment. "I have talked with her father. We had a long talk about her plans."

"Hassan, really! For Pete's sake, why can't you just discuss it with her reasonably? I can't understand your attitude to her. You treat her like a child. Why can't you treat her like an adult woman? She was woman enough for you to have an affair with for who knows how long."

"Janet, please." He looked pained and faintly

shocked. It always unnerved him when she jarred his image of her as an innocent schoolgirl.

"I'm not making a special effort to offend you, Hassan. But if we are to have any decent sort of marriage, we must be able to have some sort of open and honest discussion between us. Will you talk to Nazli?"

He spread his hands helplessly. "What do you want me to say to her? It is not so easy. What can I tell her without making her angrier than she already is?"

"I want you to find out if she still plans on going to the States, now that you and she have broken up, now that you and I plan to be married. What is there in the States that she could want?"

"Ah, now there is probably much in the States that she could want, Janet. Nazli is one of the so-called liberated Egyptian women. Don't forget she is very competent in her field. It is not unlikely that she could obtain an excellent post in the Egyptology Department of any of a dozen universities there."

"But you and I know that would not be her reason for going."

He shrugged helplessly. "That is true. But how would you propose I explain this to the United States Immigration Service? *Her* record and life history are flawless. *She* would meet all the criteria—*as I do not*—good background, no police record, well able to be self-supporting and not a charge upon public assistance. What am I to do, then?" There was no hint of anger or impatience in his tone. Hassan was being his charming best.

"Suppose I talk to Nazli and she refuses to listen to me? She could defy me. She could defy her father. What then? Do I explain to the United States of America Immigration people—I who would prefer not to call too much attention to myself. Do I say to them, 'Bar this fine young scholar from the United States of America because she is madly infatuated with me and this is annoying to my wife?' Is that what I tell them?" His voice was gentle, reasonable, kind.

Janet sagged a little on the stool. Hassan had a point. He had several points. She was going to do her best to go into this marriage commitment honestly and make the best of it for both of them. It wasn't going to be easy. Having Nazli there on the scene would make it more difficult. "Well, something has to be done," she said, speaking more harshly than she meant to.

"I know that," he replied quietly. "I will do the best I can. It seemed to me, knowing the situation, forgive me, so much better than you do, that I must first discuss it carefully with Dr. Houdeiby. He understands my wish to emigrate. He supports me in this."

"You can say that again," Janet muttered thoughtfully, remembering Houdeiby's enthusiastic efforts to push Hassan's case. Maybe he knew more about Hassan and Nazli's affair than they thought. Maybe that was why he was so eager to have Hassan half a world away. That seemed to make sense, now that she thought about it. He would certainly be one to help Hassan in dissuading Nazli from her plans.

"What did he say when you talked with him?" she wanted to know.

"He agrees with me. He will help, but sometimes these things take time."

"How much time? Did he give you a firm estimate?"

"Ah, Janet, sarcasm between us is...unseemly."

"All right, I'm sorry. But it does nag me, Hassan. How long do you think it will take?"

Again that all-purpose shrug. "How can I know? Perhaps she begins to see reason after you and I are actually married."

Janet felt a sudden chill in the pit of her stomach and slid down from the stool. "How are those arrangements coming?" she asked, not looking at him, making rather a business of gathering up her tote and tying on the head scarf she always wore against the wind.

"Almost all arrangements are in place, my love. We will have a time of waiting for some papers and such. I think, you recall, you left this part to me." He sounded diffident and somewhat uncertain, making her feel like a shrew.

"Yes, that's right. How did you arrange it?"

"I thought that here in Cairo we should have a civil ceremony, followed by the Muslim ceremony. I regret that all this will be in Arabic so you will not understand much of it, but in such way we can leave the Christian ceremony until later, when we can be in the States."

"Why?" Janet asked blankly. "There are lots of churches here for foreign residents."

"Most certainly we can do it here if you wish. I just thought it would be better in San Francisco, where you can then invite all your friends. I thought this would please you." He seemed disappointed.

"Of course. I wasn't thinking. That was thoughtful of you, Hassan. It would be better." She realized, pushing the idea away from her, that she didn't feel like a bride; she felt so unlike a bride, in fact, that it hadn't occurred to her she should be eager to have her friends come to her wedding. "Well, let's go. It's been a long day."

AFTER HASSAN HAD LEFT HER at the hotel, Janet sat a long while on her balcony. She had done her best to be pleasant at dinner and had the satisfaction of knowing that Hassan seemed less diffident and humble by the time the evening was over. She didn't want to start out the marriage, such as it was, by being a nag. No point in beating Hassan down any more than the Fates had already done. It certainly wouldn't be a perfect marriage, but it would give them each something. It would finally give Hassan the freedom he had always wanted. It would give her the family she had always longed for. A compromise, but certainly it could be made into more than half a loaf for both of them.

She had not seen Todd all day. The thought came to her out of nowhere and twisted her heart. Well, that's the way it was. She got up and went inside. Time for bed. There would be another long day tomorrow in the shed, drawing her meticulous lines. Maybe she would be alone tomorrow. Maybe Nazli would be working on those papyruses at the institute. Only then did she remember the poems.

When she was propped in bed against her pillows, she opened the envelope. There were the sheets of paper bearing Nazli's bold sprawling handwriting. There were several poems, and none seemed to have a title. Janet read the top one and was again fascinated by the elusive image of the long-ago woman, Eyes-of-Love.

O Lord of my desiring.
I have made you look upon me.
In the courtyard of the palace
I paced by, slowly, slowly,
Holding in my hand my caged and singing birds.
So you must pause and look upon me,
And at last you see me there,
O Lord of my desiring.
See my love around me shining,
As sunlight on the sand.

Janet, slightly bemused, read the brief lovely poem again, smiling to herself. She wondered if Nazli was correct and that the poems really were the compositions of Eyes-of-Love. It seemed right, somehow, and it made her own hazy image of Eyes-of-Love come just a bit clearer in her mind. She had become in a few moments more than the youthful beauty who darkened her eyelids with kohl and whiled away the time playing a game in her lovely rooms while she waited on the king's pleasure. There was just a hint of daring, a touch of humor.

"I have made you look upon me," she had written. "I paced by, slowly, slowly, holding in my hand my caged and singing birds."

Clever girl! Smiling more widely now, Janet pondered the long-forgotten girl who had become the beloved of a king. Perhaps this poem referred to the first time she had caught his attention. King or not, he could hardly help but notice her if she paced by him in the palace courtyard, holding a cage full of singing birds.

Then that triumphant line, "And at last you see me there." How long had Eyes-of-Love striven for the king's attention? Among how many others? The palace must have been full of beautiful women. And how had she been there in the palace at all? She might have lived there.

Janet searched her mind for what she knew of the ancient imperial courts, fragments from things her father had said. Yes, Eyes-of-Love could have been living in the palace precincts all her life. The royal palace itself was a small teeming city. Eyes-of-Love could have been the daughter of someone who worked there. There would have been countless priests, high in the social order, and their families. And military men. And a multitude of civil servants, those who kept the inventories in the vast storerooms and did the accounting, teachers, musicians, dancers, scribes—all well above the servant class and far, far above the slaves. Yes, Eyes-of-Love could have been only one of the innumerable dazzled young women about the palace whose most fervent desire would have been to capture the gaze of the pharaoh, who was to them both king and god.

She had done it. Janet felt a little flare of triumph. Out of the teeming mass of ambitious people who made up the royal court it had been Eyes-of-Love who had hit upon a way to catch the king's attention and intrigue him.

Janet lay back a moment, holding the poems in her slackened fingers. Eyes-of-Love seemed so much more real now. Resourceful, assertive. She had seen what she wanted and gone after it. Janet read the rest of the poems, and she had to smile at most. There was one, written apparently shortly after Eyes-of-Love had achieved a place as the king's favorite, in which she seemed carried away by her own victory and referred to herself as a sun goddess. There was another, a warm appealing little ode, apparently addressed to her parents, whose status she had advanced in her own rise to the royal circle. There was yet another in which she bemoaned an "endless day" during which she waited for him and he did not come. Janet got the idea that she had annoyed him and was being punished for it. The last one was just a few lines, expressed with a kind of frantic undertone and quite different from all the others.

> The scent of the sea
> Is in my love's hair,
> And the scent of incense and cedar.
> Turn your back upon the sea,
> And stay with me.
> Stay with me.

She wondered if Nazli had made a mistake and translated the sign for "river" as "sea," but with Nazli's expertise that didn't quite ring true. If Nazli had written "sea," the sign must have been for "sea." This poem didn't blend in with the others, all inspired by Eyes-of-Love's familiar surroundings—the palace, sunlight on sand, the winds of spring, the slow river. Here was this odd little verse that spoke of the scent of the sea in her love's hair. And it was the first time she had referred to the king as "my love," instead of "my lord." And there was something almost desperate about the poem.

Had something gone wrong for Eyes-of-Love? She had been exuberant about achieving her place as the king's favorite. Had she lost that position for some reason? Had the pharaoh abandoned her to go to some foreign kingdom? Had she somehow offended the king, her lover, so that he left her behind?

No, she couldn't have lost her place with him, because, when her life ended, she—a commoner—had been placed among the royal dead. Only the king himself could have ordered that done, so she must have had his love even in death.

Then Janet remembered something Todd had said: that the little hidden tomb had been there before the tombs of the royal wives, the queens. This love affair, then, had occurred in the king's youth, also. And grief at her death had caused him to defy sacred royal tradition and give her this burial place close to where he himself would be years later.

Or was that strange little poem about someone else—not the king at all? Thoughtfully Janet put the poems on her nightstand. Suppose Eyes-of-Love had grown tired of waiting endless days, playing games of chance in her apartment until the king had time for her. Would she—that daring, resourceful, clever girl—would she have taken another love? What a terrible gamble it would have been for both of them. And who would he have been? If he had worked somewhere in the palace, he might well have had about him the scent of incense or cedar. But not the sea. That part she couldn't understand at all. She must go to sleep. The following day would be another long one.

NAZLI DIDN'T ARRIVE at the site until late afternoon the next day. She seemed tired and strangely restless, and Janet felt a twinge of bitter sympathy for her. Nazli hungered for Hassan as she herself hungered for Todd. It was a crazy world. Janet knew that with the announcement of the coming marriage Hassan had terminated the affair between them and Nazli was spending all her nights now in her father's house.

Nazli sat in front of some unfinished work she had left the day before and didn't touch it. She had come back very likely hoping to cross paths with Hassan. Janet didn't try to fool herself about the attraction between them. That hadn't automatically been turned off when Hassan had broken away. Nature didn't work that way.

The wind had come back that day and now writhed

around the corner of the shed, voicing its mournful lament, sometimes petulant, angry.

"I read the poems last night, Nazli," Janet said. Anything to break the uncomfortable tension between them. "I hope she did write them. They are lovely."

"Yes, yes, quite." Nazli replied absently, staring somberly down at the dusty wooden floor.

"I wondered last night about how old she was. I mean, when she died. I thought perhaps she had been quite young."

"Young? Yes, that is so. Quite young, I think."

Janet was suddenly intent. "Really? Do you know that for sure?"

"For sure?" Nazli looked up at her thoughtfully. "Well, yes, almost. One cannot always tell with certitude an exact age, of course. But, yes, I would say quite young."

"Certitude." Now where had Nazli picked up that word for her patchwork English vocabulary? But even as Janet suppressed a smile she was gripped with an odd excitement. She had been right about Eyes-of-Love's youth.

"Yes," Nazli said flatly. "She was young, and then she was dead."

The statement was like a dash of cold water. Janet had fallen into the habit of thinking of Eyes-of-Love as happy, triumphant, vibrantly alive.

"I suppose Todd is still down inside?" Nazli added.

"Yes, so I understand. I haven't seen him all day."

"Okay. Then I should go down. I have something exciting to tell him."

"You don't sound excited."

"No? Perhaps not. I become tired, I think. I worked on that scroll and some other small pieces until two this morning, and then I went back at seven and worked until now I come back here. But he will be excited. Okay, I go now." She got up and started toward the door.

"I'll come, too," Janet said quickly, putting down her pen without wiping the nib. "I'm interested in Eyes-of-Love, too."

"Come, then." Nazli strode out and started across the sandy stretch between the shed and the open side of the hill.

Liar, Janet thought. She could have waited to hear more about Eyes-of-Love, but she was starving for the sight of Todd again. Suddenly her heart was pounding and her body was taut with excitement. She didn't realize until she was halfway to the opening that she had forgotten her head scarf. Her hair, short as it was, was being whipped about her forehead by the wind, first one way then the other.

Nazli had already disappeared down the shaft when Janet reached it. Scarcely aware of what she was doing, she started down. She had not been inside the tomb for days and was astonished at the progress the workers had made. Her father's makeshift hanging platform was gone, and the wall ladder had been extended to the floor. Many of the larger pieces had been moved out, and many smaller things were in some sort of careful arrangement.

The clearing of the main section of the chamber seemed to make the outsized alabaster sarcophagus, with its pale surface grimed by the centuries, a focal point. It seemed so huge for one small woman, until Janet realized that this was just the outer shell. Inside it would be a smaller one, painted and decorated and possibly studded with gems, which held the mummy. She had not really noticed the sarcophagus before, it had been so surrounded by clutter. Now it stood starkly in the center.

"It's almost cold down here," Janet said, wondering if it was just a result of some inner chill she felt momentarily about the long-gone Eyes-of-Love. That was ridiculous. Eyes-of-Love had to be dead someplace. Yet it was so difficult to think of her as anything but living and loving.

"Gets to you, doesn't it?"

Janet started at the sound of Todd's voice. He had risen up out of a corner where he had been arranging some small pots and jars on an improvised set of shelves.

"In a way," she replied. She tried not to look at him but was instantly aware of every aspect of his appearance. From the sun-bleached hair, dark with dampness, that tumbled over a sweatband, to the clear unreadable eyes, the almost too heavily muscled shoulders, naked now and streaked with dust and sweat. She made herself glance away, to find Nazli staring at her with narrowed eyes.

Without missing a beat, Nazli said to Todd, "I have a big surprise for you from the translations I did last night and today." She withdrew some flat folded papers from her jeans' pocket and handed them to him.

Todd wiped his hands on the thin denim of his pants and took them. "What's up?"

"That top one, see? I have written some about her. I have identified her father's name. He was a scribe. Something to do with the foreign trade. There was part of something about getting cedar wood from Phoenicia—a lot of that was missing. Then— that's on the second page—something about a new trade agreement and the emissaries and how long they must remain at court to work out the agreement. Then the rest of that part was too bad to read."

Todd looked up at her blankly. He had been skimming over the words as she talked. "Well, how the hell did stuff like this get into Eyes-of-Love's tomb? What would she have to do with any of that?"

"Her father, do not forget, was the scribe handling these letters, so she might know of them. The writing is hers, you know. Not a diary, exactly. More of a, ah, a recollection."

"That's the only way it would make sense. What's this here about her father?"

He looked puzzled and excited at the same time, and Janet felt an inward writhing of something close to anger. He had forgotten she was there. *What I need,* she thought, *is a cage full of singing birds to push under his nose.*

Nazli sat down cross-legged on the dusty floor. "All I could get of that was that she was the daughter of his ancient years."

"Oh, I see. These three items refer to her relationship with her father, apparently. Daughter of his ancient years, child of sunlight always by his side and daughter of the joy-filled heart."

"Joyful or joy-filled, whichever," Nazli said.

Janet felt a sudden increase of interest. She had been right in her guess. Eyes-of-Love had grown up in the palace. She might have already been a young woman when the youthful pharaoh ascended the throne. It seemed to fit, somehow. She, Eyes-of-Love, perhaps the last and youngest child, when the parents no longer expected to have another child. She could have been the pampered pet of her father's declining years. He might well have let her tag along with him at his work. She might well have played with his stylus, his ink block and other writing materials and copied the rows of tiny pictures that made up the writing, learning to write as she did so. Or he might have taught her deliberately, taking pleasure in her intelligence.

"That second phrase, Nazli, does that mean she was always with her father?" Janet asked.

Nazli shrugged. "Maybe. Could be. It might seem so."

Todd read the fourth and final sheet of paper and looked pensively at the gray sarcophagus.

"Looks as if our little friend, Eyes-of-Love, got herself in trouble, doesn't it?"

"What do you mean?" Janet asked before Nazli could reply, and reached out for the papers he was handing over.

"Read for yourself. Looks as if she took a gamble and lost."

"There certainly isn't much," she said, seeing only a few fragmentary phrases listed on the page.

"It's enough," Todd said. "That last line says it all."

Janet skipped to the last line. "Lady of the false heart and wicked beyond all. . . bringing to the god grievous displeasure and darkening. . . ."

"I don't understand," Janet said, looking up at Todd. She wished she had taken more interest in her father's work so she could talk intelligently with them now.

"Well, the terms 'god' and 'king' would be interchangeable there. Read that as 'king.' At some point she was judged to have a false heart, which caused grievous displeasure to the king. Since we already know she was the king's concubine, I think we can make an educated guess that she was unfaithful and he found out. That would finish the affair pretty fast. Remember, this is an absolute monarchy we're talking about."

"You mean she would have been punished?" Janet said reluctantly, rejecting the idea. She caught Nazli's quickly veiled look of exasperation and realized instantly that it was a stupid comment. "I guess that sounded dumb," she admitted. "I'm sure that retribution was simple and quick in those times." She looked somberly at the pale sarcophagus and somehow still couldn't believe it. She was young, and then she was dead. That stone box was supposed to contain the mummy that had once been Eyes-of-Love. One thing she knew for sure: she did not want to be down there with them when they opened it.

"When...will you open the sarcophagus?" she made herself ask.

"Day after tomorrow." Todd's tone was casual, revealing nothing of how important the event must be to him.

"What happens then?" she asked, trying not to show how much the whole thing affected her, now that Eyes-of-Love had become so real to her.

"Depends on what's in it—or what isn't," Todd answered. "Some people from the bureau will be here, and we're waiting for a couple of my colleauges from the States who want to be here, and of course some people from the universities in Cairo. If there is an intact mummy, we'll make some big headlines that might generate professional interest among Egyptophiles and increase tourist business. If it's empty, it's only of professional interest. Just another tomb hit by grave robbers thousands of years ago. One more archaeological site discovered, excavated and everything sorted and cataloged."

Something in his voice made her wince. He was tired, yes, but there was an underlying bitter kind of what's-the-use fatigue in it, too. So different from the way he had commenced the project, absorbed, excited, loving it all.

All three of us, she thought in dismay. A few weeks earlier four people had come together in Cairo, and within another few weeks they would part. Three of the four had been hurt—and badly, a kind of maiming of the soul. And all of them would go on, because life does go on. But none would ever be quite the same again. Three out of four. Not good. Not good at all.

She had an impulse to say to all of them, herself included, "I'm sorry. I'm really sorry." Instead she said, "Well, it's getting late. I think I'd better go." She turned and started up the wall ladder.

Such a long ladder, Janet thought as she began her climb. "Oh, no," she muttered to herself half-way up, remembering only now that Hassan was taking them all to dinner that night at one of the posher places he loved being seen in. Another "family dinner" to endure, with Todd behind his trusty barrier; Nazli inwardly seething; Hassan continually smoothing the surface, assisted by the enthusiastic Dr. Houdeiby at his beaming best. It would be a long grim evening for sure.

Only when she was back at the Mena House after work did Janet start wondering what she was going to wear. Planning originally on a two-week trip, she had just brought three dressy outfits: the black chiffon with the red poppy border, a long brown split skirt and two dress-up tops. She paused in front of the display window of one of the hotel's shops and looked at two elegant caftans.

Why not? She still had plenty of traveler's checks, since Hassan refused to let her pay for anything.

Inside the shop the stock was varied and exquisite and even more expensive than she had anticipated. It took almost forty minutes to make up her mind, but when she did, she was satisfied she had made the best choice possible for her coloring. The caftan was a filmy silk in palest apricot, shot here and there with delicate gold threads and the narrowest possible woven gold braid along the edges of the armholes and hem. This added just enough weight to the light garment to allow for graceful draping. The color complemented the pale creamy tan she was slowly achieving in the Egyptian sun.

Janet knew, without any regret at all, that the total effect might have been better if she had kept her long hair and piled it up, but she tried to compensate for this by using somewhat more eye make-up with just a hint of iridescent gold in the brown shadow. When she was finished, she was pleased with the total picture. Hassan would be pleased. And yes, indeed, there was something about dressing up that lifted the spirit.

When Hassan picked her up, he was delighted with the caftan. Janet was glad he was slightly late so that there was no time beyond his enthusiastic compliments to talk. She wasn't sure how she would handle it if he demanded the sales slip for the caftan and insisted on paying for it.

Their dinner reservation was for ten, and they were to meet the others in the restaurant.

"I am taking you to El Nil Rôtisserie," Hassan said in the car. He sounded pleased, so Janet knew the restaurant was expensive. "They specialize in imported American meats. It occurred to me that you might like some American food for a change. Would you like that?"

"Very much. How thoughtful of you." She put a note of enthusiasm in her voice.

"A simple American steak dinner, no? One of those crisp California salads of greens, the potato baked and a thick rare steak. Is that right?"

"Almost." She smiled. "If I can have it medium rare."

"Yes, yes, medium rare. I shall remember."

They reached the restaurant at a quarter past ten. The others had already arrived and were seated at the table, being served their drinks. The men rose as they approached—Dr. Houdeiby, looking more egg shaped than usual, with a black pleated cummerbund wrapped about his ample middle; and Todd, lean and tall with the room's subdued lights glinting on his pale sun-streaked hair.

Thankful that Houdeiby's expansive greetings relieved her of the need to say anything, Janet was seated, along with Hassan, and an order for their drinks was placed. Only then did Janet notice Nazli.

Damn. Nazli had decided to wear a caftan, too. Hers was of a heavier fabric of several blended shades—flame red deepening into a rich dark rust. Trimmed in black beads of some sort, possibly jet, whatever it was, heavy enough to drape well. There was in the same beadwork a swirling design. The whole effect with Nazli's own vibrant coloring made Janet's pale apricot fade into a pallid nothing beside it.

"Ah," Nazli cried, "you have a caftan, also. How lovely it is!" She too had used more makeup and a deeper lipstick. Her great dark eyes gleamed beneath what had to be false lashes. Just short of theatrical, the effect was stunning.

Their table, which might have looked from a distance as if they were having a good time, was a small island of unease and tension. It had really been stupid of Hassan to organize this little get-together including both his fiancé and ex-mistress. What an optimist he was. Grimly Janet made up her mind to hold up her end of the conversation if she ever got a word in edgewise. Nazli, like her father, was wildly talkative that night. There seemed to be a time-bomb ticking at the table. Janet listened almost in disbelief to the stream of chatter and laughter, some of it her own. It was as if they all thought they could smother the bomb by a wall of continual sound. But she had the uneasy feeling that the explosion would occur on schedule.

By the time dinner was served, Hassan had a sheen of sweat over his face, and an accidental touch of his hand told her it was wet, too. Todd made a minimal contribution to conversation, and Janet tried not to look at him but couldn't help herself. Every time she did, she found his gaze fixed upon her.

The expensive imported American steak might have been hamburger for all she tasted it. Janet forced herself to eat as much of it as possible, then messed her food about on the plate so it would appear she had eaten more. Minute by slow minute she longed for dinner to end so she could escape from them. But this was not to be.

"We are going up on the roof to the Belvedere," Nazli told her, stretching out a hand to stroke the delicate cloth of Janet's sleeve. "How lovely this is. So pale. So delicate." Her voice was fairly purring.

"Actually, it's pretty washed out compared to your color. We should have compared notes in advance," Janet said, and could have bitten her tongue, it sounded so waspish.

A muscle twitched in the corner of Todd's mouth, and with a sudden, almost violent motion he pushed away from the table. "Why don't we go, then?" he asked. "We'll be in time for the second show—they have an excellent dancer."

The other two men sprang up like volted puppets. The rich Todd Ballard had spoken, and they hurried to obey. Janet considered, and then rejected the idea of demanding to visit the ladies' room to freshen up her makeup first. What was the point? She might as well go along. Poor Hassan was sweating enough.

Up on the roof of the tall hotel a panoramic view of the brilliant lights of Cairo stretched out around them. The decor of the club itself was of intriguing nineteenth century Egypt. They had barely settled around a table in the bar when the lights dimmed and the floor show began.

"Now this," Hassan murmured close to her ear, "is the real oriental dancer. There is nothing in her art of the cheap so-called 'belly dance.' Watch her carefully. She is a rare pleasure."

She was, indeed. Janet was able to put aside her nervousness for a few minutes, and she became lost in the sensuous Eastern rhythms of the music. The dancer, in constant motion, performed with a kind of mindless grace, as if she were part of the music. The skillfully managed lights bathed her near nude body in moments of glow and shadow. With her mane of dark hair, her great languorous eyes and amber-toned skin, the dancer's controlled sensuousness was a poem just this side of wanton.

As the dance finished amid a thunder of applause and the lights went up again, Janet realized that Nazli hadn't even been watching. Unaware that the dance was almost over, she had just reached out a hand toward Hassan, and he, with a slight frown, had moved his own hand away. Nazli's face hardened, and she began clapping furiously. Nor had Todd missed any of the little tableau.

This was ridiculous, Janet thought in a surge of defensive anger. They treated Nazli like a child, and she deserved better. Somebody had to talk to her, discuss the situation, get things worked out and settled. She couldn't spend the rest of her life tagging around the world after Hassan in his new life. She would only be hurt more.

Janet rose from the table, picking up her bag. "Nazli," she said firmly. "Let's go freshen up a bit. Come with me in case I get the wrong door."

Nazli gave an obedient laugh. "Of course, you silly Janet. It has a picture of a woman. But, yes, I come, too." She even linked arms companionably with Janet. The fabrics of the caftans draped together, effectively washing all the color out of Janet's.

Janet stalled around in the small elegant lounge until they were alone, touching up their makeup before one of the dressing tables.

Nazli soon finished and was turning this way and that, appraising her reflection in the glass. "Okay, let us go back," she said, rising from the padded bench.

"Not yet, Nazli. Stay on a moment. I must talk to you a little while." Janet was vaguely surprised that her voice was so calm and controlled. Maybe she was making a mistake in taking matters into her own hands, but she was tired of letting others make decisions for her. She was an intelligent human being and so was Nazli. There was no reason they couldn't come to an understanding. Not the most enjoyable process in the world, but it could be done.

"Yes, yes?" Nazli sat down again. "What do we talk about?"

"We talk about Hassan, Nazli. I'm not a child, and I'm not a fool. I understand that you and Hassan had something going before I came to Egypt. That's all right. I accept that. As it turns out now— for better or worse, as they say—we've decided on this marriage. I'm sorry if that has disappointed you, but things do end. I didn't want anyone hurt. Neither, I'm sure, does Hassan. I'm sorry that things turned out the way they did. But this is the way they turned out. It's the way Hassan wants it."

Nazli's face had slowly congealed, and her eyes were downcast so that Janet could not see their expression.

"I know this," Nazli said remotely. "Hassan has told me all this. Why are you telling me again this?"

"Because I know—don't ask me how—that you are arranging to emigrate to the States. I think that would be a terrible mistake, foolish...leaving your home, your family. It will only cause embarrassment and trouble for both Hassan and me and only defeat and further heartache for you."

Janet paused, waiting for some response. None came. She went on desperately. "I have no right at all to tell you where to live in the world, certainly. But unless you have some other reason for going to the States than to follow Hassan, I ask you to please reconsider and change your mind."

"I do not change my mind," Nazli said tightly. One of her hands was sliding back and forth along the rosy edge of the marble dressing table, back and forth.

"But Nazli, you're simply laying yourself open to more hurt. It's over. Let it go. It's finished between you and Hassan."

Nazli stood up very slowly and took a few stiff steps away from the tables. Two women came into the lounge and went through the other door, speaking in a language Janet didn't recognize.

Nazli turned and faced her. "It is not finished between Hassan and me." Her voice sounded constricted. "It will never be finished. I am his wife."

"Oh, Nazli," Janet said, feeling so sorry for her she wanted to cry. "A mistress isn't a wife. You know that. Granted, maybe you felt like a wife, but—"

"*Idiot!*" Nazli blazed. "I am telling you. I am his *wife.* He marries you for two reasons only—the first reason, he is possessed by the wish to go to the U.S. Okay, I submit to this. I go, too. Second reason, he promises your father he will care for you, so it is a convenient way to do this, also. You understand this?''

''What are we talking about?'' Exasperated at Nazli's stubbornness, Janet rose to face her.

''We are talking about Hassan's marriage to me. And now his marriage to you for necessary sake!''

''What are you saying! You mean that you and Hassan *were married*!''

Recollection of Todd's comment about Muslim marriage laws darted through Janet's mind. ''Did you know that a Muslim man can divorce his wife simply by saying 'I divorce thee'?'' Her mouth had suddenly gone dry. Dear God, had she broken up a marriage by coming to Egypt?

''Did—did he divorce you?'' she asked, stricken.

''No!'' Nazli almost shouted. ''He did not divorce me. What a stupid you are. You know nothing. Nothing! I am his wife now. Right now. But he will marry you, too. He will make you his second wife. His *other* wife. Now do you understand me!''

The two women, having overheard the shouting, hurried out through the room, not looking at either Janet or Nazli.

German, Janet thought dimly, they were speaking German. ''He can't do that,'' she whispered thinly. Something had happened to her voice.

''Of course he can do that. If he wants to, he can. It is all in the laws. It says so in the sacred laws of Islam. It says so in the *civil* laws of Egypt.''

''I don't believe it,'' Janet gasped.

''See, he was right. He said you would not understand so not to tell you. But he will explain later. You will understand. He will make you understand." She strode forward and took hold of Janet's shoulders with an iron grip. "But something I want you to understand. No—don't pull away from me! You listen! You can be his other wife— but listen—you are the lesser wife, always the *lesser* wife."

Total understanding slammed itself into Janet's mind. Of course! She knew—had always known in a vague sort of way—that a Muslim man could have more than one wife. Few Egyptian men did these days, but they could if they wanted to and could afford it.

What a fool she was.

In a surge of strength she threw off Nazli's grip and pushed her away. As Nazli staggered back, Janet turned and walked out of the room. She had fainted only once in her life, and then it hadn't been a blackness but a grayish white mist that had moved in from the corners of the room to engulf her. She must concentrate now on getting away before the mist closed in.

CHAPTER FOURTEEN

JANET WAS VERY CAREFUL in her thinking, as if she were somehow holding her mind rigid, recognizing one small idea at a time. Hotel. Her room at the hotel. That meant taking a taxi. That would mean getting to the main doorway. Feeling as if she were carved of ice, she walked out of the lounge.

As she walked slowly through the main doorway into the gaudy Cairo night she found a fifty-piastre note in her hand. Tip the doorman for getting the taxi. That was right. Amazing how every thought came along in its own place, taking its turn.

In the taxi she sat back, unseeing as the night lights of Cairo streamed past her blank gaze. Deep in her mind, not to be let out, not even to be recognized just yet, was the agonizing sense of betrayal. By Hassan, her friend, her mentor, her ever-faithful tower of strength, the man she would have trusted with her life. No, it was not to be thought of yet, if ever. She couldn't stand it. If she ever did face the truth, her heart would break.

More piastre notes in her hand. They were at Mena House now. Pay the taximan liberally and well, because he had brought her to Mena House and she could hide awhile. Just until she...until she...until...."

"Janet?" It sounded like Todd, but it couldn't be. He was back at the restaurant. She pushed the Close button on the elevator panel, and the car moved upward.

"Janet?"

There it was again, a voice right behind her as she turned the key in the lock of her door. She felt a touch on her shoulder and made herself turn around. "How did you get here?" she asked remotely, staring into the distance beyond Todd's shoulder. She would never be able to meet his eyes again for fear of what she would see there—pity, derision, contempt.

"I drove. You and Nazli were gone too long. I knew something was up, so I went to investigate. I met Nazli going back to the table, so I took off after you."

"Thank you for your concern, Todd. I appreciate it, but you'll have to excuse me."

"I know what she told you, Janet. She was as defiant as hell. She was going back to the table to break the news to her father and Hassan that you know. From the look of her, she was going to throw it in their faces."

"Excuse me, please." She pushed open her door.

"No, dammit. Wait." He caught her arm. "Think a minute. They're all probably right behind me, wanting to patch things up. I don't mean to be blunt, but when you walked out, you just canceled Hassan's express ticket to American citizenship.

They'll head right for here. Is that what you want? Can you face them right now?''

She stared at him, appalled. Face Hassan with the bitter knowledge out in the open between them that she had been a dupe, a fool, that he had used her, used his friendship with her father? A shudder ripped through her. No. She wasn't ready for that yet. "Oh, Todd," she moaned.

"This way." He hurried her along the hall to another bank of elevators.

Inside the sitting room of his suite she sank down into one of the deep chairs, huddling there, unable to look at him.

"Thank you," she said. "Thank you very much. I'll stay here a little while, if you don't mind. Until I…until I work things out.''

"That may take more than a little while, Janet," he said quietly. "Better stay the night. You can have the bedroom. I won't disturb you. Can I get you anything?''

"Nothing, thank you." She had started to shiver. How strange to be cold in such a warm night. "Nothing, thank you. Nothing, thank you." She couldn't seem to stop repeating it.

"Janet! Don't hold everything in. You've been hurt. For heaven's sake cry—yell—break something—but let it out. You're entitled—" His voice broke.

Janet gave a choked strangled cry, twisting in anguish in the big chair, and the tears flowed. Sick with hurt, shame and humiliation, she tried to muffle the sounds she made, gasping out ragged phrases in a wild attempt to explain to Todd, to herself, to somebody. "My friend...trusted...helped my father. So wise...so much fun.... We laughed... and all the time he...."

Then finally, after a long time, she lay back in the chair in exhaustion, feeling empty, staring vacantly at Todd. He was on his knees before the chair, sitting back on his heels, an open box of tissues at one knee, a sodden pile of wet ones by the other.

"I'm sorry," she said dully. "Pretty awful for you, all this hysteria."

"I'll survive," he said. "Sometimes the only thing to do to hang on to your reason is to kick your heels and howl."

"It's just that...." She straightened up shakily. Her voice was thick and raspy.

"You don't have to explain to me. There's no other hurt quite like being let down by someone you care about. But there is an afterward. You will feel better. Not immediately, but eventually. It's a kind of grieving, but grief does go."

She had a quick recollection of the little boy in one of the clippings, the one about Todd being taken away from an uncle who had embezzled from his inheritance. Had he loved that uncle very much? What had he understood from the conversation of the adults around him, talking over his head?

Todd started gathering up things: balls of wet tissue; her evening bag; her shoes, which for some reason were off her feet; a damp washcloth he had given her at one point to wipe her face.

"My throat is scratchy," she said after a mo-

ment, watching his lean form move about the room.
"I guess I'm thirsty." Janet wanted to get up but
couldn't seem to summon the energy.

"I was just going to suggest a drink. I think I've
only got Scotch up here. That okay?"

"Yes, that's fine." She relaxed back into the
chair, letting her swollen eyes droop shut, hearing
the sounds of him moving about, the opening and
closing of things, the tinkle of ice, the gurgle of
liquid.

"Plain water or soda?"

"Plain, please."

Then Todd stood in front of the chair. "I made
these stiff. If you want more water, let me know."

She sipped it. "This is fine, thanks." Janet took
a swallow and in a few moments began to feel the
warmth easing through her body. Now if she could
only get it easing through her mind, maybe she
could sleep the clock around and face the next day.

"You know, Janet," Todd said after a time, "if
it will make you feel any better, from Hassan's own
viewpoint he hasn't really let you down."

Janet glanced at him sideways. "And how do you
arrive at that interesting judgment? He's secretly
married to one woman and plans to marry me,
also? That's not letting me down?"

"Not by his standards. Not really. You have to
realize you're looking at the situation as an American. He's looking at it as an Egyptian. There's a
mighty difference. Like what's-his-name Kipling
said, 'East is East and West is West and never the
twain shall meet.'"

"I know of successful East-West marriages in San Francisco."

"I know of some, too, but it takes a lot of doing on both sides. But I don't think there can ever be a complete understanding between Eastern and Western minds. The two cultures are too far apart. There can be love. Absolutely all kinds of love. Respect? Certainly. But I think that complete understanding isn't really possible. The marriages and the friendships that succeed, I think, succeed in spite of this, because both people have worked at it."

"This is funny," she murmured, "your defending Hassan."

"I'm not defending him," he said slowly, his eyes thoughtful. "I'm just explaining, I guess. Fair's fair, Janet. You can't fault Hassan for thinking like an Egyptian when he is an Egyptian. Under the laws of his religion and the laws of his nation he can take as many as four wives if he wants to. And if he can manage to obey the strict religious laws that apply to protect the wives. Are you ready for another drink?"

"Yes, please." She held out her glass. "And that sort of thing is legal in Egypt? I know it's an ancient country, but it's a modern nation now, for Pete's sake. Do Egyptians do this all the time?" Her voice was too loud, it seemed.

He laughed shortly. "No." He got another drink for each of them. "Actually, it's pretty rare now. Probably fewer than one in a hundred men have more than one wife these days."

"But the women, do they just accept it?"

"Outwardly, yes, because there's nothing they can do about it. They pretend to go along, but privately, secretly, they raise as much hell as they can to make the man pay for it. Families have split up because of it—especially when there are children from both wives."

"But I'm not an Egyptian," she protested. "He must have known that I couldn't accept it." She realized she was gripping her glass and carefully relaxed her fingers slightly.

"Of course not, but in Hassan's own mind he'd feel perfectly justified. If he thought about it at all, that is. He probably figured he could bring you around afterward. He's had quite a while thinking of you as his responsibility, don't forget and—by extension—his possession. I can't see into Hassan's head, but I'd guess it's all bound up together somehow in his thinking."

"I suppose you're right," Janet said tiredly. "I just wonder how he planned to handle it when we lived in the States. My understanding is that the U.S. laws still allow only one wife at a time." There was a bitterness in her tone. The drinks were really too strong.

Todd gave a wry laugh. "True. But my guess is that you'd have been the acknowledged wife, the one he put on display, so to speak. I think he probably planned to keep Nazli pretty much under wraps, more in the role of secret mistress. Maybe that's why she couldn't go along. Here in Egypt she'd be an acknowledged wife, with all the status that goes with it. Maybe that's the part she wouldn't sit still for, so she blew the whistle."

"Can't say I blame her," Janet said, putting down her glass, surprised to see it was empty. She really didn't need another. All she needed was to crawl into some bed and sleep forever. She got up stiffly, feeling old and brittle.

Well, at least she understood now why Dr. Houdeiby was so determined that she marry Hassan, and let him make his fortune—he wanted Nazli to have a rich husband. If Hassan got a second— "lesser"—wife in the process, apparently it didn't matter one way or the other. All the time he had been pushing Hassan at her, his daughter had been Hassan's wife.

"I've had it for today, Todd. A while ago, in a burst of generosity, you offered me your bed for the night. Do you want to reconsider that now? I can go back to my own room, I think. I'll just keep the door locked and not answer if anyone knocks."

"No. Why don't you stay here? Might be simpler. Nobody, including me, will disturb you. The phone isn't even going to ring—I told the guy at the desk nobody was home for the rest of the night."

Good old invincible Todd Ballard. He thought of everything. He never made any mistakes. He never overlooked anything. Her eyes drooped shut, and she opened them quickly. A slow heavy fatigue was engulfing her. In a moment or two she would pass into a deep sleep standing before him.

"Thanks," she said, and turned the word over in her mind with cumbersome care. It was not enough. Not at all adequate. "Thank you," she said distinctly. "Very much," she added, and turned with zombielike slowness and walked toward the bedroom.

Then she was seated on the edge of the bed, watching him from a great distance. Even his voice sounded far away.

"Good grief, aren't you in bed yet? I went down and got some of your stuff for you—you'll need it in the morning. I probably won't be here when you wake up. Look Janet, you can't sleep sitting on the edge of the bed like that. *Go to bed. Undress* and go to bed, okay? Are you going to sleep in that—that caftan thing?"

"What stuff?" She tried to focus her eyes to see him more clearly. He was bending over her, very close. He looked worried. *No need to be worried, Todd. People get over everything.*

"Stuff? Oh, the things from your bathroom—face cream, shampoo, toothbrush—that stuff. I got a few things from your closet, too. You won't want to wear that caftan through the halls tomorrow morning. You don't want to sleep in it, either. Come on, now. Undress and go to bed. Look, can you get it off or not?"

"No," Janet said. "I mean, 'not.'" But that didn't seem right, either.

Todd said something from a great distance away. Then she could feel him sitting down on the bed beside her.

"Where the devil does it fasten? Lean over here. You're going to be mad as hell in the morning if you remember this."

Suddenly she collapsed across his lap. "No," she said against his muscular thigh. "I give you permission, okay? Permission."

TODD HAD MADE one small error. He hadn't drawn the window drapes tightly enough, and blazing sunlight sliced through the room, to fall warmly across her body.

Janet drifted slowly awake. This was the day the VIPs and scholars and other interested parties would be arriving at the tomb. Well, that should keep Hassan busy representing the bureau. And the following day they would open the long sealed sarcophagus. She would have to stay for that event at least, because it would mark the end of her father's work, his crowning achievement. Then she would leave with as much grace and whatever dignity she could. For a moment she couldn't think why.

Then the next moment full wakefulness came, and with it arrived the stunning remembrance, all at once, of the night before. Janet felt herself go hot in a wash of humiliation. She would have to face them all. She twisted to bury her face in the pillow, fighting against a compulsion to gather up a few things and run. Frantic thoughts skittered through her mind: *Few things...smallest bag...out of this hotel...travel agent.* What if she couldn't get an immediate flight home? Well, then any flight to anywhere. And there at anywhere she could—

No, no matter what, she would *not* run.

Janet sat up, her hands gripping the edge of the sheet, and stared glassy-eyed at the bedroom door.

The suite was in total silence, the silence of emptiness. Todd had gone. Her lips moved into a stiff smile. One thing for Todd, when he decided to be tactful, he went all the way. Total tact. Well, she'd be tactful, too, and pretend she didn't remember that after two drinks the night before she had suddenly stopped functioning, like a broken mechanical doll.

He had even left a note. A sheet of hotel stationery had been pushed under the bedroom door:

Janet, if you want to keep busy, come out to the site. VIPs coming in today. Yusef will stop by hotel about eleven if you want a ride. Hassan won't be there. Neither will Nazli. Take care.

Todd

She didn't know how, but somehow or other he had managed Hassan and Nazli. He'd bought her a little more time to get herself together. Carefully she folded the note into a small square. She would keep this note. Someday, many years from now, when she had finished living whatever life she eventually had, some now unknown persons would find this little note among her things. One kept one's little treasures.

For now she had better shower and dress. The least she could do was vacate his suite. There would be people he would need to talk to, and he'd need his rooms.

Janet was ready at eleven when Yusef called. She

would go out to the site and finish as much as she could of the drawing in the shed before the opening. She owed her father that, even if she didn't owe it to Todd—and actually, she owed quite a bit to Todd.

Well, she would go through all the required motions, and when everything was all over and everybody had left, she would, too, as unobtrusively as she could. Janet did not know at the moment what she would do about Hassan. She would deal with that when the moment came. For now, she would deal with one thing at a time.

JANET WORKED intently in the shed through most of the afternoon, concentrating fiercely on her drawing, working with a speed she had never attained before, despite several interruptions. She hadn't counted on interruptions, but Dr. Houdeiby was apparently representing the bureau to the visitors arriving to witness the opening of that alabaster box in the tomb. She was wearing the outfit Todd had brought up from her room the night before, a cotton blouse over a halter and a skimpy wraparound skirt she had bought in Luxor. If she had known she was going to be one of Houdeiby's attractions, she would have dressed differently.

Houdeiby made three different trips to and from the site during the afternoon. Each time when the person or persons came up out of the tomb again, he dutifully brought them to the shed. His round worried face shone with sweat, and he made quite a business of presenting them to her, reminding them that this was Miss Wingate, the daughter of the man

who had discovered the hidden tomb. And Miss
Wingate had come over from the States to assist Dr.
Ballard now, he would add smoothly, editing out
such things as the little matter of Hassan and his
wife and the fact that he had lost a chance to have a
rich son-in-law. She could almost feel sorry for
him.

The sudden tinge of celebrity had surprised her,
but she managed to work around it, making up a
sort of routine that she went into as soon as the shed
door opened and she saw Houdeiby's round shiny
face and troubled eyes.

"Oh, no," she would say, "not an archaeologist.
I'm just doing some line drawings of the artifacts.... Yes, indeed, very excited to be able to see
the completion of my father's work.... No, I'll be
returning to the States very shortly. Have you seen
this chisel—or this trowel—or this drill? Yes, actually found inside the tomb...." Once she got
their attention directed to the artifacts and back to
the tomb, the visitors forgot her again, unfailingly
commenting on how odd it was to find tools inside
the tomb.

"I think I prefer Ballard's theory about that,"
one of the men said once.

"What theory is that?" she asked, disappointment darting through her that he hadn't told her
any theory.

"Why, the speed of the burial," he answered
thoughtfully. The stranger spoke with a slight
accent she couldn't place, and his fair skin was already reddening from a day's exposure to the Egyp-

tian sun. "It was obvious that the...ah...lady in the tomb had been unfaithful to the pharaoh, and so must be buried. But everything down there is all wrong. Great hurry would account for it. Great urgency to get the burial...ah...accomplished. Finished. One wonders why this was so."

After this last lot had gone, Janet sat slumped on the high stool, looking blankly at the finished drawings. Yusef wasn't coming to take her back to the hotel until after seven.

Why had they rushed Eyes-of-Love's burial? Janet faced the idea for the first time without revulsion that the king had put both his concubine and her lover to death because of their secret love. Both Eyes-of-Love and the man with the scent of the sea in his hair had died for love. He must have been one of the Phoenicians who stayed at the court to work out the trade agreement with Egypt. Eyes-of-Love must have loved him desperately—enough to risk her life for the stolen hours in his arms. One had to admire Eyes-of-Love. When she had suddenly found the great love of her life, she hadn't turned and walked away. She'd taken love boldly. Even if she had had to die for it later.

Janet felt a warmth in her face. It took a moment to identify her reaction. Shame. Countless women never encountered love at all. To encounter love and run away would be a shameful thing, and somewhere in the universe there must surely be sounds of wailing and of bells tolling because someone had found love and then thrown it away.

Idiot!

Restlessly Janet slid down from the stool and wandered about inside the shed. The wind was rising outside, and she stared out into it, watching swirls of dust and little wavelets of sand here and there. She tried to match her early image of Todd with the man she knew now—and failed. Either she had been mistaken about him, or he had grown and changed since the time he had arbitrarily stopped her father's work. She had changed, too, in these long golden troubled days in Egypt. Had she changed enough to give up her need for family, roots, commitments? Could she give these things up for a brief interval of love? Eyes-of-Love had risked everything.

Janet looked at her watch. Not yet six o'clock. If she didn't find something to do until seven, she'd lose her mind. There were still plenty of things down in the tomb she could draw. Everyone had gone now but the remaining workmen and the guards coming on duty. Todd would be around somewhere, but she hadn't seen him all day because of the visitors.

The leg bracelets with their inlaid designs of dragonflies came to mind. Todd would surely want a detailed drawing of those. She reached for her head scarf against the wind. If he had gone down in the tomb again, she could ask him. If he wasn't there, she could just take them and start.

The burial chamber when she reached it was empty, but the lights were on. Janet went to a shelf and took down the wooden box. The lid slid off. It had, sometime in centuries past, been stepped on and broken—probably when the men were frantically pushing in the last of the tomb furnishings and Eyes-of-Love's things in their mad hurry to be done with their work and seal up the tomb. Janet looked down at the heavy ancient gold rings. Had Eyes-of-Love worn these for her Phoenician lover?

With a half smile, Janet lifted the rings from the box, letting them hang heavy in her hand. Putting back the box, she slid her arms through the rings. No, they wouldn't do for arm bracelets. They had been made for legs, the slim dusky legs of Eyes-of-Love as she hurried to meet her lover.

"What on earth are you doing with those?" There was mingled laughter and worry in Todd's tone.

Janet whirled around to face him, feeling foolish, as if she were five years old and had been caught reaching into the cookie jar.

He strode across the sandy stone floor to stand before her. His jeans were dirty. His unbuttoned shirt hung open. His eyes were troubled.

"How'd things go today, Janet? I couldn't get away a minute, it seemed. Was everything all right?"

"Yes, fine. Is anything wrong?" She had been so wrapped up in her own woes she had forgotten he was under another kind of pressure. She watched him now, looking somberly at the massive alabaster sarcophagus.

"I'll know tomorrow, I guess, when we open that up. I've studied the X rays until I'm half blind, and I think—repeat *think*—there's a mummy in there.

But the shape is off, somehow." He sighed. "Well, I can't know until tomorrow, and that's that."

He turned his gaze to her again, and the leg rings were suddenly heavier. A grin tugged at his mouth.

"I hate to mention it, Janet, but those things you have in your hands are priceless. We are both aware of that, aren't we?"

"Yes. Yes, of course," she said in embarrassment. "I . . . I guess in a little fit of madness I was about to put them on for a moment."

"Put them on?" he echoed in disbelief. "On your legs?"

"Well, they are leg rings," she answered. "Hand me the box. I'll put them away." She couldn't look at him, feeling like a fool, staring instead at the gritty floor.

He reached out. Then his hand paused, just touching the rings. His fingers were very close to her arm.

Her whole body was vividly aware of him so near. She turned slightly, hoping he wouldn't see the pulse pounding at the base of her throat.

He drew back. "All right. Put them on." He spoke grudgingly, as if he couldn't help himself, his voice rough.

She sat down on the floor, trying to move briskly but fighting a sudden pull of languor. Holding the rings carefully in one hand, she tried to pull off a sandal.

Slowly he came down on his knees before her. The muscles of his thighs strained against the thin denim. Slowly he took off her sandals, and slowly he tossed them aside. She was acutely conscious of her skimpy garments now: the briefest of briefs covered by the wraparound skirt, as short as she dared wear in this country; halter top beneath a loose cotton blouse she had removed now and again while alone in the shed. The night before he had been so circumspect, removing only the caftan because she'd been only half aware. She was aware now.

She didn't want the rings on her legs. She must stop this. She should never have taken them out of the box. They belonged to Eyes-of-Love. She—that girl who risked everything for love—had put them on her slim brown legs, gleaming and scented with oil, and had gone to meet her lover.

"Wait. Never mind," Janet said, breathless. She was no gambler. She couldn't throw everything away for a brief love. "You're right. They are priceless. It was a crazy notion. I'll put them back."

"No." Just the faintest smile touched Todd's sensual mouth. He caught her bare ankle and clasped one of the rings around it. It rested there, the metal warm and heavy in the dim room.

He was careful, taking his time, being maddeningly slow. Wildfire danced through Janet's body. She wanted to writhe away from him while she still could. She couldn't control her breathing, the pounding of her heart.

Todd began to put the rings on her leg, slowly, one at a time. He was deliberate now, caressing her flesh, being seductive, tantalizing. His hands seemed to cling to her skin. "The other one won't fit," he said. "People were smaller then." He sat back on his heels, waiting.

She wanted desperately to break the spell. "They are beautiful, aren't they? In a...primitive way. The design, the style...." Her voice was unsteady.

"Yes," he murmured softly. "Primitive." Then he began to move slowly toward her. No hurry at all. Once again he had read her need in her eyes, and essentially male, he had to respond, could not help but respond.

Tremors fanned through her body. "I...must take them off," she began, hypnotized by his muscular strength, his burning topaz eyes, the tangle of his golden hair, his total terrible masculinity.

He was going to touch her now—any moment—and she held her breath, waiting. She felt his touch the instant before it came as he slid his fingers beneath her open shirt and pushed it aside, down over her shoulder. He leaned forward and began brushing his lips against her upper arm, and slowly his arms went around her and pulled her closer.

A shiver of delight went through her, and she shrugged off the shirt, letting it fall to the sandy floor. She arched back in his embrace. Without thinking, she put her hands behind her, and her fingers struggled with the loop that held the halter together.

"Here. Let me," he murmured against her throat, and turned her with rough tenderness.

There was an agonizing pause, and then the hampering cloth was gone and she felt his hands on her breasts, his mouth against the back of her neck, murmuring something she couldn't hear. And it didn't matter.

Then Janet could stand it no longer, and she twisted around to face him, straining her body against his, her mouth seeking his and finding it. Her body shook with an explosion of desire, compelling her to press closer. She must—must—merge her body with his.

There was an interval without any thought at all, an interval of soaring excitement, the intensity of which she had never imagined before. Their moving mouths locked together, tongues seeking, finding. She gloried in the heavy weight of him and the feel of the warm stone floor, unyielding beneath her. She must belong to him. She must be his, without false modesty, without shame. She must offer him her body and all its secret silken places for him to enjoy. She had no words to tell him this, only a moan, a gasp, to reveal the soaring intensity of her own pleasure. "Please," she whispered, "please."

Then—*no, she didn't believe it.* Todd was pushing her away. His strong hands forcefully broke her grip upon him, pushing, pushing her down against the sandy stone floor when she would cling to him.

Confused, rejected, incredulous, sick with desire, Janet heard him say something and knew with ugly shock that he was speaking to someone else. Someone else had come down the shaft. He was trying to get up, clamping her still blindly groping hands in his and pushing them away.

"Hosni. Go back up. I'll be with you in a

minute." His words came out in jerks of sound. "Wait for me by the Jeep."

Hosni was one of the night guards. Janet gave a strangled moan of anguish. Todd couldn't leave her now. Every cell in her body was silently screaming for him, willing for him to come back. *Please.*

"Stop that. Stop it," he whispered roughly, taking hold of her shoulders, shaking her slightly, his fingers digging in, gripping. "Janet."

"All right," she said wildly. "All right. Leave me alone. I'm sorry. I didn't mean to do that. Give... give me a minute."

But Todd wouldn't go. She huddled, half crouching, half lying on the floor, the golden rings on her bare leg gleaming. He was still there. Why wouldn't he go?

"Look, Janet, I'm sorry. Okay? I'm sorry. Look, are you all right?" His voice was ragged, fighting passion.

"Yes." She strove for her old mask of composure, her safe shield of remoteness. But instead, before she could stop herself, she reached out and almost touched the side of his strong leg. Then in another instant she halted the gesture.

A tide of angry humiliation engulfed her. *He doesn't have to leave,* she thought wildly. *He doesn't want me.* It was too big a claim on his freedom. She was different from the other women he had known. She would make demands, want commitments, and he knew it. *He doesn't want me.* The idea of Todd's shattering rejection persisted even as her rational mind knew that he did want her, that he would have taken her there on the un-yielding stone floor if the night guard had not come down the shaft.

"Well, I'll go—" It was almost a question. Todd still lingered uncertainly. "We can...talk about it later." His voice was steadier now, more con-trolled.

"If you wish." Janet made herself speak careful-ly, a word at a time. "It doesn't matter. I'll put the rings back where I got them. I think it's almost time for Yusef to come for me. I'll wait in the shed." She began to take the rings off. Slowly.

"Maybe later this evening," he began tentatively. "No, damn it. I'm up to my eyes in guests. I'll have to—"

"Never mind, Todd. Forget it."

He was leaving. Going. Gone now. Without rais-ing her head and looking, Janet knew it, and then realized she was crying. She tried to wipe the tears away but more came. Sand got in her eyes. It hurt.

I should never have put them on, she thought. *They don't belong to me. They belong to Eyes-of-Love. They're her rings.*

Janet sat on the floor for a long time, holding the rings in her hands, until she knew Todd had gone about his work.

When she reached the top of the shaft, Todd and the guard were nowhere in sight and the angry wind had increased. A blast of it whirled around her fiercely, dragging at her head scarf and making her squint against the flying sand. She ducked her head and made for the shack, darting inside and slamming the door. The wind whined and growled around the corners, and the air conditioner gurgled, choked and then resumed its muttering hum.

Fool, Janet thought, fool, and stared unseeing out the window at the blowing sand.

Well, the following day would finish it. All the VIPs would be there and the sarcophagus would be opened. There would either be an intact mummy, or there wouldn't. Then she could escape. There would probably be some final scene with Hassan— she would cross that bridge when she came to it. She felt a reluctant sense of gratitude to Todd for whatever it was he had done to keep Hassan away from the site that day. He had made one of his behind-the-scenes adjustments to free her from both Hassan and Nazli for that one day at least.

"Somebody should get something out of it." The echo of Hassan's words, spoken by the sacred lake at Luxor, came and went in her mind as the loud sound of a Jeep starting reached her. She went to the other window. Todd was leaving now, going someplace else. She saw the back of his head, his strong neck and shoulders. He was saying something to the guard, Hosni, who clung to the side of the Jeep. He had won over all the workers very early; their loyalty to him was intense. Hosni jumped clear, and the Jeep roared away. "Wait. Don't go," she wanted to say. She loosened her grip on the dusty window ledge and flexed her fingers. If only Hosni hadn't come down the shaft. If *only*. She watched the long funnel of sand and dust behind the disappearing Jeep.

Almost immediately she heard the sound of another vehicle. That would be Yusef. She snapped off the air conditioner and the light over her drawing surface. Then she turned to pick up her tote bag from the shelf where she kept it, dropped it and watched in disgust as it spilled its contents over the dusty wooden floor.

Perfect. Just perfect. If anything else could go wrong, it would. Janet began to gather up her scattered possessions and push them willy-nilly back into the bag.

Two hotel-room keys?

The hotel wouldn't like that. One was supposed to hand it in at the desk whenever one left. They were fiercely protective about the room keys.

Yusef, outside, beeped the horn gently in case she hadn't heard him drive in. Well, too bad, hotel. She had both her room key and Todd's. At least she should have given Todd his. At least she owed him common courtesy.

Then she paused, holding the key with its heavy metal tag in her hand. Her fingers closed over it slowly. For a moment she had the odd feeling of standing on the edge of a precipice. No. She was no gambler. She needed time to think. But Todd would be busy with all the visiting VIPs until late, probably very late.

There was time, hours of time.

Still holding the key in her hand like a talisman, she opened the shed door and ran outside toward the car, letting the wild spring winds of Egypt wrap themselves around her.

CHAPTER FIFTEEN

JANET TURNED THE KEY in Todd's sitting-room door at half-past one. She had knocked softly and got no answer. He had to be there. They wouldn't have made a long evening of it, knowing they must be at the tomb site in the morning. The room was empty and silent: one lamp cast a glow over the littered coffee table by the windows and the scatter of chairs around it. They stood at odd angles, just as the men had left them when they had got up to go.

He was already in bed, then. A slow tingle of shock crept up her spine. Janet paused in the middle of the room and looked at the bedroom door. She had made the right decision, and in his rooms she knew there was no other way for her. She was filled with a wild sweet yearning simply to walk into the bedroom and crawl into bed with him. He had wanted her badly enough—he'd made that clear.

She would have him for a while, at least. How long did his affairs usually last? A week? A year? It didn't matter. Janet had thought a long time about it—all the time she showered and washed and brushed her hair to a sheen, all the time she had rubbed scented lotion over her body.

She had worn her brown evening skirt, amber top, her brown sandals and nothing else.

Todd would be asleep. Her breath caught in her throat with the rising of deep excitement and longing. In a moment, in just a moment, she would see him sleeping, and then in another moment. . . .

She turned the doorknob of the bedroom door carefully and pushed open the door. He had left the light on.

"Who is it? Janet? What are you doing here? What's wrong?" He was sitting up in bed, bare to the covers, reading a sheaf of papers. He tossed them aside and started to throw back the cover and get up. "What's wrong?"

"Nothing! Nothing's wrong," she said hastily, color flooding her face. "Where. . .where's your robe?"

"Oh, *wow!*" He slid back under the covers again. "Sorry. It's over there. On the chair."

The sight of his naked body had sent raw shock zigzagging through her like lightning. On unsteady legs she went to the chair and picked up the cream-colored cotton robe and tossed it over to him, then turned her back while he put it on.

"Okay, Janet, what happened? Nothing's wrong? Are you sure?"

"Yes, I'm sure." She turned to face him. He was by the bed, tying the sash of the robe about his waist. It was a short wraparound, and he had crossed it over in front and pulled it tight.

"And your next question has got to be, 'Then what are you doing here?'" Her mouth had suddenly gone dry. This wasn't the way she had planned it.

"Close enough." He was looking at her intently, his face closed and blank, his eyes revealing nothing. But she knew from experience that he had seen everything about her—the way the blouse lay against her breasts, the gleaming skin of her leg through the split in the skirt.

She swallowed hard. "I think I'll just give you the simple truth," she said finally.

"The simple truth would be appreciated." He was smiling just slightly. "It's something I don't get a lot of." He was coming toward her. He had rammed his hands, fists, into the pockets of the robe and consequently drawn the fabric tight around the curve of his body. "Would you like to do something? Like sit down? Or have a drink? If you want a drink, I'll ask you to mix your own. The last time I made you drinks you zonked out."

Janet sat down suddenly on the padded bench in front of the window and passed her tongue over her lips. Dragging her gaze away from Todd's face, she looked determinedly at the floor in front of him. His feet were bare. He had good ankles, tapering up into strong, well-shaped calves, like a male underwear model. Good legs. Very good legs.

"I've been thinking things over all evening." That sounded like the right beginning, and her voice was surprisingly steady and firm. "And I decided that you were right about several things and I was wrong." She paused, trying to phrase her next sentence.

"About what, Janet? Which subject? We've had a number of differences, as I recall. What is it that we're talking about?" His voice was cautious.

"Us, I guess. You've made a number of... passes, and I was...wasn't free. Well, I'm free now." She looked up at his face, loving every line of it. "I changed my mind. I thought maybe we could...work something out. I mean, what I mean is, actually, I came here tonight with the idea of seducing you, I guess."

"Janet?" he whispered, and took two strides to stand in front of her. "You don't mean that. You've had a bad shock from Hassan. You've had some rotten luck with your love life, and you're hurting." He reached out as if he couldn't stop himself and smoothed her hair. "Don't add this to your other problems."

Without volition she reached out and clasped her arms around his waist, pressing the side of her face against his hard stomach. "It's what I want," she said fiercely. "I'm not a child, Todd. I've learned a lot in a short time here in Egypt. I know what you and I can do to each other across the room without even touching."

"Janet, don't. Don't. You're rushing in without thinking. Give it some time." His voice was unsteady.

"I'm not." She pulled away slightly and looked up at him, her hands irresistibly sliding down over the curve of his buttocks. She felt a shiver go through his body. "You see?" Janet asked softly. "You see? You were right about that, too. The attraction is there. And the job here is almost finished. I can stay until it is. Then we can both go—each in a different direction, if that's the way it works out.''

"Don't," he grated, taking her arms in his strong grasp and pushing her back. "Don't talk like that, Janet."

Todd wrenched away from her, crossed the room and stood next to the bed with his back to her. She was after him in an instant, sliding her arms around him, caressing his chest, pressing hard with the heels of her hands, pressing her face against him and moaning, "I need you. I need you," against his muscular back.

He groaned and tried to twist away, but Janet clung, pulling the sash of his robe and letting it drop open, passing her hand over his navel.

Todd sucked in a quick breath, and his hand clamped an iron grip on her wrist, wrenching her around in front of him.

"Janet! Oh, *Janet*!" His voice was thick, tortured.

She knew a moment of exultation. "You see? You see? You can't stop this." Her voice was shaky.

He caught her by the arms and sat her down roughly on the side of the bed. "Damned right!" He tied up his robe again quickly. "Janet, if you came on to any guy like this, I can guarantee he wouldn't resist. You'd have to have two heads or something to turn him off. *Sit* there a minute. Let me think!"

"I already thought for both of us." She pushed her sandals off and with trembling fingers unfastened her blouse and tossed it on the floor. She stood up and let the skirt slide off.

"Janet!"

She stood before him, her arms at her sides, palms turned toward him. "Don't you remember?" she prodded softly. "This was what you wanted in the first place?"

"But that was...things have...you've been through...."

She turned sideways and slid into his bed, looking at him wide-eyed, waiting.

Todd said something in a choked voice—Janet couldn't understand what—and let his robe drop to the floor. She shut her eyes for the delicious moment when she felt the bed move beneath his weight. Then his hands—wonderful, strong, gentle hands—were on her body, caressing, stroking, as she had longed for him to do. His mouth, murmuring half words she didn't need to understand, moved ever so lightly against her shoulders, her throat, beneath her chin, over her breasts.

There was the slow increase in the pounding of her heart, and mounting excitement throbbed through her body. It was heightened by an underlay of apprehension lest he move away, lest he change his mind and stop. So Janet had to hold him, entice him, closer always closer, exulting in the sheer beauty of his strong male body. She had to twist her fingers in his hair and press his face between her breasts. Or when his lips brushed across her jaw she had to turn her head—just enough—so that his mouth had to meet hers again—it had to—and he could not escape it. It was as if she were coming alive in his hands in ways she had never been alive before, and she wanted in return to please him, to excite him to a peak he had never known before.

There was between them an insatiable devouring need now, and she could not wait to welcome his body into hers. She must stroke him, kiss his smooth skin, knowing and not caring that she could tell him how much she loved him only in little moans. "Oh, Todd...Todd." Or a few words, "Yes...oh, yes," or one word, "please." And there must be no pausing, no holding back the rising waves of sensations in the shattering shuddering climax of their belonging to each other.

Then for a time they lay facing each other in exquisite lassitude, when it was an effort to trace her finger down the hill of his chest, when she had to keep her eyelids from closing or else lose the shared gaze of wonder that spoke messages of love without words. Only now and then they talked.

Once she whispered, "You didn't turn off the light."

And he answered, "No, did you want me to?"

And she smiled and said, "No," knowing that soon, in just a little while, she would feel again the rising tension of arousal.

Later Todd awakened her in the dark with whispers spoken into her neck. And he pulled her across his body, holding her, and stroked her back slowly, up and down, up and down, until she writhed and twisted in his grasp, struggling up out of sleep, filled with desire again.

Sometimes in the intervals between lovemaking they talked to each other awhile before sleep came again. All too soon there was a crack of pale gray light between the drapes at the window.

"I haven't hurt you, have I?" Todd murmured once.

Janet placed a finger across his lips. "No," she whispered. "It's perfect . . . perfect."

He clasped her hand loosely, kissing her fingers between words. "I wondered a little. You seemed— I didn't want to—don't laugh—"

"Did you think at first I was a virgin?"

She could feel him smile against her fingers. "No. But, well, sometimes you seemed . . . not naive exactly, but uncertain?"

"Let's just say my experience isn't as great as yours—but I did have two relationships. During college."

His body went quite still for a moment.

"Well, maybe not exactly relationships. More like encounters, I guess."

"And that's it?" he asked after a moment.

"Yep. I didn't pursue it in either case. I didn't think it was that great either time. Not like this."

She could feel his mouth, against her palm now, smiling again. "I thank you," he murmured. "My ego thanks you. Whenever you're interested in another encounter, just ask."

It was as if they had both been starving and could not assuage their hunger as they aroused themselves from exhaustion again and then again.

Once when Janet flinched Todd said, stricken, "I'm hurting you now." And she, afraid he would stop, lied quickly, "No, not at all. Not a bit."

The crack of sky showing between the drapes was pale pink when they awakened again.

"I'm starving," she said. "I'm famished."

Todd went foraging in the sitting room and came back with some peanuts left over from when his guests had ordered drinks and snacks the night before. They lay, bodies touching, eating the peanuts and talking now and then between comfortable stretches of silence.

"I never thanked you for keeping Hassan and Nazli out of my hair," Janet said. "Will he be there tomorrow? I mean today."

"He should be, because of the bureau. Do you mind?"

"No, not really. What did you say to him? Was there some sort of confrontation?"

"No. I was icy polite—really at my best. Don't laugh. It wasn't easy. I was angry clear through."

"You would have preferred the classic he-man confrontation, I suppose?"

"No, not really. But I am your basic direct-action type. I kept wanting to punch his face in."

"Well," she sighed. "It doesn't seem to matter now."

He brushed salt from his palms and half turned toward her, propping himself up on one elbow.

"No, it doesn't." His voice was soft and lazy, contented. "My life has taken a turn for the better, and somehow or other I don't think I can be mad at anybody. And Hassan being Hassan, I have the feeling that he'll pop up again. I'll probably end up doing something for him. He's got plenty of brains, you know. If I do end up helping him some day, would you mind?''

"Mind? No, not really. He was very good to my father. I wouldn't mind."

"I'm glad in a way. I can't help admiring the guy. He's a world-class con artist, Janet. That's pure expertise. I admire expertise in anything."

"So do I," she teased, reaching over to stroke his body. "I'm glad you didn't punch him."

He grinned. "My self-control was excellent."

"It isn't always, though, is it?" she murmured, and knew the inner swell of exultation as she saw the beginning of desire in his eyes and waited, holding her breath, for him to move closer again.

When she left, creeping silently out of the suite, he was deeply asleep and the morning sky was a scarlet line between the drapes.

She strolled leisurely through the halls back to her own room, feeling intensely the joy of being alive, and thought how lovely were the mellow old walls, how beautiful the strip of oriental carpeting. Oh, Eyes-of-Love had been right to throw it all away for love. In her own hallway she had to pause and stare intently at the watercolor pictures of village life. How exquisite. How perfect. How foolish not to have really noticed them before.

She showered and shampooed for the day and examined her body with utmost care, that slim pale body that could drive her lover out of his senses.

Lover, she thought in a surge of awed delight, beautiful, beautiful word. *Lover. . . lover. . . .*

SHE HAD COME A LONG, LONG WAY, a million miles from the woman she had been for a moment the day before, hurt, feeling abandoned, there on the stone floor with the golden rings on her leg. Never again would she feel like that. Nothing at all could happen to her for the rest of her life that could shake this inner confidence and poise she now had. If this was what being loved did for a woman, then Eyes-of-Love had indeed—indeed—been right.

Well, enough daydreaming. She'd better order up some coffee. This was to be the big day at the site, and Todd wanted everyone to get an early start. He wanted the whole thing over by afternoon so they could return to the hotel for a press conference.

When she was half finished with her coffee, Hassan came. When she opened the door at the sound of the knock, he was simply there. He looked ten years older. The day before she might have shut the door in his face. Now she couldn't. Maybe he loved Nazli as much as he could love anyone. People did wild things for love.

"Come in, Hassan," she said, and shut the door. "Please sit down. I'm just having some coffee. Would you like some? I'll have the waiter bring another cup."

"No. No, thank you." He stood there uncertainly, looking at her. After a moment, as if suddenly remembering what she had said, Hassan glanced vaguely around and settled heavily into the chair opposite the coffee table.

"I...want to speak with you," he began, sounding more tired than she had ever heard him. It was as if he were pushing the words out one at a time, and it seemed to take all the strength he had. His well-shaped hands lay lax in his lap, hands that had tugged stones out of the rubble, had pushed the ancient waterwheel and steered the taxi through teeming Cairo streets. He had lost his big dream of sliding into the States silently to amass his dream fortune, and it had cost him dearly. Her throat tightened.

He leaned forward with an effort. "Is there *no* possibility—a temporary marriage, perhaps?" he began humbly.

"None," she said with gentle understanding. Being Hassan, he had to try.

He gave a sigh and leaned back in the chair, his eyes drooping half shut. "I rather thought not." A long, not-uncomfortable silence stretched between them. Finally he straightened in the chair. "I think I should explain how our thinking differs, my dear. I don't want you to think so ill of me."

"Hassan." She leaned forward and touched his hand briefly. "You don't need to explain. I was upset at first, but I...got over that. Todd talked to me about it, explained your reasoning, more or less. I think I understand. It's all right."

"Ah, yes," he murmured, "Todd. May we speak of Todd for a moment?"

She felt herself retreating. "There's no need to

speak of anything, Hassan," she said carefully. She didn't want to share with anyone yet what she now had with Todd. It was their own.

"Ah." Hassan tightened up, his wise haggard eyes gazing at her, through her.

She watched a tremor of shock go through him. A dull color rose in his face. He *knew*. Without being told he saw and recognized the subtle changes in her.

"Oh, my dear girl! I feared this. I feared it." He wrenched himself out of the chair in a rush of desperate energy. "I see it in your eyes—in your body. He is your lover now, yes? Oh, Janet! It is my fault! Mine. He will hurt you. You should not...."

She stood up to face him, experiencing a moment of pure disbelief. In all her years of knowing Hassan she had never understood him at all, and she never would. "Hassan, don't. This is my affair. I am not a child."

At her firm tone he turned and started pacing the room. He pushed his hands through his hair distractedly. "Well, then, you must marry him. Yes, that is so. We must see that he marries you. That will solve it all. You would be secure, Janet, you see? He has plenty of money. Plenty. I can tell you right now how much he is worth. I can—"

"*No.* Don't tell me anything!" Careful. She must go slowly here. Somehow she must hold fast to her right to control her own life and at the same time do nothing to further hurt the desperate disappointed man before her.

"Hassan, you are not my keeper," she said kindly. "Whether or not there is a marriage doesn't matter. It's between Todd and me. Only us. I understand this and accept it. I'm not being hurt by this. When this—what I have with Todd—comes to an end, I will leave it a much richer woman than I was. And it has nothing to do with money. Nothing at all."

Hassan looked at her from across the room, trying to understand. "Why?" he asked slowly. "You do not want to marry him? Because of what you said before—that he caused your father's death?" And before she could protest and explain, he rushed on. "Don't do that. It is not correct. I mean, not true." The color of his face darkened with embarrassment. "Your father was dying, anyway, Janet. But he did not want you to know. He forbade me to tell you then. Later I did not tell you for my own reasons. I—I'm sorry about that now. It was one of the reasons he worked so long, so hard. He had a— what is it— a compulsion to finish, even if it killed him."

Janet looked at him with hopeless dismay. If only he had told her the truth. But he hadn't, and she had carried the rage against Todd in her heart too long and had bludgeoned him with a guilt that wasn't his.

"It...doesn't matter now," she said quietly. "I managed to come to terms with it myself."

"I have proofs if you still doubt. He is innocent. If you wish to. . . ."

"Never mind. Thank you, anyway."

"Then you must marry him," he persisted. "It is important for you to have the security—"

"*I* am my security, Hassan. And I don't expect you to understand that any more than I understand your thinking."

"But you must have something," he said desperately.

She went to him and placed her hands upon his shoulders. "I have something," she said. "It may not be what you want for me, but it's what I want. Let's just agree at last that there is a limit to how well we communicate. Let's just accept this, Hassan. Be a good friend and let me alone?" She made it a question.

"I don't know," he said, deeply troubled. "I don't understand, as you say. I don't understand."

She shut the door behind him with a soft sigh of relief. There was a finality to it, like shutting the door on a part of her life that was completed.

JANET HAD RESOLVED to stay as far from Todd at the tomb as she could. He'd have his hands full that day, and she didn't want to distract him. She had overcome her reluctance to be in the chamber at the opening, since her presence seemed important to Todd.

"Why?" she had asked him softly during the night.

"Can't explain, exactly," he had answered after a time. "But it seems right for you to be there at the end of it. It's your father's discovery, and he—well, it evens things up, somehow. Humor me, will you?"

She paused now before going down the shaft and

looked around the windblown desert surface about her. All the workers had gathered in small groups. A dash of sand hit her in the face, and she felt the grains sliding down between her breasts. Somehow the wind didn't seem to bother her now. It would go soon. The desert wind had come and gone for thousands of years. It was just another part of Egypt.

"Are you coming up or going down?" It was Nazli's voice, sounding uncertain and tentative. Clearly she did not know what approach to use this morning.

"Down," Janet answered, smiling. She wished Nazli a long and happy life, but she didn't quite know how to put that into twenty-five words or less, and time was short.

Inside the chamber there seemed a great crowd of people, a few workmen and all of the visitors. It might not be more than a dozen or so people, she supposed, but it seemed like too many to crowd into Eyes-of-Love's final place. It was an intrusion.

Todd was talking with another man who was examining the edge of the big sarcophagus. Her eyes met Todd's for an electric glance, and she looked away quickly. It was then that she noticed the massive lid was off and standing tilted against the wall.

"When did they remove the lid?" she asked the man who stood next to her, one of the visitors she had met yesterday.

"Early this morning, I understand, Miss Wingate. The workmen were brought down to remove it." He spoke with a faint accent under which was a controlled excitement. "The mummy case is there—

all intact, it seems. Step over to the side and look in.
We all have.''

The man in front of her turned and recognized
her. ''Ah, yes, my dear. Here, let her through. It's
Miss Wingate.'' He tapped the man ahead of him
briskly on the shoulder.

Holding her breath, reluctance dragging at her
feet, Janet smiled blankly and went to the side of
the great alabaster box and made herself look over
the edge. An odd feeling of relief filled her. She
wasn't sure why. Perhaps it was because she always
thought of Eyes-of-Love as living and active, going
about her affairs in the royal court. What she
looked at now was simply a mummy case, beautifully painted with exquisite designs. An object one
would view in a museum, and just as impersonal.

''Excellent example of Old Kingdom work,''
someone behind her said. ''Beautifully preserved.''

As soon as she could, Janet stepped back into the
group again and watched as two of the men reached
inside to lift out the case. Todd was speaking to the
group now.

''Now we will see what the X rays refused to tell
us. All of you examined them last night, and as you
all saw, they were inconclusive.''

Slowly, with infinite patience, the men lifted the
mummy case from the alabaster sarcophagus and
placed it gently on two padded sawhorses that had
been set up. Gently and ever so slowly they began to
ease off the upper part of the case. It seemed to take
forever.

Janet inched her way back, farther into the

group, away from the case. The silence in the room was thick. The painted lid was placed carefully upon the floor out of the way, and several men stepped forward to look into the lower half of it.

Janet watched Todd's face and saw the look of brief surprise that crossed it. Then his features settled into his most blank and unrevealing expression. She knew instinctively that he was hiding disappointment, and she ached to comfort him. A murmur arose around her, a phrase from one, the fragment of a sentence from another.

"Wood, by Jove, but this is fabric—what's left...a statue of some sort...no, man, just odd blocks of wood...cedar, I'd wager. But why would they—well, the mummy was obviously stolen for the jewels, but *before* the burial, why else put in something to make up the weight."

Eyes-of-Love wasn't there. She had never been there.

Sorry as she was about Todd's disappointment, Janet felt a sense of satisfaction. She backed inch by inch toward the wall, unnoticed by the fascinated scholars who surrounded the mummy case.

Somehow that clever devious girl of long ago had tricked them all. No one had stolen her mummy. She hadn't died when the king commanded it. Being Eyes-of-Love she had managed—somehow or other—to meet her lover and run away with him. They had got away together across the sea. It had to be! A half smile curved Janet's lips. She *wanted* to believe it.

But surely such an event couldn't be. The

pharaoh of Egypt at that time, born a man, treated like a god, had been a power in the world. He would have sent for them, had them dragged back as soon as he found out.

If he found out.

But what of the men whose business it had been to see that Eyes-of-Love died for her crimes? What would they have done if she'd got away? Those were the times when a king might kill the messenger who brought the bad news, so what would they have done?

The king was never told.

Janet felt certain of it. Who would have dared tell him? No, they would have retreated into an uneasy conspiracy of silence to protect themselves, to save their own lives. Of course they would have.

But Eyes-of-Love had cast her spell over the king too well. She had made him love her too much. If pharaoh's pride had demanded her death, pharaoh's grieving heart had compelled him to have her entombed in a royal place. The courtiers would have had to go through with the funeral ceremonies. And that's why they hurried with such frantic haste, sick with fear that the angry grieving king would take it into his head to look just once more upon the face of his favorite. That's why all Eyes-of-Love's things had been pushed in helter-skelter. That's why the workers hadn't even paused to clear away their tools. They'd had to finish and get out and seal it all up, then go and lie to the king that it was done.

Janet held on to the metal rung of the wall ladder

and took careful breaths to quell her excitement. She was understanding with great clarity the fascination this work held for Todd and had held for her father.

She would tell Todd. That evening she would give him the Janet Wingate theory of what had happened—what she believed had happened. Maybe he could use it. Maybe it would be of value to him.

The crowd was beginning to disperse now. There was a general drifting toward the ladder, and Janet stepped aside. The whole mood of the group had plummeted, though they tried to hide it under polite comments to one another, about going up into the windy outside again, about the coming press conference at the hotel. There were even some little halfhearted jokes dear to the hearts of all archaeologists.

What a letdown for them all. Janet mounted the ladder with the others. There was a lot still to do. After the press conference, all the visitors, each one important in his own right, had various appointments in various places. They would be coming and going. Todd, because of his work, but more because of his connection with the Ballard Foundation, was booked almost on a minute-by-minute basis. Every visitor had some private project at home, some absorbing interest, that could use an infusion of money from the wealthy Ballard Foundation. Something else became clear in her mind. No wonder Todd's barriers were so well-erected, and his ways of withdrawing so adroit.

She found that she herself, as Janet Wingate, was in some demand, also. It was a new experience, not unpleasant, as she learned, working her way through it. Some of the people had known her father. Some of them had surmised that she had some professional or unexplained connection to Todd Ballard. The experience offered her a new challenge and one she thought she could handle pretty well, with a little practice.

IT WAS AFTER MIDNIGHT when she finally turned the key in her lock and opened the door to find the lights on and Todd asleep in a chair. He'd been waiting for her. *My lover,* she thought, *my lover.*

"Hey," she said softly, touching his hair. "Wake up."

He muttered something unintelligible and opened his eyes.

"Wake up and come to bed. You'll break your neck sleeping like that." She couldn't help smiling. He seemed so utterly gorgeous.

He got up slowly, grimacing and rubbing the back of his neck. Then he smiled. "What kept you? I got away an hour ago."

"I'm not sure," Janet said, easing out of her high-heeled sandals. "There were so many people, and everybody wanted to have a few words with me. How did you manage?"

He grinned. "I'm better at disengaging than you are. It's a learned technique. Takes a while."

"Todd," she said thoughtfully. "Speaking of disengaging. I think there is one thing we want to be sure we both understand."

"And that is?"

"When I came in to seduce you—" a fleeting smile touched her lips "—I did make it clear, didn't I, that you're not to feel committed in any way? When you want to...disengage, then do it. No hard feelings. Even if I'm not ready for it yet, even if I don't want it, I promise you I won't lift a finger to try and stop you. When you want your freedom—just go."

He was silent a long time, looking at her somberly.

"Your timing is off," he said finally. "*I've* been thinking about *you*. For some time."

"Oh, Todd." She made herself laugh. "When have you had time in the past few days to think about me?"

"I'm never *not* thinking about you, Janet. Since the day I met you. And that's a fact. No matter what I'm thinking or doing or saying, you're in my mind, Janet, at some level all the time."

Janet widened her eyes because she was afraid she was going to get teary. "It's...been pretty much that way with me, too."

Todd came and stood before her, not touching her yet. But she knew he would. He was half smiling now.

"And I appreciate your kind offer to free me even if I don't want to be free. The way I've felt for a long time, I don't think that's going to be a problem. I told you—oh, quite a while ago—that I was falling in love with you. I think maybe the next logical step for us is to marry—wouldn't you say so?"

Totally unprepared, Janet simply stared at him blankly.

"But Todd," she managed finally. "You've said. . . you've implied. . . I mean, I understand that with your background you might be wary of commitment." A slow rapture began to fill her. "Todd, are you sure—are you *sure*?"

"Yes, I'm sure." His voice was husky. "I've been sure for quite a while. I was going to wait some sort of 'decent interval' until I felt you were over the shock of Hassan, but. . . ." He grinned faintly. "You rushed me into it, I guess. I knew there was no need to wait when you came to me the way you did. I knew then that it was right for us, and now, no waiting around. You do think it's right, don't you? I mean, for a permanent till-death-us-do-part commitment?"

"Oh, yes, right. Absolutley right." Janet was half laughing, half crying. Then they were in each other's arms and the magic was beginning all over again.

And somewhere in the back of Janet's mind she remembered that she hadn't told him yet about Eyes-of-Love and what had possibly—or probably—or must surely have—happend for her.

Todd instantly sensed her distraction. "What is it? What's the matter?"

"Nothing," Janet replied. "Nothing. She would tell him later, much later, or whenever they had the time.

Eyes-of-Love would be the first to understand.

ABOUT THE AUTHOR

Virginia Myers wrote her first novel when she was only thirteen. Since then she's been prolific, producing short stories, mysteries and both historical and contemporary romances. Her job history has been equally eclectic; Virginia has worked in social welfare, insurance, publishing and teaching.

A born organizer, Virginia is an active committeewoman in her church and community in Seattle, Washington. Recently she coordinated the program at the 28th Pacific Northwest Writers Conference.

Sunlight on Sand was inspired by a lifelong fascination with Egypt and Virginia's travels to that country. The author describes her first Superromance as "my favorite kind of book— a love story with a happy ending."

LaVyrle Spencer

Sweet Memories

a special woman...a special love... a special story

Sweet Memories is the poignant tale of Theresa Brubaker and Brian Scanlon, separated by Brian's Air Force officer training, but united in spirit by their burning love.

Alone and unsure, Theresa decides on a traumatic surgical operation that proves devastating for both her and Brian, a proud sensitive man whose feelings of betrayal run deep. Through the tears and pain, Theresa emerges from her inhibitions a passionate, self-confident woman ready to express her love.

Available in May wherever paperback books are sold, or send your name, address and zip or postal code, along with a check or money order for $4.25 (includes 75¢ postage and handling) payable to Harlequin Reader Service, to: Harlequin Reader Service

In the U.S.	In Canada
P.O. Box 52040	649 Ontario Street
Phoenix, AZ 85072-2040	Stratford, Ontario N5A 6W2